"The truth is, _____ something for _____ passion than racing," Ramon announced in a firm voice.

"Hard to believe, is it not? Racing has been my life for over a decade, but with my brother so happily married and starting his family I find I can't wait to enjoy the same. I'm deeply in love and, well…"

He moved around Isidora so he was no longer behind the podium and sank to one knee beside her.

A massive gasp went through the crowd.

The cacophony of flashes and clicks increased, but the shouting of questions ceased. An eerie expectancy characterized the wordless explosion of repeated shutter-click-flash. The lights strobed against his skin as he looked up at Isidora's incredulous expression.

She paled as comprehension dawned. Her eyes showed white around her gray irises. One hand came to her mouth and she might have said, "Don't you dare."

"You said if I quit racing you would marry me. So, *mi corazón. Now* will you make me the happiest man on earth?"

The Sauveterre Siblings

Meet the world's most renowned family...

Angelique, Henri, Ramon and Trella—two sets of twins born to a wealthy French tycoon and his Spanish aristocrat wife. Fame, notoriety and an excess of bodyguards is the price of being part of their illustrious dynasty. And wherever the Sauveterre twins go, scandal is sure to follow!

They're protected by the best security money can buy—no one can break through their barriers... But what happens when each of these Sauveterre siblings meets the one person who can breach their heart...?

Meet the heirs to the Sauveterre fortune in Dani Collins's fabulous new quartet:

Pursued by the Desert Prince

His Mistress with Two Secrets

Bound by the Millionaire's Ring

Available now!

And look for

Trella and Prince Xavier's story

Coming soon!

BOUND BY THE MILLIONAIRE'S RING

BY
DANI COLLINS

First Published in Great Britain 2017
By Mills & Boon, an imprint of HarperCollins*Publishers*
1 London Bridge Street, London, SE1 9GF

© 2017 Dani Collins

ISBN: 978-0-263-92542-5

Canadian **Dani Collins** knew in high school that she wanted to write romance for a living. Twenty-five years later, after marrying her high school sweetheart, having two kids with him, working at several generic office jobs and submitting countless manuscripts, she got The Call. Her first Mills & Boon novel won the Reviewers' Choice Award for Best First in Series from *RT Book Reviews*. She now works in her own office, writing romance.

Visit the Author Profile page
at millsandboon.co.uk for more titles.

Dear Reader, for being such a passionate,
wonderful fan of romance.

CHAPTER ONE

Isidora Garcia didn't glance up as her boss entered her office. She recognized him in her periphery and was only a little surprised he was here in Paris. He was a new father, but when there was a crisis with one of his sisters, particularly Trella, he waded in without hesitation.

"I just saw it," she assured him. "I'm emailing—"

She cut herself off as preternatural knowledge struck. Her body tingled and her skin felt stroked. Her fingers became clumsy while her blood grew hot and thick in her veins.

She didn't have to look up to know that was not Henri Sauveterre advancing on her. It was his twin, Ramon.

A flash of intense vulnerability went through her. Treachery. Anguish.

She clamped down on the rush of emotion, hiding it behind a falsely cool lift of her gaze to the man who looked identical to the one who had arm-twisted her into taking this position. They were both ruthless in their own way, but at least Henri wasn't cruel.

"I didn't know you were in Paris." Her voice came out steady enough to hide the tightness that invaded her throat.

Like Henri, Ramon's dark hair was cut short, but had a tendency to spike on top. His clean-shaven, spectacularly handsome features were sophisticated without being pretty, angular without being rugged. His Sauveterre eyes were green when they were amused and gray when they were not.

His irises were somewhere between slate and ash this morning, making a knot of tension coil in the pit of her stomach. His sensuous mouth sat in a flat line. His honed physique flexed beneath his tailored suit as he set his hands on her desk, leaning in to confront her.

"Why aren't you doing your job?"

His lethal tone cut her in half, sending a burst of adrenaline through her.

Oh, she hated herself for still being sensitive to his every word. Him, with his superiority, and opportunistic streak, and complete lack of conscience. She wanted to hate him. Did hate him. But she remained susceptible. In fact, it was worse, now that she knew how brutal he could be. At least when she'd been young and stupid, she hadn't feared him.

She took a firm grip on herself and tried to hide her dread by casually looking back at her screen. She couldn't absorb what she'd been writing. She waved at her keyboard, aiming for nonchalance. "I'm doing it now. If you weren't interrupting me, I could get on with it."

She managed to sound composed and begged her hand to stay steady. She didn't want to reveal the fine trembles that worked upward from a deep, inner flutter in the pit of her stomach.

Because even with hatred and fear gripping her, she found him utterly compelling.

"What can you possibly do at this stage?" he growled. "The cat is out. Why didn't you prevent it?"

"Prevent your sister's pregnancy?" Her pulse hammered once, hard, as she met his gaze, but she managed to tilt her mouth into a facetious smirk. "Not in my bailiwick, if you can believe it. I've had three discussions with her, suggesting we leak the news in a controlled way. She chose to stay mum."

Pun not intended. Trella was tall and a wizard with cutting cloth to create the effect she wanted, but she was five months along. She couldn't hide it forever.

"You should have had a fourth discussion. And a fifth. Your father had the contacts to keep these things under wraps. Why don't you?"

Her heart stalled. Oh, he was not going to bring her parents into this, was he? That was *such* dangerous ground.

At least it flipped her out of defensive mode into a willingness to go toe-to-toe.

"Even my father can't control every person with a social media account. The photo was posted by a woman visiting her mother at the hospital. You took Trella there yourself—in that car everyone notices. Of course people watched to see who got out."

She punctuated with a look that said, "Take some responsibility for a change."

"The only reason it took this long for the trolls to call it a baby bump was because they were having so much fun shaming her for gaining a few pounds." Then, as she remembered his sister-in-law had delivered twins by emergency cesarean a few days ago, she asked, "How are Cinnia and the babies?"

"Fine." He pushed off the desk, expression blanking to aloofness—it was the way he and all his siblings reacted when questioned about their family, even when the inquiry was sincere.

The Sauveterre twins had become media sensations the minute the second pair, Angelique and Trella, came along. Born to a French tycoon and his Spanish aristocrat wife, the children had been mesmerizing in their mirrored resemblance and elegantly perfect lives.

Then, when the girls were nine, Trella had been kidnapped. She was recovered five days later, but rather than give the family breathing space, the media's microscope had focused even more intently on their slightest move. The pressure had sent their father into an early grave and the fallout had continued for years.

Angelique—Gili to her family—seemed to have found some happiness, though. She was secretly engaged to her soul mate, Kasim, which was why the family had convened in Spain.

Their celebration had been cut short when Cinnia was rushed to hospital.

Trella had jumped into Ramon's distinctive Bugatti Veyron to chase the ambulance with him. Not content with the limited edition Pur Sang, worth millions, Ramon had had one custom-built to his own specifications. It was fully carbon this and titanium that, didn't have a lick of exterior paint and topped out at a speed of over four hundred kilometers an hour.

Isidora was dying to ask if it had air-conditioning.

Worried for Cinnia, Trella had leaped out of the car without taking due care over how much midsection she showed.

Any casual snap of a Sauveterre went viral. And one that allowed the public to speculate on a secret pregnancy and the identity of the father…? There was no containing such a nuclear bomb.

Isidora knew all this because she had grown up with the girls. Her father had worked for Monsieur Sauveterre. She'd had tea parties with the girls before Trella was taken and still had slumber parties with them. She cared deeply for them and wanted the best for the whole family.

That was why Henri had hired her. He trusted her with his sisters and all of the family's most delicate PR announcements—most recently a statement that he and Cinnia had spoken their wedding vows in the hospital with their newborn daughters in attendance.

None of that mattered to Ramon, however. To him, she was an outsider, not entitled to anything more than criticism and a pat. *Fine*.

Fine. It didn't hurt. She was so past yearning for his positive regard.

"I was hoping you were Henri." For a million reasons. "I was going to suggest taking the family portrait with Cinnia and the babies sooner than planned. I'm inundated with requests. Releasing photos might divert this focus on Trella."

"By all means, let's make sacrifices of my brother's innocent children before they're a week old."

She was only trying to help. Swallowing back a lump that formed behind her breastbone, she rose to walk a file to the cabinet in the corner, mostly as an excuse to put distance between them. "Do you have another suggestion?"

"Yes."

Oh, that supercilious attitude grated. If her father hadn't badgered and cajoled, if Henri hadn't offered her disgusting amounts of money, if she didn't adore Trella and Angelique and now Cinnia, and want to protect her friends as much as Henri did, she would quit this job. Even this little bit of interaction with Ramon was too much.

"I'm all ears," she said without turning around. She shoved the file into the cabinet, feeling a burning sensation streak down her back. He was *not* looking at her butt and she was *not* wishing he would. Seriously. She consciously tried not to tense, but she needed to resist him. She was so *done* with this man!

"Arrange a press conference," he said. "I'm announcing my retirement from racing."

Isidora had the nicest ass he'd ever seen—and he was a connoisseur.

When she turned with surprise, one arm remaining atop the filing cabinet so her buttons strained across her breasts, he stole an appreciative glance at that, too, before lifting his gaze to her astonished expression.

Auburn brows framed warm brown eyes. Her gold-tipped lashes were thick and lush. Her glossy hair, which had toned down from a bright copper as a child to a rich burgundy wine, was pulled back in a clip. He couldn't help imagining it falling freely around those high, honey-toned cheekbones. She wore little makeup, needing nothing to give her skin that glow of health, or shape her plump lips.

He typically stuck with overt beauties, ones made with a generous hand that exuded sexuality. When it came to physical companionship, he preferred obvious women and uncomplicated encounters. Indifference was his goal. He didn't objectify women, but they objectified him. He was fine with being trophy-hunted. He gave as much pleasure as he took and they both walked away unharmed and completely satisfied.

Isidora had never offered anything so simplistic. Her years of doe-eyed hero worship had reflected yearnings and expectations he could never fulfill. So he had done her an enormous favor five years ago. He had let her believe he had slept with her mother. That adolescent crush of hers had needed to be crushed.

She still hated his guts for it. Overnight, she had stopped accompanying her father to the office or Ramon's races. She continued to visit his sisters, but sent regrets to any parties the Sauveterres invited her to attend. While completing her degree in public relations, she had maximized work-abroad opportunities. On the few occasions Ramon had crossed paths with her, she had left the room as quickly as she politely could.

That's how he'd made such a study of her ass.

Her contempt had finally gotten to him last year, when he'd seen her at her father's sixty-fifth birthday party. He had rivalries in business and on the track, but no one outright hated him. Isidora had been all grown up, incandescent in a sapphire-blue dress. Surely she was far enough past her childish infatuation to hear the truth and get over her anger.

"I want to bury the hatchet," he had said when he'd cornered her into a waltz. "Let's go somewhere private, talk this out."

"Is that what you're calling it these days? Burying the hatchet?" Her tone had been glacial. "No, thanks." She had walked away before the song finished.

Still acting like a child, he had deduced, but he had her attention now.

"You're retiring," she repeated now, with disbelief. "From racing."

"Si." It was the least he could do for his family.

"But you're still winning. Your fans will be devastated."

"I have sufficient fame and money."

"But… You love it. Don't you?" She closed the file cabinet and faced him, weight hitched to one hip so her knee peeked out the slit in her skirt.

Definitely no longer a child, his libido took great care to note.

"It's just a pastime." Psychologists would say his need for speed was compensation for failing to catch up to Trella when she'd been kidnapped. That might have been true in the beginning, but he was genuinely fascinated by the mechanics of high-performance engines and loved competing. Nevertheless… "This is something I've been considering for some time. I'll continue to sponsor my team and stay involved that way." These were the pat answers he would give the press this afternoon.

"It seems extreme. Trella's pregnancy can't be denied. Not forever."

He folded his arms, not used to defending his decisions to anyone. He didn't bother to soften the condescension in his tone as he explained, "I'm choosing to announce it now to distract from the rumors about her, but quitting racing was inevitable once Cinnia turned up pregnant. Henri can't travel as much as he used to."

He and Henri jointly ran Sauveterre International, but work had been Henri's sport of choice for mental distraction. Ramon had never shirked his responsibilities, but he had never felt guilty handing something to his brother if he had to race.

Henri had greater concerns now. Ramon was more than willing to pick up the slack so his brother could look after his young family.

"So you've been planning this all along?"

"I knew once the babies came, my role would change."

"We all knew you were taking over this office so Henri could move to Madrid, but I don't think anyone expected you to quit racing."

"We planned to make all the announcements next month. With the babies coming early, we've moved up the timetable. I will begin restructuring today. Starting with you."

Her eyes widened. "Me? I arranged a transfer to Madrid. It takes effect with Cinnia's due date, but— Are you saying that with the babies coming early, I need to move that up?"

"You're staying here." He probably shouldn't take so much pleasure in making that statement, but he found enormous satisfaction in it. "My sisters came to Paris with me. They're sorting things at Maison des Jumeaux in preparation for Angelique leaving. Her engagement will be announced soon and there are details with Kasim's family that need your delicate touch."

Isidora's jaw dropped behind her sealed lips, making her cheeks go hollow. Her thick lashes quickly swept down to disguise what might have been a flash of…fear? No. Fury? Why? He wasn't being sarcastic about her delicate touch. She was very good at her job or she wouldn't have the position she held.

He wasn't in the habit of giving anyone ego strokes, however, so he simply continued. "With Trella in the hot seat again, I'll do my best to draw fire with the retirement announcement, but you'll have to manage all of that, as well as the press releases on the restructuring."

"I can do that remotely." She folded her arms, posture stiff and defensive, face turned to the window, where vertical blinds held out most of the July sun along with the building's excellent view of the Seine. "I'll speak to Henri—"

"He just brought home *twins*, Isidora. He's working as little as possible and mostly from home so he can enjoy his children and support his wife. Henri is not your employer, *we* are. We speak for each other and this is something we decided together."

"You decided between you to deny my transfer? Without discussing it with me?"

"Yes." It hadn't even been a discussion. As often happened, Henri had voiced what Ramon had already been thinking. "It's a matter of response time. *Some* of your work can be done remotely, but when a crisis arises, like today's, we need you on the spot to defuse it."

Her mouth tightened. He could see her wheels turning, searching for an alternative. He knew why she was acting like this and he was losing patience with it.

"Perhaps we could coax your father out of retirement?" he said facetiously.

"Don't think I'm not tempted."

"Stow your grudge, Isidora. You're a professional. Act like one."

She lifted haughty brows. "It's not *my* ability to keep things professional that I'm worried about."

"If I was the least bit interested in frostbite below the belt, you'd have something to worry about. I'm not."

He always hit back. *Always*. It came from never wanting to be a victim again.

But when her nostrils pinched and she sniffed like she'd taken a hard jab to her slender middle, he felt a pang of conscience. A shadow of hurt might have flickered in her eyes, but she moved behind her desk, ducking her head and sliding a nonexistent tendril of hair behind her ear, the screen of her hand hiding her expression from him.

When she lifted her face again, it was flushed, but her expression was one of resolve. "I'll hand in my resignation by the end of the day."

The floor seemed to lurch beneath his feet. Her antipathy ran that deep?

As he searched her gaze, unable to believe she was serious, her pupils expanded until her eyes were like black pansies, velvety. Yet disillusioned and empty.

For one heartbeat, the world around him faded. A quiet agony that lived inside him, one he ignored so completely he barely knew it existed, seared to life, flashing such acute pain through him that his breath stalled. Fire, hot and pointed, lit behind his breastbone.

He slammed the door on that dark, tangled, livid place, refusing to wonder how she had managed to touch it by doing nothing but trying to retreat from him.

Why would she even suggest it? The job she held, as someone still fresh from school and not yet twenty-four, was unprecedented. Nepotism had played a part, sure, but she brought a rare and valuable quality to the position: trustworthiness.

Ramon would not be the reason his sisters lost a precious ally.

He wasn't a man who begged, however. Racetracks were not conquered by being nice. She already hated him so there was no point in trying to charm her. Meanwhile, that strange split second of confused feelings left him with the scent of danger in his nostrils. It fueled his need to control. To dominate. To conquer.

He came down on her with the same lack of mercy he showed anyone else who might threaten him or his family.

"*Cariño*, let me explain what will happen if you resign." He moved to lean on her desk again.

She was standing now, blinking with wariness. She stiffened, but she didn't fall back.

He caught a light scent off her skin, something natural and spicy with an intriguingly sweet undertone. Herbs and wildflowers? The base, primitive animal inside him longed to get closer and find out.

Perhaps he would get the chance, he thought darkly, as he continued.

"I know you've signed confidentiality agreements, but given your antagonism toward me, I don't trust you not to take what you know about us to the highest bidder. I will make your life extremely difficult if you walk out of here. There won't be other jobs available to you. Not at this level."

A renewed flush of color swept across her cheekbones. "If that's your way of trying to make me warm up to you, 'hash-tag friendship fail.'"

"Prove your loyalty to our family. Do what we pay you very well to do."

"Me." She pointed at her sternum. "You want *me* to prove *my* loyalty to *your* family."

"Yes. And quit editorializing on mine." He ignored a stab of compunction. "You know *nothing* about my capacity for loyalty or anything else."

"I know what I need to know," she assured him bitterly. "But if you're going to make threats against my career, fine. I'll take the high road and show you what loyalty really is. I'll stay because I care about your sisters and because my father *would* come out of retirement if I quit. His devotion to your family is that ingrained. I never told him that you slept with his wife or he might feel differently. And don't say they were divorced!"

She jabbed her finger at him.

He narrowed his eyes, warning her she was standing on the line.

"It would gut him to know what you did and unlike you, I'm not someone who enjoys making other people miserable."

"I said 'difficult,' *hermosa*. If you want me to make your life miserable, I can arrange that quite easily."

"Job done, *hermoso*," she said with a smile that went nowhere near her eyes. "Will you excuse me? I have a press conference to arrange."

"Isidora," he said gently, without moving. His eyes clashed with her gaze in a way that kept his muscles tight and his skin tingling with exaltation in the battle. "*I* care about my sisters and your father. That's why I'm allowing you to continue with us, and not firing your ass for insubordination. Mind your manners, or you will discover *exactly* what kind of man I am."

CHAPTER TWO

WITH FURY BURNING a hole in the pit of her stomach, Isidora did her job and sent out the notices that a press conference would be held in the media room of Sauveterre International's Paris tower. The skyscraper in Madrid was its twin, built the same year on the same specifications. Until today, Ramon had worked out of that office, which was why she had not requested a transfer back to her home country, where she could be closer to her parents.

She desperately wanted to call her father with the news that Ramon was retiring. Her father had been a fan of all types of racing long before his client's son had begun entering grand prix races at a mere nineteen years. After showing some talent for racing while learning evasive driving, Ramon had spent an inheritance from one of his grandparents on a car and team, much to the late Monsieur Sauveterre's dismay. Ramon had won that first year and had won or placed in nearly every race since.

Some of Isidora's most cherished memories involved catering to her father as he parked himself in front of the television for a twenty-four-hour endurance race, or biting her nails alongside him as cars zoomed through the narrow streets of Monaco. In the beginning, she hadn't been so much a fan of racing as she was of her father's passion and delight in having a companion while he watched.

Of course, by the time she was twelve, she had definitely been a fan of one particular driver, heart pitter-patting as Ramon rocketed through turns and occasionally spun out only to straighten and take over the lead once again.

Ramon's winning streak, coupled with his Sauveterre name and the fact he represented both France and Spain, made him more than a darling in the racing world. It set him on a level beyond infamous. Demigod.

He had certainly dazzled her young heart.

But after That Day, which had actually been an early morning, when she had bumped in to Ramon leaving her mother's house wearing rumpled clothes, a night's stubble and a complete lack of remorse, she had stopped watching the races with her father. She had claimed she was too busy with university, and would go to her deathbed before she admitted she had watched alone, in dorm rooms, or plugged into her laptop, tucked away in a solitary corner of the library.

She hated Ramon Sauveterre, but she had always needed to know he survived to race another day. How could she be disappointed on his behalf that he was giving it up? She ought to be doing a happy dance that he wasn't getting what he wanted for a change, the arrogant, heartless tyrant.

Her father would be even more devastated, but as the former VP of PR for Sauveterre International, he would understand. Even she had understood, before embarking on this profession, that when it came to publicity, Ramon stole the lion's share of attention as a way to take the fall for his family, particularly his sisters.

That behavior had continued even as she'd taken over her father's position. Since she had come aboard earlier this year, she had watched it happen—if somewhat mysteriously. Ramon had to be the source of the leaks, but he took care of them in his own way, never involving her and never charging into her office to demand why she wasn't preventing *his* scandals from going viral.

Still, his escapades always seemed to hit the light at the right time to pull attention from his siblings. When Angelique had been called a two-timer because photos of her kissing not one, but *two* different princes had turned up, photos from one of Ramon's "private" parties had surfaced. He had been half-naked and canoodling with a stripper on each knee. When Trella reentered society via the wedding of a family friend, causing a social-media riot, a tape of Ramon's blue-streaked voice mails had taken over the talk-show circuit. The minute Cinnia's twin pregnancy had become a target, an online feud had erupted between Ramon and a fellow driver.

So, in a way, she wasn't surprised he was announcing his retirement when a secret as big as Trella's pregnancy was hitting the airwaves. It just made Isidora...sad. And sheepish, for calling him faithless.

Not that she would admit that after he had threatened her job and future, the power-drunk bastard. Why did he have to be so hard on her? What had she ever done except like him a little too much?

She smoothed her hair, painted her lips a demure pink and told her throat to stop feeling so raw at the injustice.

She texted Ramon that she would wait for him at the elevator, but Etienne joined her first. He had been her father's protégé and had taken her out a few times last year, breaking it off when their sex life hadn't progressed as he had desired. She had gone to London to finish her degree and had been quite happy to never cross paths with him again.

Then her father had retired and Henri had used a

press-gang of euros and guilt trips to bring her aboard.
Etienne had believed he was a shoe-in for her father's
position. Instead he had wound up answering to *her*. He
was *not* happy.

"So it's true?" he said, his tone bordering on belligerence.

"What's that?"

"Trella is pregnant?" His tone rang with *obviously*.
"That's what this press conference is about, isn't it?"

"I'm need-to-know, same as you." She pretended to
read something on her phone. "But today's announcement is on another topic entirely."

A beat of silence, then he asked, "You're not going to
tell me what that topic is?"

"You'll find out in five minutes. That's why I invited
you to hear it firsthand."

He swore, muttering something about favoritism.

When she made no response, he said, "So you don't
deny it?"

"Deny what?"

His jaw clenched, then he spat out what had clearly
been chewing at him. "You were hired because of your
father. You're not even qualified. You don't have my experience."

"I was given a chance because of him, yes. But if I
stuff things up, I can assure you they will have no qualms
about letting me go."

A door closed down the hall and they went silent as
Ramon's firm steps approached. She pasted on the same
composed smile she would use to introduce him to the
rabid hounds of the press.

"Henri." Etienne greeted Ramon with a deferential
nod. He waved at the elevator she'd been holding, inviting Ramon to enter ahead of him.

"Ramon," he amended as he stepped into the car.

"Of course," Etienne said, visibly flustered as he came in last and pressed the button for the bottom floor. "The memo didn't specify." He sent a malevolent look at Isidora. "I didn't realize you were here. I suppose your brother is still in Spain with—"

"Bernardo never had a problem telling us apart," Ramon interjected. "And neither does Isidora. It's a quality we appreciate in those closest to us. Don't ever gossip about my family again. I have no qualms about letting *you* go for *that*."

It wasn't working. After a brief ripple of flashes and murmurs over his announcement, the callouts quickly turned to Trella.

"Can you confirm the pregnancy?"

"When is she due?"

"Who is the father?"

"Ladies and gentlemen, please confine your questions to today's topic." Isidora leaned her fragrant hair under his nose so the microphone picked up her well-modulated voice. "Ramon is retiring from racing to free up his time to restructure the company. These are details that will be of interest to your financial and market readers as well as the sports fans."

Such a smooth, unruffled command as she stayed on message, just like her father. As competent as she was, however, Etienne was right. She lacked experience. She didn't have Ramon's well-honed skill for manipulating the press—techniques he had learned from her father under the worst possible tutelage.

"Cuánto lo siento," Bernardo had said fifteen years ago, pleading for Angelique's forgiveness while Ramon had held her small, sweaty palm in his equally clammy hand.

The police thought a public plea for help would urge people to come forward with tips that could rescue their sister from her kidnappers.

"Emotions move people, Angelique," Bernardo had said. "I don't mean to cause you more pain. *Lo siento mucho.* I know you're frightened and hurting, but please don't try to hide your tears. People need to see how you are feeling. This is what makes it stick in their minds and moves them to act the way we need them to. *Lo lamento mucho.* I wish I didn't have to ask this of you, but I need you to reveal your heart to the camera."

It had been a disgusting thing to ask of a nine-year-old girl. Using her terror and anguish had bordered on exploitation. Their father hadn't been able to watch, too filled with self-contempt at putting his shy, sensitive daughter through such an ordeal when she was already so traumatized. But they had been desperate, all of them.

Their father had held their weeping mother in the other room while Henri stood beside the camera, so Angelique could look at him as she pleaded for Trella's return. Henri had worn the same ravaged expression that Ramon had felt upon his own face.

They had all developed a deep, deep hatred of the public attention that had never been invited and had turned their family into a target in the first place.

After Trella was rescued, and they were trying to move on with their lives, they had all found different ways of coping with the continued attention. Henri stonewalled at every opportunity. Angelique accepted and ignored. Trella had retreated to seclusion, becoming an elusive unicorn who had gone several years without being photographed.

Ramon preferred to play them at their own game. He didn't care what was printed about him. It amused him when the facts were wrong, especially when those "facts" came from him. One of his fellow racers had gleefully exchanged a volley of insults with him for several weeks earlier this summer, to take the pressure off Cinnia as she floundered under the weight of two babies and more attention than anyone should have to suffer—especially if they hadn't become inured to it the way the rest of his family had.

Now another baby was on the way. Ramon would quietly strangle his sister at some point for getting herself into that situation, but that was a job for another day.

Today's task was to protect that unborn Sauveterre. And Trella. Despite the progress she had made in the last year, she was still very fragile. She had barely survived her kidnapping. The critical press that had dogged her for years after had made every effort to finish her off. Ramon was very cognizant that a renewal of that harsh focus could give her a setback.

"Is it true that Trella watched some of your races last year, by pretending she was Angelique?"

Yes, and that was a can of worms that needed to stay closed. Ramon *had* to bring the focus back to him. Leaving racing wasn't doing the job. The dry topic of restructuring a corporation was certainly not holding anyone's attention.

Emotions move people. Reveal your heart to the camera...

His mind raced to find and evaluate options, quickly discovering the line he would have to follow if he wanted to stay in front of the pack.

"The truth is, I've discovered something for which I feel more passion than racing," he announced in a firm voice. "Hard to believe, is it not? Racing has been my life for over a decade, but with my brother so happily married and starting his family, I find I can't wait to enjoy the same. I'm deeply in love and…well—"

He moved around Isidora so he was no longer behind the podium and sank to one knee beside her.

A massive gasp went through the crowd.

The bombardment of flashes and clicks increased, but the shouting of questions ceased. An eerie expectancy characterized that wordless explosion of repeated shutter clicks and flashes. The lights strobed against her skin as he looked up to Isidora's incredulous expression.

She paled as comprehension dawned. Her eyes showed white around her gray irises. One hand came to her mouth and she might have said, "Don't you dare."

"Lo siento, mi amor," Ramon said with loud pride over the mechanical clicks and pops. "I cannot sneak around any longer, trying to keep this quiet. I love you too much."

He couldn't recall ever saying those words to anyone except his mother and siblings. It felt strange, pulling disturbingly at that inner door he kept so firmly closed. The push-pull gave his voice the appropriate amount of unsteadiness as he continued.

"You said if I quit racing, you would marry me. So, *mi corazón. Now* will you make me the happiest man on earth? Our fathers would approve, you know they would." He added the last as a reminder of where her loyalty should lie.

He had to give it to her. She had studied well under Bernardo. Her eyes filled with glossy tears and she didn't try to hide them. Her fingers against her lips trembled. Her other hand was cold when he took it in his, her fingers lax with shock.

The white fingers against her mouth curled into a fist.

"Was that yes?" He pretended he had heard a response no one else could and leaped to his feet. As he crushed her to his front, he played up the joyful act as he exclaimed, "She said yes!"

Then he dug his fingers into her hair, tipped back her head and kissed her.

She stiffened. Her breasts crushed into his chest as she sucked in a shocked breath.

He closed his grip on her more firmly, subtly, but implacably. *Do this*, he urged, but even he had his limits when it came to cold-bloodedly achieving his goals. Rather than force the kiss upon her, he brought all his sensual skill to bear and *persuaded* her to accept it.

Oh, this rat wasn't content to threaten her job or break her heart. He had to knock her self-esteem into smithereens. He rocked his mouth across her lips in exactly the way she had fantasized all through her teen years. Confident, hungry, enticing. Like he *loved* her.

Exactly as he'd just said he did.

She couldn't let his declaration affect her. It was a lie. She wanted to scratch his eyes out for playing with her like this.

Her own eyes stung, as if they'd been scraped raw behind her eyelids, but her self-control checked out. The besotted girl who had fallen in love so long ago came running out of her room, where she'd been crying into a pillow for five years. She threw herself into Isidora's body, heart singing with joy. She offered her mouth and drank up the sweet sensations that washed over her as Ramon acted, finally, like he wanted her.

Everywhere they touched, her skin bloomed with heat. Her bones turned pliant and the betrayal of his putting her on the spot like this evaporated. *Her*, the girl who had crushed so hard on a boy who was too old for her, the girl who had been ignored, rejected, then brutally passed over for her mother, the girl who had dealt with those horrible feelings of treachery and rebuff… She kissed him back.

She wasn't terribly experienced and that was his fault, too. These were the arms she had wanted from the first. These were the lips. This was the man.

He drew back and she realized he had one possessive hand drawing slow circles on her butt. That's why flutters of excitement were working up her lower back and into her loins. The fireworks that had been going off behind her closed eyelids were actually flashes. The roar in her ears was excited laughter and cheering. Sly jeering.

At her expense.

Oh, this mean bastard of a man. He didn't even let her go when she pressed her weak arms against his chest and tried to make space to catch her breath.

His embrace tightened to keep her smeared across his front. All she could do was hide her face by resting her ear against his chest and look toward the back wall—where Etienne stared at her with his lip curled in contempt.

"You—" So many filthy names crowded her tongue as Ramon closed them into his office minutes later that she couldn't pick one. "How *could* you?"

Her chest was tight, her voice fractured. Her entire world was topsy-turvy and it didn't help that she was in the mirror image of Henri's office, situated on the other side of a pair of connecting doors to her right. She definitely felt as though she stood on the wrong side of a looking glass.

Ramon threw off his jacket and slung it over the back of the sofa as he passed the conversation lounge. He dug his ringing phone from the pocket of his pants on his way to his desk in front of the tall windows.

"I need to take this. Stay here until you can find a suitable glow of delight. You looked like hell as we left. Good thing they only saw the back of you. *Hola*."

"Are you serious?" a woman's voice said. It sounded like Trella, but she and Angelique sounded very similar.

Ramon propped the phone against his laptop dock and glared at it. "This is your fault. Say 'thank you.'"

Definitely Trella.

"Why would you do something like that to poor Isidora? She didn't know it was coming, did she?"

"Did I take you by surprise, *mi amor*?" He turned his head to glance at where she stood like a whipped dog, hovering inside the closed door, trying to find her bearings among the cool masculine colors and implacable lines of the décor.

"Izzy's with you? I'm so sorry, Izzy." Trella was one of the few people who could get away with calling her that.

"It's fine," Isidora lied, forcing herself to move until she was close enough to see both Trella and Angelique in the screen, but not so close she joined Ramon in the tiny window. "I should have found a way to defuse those photos before they became more than we could contain. But we'll need a statement from you. There's no more avoiding it."

"It's not your fault." Trella spoke in the same pained tone she had used each time Isidora had tried coaxing her toward a disclosure. "I know I have to cop to eating for two, but I don't want…"

To tell the father. That was obvious, since she refused to name him even to her family. They all had a very good idea, however. Isidora had concluded herself that the man in question had to be Prince Xavier of Elazar, who had been photographed kissing "Angelique" earlier this year.

As Ramon had said himself, Isidora had never had a

problem telling the twins apart. She had known straight away that *Trella* had been caught kissing that particular prince, while Angelique was the twin in the photos with Kasim.

Did Prince Xavier know which twin he had kissed? That was a question for another day. She imagined Angelique's fiancé, now *King* Kasim, must have some opinions on the matter as well, since his intended appeared to have two-timed him. But Angelique had never said a word on the topic. Today, she showed nothing but loving protectiveness as she looped an arm around her sister and gave Trella a comforting hug.

"Why don't I walk over right now and we can discuss some angles," Isidora suggested. She could use an excuse to leave the building and get some air.

"Pahahaha!" Trella sputtered.

"You can't!" Angelique cried at the same time, urgently shaking her head.

"Why not? Is there something going on at the design house—?"

"You're one of us now, *moza amiga*." Trella leaned forward as though speaking to a child. "You travel by armored tank and avoid leading the hunters to the door. Seriously, *hermano*. What were you *thinking*?"

"What do you mean?" Isidora asked, even as reality began to sink in. Declaring a fake engagement, putting her on the spot in front of the cameras like that, had been awful, but the greater ramifications began to strike her consciousness.

No. The explosion of excitement downstairs had been for Ramon. Hadn't it? The paparazzi wouldn't think they had found a fresh target in *her*, would they?

She had never thought of herself as naive, but suddenly saw herself as the world's most gullible idiot.

"Have you talked to your parents?" Angelique asked with concern, voicing what was finally hitting Isidora's sluggish brain. "They're probably getting calls."

Her mother.

Isidora touched her brow. All those years she had spent lying to the world, including *to her own father*, spinning and downplaying her mother's affairs so their family wouldn't be talked about and vilified. Now every single tryst would be dug up. Her mother's past lovers might even throw their names into the ring of fame, just to have their moment in the spotlight. It didn't matter that her parents had eventually divorced over Francisca Villanueva's infidelity. She had cheated on Bernardo Garcia dozens of times and he would be forced to relive all of it. He would be humiliated all over again.

Isidora flung around to face Ramon. Of all the things he'd done, this was, by far, the worst. "I will never forgive you for this."

CHAPTER THREE

Isidora's mother answered her call with "Oh, *mi cielo.*
Henri just called. Such thrilling news! You've always
loved Ramon so much—"

"Henri called you?" Isidora interrupted, praying her
mother's voice hadn't carried.

Ramon was focused on his own phone as it buzzed
with incoming texts. *"Si,"* Ramon said to Isidora. "Henri
was watching the press conference. He's sending a car
for your mother now."

"Henri is worried reporters will descend on you," Isidora informed her mother.

Francisca would definitely say the wrong thing if she
knew the engagement was a publicity stunt. Isidora didn't
clear up her mother's misconception, and just said, "You
should pack, Mama. Don't keep them waiting."

"Where is Ramon? I want to give him my love." It
was a twist of the knife her mother had plunged into her
heart five years ago.

Isidora didn't waste hatred on her own flesh and
blood, though. She didn't even bother speculating why
her mother had taken Ramon to her bed when she had
known how her daughter felt about him. She had pro-
cessed long ago that her mother had an illness. An ad-
diction. It looked like a dependence on sex, but it was

actually a broken, empty soul starving for love and admiration. She was permanently an abandoned adolescent, like a broken runaway, with the same lack of judgment and gaping emotional needs.

Isidora would never feed in to that heartache by rejecting or reviling her. She did what she could to protect her. That's why she held Ramon in such contempt. How could he take advantage of someone so vulnerable?

"Henri has spoken to both your parents. He's bringing them to Sus Brazos for a few days while things blow over," Ramon told her.

Don't put them together, Isidora wanted to protest. Her parents were weak-willed where the other was concerned. It always ended the same, with her mother cheating and leaving for another man while her father nursed a freshly shattered heart. The hairline fracture left in Isidora's heart pulsed with an old ache as she contemplated another round of emotional turmoil.

"Is that the doorbell, Mama?" Isidora broke in to her mother's breathy ramblings. "Tell the staff to ask for identification. Call me when you're settled. *Te amo*."

Isidora ended the call and sent a text to her mother's housekeeper with the same instruction about checking for identity.

"So," Ramon said as their flurry of communication ended and they set aside their phones.

"Why?" she cried. "Why would you *do* that?"

Why had he said he *loved* her? It made it all the more hurtful. Thorny vines were tangled around her insides, squeezing and prickling. Half of it was self-recrimination. She would love to say she had gone along with it because she was a professional willing to sacrifice herself on the altar of her career. In truth, she had been so stunned, so *appalled* that he would exploit her old feelings in such a careless manner, she had been struck dumb.

"You know why. The retirement announcement wasn't working."

"Why *me*?" It was cruel. Her cheeks and throat and chest still burned, but when had he ever cared about hurting *her*?

"Was I supposed to come out as gay and propose to Etienne?" So blithe, shrugging off the damage he'd done. "I admit, that might have created a more effective stir, but maintaining *that* ruse for any length of time…?"

"Do you honestly think anyone is going to believe we're a couple?" She wanted to *kill* him.

"That's up to you, isn't it? I'm serious about you working on looking more pleased about marrying a Sauveterre. We have an image to maintain," he added with a disdainful tilt of his lips.

"Quit making jokes! This isn't funny." Her pulse raced like she was being chased through a dark forest by a pack of wolves. "I am *not* marrying you."

"No," he agreed, the single word dropping her old hopes like china on concrete. "But you will play the part of my fiancée until the attention on our family dies down."

"Oh, right. When has that ever happened? No, Ramon. I refuse. Go ahead and fire me for insubordination. *Make my day.*"

He folded his arms and leaned his hips on the desk, his expression bored. "Are you done?"

"Are you implying I'm overreacting?" She was trembling, hands fisted at the ends of her tensed arms, entire body twitching with fight or flight. *"You're ruining my life."*

"Please," he scoffed. "This is your job. You're in front

of the cameras all the time, standing next to one of us, making statements that say nothing. It's more of the same."

"It's *not*. I'm fine as a Sauveterre minion, but I don't want to be the main event!"

"You're not a minion." He drew back a little, sending her an annoyed frown. "You're part of the inner circle. You know that."

"Since *when*?" His siblings might treat her that way, but *he* certainly didn't.

"I wouldn't have gone down today's route with anyone else, even if there had been other choices. We trust you. This is obvious by the position you hold. How is this news to you?"

"*You* trust me?" She refused to let herself believe it. Wouldn't allow it to be important. "After what you said this morning about making my life difficult? Or was it miserable? Either way, you're ticking all the boxes, aren't you?"

He didn't move, but his expression hardened. "Let's talk about how I really ruined your life, shall we? Clearly we have to get that out of the way before you'll be able to act like a grown-up."

No. She felt her throat flex as it closed around a cry of pain, like an arrow speared into her windpipe. Without a word, she spun and headed for the door.

A *snick* sounded as she approached it. Oh, he had not just locked it. She gave the latch a furious wriggle and yanked on the door, but nothing happened. It was oddly frightening. She didn't fear him exactly, but she was terrified of the feelings he provoked in her. They were always off the scale. And to lock her in and insist she talk about *that*?

No. Clammy sweat broke out on her forehead. Her hands and feet went icy cold.

She spun to see him behind his desk. His hand came away from a panel that he casually closed so the surface of his desk was smooth and unbroken once again.

"Why are you such a horrible person?"

"You know why. That is what I've been saying." He spoke in a flat, implacable tone. The fact that he didn't deny being reprehensible did nothing to reassure her. He moved to the wet bar near the sitting area and pulled out a bottle of anise. "Your preferred spirit, I believe?"

She didn't answer, thinking it strange that he would know that. It was a common drink in Spain, though. It was probably a lucky guess. He poured them each a glass.

"You know our family history, Isidora. You played with my sisters when they had forgotten how. You visited Trella when she imprisoned herself in Sus Brazos. You showed a preference for me when every other girl on the planet couldn't tell me apart from my brother and didn't bother to try. Come. Sit."

She stayed stubbornly by the locked door, arms folded, face on fire. She stood there and hated him for knowing how infatuated she had been. For talking about it like it was some cute, childish memory. Nostalgia for a first pet.

Most of all, she hated him for making her stand here and relive the morning when two of her most painful experiences collided and became an utterly unbearable one.

He leaned to set her drink on a side table and sipped his own, remaining standing, flinty gaze fixed on her resentful expression.

"I was flattered, but I couldn't take you seriously. You were too young."

She had known that. Eight years was a big gap and aside from a handful of boyish pursuits, he and his brother had always been beyond their years. Their sister's kidnapping when they were fifteen had very quickly matured them, then their father's early death had forced them to take control of an international investment corporation at twenty-one. They had been carrying tremendous responsibility for a decade. In many ways, Ramon was still too old for her.

"I don't care that you never wanted to date me." Lie. She cared. His disinterest had been demoralizing. "What I can't forgive is that you slept with my mother."

"I didn't sleep with her," he growled.

She snorted and looked away, working to keep her face noncommittal while she was dying inside, aching to believe that, but she wasn't stupid. The fact he would lie to her face about it made it even worse.

"Did you ask her?" he prompted.

"No!" As if she wanted details about any of the men her mother slept with, most especially *him*. "I didn't have to, did I? The evidence spoke for itself."

"The evidence," he repeated, tone light yet dangerous, increasing her tension.

"You were half-dressed, wearing a night's stubble, and the hood of your car was cold. It doesn't take a forensic scientist to figure out where you spent the night."

"I've never denied spending the night."

"In her bed. Two pillows were used. I *looked*."

"I reclined *on* her bed while she changed and removed her makeup. We were talking. Nothing happened. We went back downstairs and drank enough that I decided to sleep it off on the sofa. I woke when I heard you come in. I tried to tell you this at your father's birthday. You walked away."

"Oh, please. Once she realized I'd come home, she didn't say, 'Oh, by the way, Ramon spent the night, but it was completely innocent.' She asked how long I'd been there and looked guilty as hell."

"That—" He pointed at her. "That is the real evidence, isn't it? You don't think your mother can't bring a man home without making love with him."

True, but that was such a complex issue for her, she refused to go there.

"You've hit a hard limit, Ramon. The way my mother lives is not up for discussion. I *will* walk. And that's not why I think you're the scum of the earth."

His head went back as though the cold iron in her tone caught his attention. After a brief pause, he said, "If you're thinking *I'm* the one who can't spend a night with a woman and not have sex, you're wrong."

He was talking about Trella, she supposed. Her friend's struggle with anxiety was something that turned Isidora inside out every single time she thought about it, but she refused to let herself soften with empathy. To give him the benefit of the doubt.

"You want me to believe that's what you were doing that night?" She burned afresh with outrage and scorn. "Letting my mother cry on your shoulder? Then why didn't you say so when we met in the lounge? I asked you what you were doing there and you said she had been looking for company so you came home with her. You knew what I took from that. You knew *exactly* what I was thinking. If you didn't have sex with her, why did you let me believe you did?"

"Because you were eighteen and still carrying a torch." His voice was a sledgehammer. "It had to stop."

This moment was every bit as hard a hit as that moment had been, completely destroying any shred of hope she might have clung to. For a few seconds, she couldn't breathe. The agony was that all-encompassing.

She wasn't *still* carrying a torch, was she? She would swear she hadn't been.

Until he had kissed her. Something tentative had begun playing in the back of her mind in the last hour, though. She was waiting for time alone to relive that kiss and properly savor it. To build it into something it would never become.

How pathetic.

He was right. This childish yearning had to stop.

As the silence lengthened, something tickled her cheek. She wiped at it, discovering it was a tear.

He released a heavy sigh, which scored, speaking as it did of his impatience with her intense feelings where he was concerned.

She was equally exhausted by it herself. She really was.

Last one, she vowed. That was the last tear she would ever cry over this man.

Because it didn't matter if he had slept with her mother or not. What he was telling her, then and now, was that he would never be interested in her. Not as anything but a fake fiancée. A prop for one of his PR tricks.

She *had* to move on.

She nodded with understanding, feeling disconnected from her body. The muscles around her mouth twitched and she thought she might be trying to smile, but it was the kind that came when the tragedy was too great for any other emotion but laughter at how punishing life could be.

"Tough love," she said, voice jagged beneath the irony.

He swore and she heard him exchange his empty glass for the one she hadn't touched. He knocked back that shot and his breath hissed again.

"It was a test. You passed."

"Because I didn't turn on you and your family?"

Such a cold bastard. What had she ever seen in him?

Aside from his incredible devotion to his family, of course. And his unbending will to win, his lust-worthy looks, his charisma, brilliant intelligence and unwavering confidence.

She wanted to turn on him now.

But she couldn't. It wasn't in her to walk away from people who needed her. Even when her own heart was twisted beyond recognition by staying.

That was her specialty, in fact. Wasn't it? Helping her father and mother navigate the pain they caused each other, standing by both of them while they went through it. She carried on, fractured and battered by a heartrending personal life. Why should her professional life be any different?

Forcing herself to move, she closed herself into the powder room and checked her makeup. There was an emotive redness around her eyes and her lipstick was faintly smudged. She smoothed her hair and used a damp tissue to repair her lips, all the while thinking of the times her father had said he was proud of her. Not just for following in his footsteps, but for other things, too.

That love of his had pulled her through a lot—the devastation of learning he wasn't biologically her father, for instance.

Bernardo was her anchor, her moral compass, her silver lining in a world too often clouded and stormy. He was the parent her mother was incapable of being.

He would never wind up in such a ridiculous position, but if he had to choose whether to work with a Sauveterre or against one, she knew what he would do: whatever was asked.

He would stay loyal to the offspring of the man who had convinced him to accept the child her mother had passed off as his own.

Isidora owed the Sauveterres for the man she called "Papa," not that they knew it.

At least, when this was over, she would feel she had settled that debt.

Ramon savored the subtle bite of the anise, letting the fragrant sweetness roll on his tongue, thinking it was not unlike Isidora's personal flavor. *That kiss.* As he finally had a moment alone, he gave in to the memory of driving his tongue into welcoming heat. He had half expected her to drive her knee into his groin, but the kick of her response had been even more devastating. That hadn't been mere surrender. It had been a chemical explosion that had burned away everything he understood about kisses and women and sex.

What the hell?

He had held many beautiful women. None had sparked such a profound reaction in him. He had lost himself for a moment, absorbed in a vast landscape he instinctively knew would take a lifetime to explore.

Then the insanity of their public location had struck. He'd pulled out of the worst tailspin of his life, dazed and, yes, instantly defensive at having his thick shields penetrated so effortlessly.

If he had realized they were so sexually compatible—

No. He poured a third drink, refusing to go back and reexamine the turns he had already made. That was his brother's MO. Henri liked to track results on spreadsheets and weigh options as he made projections and charted his next moves. That invariably resulted in accurate predictions that efficiently achieved the result he wanted, but it wasn't Ramon's style. He let his gut pick the goal and shot toward it via the swiftest, shortest line, making corrections as problems cropped up.

His aim was to protect his family, first and foremost. Always. He never let his libido distract him. It was a weakness. Strength was his only option. Too many people depended on him, especially now that Henri had a wife and two defenseless infants to look out for.

But Ramon did have weaknesses. Some of them came around annually as a long, dark night of the soul. When he was not in a position to spend those nights with family, he sought company, usually female. That was how he had come to enter a bar in Madrid and find the ex-wife of his father's best friend, five years ago.

Francisca Villanueva was a delicate soul who carried a lot of pain. He had taken her home to keep less honorable men from taking advantage of her. He couldn't save her from herself indefinitely, but he could for a night.

She had made him laugh and revealed her own pain, exposing more cracks in her family than he had ever guessed from Bernardo's composed demeanor or Isidora's sunny smiles.

Coming face-to-face with Isidora as he left the next morning had been like one of those moments on a racetrack, where a split-second decision had to be made.

Isidora had been making calf eyes at him since adolescence. The longer her legs grew, the more difficult it was to ignore her. Temptation had been closing its grip on him as she blossomed into an ever more alluring woman, but she was too young and inexperienced for the light, temporary affairs he offered.

As her smile of delighted recognition had faded into confusion and suspicion, then betrayal and devastation, he had let the disillusionment happen.

He could have corrected her assumption. He could have told her that his night with her mother had been wine and conversation and a chaste kiss on the cheek when her mother went to bed alone. He could have kept Isidora's fixation on him alive, but to what end? He was never going to marry her. It wasn't personal. He would never marry anyone. Children were completely off the table. His siblings might be changing their minds about opening themselves to liability, but Ramon hadn't and wouldn't.

So what had been his alternative in that moment? Encourage Isidora to keep mooning after him? Eventually date her, sleep with her, *then* break her heart? No. He had used the opportunity to cut her off the lane she was on. Cruel, yes, but a type of kindness. She was on track to crash and burn otherwise.

He had not foreseen that Henri would hire her years later, but he couldn't argue with the appointment. Isidora had grown into a composed, accomplished woman with cutting-edge PR skills, and who possessed wit and intelligence. Most of all, she brought to the table a deep understanding of their family dynamics, allowing them to skip past painful history lessons.

Ramon accepted that she was angry. Hurt even. That she didn't want to lie about their being engaged. His proposal had been another reflexive move. Cruelty without kindness, but there was no backing out. They would have to make the best of it.

He stroked his thumb on the curve of the glass he held, trying not to fall back into dwelling on how exquisite her response had been. It was a dangerous distraction when he needed to stay focused on what his family needed.

The powder-room door opened and Isidora came out wearing an expression that was both calm and— Was that a light of joy as she let a broad smile take over her face?

It kicked him in the chest. *Dios*, there really was no ignoring how lovely she was.

"Better?"

His ears rang so loudly it took him a moment to catch the sarcasm.

"You said I could leave when I managed to look happy about this. Good enough?" She dropped her smile.

The radiance in her expression dimmed so fast and sharp, he felt it like the chill when the sun went suddenly behind a cloud.

"You'll need a retirement party and an engagement party," she continued matter-of-factly. "Two different ones, to maximize the coverage." She crossed to where she had left her phone. "We should do something around all the restructuring and promotions, too. We'll call them team-building sessions, but something visual, like zip lines or a fun run. We'll link it to a charity for a higher profile. You and I can make appearances, invite the press to watch you shake hands with your new CEOs. If I'm going to all this trouble to snag news coverage, Sauveterre International should benefit. I'll need a ring. Something flashy. Gaudy, even. The gossip outlets are on ring watch with Angelique so let's give them something to notice. I won't keep it, so I'll arrange a loan—"

"I'll get the ring," he interjected, not quite trusting this abrupt switch in attitude. "You're doing this, then? No more arguing?"

"Oh, I'm sure we'll argue, but you haven't given me much choice, have you?" She took a moment to set her shoulders and lift her chin, as though bravely facing down a firing squad.

Was it really such a monumental favor? He hitched his hands on his hips, wanting to roll his eyes. "You'll be compensated."

"That's not what I'm after." She flashed him a cross look, offended. "I'll always do what I can to help Trella.

All of your family. But… How long does this have to last? Three or four months?" Her brow furrowed with calculation. "Once Trella has her baby and Angelique announces her engagement, you and I can have a nice public breakup, yes? Unless something else comes up along the way and we need a story?"

Ramon knew when to push an advantage and when to simply hold on to one, but it still bothered him as he said, "That sounds appropriate."

"It will make sense that I leave the company when we part ways. You should talk with Henri about how you plan to replace me."

A reflexive protest rose, but she was right. He would facilitate her finding a good position as part of her compensation. After a suitable period, if they needed her, they could pull her back.

She cut him a glance and briefly bit her lip. The self-conscious color in her face increased. "Etienne would seem the natural choice for my position. If that's what you're thinking, I should disclose something."

He narrowed his eyes, not wanting to believe what had just leaped into his brain. "Continue."

She tucked a wisp of hair behind her ear, cleared her throat and smiled flatly. "He expected the promotion into my father's position. He's been upset about my receiving it."

"So? We make our decisions based on what's best for us."

"I know, but…" She clicked off her phone. "He worked under my father for the four years I was at school. I've never advertised how close I am with your sisters so he doesn't realize why you chose me. He feels passed over—"

"I don't care about his dented ego, Isidora. Why would I?"

"I'm telling you why." She dropped her phone into the pocket of her jacket and smoothed a fingertip along her eyebrow. "If you think he'll be appropriate to take my job, we should bring him in on this. Tell him the engagement is fake so he feels part of the team. He already thinks I earned my way on my father's coattails, but he and I used to date and—"

"You *slept* with that idiot." For some reason, Ramon had believed she was still a virgin. He knew it was outlandish, but she projected such innocence at times.

She lowered her lashes now, blushing like a new bride.

Of course a woman her age would have had lovers. He didn't know why it was such a surprise. Maybe because his sisters had never breathed a word about her dating exploits. Her father had spent Isidora's adolescence closely monitoring her virtue—which was absolutely no surprise given her mother's behavior. That vigilance of her father had been yet another reason Ramon hadn't so much as glanced in her direction, but he had honestly believed her attention had never strayed from *him*.

Despite the pains he'd taken to ensure it would.

So why did it bother him to discover she had followed her urges to other men? Maybe because he couldn't help wondering if she'd kissed them the way she had kissed him today. Had Etienne enjoyed fully the passion Ramon had only tasted?

Dios. It was one thing to know she had men in her past, quite another to pass the lothario in the hallway. To wonder if she carried a torch for *that* man.

"Etienne is not an idiot," she said stiffly. "He's dedicated and smart, otherwise my father wouldn't have apprenticed him and I wouldn't have kept him on. The important piece here is that he could become a liability if not handled carefully."

Ramon choked out a laugh, astonished by how much aggression filled him—he made his voice as callous and dispassionate as he possibly could.

"You're adorable. How have I treated you, Isidora? And you have value to me. You think I'm going to put on kid gloves for a spineless twit nursing entitlement issues? What did I say to him before the press conference? As far as the world is concerned, you just became part of my family. If he treats you with anything less than the utmost respect, if he makes one wrong step for any reason, he will lose his job." It was the same lack of mercy he showed anyone, but the clench in his chest pushed the words out with added vehemence. "More, if I judge him to be any sort of threat beyond rumor-mongering."

Her lashes went down and her cheeks went hollow.

"Do not even think of telling him that. If he needs it spelled out, his job is already lost." He couldn't countenance her wanting to protect the man. Did she still have feelings for him? "Only my siblings will know our engagement isn't real," he stated, halfway to firing Etienne for no other reason than that he existed. "Otherwise we'll be dismissed in a day and the press will go straight back to crucifying Trella."

"Fine," she said in a small voice. "But I have to tell my father it's fake."

"No."

"Yes, Ramon." Her lashes swept up, but rather than vehemence, he read a surprising vulnerability. Her voice held a tiny fracture. "He'll assume it's a stunt, same as your family did, but he'll expect me to confirm it. The alternative is for you to ask for my hand like a proper suitor and I won't let you lie to him. Not about that. It was bad enough you—" Color bled across her cheekbones and she clammed up, jaw tightening.

Said he loved her?

Something seesawed in his chest, but he had to agree. There was too much history with Bernardo. He'd been a true friend to their father and later a very trusted advisor to him and Henri. He couldn't disrespect Bernardo with any sort of lie.

"I'll speak to him," he promised.

"Thank you," she said stiffly.

"Good. Now let's get to work." His thoughts expanded as everything he had come to Paris to implement was now filtered through a fake engagement. He moved to his desk and opened the panel to release the doors, then asked his PA to assemble key personnel in the boardroom.

Isidora lingered.

"I thought you were anxious to escape? Call Julie," he told her. "She coordinates my calendar with my race schedule. Ask her to plan the retirement party in Monaco. Then join us in the meeting."

"Yes, fine," she said, brushing a hand through the air. "But I just want to be clear. No more passes like today." Her cheeks went bright pink.

"It wasn't a pass. It was a performance. More will be necessary."

Her jaw tightened. "Keep it to a minimum. I won't sleep with you."

It struck him that he had tied himself to the one woman he shouldn't sleep with, even if she wanted to—which he had taken great pains to ensure she didn't. *Dios!* Celibate? Him? He had to bite back a curse of self-disgust, but as he thought again about how open he'd left himself when he'd had her in his arms, he knew it was better to keep a lid on things.

"You weren't invited to," he stated.

Her stunned expression went stoplight-red, flashing blunt injury before she spun and treated him to a view of her rigid spine and spectacular ass. The door slammed loudly behind her.

CHAPTER FOUR

ISIDORA PASTED ON a smile as fake as her engagement and allowed Ramon the Rat to take possession of her life.

She knew how the Sauveterre men worked. There was no option to lead, only to follow or get out of the way. She had agreed to follow. As she sat through the meeting, she felt herself sucked along the slipstream of his accelerated pace. He snapped his whip over the team, pacing behind her and pausing only to consult with her in an offhand way as he threw out dates and locations, names and promotions.

"You agree, *mi amor*?"

"Of course, *cariño*," she murmured, smiling and smiling her manufactured joy until her face ached. Trying to hide that she was dying inside.

She didn't know how she would get through this.

The news that he hadn't slept with her mother altered her feelings drastically. Of course she was relieved, but the resentment that had been a form of protection had been burned to the ground, leaving her suddenly susceptible to the powerful attraction that had always gripped her.

Which had made his shot about not inviting her to sleep with him quite the poison dart. Her insides were still seared raw. What was it about this man that made her so ultrasensitive to him? Was she missing a vital gene of self-preservation? She really was her father's daughter, if that was the case.

Ramon had gone to incredible lengths to rebuff her and still didn't want anything to do with her. That indifference of his had done a number on her self-esteem in her teen years, but after a lot of travel and hard work at school, not to mention dating men who actually seemed to *like* her, she had built up her confidence. Maybe she hadn't fully escaped her fascination with Ramon, since she had never been drawn enough to other men to sleep with them, but she knew they found her attractive. Not that she needed a man to validate her. Her work ethic was solid and the work she did well-received. She had started today feeling like the confident, professional woman she had fought to become.

But she was back to feeling like an adolescent with an inferiority complex.

No. She had a thick skin in every other area of her life. Control, composure and staying on message, were her stock in trade. He had said this was just an extension of her job. She had to be as unaffected as he was.

As the meeting broke up, he chivalrously helped her with her chair.

She exerted supreme effort and kept her inner turmoil from her face, feeling brittle as she said, "Good meeting." She made to step past him.

His heavy hand landed on her hip, urging her to stay and face him. Her stomach trembled in reaction. The intimate tone of his voice picked at her composure, threatening to unravel it.

"We should celebrate."

It's for show, she reminded herself, holding very still, trying to ignore the gaping canyon of yearning that opened inside her. His light touch sent licks of fire up her side and down her thigh. She told herself it was okay if her cheeks revealed the heat radiating from her core, that she was supposed to be dazzled by him. She gave in to his power for one moment and let her adulation of this particular god shine through her expression.

A startled spark flashed in his gaze, exciting and terrifying at once. His other hand came to her other hip and his fingers tightened. His attention slid to her mouth.

Her lips tingled as though he'd grazed them with his own. The memory of their kiss was right there, making her heart begin a rapid drumbeat.

You weren't invited to.

She had folded like a cheap tent for him the first time, but a jagged catch of humiliation kept her from doing it again.

She didn't care if they had an audience to amuse. The people filing toward the door were sending them curious smirks, but sick horror took hold in her, tensing her with resistance. She would not allow herself to become a laughingstock.

"Let's keep the PDA to a minimum in the office, *hermoso*. No need to embarrass anyone." She set her hand firmly on his chest, face averted. "I'll go make a reservation for dinner."

His strength was such that he didn't have to exert himself one iota to keep her exactly where she was. "I'll arrange it."

"You mean you'll ask Monique to do it?" She batted her lashes as she mentioned his PA. Engagement banter. So cute.

"I said *I* would." His voice was laconic, his expression arrogant. Yet watchful enough to make the moment feel bizarrely lethal.

She was in the cage with the tiger. His tail was twitching, but he wasn't hungry. Not for her. She was safe. For now.

"Seven o'clock?" he asked.

"Can't wait." She tried again to pull away and this time he allowed it.

And she knew she was deranged on some level because disappointment clawed in her chest.

Isidora did her own makeup and hair, then put on a dress her mother had bought for her when they were shopping on her last birthday. She had only tried it on because her mother had insisted.

"You have such a beautiful figure, *mi angel*. Why don't you show it off?"

Isidora had bit back observing that her mother did enough showing off for both of them. "It's not exactly office attire, Mama."

It was a strapless cocktail dress that hugged her curves in what looked like ribbons of liquid gold. The tails came together in a bow between her breasts, leaving a peeka-boo cut out over her diaphragm.

"You work too hard. Dance!" Her mother had bought her a pair of gold heels to go with it. "Enjoy your youth. Live your life with *entusiasmo*!"

Francisca was an heiress who had grown up with ev-erything except love and discipline. The expense of a designer outfit for her daughter was nothing compared to what her mother spent on herself each month. Isidora had accepted the gift, fully expecting it would collect dust in her closet.

She never wore skirts this short. Given her mother's lack of modesty, she compensated with conservative styles and even more conservative behavior. Ramon's sisters could easily get away with showing this much skin and still look respectable, but Isidora felt positively loose and looked…ah, hell. She looked like her mother. Not so much physically, but in the come-hither display of her wares.

She never dressed like this, especially for a man. Ramon's constant rejections during her adolescent years had killed that in her.

She might have panicked and changed, but as she took note of the text that Ramon was on his way, she noticed things were heating up online. Ugh. She checked the rest of her notifications with dismay. She would have to discuss that with him.

In danger of running late now, she closed the door of her flat and descended the two flights of stairs to the lobby, realizing as she arrived on the bottom step that the noise she had dimly assumed was a neighbor's television was actually a crowd gathered outside the glass doors of her building.

Aside from a handful of photographers, her arrival home from work hadn't drawn much notice, but in the hour she'd been dressing, a hundred people had gathered. Maybe more.

She instinctively hung back until a black car pulled up to the curb.

An excited murmur grew. Ramon's guard stepped from the passenger seat, took a reading on the crowd and directed people to part, waiting until there was a clear path to the building's door before he opened the rear door of the car.

Ramon rose with his easy grace. The crowd roared with approval.

He paused to give them a nod, utterly breathtaking in close-cut pants and a light blue pullover beneath a linen blazer. He really was too beautiful.

Isidora snapped out of her admiration and quickly moved through the lobby and out the doors, intent on keeping the spectacle to a minimum and allowing them to hurry away.

As she appeared, another roar went up.

She paused reflexively, not expecting the reaction. She was no one. Fake, fake, fake.

They didn't know that, of course. They went wild.

She found her party smile and waved a greeting.

Was this what it was like for them? Pretending to be happy about the attention? Pretending she enjoyed the claps and calls of her name?

Wait. Was that a curse? A *boo*?

She faltered, glancing to the right where someone said something she didn't catch, but his tone was aggressive.

The mood of the crowd shifted. The excited babble grew bothered as people jostled. She heard someone say something about her destroying the sport.

It was unnerving and she took a few more steps forward, but there were no ropes or other obstacles to hold people back. The crowd on either side had pressed into the space, narrowing her path, and a woman stumbled into her way, crying out a protest at being shoved. The milling bodies grew more unruly and an unseen hand reached for Isidora, hard fingertips skimming her arm.

Startled, she jerked from the touch, staggered in her heels and wound up bumping into someone on the other side.

Like walls closing in, strangers pushed into the space between her and Ramon, blocking her from both him and a safe retreat into her building as they started to surround her.

She grew scared. Truly scared. She looked for him,

but another touch on her arm had her jerking her head around.

She was given a hard yank and lost her footing. She stumbled toward the sidewalk, hands outstretched.

Ramon was unsurprised that a crowd had gathered outside Isidora's building. It was routine when he started dating a woman that fans and paparazzi tried to catch a photo of him with his new woman. It was the reason women threw themselves at him—for the notoriety.

He had expected to go into the building and escort Isidora out. That was also routine. He was a gentleman who offered door-to-door service, but she stepped out as he arrived, then paused in surprise as the crowd reacted.

He, too, reacted. His breath left him as he took in the vision she made of polished gold against the weathered stone of her building. She was an award statuette come to life, loose auburn curls gently shifting around her bare shoulders, her legs pale, delectable stems that begged for kisses upon every inch.

His gut tightened exactly as it had when he had stood in his boardroom, keeping her standing before him, feeling her hold him off even as she turned her sunny expression up to him.

He had basked in the glow of her smile like a cave dweller in springtime, startled by how good it felt. He had missed that light. That warmth. For a few seconds, an unidentified tightness in him had eased. He had wanted to kiss her again. Hard and deep. The kind of kiss that didn't stop until they were both replete.

He wanted to make love to her. He could lie to her and pretend he didn't, but he couldn't lie to himself. What man, looking at her now, would *not* want to carry her to the nearest bed? She was breathtaking.

Desire like he had never known crystalized in him, far more potent than the generic sexual hunger that pulsed in his loins for any woman who gave him a signal. His body suddenly demanded *this* woman. He needed *her* capitulation. *Her* writhing body beneath his.

Pure lust blinded him as surely as their kiss had—which became a near fatal mistake as the crowd turned on her.

It was not something he had ever experienced. Female fans might say jealous things about his dates online, but no woman he'd ever been with had ever been assaulted.

Nevertheless, in seconds, the avid excitement in the crowd became stained with hostility. Outright aggression. Isidora was shoved and started to fall.

He reacted with the reflexes he had honed on the track and hardened with physical training, which included military-style fighting. He shoved aside whomever stood between them, swept her up and growled, "Get back or I'll kill you."

Not his usual urbane reaction, but he was incensed. Shaken. Utterly feral in that moment, unnerving himself and terrifying pale faces into backing off with wide-eyed alarm.

Oscar, his day guard, was right there, arms spread to ensure the press of bodies gave them room to reach the car. Ramon slid Isidora into the back seat and threw himself in behind her, slamming the door to lock them in. His heart jammed and his temperature redlined.

"What the *hell*?" he groaned as Oscar leaped into the passenger side and the driver took off down the street, pressing them into their seats.

"I had no indication—" Oscar stammered.

"It's because you quit racing *for me*," Isidora said in a small, breathless voice. She was white as a sheet, looking back through the rear window at the uprising they had barely escaped.

"Qué?" He couldn't process that she had an answer when his security guard didn't.

"Some, um…" She cleared her throat, visibly trying to regain her composure as she faced forward and folded one trembling hand over the other. "Some of your fans think your proposal was romantic, but some are blaming me for their favorite driver leaving their favorite sport."

"You knew this was brewing and didn't warn me?" The top of his head nearly came off.

"I started seeing the posts a few minutes ago." Her face was drawn, her tone distraught. "I was going to tell you now. When I saw you."

"It's protocol to forward security concerns the second threats are recognized."

"When they target you or your siblings. They weren't saying anything against you, so I…" Her eyes nearly ate up her face at whatever was in his expression. Her voice became so thready, he barely heard her. "I didn't think—"

"No. You didn't. You put me in danger, Isidora. All of us." He waved at Oscar and his chauffeur, then pulled out his phone and connected to the man who held the contract for Sauveterre security.

"We need a full detail for Isidora. Everything my sisters have."

A preliminary backup team was immediately organized to join them at the restaurant. A promise was made to have everything in place by morning.

"I thought they were just trolls," Isidora muttered.

"And I thought Trella's kidnapper was just Gili's math tutor. *Anything* could have happened back there." He was still beside himself, his thoughts in the darkest places because he had learned the hard way that those places were real. "You could have been trampled. Beaten. Thrown into the street under a car. Stolen and raped and killed. *You should have warned me.*"

What if that had happened? What if it had been his fault?

She pushed back into her seat, lips white, chin crinkled, eyes blinking hard. Her knees were pressed together tight, her painted fingernails clutching her elbows. With a little sniff, she turned her face away and her throat flexed.

"Scared? You damn well should be!"

She hated him *so much*. And she would not—*would not* let him make her cry.

"Whose fault is it that they hate me?" she choked out. *"Yours."*

"You think I don't know that?" he roared.

She jolted and even the driver was startled because the car juddered before he smoothly changed lanes and carried on.

With a curse, Ramon leaned forward and closed the privacy screen.

"*This* is why I'm such a bastard. *This* is why I don't compromise. *This* is why I can never be the man you wanted me to me." He sat back, fist hitting his thigh. His voice held a note of uncharacteristic defeat. "I could never ask a woman to put up with this for the rest of her life."

Your brother did, she wanted to snap out, but Henri and Cinnia had broken up and only came back together when Cinnia was noticeably pregnant. If she hadn't been carrying a Sauveterre, Isidora was pretty sure both brothers would have remained bachelors their entire lives.

She privately believed Henri had been glad to have the excuse to get back with Cinnia. He had sounded indescribably pleased when he had told Isidora they were married, but Ramon seemed resolved in his detachment.

And looked surprisingly lonely in it. He stared ahead, his profile a study in carved planes and stark shadows.

"I'm sorry," she said in a subdued tone.

"You should be."

Why did she even bother? She looked out her window again, shoulders aching where she refused to let them slouch, trying not to breathe so he wouldn't hear her sniff.

As he waited for Isidora outside the powder room on the top floor of the Makricosta Elite, Ramon was more keyed up than before a race.

He had set her up for harm with his proposal.

From the time he was fifteen, after Trella had been stolen and recovered, he had settled into a mostly unspoken agreement with his brother. Neither of them would pursue a serious, long-term relationship. A Sauveterre wife, and most especially a child, would be endangered simply by carrying their name.

Cinnia's accidental pregnancy had forced his brother to change his mindset, but Henri had had feelings for Cinnia from the beginning, whether he had admitted to them or not.

Ramon kept his heart far more guarded. The logistics of protecting the people he cared about was a big responsibility, but that wasn't the only reason he refused to marry. He had the money and resources to ensure the best if it came down to it. No, the real issue was the emotional cost. The idea that a woman he cared about, or a child he loved, could be taken and harmed as Trella had been, closed such a fist of terror in Ramon, he could barely withstand it.

He didn't like being that vulnerable. He was very judicious in how much he cared and for whom. It was why he strove for indifference in his sexual relationships.

His proposal to Isidora had been a stunt. It was supposed to look gallant. In the back of his mind, he'd been aware that extra security precautions would have to be taken. Any woman who was attached to him was entitled to his protection. His team knew the drill.

But this sort of attack? The preliminary report on the social-media diatribe had since come through and the vehemence against Isidora was unnerving. Ramon felt like an idiot—not something he was used to. He was furious with himself for not anticipating it. He knew how much evil existed in this world. How had he not guessed this could happen?

Fear for her pierced his thick shields and maintained a thorny hold on him. He did what he could to alleviate it by biting out terse orders at his guard. "Send a team to her apartment. She's not going back there. She'll stay with me."

Oscar nodded as he texted.

She emerged, pale with stark shadows in her eyes, and checked when she saw him. Whatever was in his grim expression made her sweep her lashes down to hide her thoughts before she lifted her chin.

"You didn't have to wait for me. I'm perfectly capable of finding my way to the table without getting egged."

It hadn't even occurred to him to go ahead. He thought of all the times Trella had asked him to wait outside a bathroom door, suffering panic attacks so debilitating she had been afraid to be alone for five minutes. For once it had been his own apprehension that had kept him standing sentry.

"Let's not test that."

She flinched at the rasp in his tone.

He grimaced, but only waved at her to precede him.

The maître d' greeted them warmly and showed them to their best table, where a bottle of Dom Pérignon stood chilled and ready. The table was set with bone china, gold cutlery and gold-rimmed champagne flutes. Rose petals adorned the white cloth. Three glittering candles stood sentinel over a delicate spray of white orchids with pink centers. The exotic blooms curled around a small velvet box in a fragrant embrace.

Which is when Ramon remembered placing a request for some pageantry this afternoon, after Isidora had looked so pithy about his making a reservation, like she knew damn well he didn't call restaurants himself.

He didn't, but he had a competitive streak a mile wide. It demanded he prove someone wrong even when they were right.

"I'll give you a moment." The maître d' retreated.

Isidora said nothing, just stood there staring, freshened lipstick seeming stark against her pale face.

In his periphery, he noted that people were openly watching.

"It was supposed to be a joke," he groaned beneath his breath.

"I know." Her voice was faint. She brought her hand up to steady her trembling mouth. The sheen on her eyes grew thicker.

She'd had a shock, he realized belatedly, and he'd been treating her like the altercation at her building was her fault. It wasn't. It was *his* fault, for being who he was. Nothing could change it, either. He had had come to grips with that years ago.

She, however, had been on the sidelines. Until today, she hadn't known how it really was, and that was only the tip of the iceberg.

He reached out on instinct, pulling her trembling body into his.

She stiffened, arms cool and hesitant as they tucked like bent wings into the space beneath his jacket, against his rib cage. He smoothed a hand down her tense back, startled by how slight she felt. This spine of hers was hammered steel. He'd seen it in the way she had shown it to him for five years.

The competitor in him loved the challenge this narrow back represented. As she had held him off after their meeting, disparaging what was a typical effortlessness when it came to seducing a woman, the idea of showing her he was perfectly capable of romance had seemed inordinately pleasing.

Then, everything had turned inside out.

This wasn't a game. He had endangered her with this engagement and they couldn't call it off because he wasn't going back to racing. For the next few months at the very least, she needed his protection.

All they could do was play the part and hope that the impression of true love turned the tide.

"Let's get this over with," he murmured, reaching for the velvet box.

Isidora made a choked sound, too disheartened to be a laugh.

For some reason, the sound hit like a missile, landing in a place he hadn't known was unguarded, making him uncharacteristically unsure as he revealed the oval-cut diamond. It reflected the peacock-blue topaz stones that flanked it. On first glance it was beautiful in its simplicity, but on closer inspection, the complexity of the cut and setting became a reward for a lengthier study. It was quietly radiant, much like its new owner.

Ramon said what had been in his mind when he chose

it. "It's not on loan. I want you to keep it. As a thank-you for doing this."

Isidora's expression revealed nothing. Her hand held a fine tremor as she allowed him to work the ring onto her finger, but that was her only reaction. Her face looked like it was made of porcelain.

He was unaccountably disappointed. He'd chosen this piece because he had genuinely thought she would like it. Most women grew quite exuberant when offered jewelry.

"You don't care for it?"

"It's beautiful." Her voice sounded constricted. To anyone overhearing them, she would have sounded as overcome as a newly engaged woman ought to. Her lashes flickered as she took in the extravagant display once more.

Finally, she looked at him. Her eyes were bruised mauve in the candlelight, filled with the disillusionment he'd seen the morning at her mother's.

"It's the proposal of my dreams."

Ah, hell.

He took in the image he'd projected with this setup, seeing how thoroughly he had played to every woman's fantasy, not thinking that this particular woman would have imagined this moment, with him, over and over, once upon a time.

"No other man could ever top it." Her smile was harder than the diamond she now wore. "Thank you."

It was supposed to be a joke.

His ribs felt like they'd curled to bite into his lungs.

She barely spoke through their entire dinner.

"Are you high? I am not moving in with you." Seriously, could this day get any worse? Ramon's driver had just missed the turn to her flat and Ramon had thought that was the right time to mention he wanted her to live with him for the duration of their engagement.

Like. Hell.

Dinner had devolved into a series of selfies with restaurant patrons unable to resist a snap with the infamous Sauveterre. Neither of them had protested the rudeness. It had saved them from speaking to each other.

In the privacy of his car, however, she had plenty to say. Pointing at the ring on her finger, she said, "Exactly how much cooperation do you think this buys?"

"As much as I require."

His face was impossible to read in the uneven flicker of light beyond the car, but the air seemed to crackle. Her ears pulsed with the suddenly hard beat of her heart. It seemed to fill the canned space they occupied, the back seat suddenly far too small for the two of them.

As the silence played out, a weird fear accosted her.

Let him say he thought he owned her. Let him reach across and act like he would prove it.

She wanted to believe this sting in her veins was readiness to scratch his eyes out if he tried, but deep down she knew what really scared her. That she might let him touch her. She might even like it.

"The fact my team was able to empty your flat, robbing you blind without one person trying to stop them, tells me how effective your security is." He was contemptuous, not contrite, and returned his attention to his phone.

Or maybe her deepest fear was that he would never touch her again.

A huge lump lodged in her throat. She fought back the sense of rawness, of fresh rejection, clinging instead to anger at his high-handedness.

"So I don't have anything to go home *to*? I have half

a mind to report you to the police." The zip of motor scooters flying up beside them, trying to get a snapshot of them through the darkened windows, dissuaded her.

But did he have any idea how badly he'd hurt her today? Mocking her most cherished dream, saying things like "let's get this over with"?

"Can't I go stay with your sisters at Maison—"

"It's a big space," he interrupted, biting off each word. "You won't see me if you don't want to."

It was. The six-bedroom penthouse belonged to his family and she took a room at the far end from his.

For the next week she passive-aggressively texted him, rather than walk down the hall to speak to him. She didn't eat breakfast with him, taking care to eat while he worked out.

She had to join him in the car to go to work, but she did her best to keep to her own office through the day. He was busy with the restructuring and she was busy planning their fake engagement junket. They worked late every night, which allowed him to cry off his many social invitations, thank goodness. They ate whatever dinner his housekeeper left for them, but she avoided him then, too. She worked out while he ate, then ate alone in the kitchen while he watched the news in the lounge.

She knew she was being childish, but every single minute in his presence was excruciating. When she had to act the part and set her hand on his arm or go up on tiptoe to peck his cheek, she felt worse than an open book. She was a story being read aloud, one that was gauche and predictable.

His scent would intrigue her nostrils, the feel of his stubbled cheek would brand her lips and she would have to fight the urge to draw out the contact. Her physical infatuation was as strong as ever and she was terrified he knew it.

Being alone with him was a million times worse. She was sensitive to his disapproval, and his ignoring her stung. She felt utterly defenseless. It was exhausting.

Now they had arrived in Monaco. Instead of being hands-off, ostensibly out of respect for office sensibilities, more overt displays of affection would be expected. They faced a string of parties and public appearances.

She didn't know how she would keep herself together, especially when she saw what close quarters they'd be in.

His pied-à-terre in the Carré d'Or of Monte Carlo was at the top of a former hotel. Its quirks of low ceilings and small rooms had been overcome with a clever layout and the opening of walls into grand archways, giving the space a wonderfully bright and airy feel. Its terraces overlooked the beach and sea, as well as the race circuit.

Under other circumstances, she would have been charmed beyond words, but it had only one bedroom. One *bed*.

"I'm not staying here," she stated when they were alone, the chauffeur having exited after dropping their luggage.

Ramon lowered the phone he was reading, the distracted lift of his head arrogant in the extreme. While she drowned in awareness every minute of every day, he barely noticed she was alive.

"Why do you say that?" he asked absently.

His power-soaked good looks were on full display in a collared shirt that clung to his shoulders and tailored pants that hung with sharp creases to his polished Italian shoes. He'd always been clean-shaven, but hadn't shaved today. The light stubble accentuated his masculinity. One glance from his gray-green eyes used to destroy her, and in one glance, she nearly succumbed all over again.

"Because there's only one bed." She hid her blush by glancing at the sofa, not keen on sleeping there, either. She had a good idea what had gone on here over the years. "This is where you bring your groupies after races, I presume?"

With one dismissive blink, he said, "I deliver."

Gross.

"Well, I don't," she stated firmly, and started to retrieve her luggage.

"It's one night." His tone hardened. "It's the most secure building in the city and my team knows the neighborhood. This is where we're staying. Use the sofa if you don't want to share the bed."

He went back to his phone like he didn't care if she camped in the bathtub.

He had a point about security. How did he live like this? She didn't want to soften toward him at all, but she was being handled by the kind of detail that followed him and his siblings and it was claustrophobic. She couldn't help feeling sorry for the bunch of them because she felt plenty sorry for herself.

She would prefer to be under protection than without it, though. The threats against her hadn't grown worse, but they were still awful. She knew the safest place she could be was at his side. In his secure flat.

She'd be safest of all in his bed, no doubt. He had never been interested in her and had shown more attention to his phone this week than to her. She was little more than someone's dog he was minding. *Here girl, sit. Stay.*

Blowing out a breath that made her fringe tickle her eyebrow, she threw her suitcase onto the bed and opened it, took out her makeup bag and locked herself in the bathroom.

She had squeezed in a fitting with his sisters the day after her "engagement" and they had put a rush on several items for her. Tonight she would wear a backless jumpsuit with a halter front in emerald-green. The vague nod to his racing overalls had seemed cheeky and fun when she'd chosen it for tonight's party, but as she pulled it on, insecurity struck.

It clung to her backside and thighs, coating her curves in shimmery green.

Ramon hadn't said anything about the gold dress she had worn to their engagement dinner. She had kept to her own outfits since, telling herself she didn't care what he thought of her, but tonight she would be judged against every supermodel who had ever dangled from his arm. She had to look her best.

She curled her hair, then shook the loose ringlets around her shoulders. The sparkle of her gold pendant drew attention to her cleavage. With the sinfully high shoes she had charged to Ramon on a passive-aggressive whim, all she could think was that she looked like she was trying too hard.

Insecurity struck as she relived all those times she had thought combing her hair a different way might be the ticket to finally catching his eye. Nothing she'd ever done, whether it was a new shade of lip gloss or a pricey push-up bra, had ever prompted the tiniest show of interest from him. She didn't want to be that girl again, obvious in her yearning and devastated when she fell short.

With a glance at her suitcase, which had nothing else to offer because they were only here one night, and a glance at the clock, she knew she was stuck. It wasn't as if she wore a minidress and bare legs, she told herself as she left the bedroom, heart in her throat.

At the sound of the door, Ramon stood and pushed his arms into a dark blue jacket over a pale gray shirt he wore open at the throat. He finished reading and dropped his phone, freezing as he glanced toward her. He took his time drifting his gaze from her carefully made up smoky eyes to her pedicured toes in rose pink.

The only noise came from the distant move of traffic far below the open terrace windows. As time inched along, her insides wobbled.

"Will I do?" she challenged, and did a slow pirouette, mostly so she could turn her back on him and gather her composure. She gave her hair another flip and felt his gaze strike her butt like a spank.

Get a grip, Isidora.

"Blame your sisters if you don't like what you see." She faced him again, and pretended her clutch needed a thorough inventory of its lipstick, mobile phone and credit card.

"I do like it," he said, voice hitting a low note that made her belly contract. He finished shrugging on his jacket. "You look beautiful."

"You don't have to be polite," she said flatly. "I mean, be polite, obviously, but don't say things because you think it's expected. I know I'm a scarecrow in your eyes. This extra effort is for the cameras, not you." She shook out a black chiffon jacket, startled when he was suddenly right beside her, taking it to hold it for her.

He smelled divine and looked sexy as anything with that five o'clock shadow and his dark brows pulled into a frown of admonishment. "I've always thought you were beautiful."

He sounded sincere, but it only made her sternum ache that he wasn't being honest with her.

"Seriously, save it for someone who wants to hear it."

He narrowed his eyes. "It's time to get over your anger, Isidora. Life's too short."

"I'm doing everything you ask," she snapped, taking back her jacket and tugging it on. "What else do you want from me?"

She flashed a look up, expecting the tired, remote look of boredom he seemed to have carved specially into his face for when he looked at her.

There was an eerie stillness in his stony expression, but the spark in his eyes turned them electric green. The air shimmered as though heated, spilling excitement, heady and thrilling, through her.

It was her turn to stall with one arm in a sleeve, grappling with an outlandish impression that she was not the only one fighting attraction. More like they were both fighting this *thing* between them, but the more they chipped at it, the closer they were to crumbling and crossing to the other side.

He was a formidable man. He had a special hold over her, but in that moment, she didn't feel small and helpless. She felt exalted. Empowered.

At the same time, attraction didn't merely tug at her. It drew her taut from the inside, threatening to swallow her whole.

He's doing it again.

With a muted gasp, she forced herself to pull back a step. Her heart thundered with panic, which she hid by finishing the yank of getting her jacket into place, nearly tearing the delicate fabric in her haste.

"Ask me that again when you're ready to hear the answer." His voice coiled around her, squeezing until she could hardly breathe, holding her in merciless thrall for one second as he lazily reached for the door.

He held it open, sending her an unreadable look as he waved an invitation for her to escape this airless apartment.

CHAPTER FIVE

RAMON'S RETIREMENT PARTY was held in the rooftop ballroom of a casino. A band played all the latest hits and a disco ball sent rainbow flecks bouncing off the mirrored columns that stood between draped alcoves. The guests, some of whom he considered friends, others merely faces he knew, were taking full advantage of the open bar, dancing in a crush on the floor and gambling enthusiastically where tables were set up in an adjoining room. It was a photo op and give-back to the racing community that had embraced him all these years. No expense had been spared.

Ramon liked parties. He was the extrovert of the family, but he couldn't seem to relax and enjoy this one.

"She's not what I expected," one of Ramon's toughest competitors, Kiergen Jensen said, as he gazed at Isidora dancing with Ramon's test driver. "Too nice for a man who stops at nothing to win."

Here, at least, Isidora wasn't being vilified for his departure from the track. She was lauded. His rivals were ecstatic they had a shot at the championship without him in the way and admired her for stealing the heart of such a confirmed bachelor.

Little did they know she hated him more than ever.

She had a right to be angry. He had put her in danger

and made a mockery of her childhood dreams. The job she had already struggled to prove wasn't pure nepotism had been turned into something even more blatantly biased. She had made it clear she wanted him to leave her alone, so he had.

But her enmity grated at him.

He had moved her into his space, something he had never done with a woman in his *life*. She resented it, and had gone back to leaving a room if he entered it. At work, she did a credible job of gushing if put on the spot, but she made sure everyone knew they intended to behave professionally. It was her way of avoiding physical contact. When he did have to act like a smitten suitor and take her arm or press a hand to her back, she stiffened. It was subtle, but he felt it. She didn't even want a compliment from him.

He was an egocentric man. He looked after himself, but had the capacity to love and worry for his family. He had even made accommodations in his life for his infant nieces. That's how he'd wound up at this retirement party. But he didn't reserve a lot of bandwidth for worrying about anyone outside his chosen few. Using Isidora for his publicity stunt had been expedient. Whatever cost she incurred as a result could be compensated monetarily. Her feelings had never been much of a factor in this.

So why did her antagonism bother him so much?

Then, as they were leaving to come here, it had become obvious. *Sexual tension.*

In the privacy of his apartment, with no one to see it, she had revealed—very briefly—that she was still attracted to him. Which was adorable, given their history.

He really wished he could dismiss the discovery that cavalierly, but he'd taken it like a bullet to the chest. He'd been aware of her all week. Hell, he'd always been *aware* of her. Now that she was grown and under his nose, it was impossible to ignore how alluring she was. She could wear subdued business attire and a sober office persona, hold herself beyond his reach and mutter pithy comments under her breath, but that had only fed his intrigue. Turns out, he had a depthless appetite for sexy-librarian fantasies and they all starred her.

Then, tonight, he had nearly popped a blood vessel when she had emerged looking chic and feminine in a skin-tight suit that revealed more than it disguised. She was utterly delectable and Kiergen wasn't the only one to notice.

The entire room, heavily weighted to high-octane men, found her mesmerizing. Why wouldn't they? She had her mother's ingenuous way of tilting up a wide-eyed gaze so all a man could think about was taking her under his wing. She also possessed her father's ability to draw people out. Her natural empathy made her anyone's immediate best friend. Add in her quick wit and unstoppable smile and she was irresistible.

She didn't lap up the attention the way another woman might, either, which only added to her attractiveness. He *felt* lucky to be with her, which was a singular sensation for a man who had always been the prize.

"I'd do whatever she asked of me, too." Kiergen's eyes stayed a little too long on Isidora's hips as she enjoyed herself on the dance floor.

"Hey." Ramon waited for his friend's gaze to track back to his, then shook his head. He meant it, and Kiergen knew it, which wasn't comfortable. Ramon hated being obvious. Revealing any detail about his wants or intentions, about what he valued, was something that could be used against him. He rarely exposed his throat.

He couldn't stop himself, though. With one question,

Isidora had released a roar of desire in him. *What else do you want from me?*

The list had been so long, he hadn't known where to start, but the way her tongue had absently dampened her lips had given him an idea.

He couldn't stop wondering what would have happened if she hadn't dragged her antipathy back into place along with her filmy wrap.

They wouldn't have made it to this party, that was for damn sure.

The song ended and she motioned that she needed a drink. She wound her way through the crowd toward him and Ramon handed across the glass that had been delivered while she'd been dancing.

"I had my chauffeur bring this up for you. For your father," Kiergen said, giving her a key fob that advertised his team logo.

Isidora had already fan-girled over Kiergen, claiming she and her father were both avid race followers, even though Ramon would have sworn she hadn't watched in years. Certainly not in person.

Her fawning over Kiergan had been annoying enough. Now Kiergen, the narcissist, was trying to keep the admiration train going with his penny candy swag.

Isidora's face brightened all the same. "I would have settled for a selfie, but thank you so much."

"We can do that, too." Kiergen's arm looped casually around her shoulders as she took the snap. He sent another smirk Ramon's way and hardened his arm to keep her close as she lowered her phone. "But now you have to answer something for me. I'm dying to know if you've ever kissed Henri."

Isidora pulled away in shock. "What?"

Ramon knew what was coming and his hackles rose even as Kiergen thumbed toward him.

"This one tried to kiss Cinnia. Did you never hear that story?" Kiergen grinned his enjoyment as Ramon glowered a warning. Isidora wouldn't see the funny side of it.

Kiergen couldn't resist, however, and launched into the tale that had become a small legend in their circle.

Shortly after Henri and Cinnia had become exclusive, Henri had brought her to watch one of Ramon's races. The next morning, as their usual group had gathered for breakfast, Henri had stepped away to take a call.

Ramon had been puzzled by his brother's fascination with her. Until Cinnia, neither of them had stuck with any particular woman more than a handful of days, let alone gone back for a particular one and locked her in for the foreseeable future.

Ramon had been high on his recent win and, well, sometimes brothers were jackasses to each other for the sake of it. Whatever had possessed him, he had mimicked Henri's preferred French greeting, moved behind where Cinnia sat, set his hand on her shoulder and leaned in to kiss her just as if he was Henri.

Maybe it had been a test. His brother was plenty sharp enough to look after himself, but there had been a part of Ramon that had needed to know how sincere Cinnia's feelings for Henri really were.

"We all thought he was Henri," Keirgen was saying. "For about one second she did, too. Then, right before he kissed her, she screamed. Jumped a meter. I thought she was going to punch him. Henri came running, ready to draw blood. The look on Ramon's face was the most priceless. He didn't expect her to know the difference. We all lost it." Kiergen was still laughing, two years later.

Isidora chuckled politely, shaking her head. "No, I've never heard that story. Poor Cinnia."

"Lucky Henri. But now I have to know, have you done the kiss test? Did you pass?"

"I'll pass on doing the test! Cinnia would punch *me*."

"Ha! Perhaps you're right." Kiergen was plainly disappointed, though. He asked after Cinnia and Henri, then moved on, leaving them alone.

Ramon watched Isidora's head bob lightly in time to the beat as she sipped the last of her drink. He was about to ask her to dance when she said, "I did, though."

"Did what?"

She kept her eyes on the dancers, speaking just loudly enough for him to hear her over a song about loving cheap thrills. "I kissed Henri."

It was time to switch to water. She kept working up a thirst on the dance floor, then draining gin-and-tonics. That was her third. Fourth? If she was losing count, it was definitely time to switch. Also her tongue was getting way too loose if she was starting to think that baiting her fiancé was a good idea.

Perhaps he thought so, too, because he plucked her glass out of her hand and gave it to his guard, then caught her elbow and spun her a few steps, pulling her behind a heavy curtain.

"What…where—?" She had thought the drapes decorative, but they disguised alcoves where chairs were stacked. The towers at the back reached to the ceiling, while others sat two and three high near where they stood crowded into the small space at the front.

"When?" he demanded, hands firm on her upper arms.

She automatically brought her hands to his chest and— Oh. Her fingers splayed against the firm heat of his chest, instinctively wanting to feel as much of his muscled torso beneath fine linen as possible.

"Isidora. When did you kiss Henri?"

Her light press into his chest was no match for his strength. He drew her closer so his mouth brushed the hair near her ear, causing a frisson of tickling sensation all the way down her neck and farther to the base of her spine. "Tell me."

"I don't know." How was she supposed to think, surrounded by his masculine scent like this? Ever since that moment at the flat, she'd been wondering if she had imagined the flash of carnal heat in him. She knew it had happened on her side, but him?

I've always thought you were beautiful.

He was such a liar! He hadn't even known she was alive. Still didn't.

Did he?

"Since Cinnia?"

"No. Long before. I was visiting Trella at Sus Brazos." She threw back her head, but it was nearly impossible to see him in the thin sliver of light that came in over the top of the drapes from the dimly lit ballroom. "I wasn't at university yet."

"Are you serious?" His hands tightened on her arms. "And he kissed you? Or did you kiss him?"

She wanted to kiss *him.*

Oh, she was sorry she'd been drinking. All her defenses were slipping away like scarves off an exotic dancer. Her body wanted to sway and slither against him. *Come hither, virile man.* She really was just like her mother.

And deep down, despite her continued lectures against that silly child who had been so infatuated, she wanted to believe that he did, indeed, think she was beautiful.

She wanted to prove it. She wanted to bring him to his knees with lust and adoration.

"Why does it matter?" she asked, nudging her nose against his stubbled jaw, feeling his hands flex on her arms and finding it erotic to be trapped in his hold like this. Since when did she have a kink for restraint?

"It matters. How old were you exactly?"

"I don't know." She grew a little drunker as she realized how invested he was. She couldn't resist taunting. "Sixteen?"

His grip tightened to just short of painful. "Which would have made him twenty-four. I'll kill him."

She smiled at how incensed he was. "Relax," she chided. "It was my idea. I came up to him like this." She shifted enough to feel his stubble graze her lips. She stepped in so her arms looped up behind his neck and her body brushed his. "*He* didn't scream when I did this…"

She went onto tiptoes so she was leaning against the taut line of his body and pressed her mouth to his, vaguely remembering the feel of a warm mouth that had parted with a smile, not anything resembling passion or reciprocation.

"I'm not Ramon," Henri had said, gently but promptly easing her back onto her feet. "And I'm not going to tell him, if that's what you're hoping. But thank you. That was very nice."

It had been a very adolescent move, both an attempt to prompt Henri to tell Ramon, hopefully inciting possessiveness, and an exploration of her feelings for the wrong twin. The peck had amounted to a Christmas kiss. Henri had essentially patted her on the head and told her to go play. Only the compassion in his eyes had kept the moment from being completely humiliating.

Ramon didn't express humor at the touch of her mouth. Or stop her.

He slid his arms around her so they banded across her back and held her in place as he stole control of their kiss.

She might have groaned as his mouth crushed hers. It was impossible to hear over a song blaring about not being able to stop the feeling.

A shudder of relief went through her as he slaked a thirst she'd suffered for years. It was not unlike falling into bed after a long day. Like tasting a rich dessert as it melted on her tongue.

Like kissing a man she had always found insanely attractive.

Don't *do* this, she warned herself, but couldn't resist. He kissed like the expert he was and his abundant skill made her furious enough, jealous enough, to kiss him back without inhibition. In silence, using only the rock of her mouth beneath his and the spear of her tongue into his mouth, she mused, *Feel that, Ramon*?

She *was* beautiful. In that moment, she was confident in her attraction. Arrogant. Other men came on to her. They were going crazy for her tonight. Why not him? He didn't know what he was missing. This. This is what he could have had all this time, if he had only asked.

She dug her fingers into his hair to draw him down and pressed her mouth more firmly to his. She stroked her tongue against his and groaned again, unreservedly, strong enough he must have felt the vibration in her throat. Arching her back, she rubbed her breasts against his chest, following the beat in the music that throbbed around them.

Their kiss became a dirty dance. He dropped his hand to her backside and firmly snugged her hips into his, working with the pulse of the song. His other hand brushed aside the front of her jumpsuit so he claimed her bare breast, his palm hot. He splayed his fingers and massaged, tongue stabbing against hers.

He was hard.

Mind blown, she rocked her hips between his firm caress of her cheek and the ridge of flesh that proved he found her desirable. That reaction in him ought to make her feel superior. She should have pushed away at that point to give him a scathing and triumphant "ha!"

But the allure of rubbing against him was too much. The tips of her breasts ached. Her loins felt hollow and needy. She couldn't resist staying exactly where she was, moving against him in time to the music.

He kept her against him as he turned and shuffled backward, drawing her down as he sat. She flowed weakly, like she was under a spell, more than happy to let him pull her astride his lap as he lowered into a chair. Both his wide hands slid to her lower back and cupped her butt to pull her hard against his fly.

A flash of sensation went through her, so sharp she threw back her head and let out a gasp, seeing nothing but shadows moving on the ceiling, as dark and mysterious as the sensations that flowed through her.

That moment might have given her pause, but he kissed her throat. He cupped her breast and plumped it again, dipping his head to bite gently at the upper swell, then flicked her nipple with his tongue.

She arched, wanting that tease, but wanting to rock herself against that hard ridge between her legs.

His hand on her hip urged her to move against his fly, to take up the rhythm of the song again, while he pinched her nipple and lifted his head to kiss her once more.

At the edges of her consciousness, she knew this was filthy. They were practically in public. He must have snuck behind a thousand curtains with other women, given how quickly and easily he had lured her here.

But with her knees wide and her heeled shoes braced on the floor, *she* was the woman pressed sex-to-sex with him tonight. The only thing between them was a few layers of fabric and they might as well have been naked for all the dulling of sensation.

And she was mad at him. Mad *for* him.

Maybe she thought she could make him break first. She wasn't really examining her motives, just reacting to the pleasure of rubbing against him while being in the control position, riding his lap, driving him crazy.

"Do you like that?" She caught at his earlobe with her teeth, arms folded behind his neck, breasts mashed to his chest.

His fingers dug in to the seam that traced the cleft of her butt. He bit out a really graphic curse of agreement. "Keep going."

She faltered. He was hard all over. He had admitted he enjoyed what she was doing to him. Here was the point she should pull away and show him she could take him or leave him. If she kept going…

How far did he expect her to go?

He bared her other breast, the cool air erotic and dangerous. Stimulating. The brush of his fingers against her aching nipple sent a spark of acute need into her loins. Heat flooded into her chest, making her breasts feel fuller and more sensitive. Her sex grew needier. Greedier.

Instinct made her take up the rock against him again, or maybe it was his hand on her butt.

This was getting out of control. Either way, lightning streaked into the place between her legs.

She shifted her grip to the back of his chair while his flat hand against her tailbone kept her hips tight to his. He lifted into her, continuing to excite her as he caught her mouth in a kiss that was insanely wicked. His tongue sought hers as he practically made love to her fully clothed in that chair, lifting her higher into the cloud of acute arousal. Driving her toward climax.

She was a virgin, but she knew how to give herself an orgasm if she wanted one. She had never felt a strong need for a man to perform that duty, but here she was, legs splayed, encouraging the lethal thrust of his hips against her. It was primal and, damn, he knew exactly how to play against her button of nerves like a bow against strings.

She had no will to stop his pushing her toward the brink, loving everything he was doing to her, no longer caring where she was, only wanting *this*.

She wanted that rush, wanted to feel it here, in his arms. Ramon's arms. Ramon's hips rolling against hers until she quivered on the edge.

The tension grew so intense she tried to close her thighs, but she couldn't. She was at his mercy, the coil of desire pulling into unbearable need that made her catch back a sob.

She clutched the back of the chair and closed her teeth on his bottom lip, trying to fight the rising wave, but he palmed her breast and kept up the relentless lift of his hips against hers. Shivers went down her spine, making her shoulder blades flex. She arched as the tingle spread across her lower back, then poured like liquid pleasure through her loins and thighs.

Release shuddered through her in a rush of joy. Sexy, hungry pulses followed, making her grind against him with abandon, eager to wring every last clench of deliciousness from their encounter.

It was so good…so good.

And so solitary.

She felt the dry laugh that went through him. The hoarse sound could have been a saber, it rent her so badly.

She wilted into his caging arms, shaken and breathless. Defeated.

This man had possessed her attention for far too long and now owned what shreds of dignity she had managed to preserve.

This was the most humiliating encounter of her life.

And there was no coming back from it.

CHAPTER SIX

"COME HERE," RAMON said the second he closed the door of his flat.

He could barely speak and didn't even remember getting here. He vaguely recalled a quick exit through a service door and a brisk walk through a bustling kitchen to the underground car park. That sort of disappearing act was exactly what he paid his security service to provide.

All that mattered was that he had her alone now. Properly alone, where he could strip off that maddening jumpsuit and satisfy both of them this time. If she had been wearing a dress tonight... But she hadn't been and damn it, he was *aching* to finish what they'd started.

She sent him a baleful glance. "Where are the extra blankets? I'll take the sofa."

She clutched her sheer black wrap like it was a trench coat, her mouth clean of lipstick from their kisses, her eyes dark with betrayal.

"Qué?" His voice came out harsher than he intended as he clung to something he could see was already moving beyond his reach, even before she spoke again.

"I told you I wouldn't sleep with you."

Then she had lap-danced him into believing she wanted to. She had come apart in his arms with such abandon, he'd nearly exploded. His heart was still thudding, hammering an obsessive pulse in the stiff flesh between his thighs.

Want. Need. *Have.*

But the wariness in her expression put the brakes on that. He firmly believed in a woman's right to change her mind, but he searched her expression, trying to understand how they had gone from ecstasy to aversion in a five-minute car ride. It put his lungs in a vise.

"Why did you say you wanted to leave, then?"

I want to go. The crack in her voice and the final twitch of postclimax that had shivered through her as she'd sat up, pressing her weight into his straining flesh, had been all the excuse he'd needed for a very swift and wordless departure from his own party.

"I couldn't face people after that!" She hugged herself, eyes wide and appalled.

"Dios," he muttered, not expecting her to be shy about it. "No one knew what we were doing. They didn't even know where we were."

"Oh, please." Her fingertips were digging so hard into her upper arms, she was going to leave bruises. "Everyone wants to know where you are and what you're doing at all times. I guarantee someone was watching and that your friend Kiergen will be adding this to his roster of stories. 'Remember that time Ramon pulled his fiancée behind the curtain for a blowie?'"

"Well, he'll be wrong, won't he?" Her crude talk didn't bother him so much as the fact she might be right. But he had had to become inured to gossip long ago. *"Who cares* what people say? We know the truth. That's all that matters."

"I care! And the truth isn't any more palatable." She let out a choked laugh. "I criticize you for not being able to share a night with a woman, but I can't even share a chair." She hung her head into her palm.

"We are *not* still fighting about your mother." His teeth came together and the rest came out between them. "I didn't have sex with her. Believe me this time because I'm not going to say it again." Inside his pocket, his hand closed into a fist.

She averted her face, but he watched her profile struggle with anger and a despair that made his chest feel tight.

"Whether you did or not doesn't matter. I'm sure you're both well over it by now. But I'm not like that, okay? I don't sleep around. I don't have sex in public. *I'm not like her*, Ramon."

Ah, hell.

"I know you're not like her," he said more gently.

Her head came up to send him a look of misery. "Judging by tonight's performance, are you?"

Which is when he realized this wasn't a case of self-consciousness or embarrassment, but shame. Deep shame. Her face was an agonized red, the corners of her mouth dragged with disgrace. She wore the cloak of someone who didn't know how to hide from herself.

"Don't." The word came out from deep in his chest, where a pressure settled, heavy as a piano. He couldn't bear that she regretted one of the most erotic and exciting experiences of his life. "Isidora—"

He started forward, but she retreated. Recoiled. She caught at the back of the chair that she bumped into, swaying before she gathered her excuse for a jacket around herself again.

A breath gusted out of him, leaving a hole in his chest.

"You know I'm not going to force you into anything. Don't you?" He was surprised his voice was so steady when he felt so flabbergasted.

"Except an engagement?"

"Sexually," he clarified. "You know enough about Trella's experience to believe me when I say I would never take advantage of a woman that way. That's why I was angry with you that morning at your mother's," he added with a return of ire. "You knew me. I was offended that you jumped so quickly to thinking I'd had sex with her."

"Oh, my fault! Silly me, making things up for no reason."

Dios. "All right, I know why you assumed I had—"

"No, you don't know!" Her jagged voice brimmed with acid.

He did. He had lived in Madrid on and off all his life. Gossip about her mother had always been rife.

"She had a rough childhood," he reminded her. "She told me that night how she'd been bounced between guardians, everyone fighting over her money and not giving a damn about her."

Francisca had married way too young and her first husband had abused her. The second had been too old, but had doubled her fortune when he died, turning her into the merriest of widows. By the time she had been pregnant with Isidora, not even thirty yet, she was entering her third marriage with Bernardo.

"If she was a man, no one would care how she conducts herself. People shouldn't judge her just because she's a woman. You shouldn't."

Her jaw dropped. "Don't you *dare* tell me how to feel about it! Did anyone ever ask you if your knees were as loose as your mother's? Were you ever refused service in a restaurant, in front of your friends, because your mother had slept with the owner's husband? How many times did you lie to your father about why a man was in the house, because you didn't want to hear another fight go on for days, and were afraid he would leave for good if he knew the truth?"

At the mention of her father, his chest grew too tight for his ribs, but he couldn't pile on her pain by telling her Francisca had confided to him that Bernardo wasn't her biological father.

"Isidora—"

"I don't tell you how to feel about your past, do I?" Her hands flung through the air in agitation. "And for your information, I *don't* judge her. I don't care how many men she sleeps with. I care that she's hurting so badly she can't stop herself. I care that I can't fix her. I care that men take advantage of her and people say things behind her back that only hurts her more."

"Well, I didn't take advantage of her," he growled. "We *talked. Bueno*? About *my* past. It was the anniversary of my father's death, Isidora. It pisses me off that you've never figured that out, which I know isn't fair, but you know everything about me. I didn't feel I should have to tell you. I didn't want to be alone that night and your mother was the perfect companion. She knew Mama from their boarding-school days. Papa had managed her trust from the time she had access to it. She talked about their wedding day. Told me stories I'd never heard, from when they were young and happy. From before." Before Trella's kidnapping, he meant. "Don't begrudge me that. I needed it."

She stared at him, motionless but for the throb of the artery in her throat.

"It's the truth," he said, trying to impress it through her brain, *needing* her to believe it.

"Then why…?" The profound hurt in her eyes twisted up his insides. "Why didn't you just tell me that?"

"Because I was angry." Tempted. Stung. He shook off the confusion that had driven him that morning. The sudden want as he'd realized she was a grown woman and the sight of the dead end they were doomed to hit. "Nothing was ever going to happen between us. You're the daughter of my father's friend. My sisters' friend. Was I supposed to lead you on? Date you and dump you? *Marry* you? I'm never going to marry anyone and *you*, in this position of having threats online and a damn army protecting you because of *me*, have to understand why I say that. So tell me, Isidora. What the hell was I supposed to do about that damn crush of yours except kill it so you could get on with your life?"

She sucked in a breath as though it was the last one she would ever take.

After a moment, she swallowed loud enough for him to hear. The glow that was brimming on her lashes threatened to spill onto her cheeks.

"So what was tonight? Pity? Throw a bone to the girl who used to love you?" Her brow flinched in acute humiliation.

"No." His ears hung up on *used to* while the rest of him tried to figure out what it *had* been. Sex didn't have hidden meanings for him, but even he knew it hadn't been the sort of quid pro quo he usually engaged in. The idea of her kissing his twin had set something alight in him. The sense of competition that had come over him had been the least friendly he'd ever felt toward Henri. It had been downright savage. Territorial.

That's what had driven him to kiss her, at least. A completely uncharacteristic possessiveness had gripped him as he'd held her, making him want to erase thoughts of any other man from her mind and replace them with himself.

Lust had taken over. She'd been so responsive—her breasts were perfection, her weight on him pure seduction, her abandonment to their lovemaking completely enthralling. He was a very experienced man, yet he would never forget something that amounted to adolescent petting behind the bleachers.

"You kissed me. I thought it meant you were willing to settle for an affair." It sounded lame even to his ears. He wasn't surprised she only shook her head.

"Maybe I would, if I thought you wanted *me*, and not just the woman you were stuck with because of this stupid engagement."

"I want you." How could she doubt it? "Look in a mirror. Of course I think you're beautiful. Of course I want to sleep with you."

"Because I'm *here*. Not because I'm *me*." She pointed to where her pendant hung against her bare breastbone. It swung forward as she leaned into her words. "In the entire time I've known you, you've never treated me as anything but a giant pain in your behind. Henri used to at least have a conversation with me, but not you."

She pointed at him to punctuate.

"I was that thing you had to endure coming into your house because I happened to be friends with your sisters. Then you did me this great favor of shattering my heart by appearing to sleep with my *mother*."

She straightened, shoulders back, chin up.

"Five *years* go by and do you *ask* me to help with your sister? No! You threatened my job and pressed on my loyalty to your family. And now, after all of that, I'm supposed to fall down with gratitude that the great Ramon Sauveterre has decided I'm physically attractive enough that he's *inviting* me to have an affair? Thanks a bunch."

This time, her hostility didn't grate. That vilification

clawed past his thick skin to the center of his soul, which he suddenly feared was a vacant space. She'd pulled back the curtain, pointed and made him feel small. Dishonorable.

"So that's a no, then?" He took refuge behind sarcasm because no one was supposed to be able to hurt him. Not this badly. Not by holding him up to the light and finding such an ugly angle.

He feared the rasp in his voice gave away what a direct hit she'd scored, but she only widened her gray eyes in disbelief. Then she shook her head like she should have expected his callousness.

"When I was young, I used to think your past made you afraid of being hurt. I told myself that's why you wouldn't love me back. It made the rejection easier. But you're actually just a self-important, unfeeling bastard, aren't you? Here's news. Some people react to life's tragedies by being nice. They try to make the world a better place. They don't ruin it for everyone else. I will never forgive you for forcibly dragging me back to your side so you could teach me again that you're not worth my time."

She turned toward the bedroom, one wrist coming up so she could use her sleeve against her cheek.

"Isidora."

"Really?" she cried. "I have to spell it out?" She kept her back to him. "That was a hard no, Ramon. Step outside if you want sex. I'm sure you can flag some down with that charm of yours. I'm going to have a bath and sleep on the sofa."

"Take the bed. I have some calls to make."

"So noble."

As he heard the tub faucet start, he moved to the cabinet in the lounge and poured himself a strong start on a terrible hangover.

* * *

They both wore sunglasses the next morning. Isidora was trying to hide that she had cried—yes, again—over that stupid man.

She didn't know what was up with Ramon, though. She didn't think he'd had that much to drink at the party, but he informed her flatly that he had called in their regrets for a brunch they were supposed to attend. He had a tall cup of the coffee she'd made, but didn't touch any of the pastries she had sent up.

That suggested an unsteady stomach. She noted a near-empty bottle of Scotch on the end table in the lounge as he moved into the shower she'd vacated, but she didn't ask.

She wouldn't spare one word in his direction if she didn't have to.

And she personally wouldn't touch alcohol again for a long time. She was still writhing internally at how she had behaved. The part where she had climaxed on his lap was bad enough, but then she had bared her soul and he had only scoffed at her history of unrequited love like it was a skinned knee.

The next few months were going to be interminable.

As if to prove it, they met Kiergen in the lobby as they were leaving. Apparently he had a flat in the building, too.

"Where did you two get off to? As if I didn't know," he said with a playful leer.

Before Isidora could smile weakly through her squirming blush, Ramon said bluntly, "A personal matter came up."

Kiergen's smile gave way to concern. "I hope everything is all right? Are you still coming to the brunch?"

"No. Excuse us. The car is waiting." He hurried her

out, leaving Kiergen sounding worried as he called out a wish that they travel safe.

As they settled into the cool leather seats and the car pulled way, she glanced briefly at Ramon. He really was a master class in manipulating his own image. Now Kiergen would go to the brunch with genuine concern over this "personal matter." Speculation would abound, and no one would be aware it was pure red herring.

Was she supposed to thank him for covering up her lunacy?

She churlishly chose to read emails instead, doing her best to ignore him while feeling slighted that he did the same.

They had a milk run of business engagements for the next few days, crisscrossing to Italy and Germany before coming back to France. She was mostly arm candy at luncheons and cocktail parties as he shook hands and took photos with newly promoted executives.

It was nice to see a mix of women taking management positions and the conglomerate wasn't named Sauveterre *International* for nothing. At least it gave her a broad range of people to chat with as a buffer against him.

They were able to avoid all but the bare minimum of physical contact, too. If they kissed, it was a perfunctory performance—not unlike the kiss she had exchanged with his brother, if distinctly less warm. And while they smiled at each other when they had to, they spoke as little as possible.

It was a delicate balance on the edge of a razor blade, cutting into her relentlessly as they crawled along with this charade.

So, even though she was loath to be without external distractions to keep them apart, it was a relief to board his yacht to sail across the Mediterranean to Málaga,

Spain, where their official engagement party would be held.

To the long-lens cameras spying on them from afar, they appeared to be on a prehoneymoon. In reality, Ramon worked tirelessly from his onboard office. She answered emails and wrote press releases while sunbathing in her bikini. They saw each other over meals and confined conversation to work-related topics.

One day, she kept promising herself, she would be over Ramon and would fall for a man who adored her. Their passion would overshadow that bit of petting she had shared with Ramon. They would marry in a dream wedding, have a handful of children and this gnawing ache inside her would subside.

But that was many days away. She still had half of *this* day to get through.

She gave the purser a brief thank-you smile as she took her seat across from Ramon at lunch. He wore a collared short-sleeved shirt and casual shorts with deck shoes. She had shrugged on a simple red sundress over her bathing suit since they were eating poolside.

"Did you see that email about—"

"Yes. I told them not to bother."

It was exactly the minimum exchange they had been keeping to for days. Was he sulking because she had refused to sleep with him? She might think so if he wasn't so completely unmoved.

He was back to ignoring her the way he had most of her life. It stung. She didn't expect an apology. He was hardly the type to go that far, but she would prefer anger, if that's what he felt. Some kind of emotion. This stiff politeness was horrible. And why did it make her feel like she was at fault? Was it a woman thing?

She bit back a sigh and declined a glass of wine.

Taking her cue from him, she picked up the phone she had set aside. It was pinging with a notification anyway. Before she could read it, Ramon let loose a string of sharp curses.

"What?" she prompted, sensing disaster and hurrying to unlock her screen.

Ramon saved her the trouble by turning his phone so she could read the alert Etienne had just sent.

This English translation just hit. It's been circulating in Arabic for an hour. The queen mother of Zhamair is quoted as stating her future daughter-in-law was not the twin in the photo kissing the Prince of Elazar last spring. True? How do I respond?

Trella still hadn't publicly confirmed or denied her pregnancy. Now she was exposed as having been with one of the most sought-after bachelors in Europe, one who was rumored to be on the brink of an engagement to someone else. Isidora had been doing her job, keeping up with online gossip about the prince. She'd been secretly worried for her friend. If he married while he already had a child coming with Trella, that would be disastrous!

She blew out a dismayed breath. "There's no pretending Kasim's mother is not a creditable source, is there? I mean, I've always wondered why Kasim allowed people to think Angelique had been with both him and the Elazar prince, but why would his mother go on record with such an inflammatory statement?"

"Kasim kept quiet because Gili asked him to. That smudge on her reputation is the reason they haven't announced their engagement. His highest-ranking advisors made it clear they wouldn't accept her as queen. My guess is that his mother chose to repair Gili's reputation

by annihilating Trella's. I've met her. She takes things
into her own hands without a sense of consequence." He
was furious. She could hear it in his voice.

"I'll tell Etienne we're handling it." She began texting.

Ramon's phone buzzed and he swore again, then
hitched his chair around to her side of the table, so they
sat side by side and could both see his screen. She tingled
with awareness at how close he suddenly was, but the
message coming through from his sister was so shocking, it demanded her complete attention.

Apparently I'm married.

Angelique attached a breaking news story that contained a brief video of Kasim. He exited a closed-door
meeting to be confronted with the storm surrounding his
mother's statement. Reporters were demanding he respond to whether he intended to marry Angelique. Surely
not, given all this controversy.

His reaction, released minutes ago, was already going
viral.

Isidora had only met Kasim once. He would have intimidated the heck out of her even without the title of king
of Zhamair. He was tall and dynamic. The only things
remotely soft about him were his long-lashed, dreamy
dark eyes. They were especially heart-melting when his
gaze rested on Angelique.

The rest of him was short beard, desert garb and an
uncompromising air. His essence of supreme power came
through even on the small mobile screen as he spoke in
Arabic, his implacable words translated as English sub-
titles beneath his unyielding image.

"Let me resolve this once and for all. *We are married.* I
am king. If I say she is my wife, she is my wife. Treat her
with the respect my queen deserves. Gossip and speculation will not be tolerated. Move on." He walked away.

Oh. She couldn't help the small chortle that pushed into the back of her throat. That was one way to handle it.

A quick flick to the social sites on her own phone showed the video was already looped to a GIF meme and beginning to trend. *If I say she is my wife...*

"So much for worrying about an engagement announcement." Isidora used a weak laugh to cover how envious she was. Kasim's defense of Angelique was ruthless and sexist, sure, but swoon-worthy.

Ramon immediately placed a video-chat call to his sister. Angelique appeared next to Trella, with their office at the design house in the background.

"Wait," Angelique said breathlessly. "Henri wants in." She tapped and added his image to the screen.

Ramon's twin held an infant swaddled in a pink blanket. Henri's jaw was shadowed in stubble, exactly like Ramon's. Their mother sat on one side of Henri, Cinnia sat on the other. Cinnia had a blanket draped over her shoulder, presumably nursing their second newborn. Cinnia looked tired, but healthy and happy as she said a warm "Congratulations!"

"Thank you." Angelique wiped at the tears tracking to the corners of her smiling mouth. "That's not the way we meant to do it. He just...said it. He's not the least bit sorry and neither am I."

She sighed, but it was a blissful one. Then she fanned her streaming eyes. "I don't know why I'm crying. I'm *happy.* And relieved. His mother was trying to override resistance to our engagement. She wanted to start planning the wedding, but now it's done. I'm married!" Her hands went up in bemusement.

"So no proper wedding?" their mother asked with a disappointed throb in her voice. "Henri's was in the hospital. I was so looking forward to a big affair with yours, Gili."

"We'll plan something, Mama," Angelique promised. "But right now a plane is waiting. I'm flying to Zhamair as soon as I throw a few things in a bag, but—"

She looked to Trella, who drew her in for a warm hug, then dried her sister's cheek with a gentle touch. "Our leaky little Gili is married. Don't worry about me. Go. Pack. Be with your husband."

Angelique was obviously torn. She looked to the screen as she rose. "Kasim's team will take care of my PR going forward. I hate to leave you all in the lurch—"

"You're not," everyone said in unison, making her laugh-cry again. "I love you all *so much*."

"We'll issue a statement that we're very happy for you," Ramon said. "Which we are. Will you come to the engagement party this weekend?"

"I have no idea. Kasim said something about honeymooning at his oasis." She blushed. "Either way, you'll all come see me soon?"

"Count on it," Henri promised, which was quite an offer considering he literally had his hands full. As if on cue, the daughter he held began to fuss. He exchanged a rueful look with his wife. "Time to switch out again. We have to go. But Trella—"

She bowed her head against her hand. "I *know*."

"I've got this," Ramon said to his brother. "Take care of your *chicas. Besos*, Mama."

His mother blew them a kiss and Spain signed off. Angelique walked away, presumably to pack. Trella lifted her face from her hand. She sighed as she looked at her brother through the small screen. "Don't start."

"*Is* the prince of Elazar the father?" he asked. "Have you told him?"

"No."

"No, he's not the father? Or no, you haven't told him?"

She skipped past clarifying. "For Kasim's sake, Isidora can confirm that I was the twin in the photo. Hold off on announcing the pregnancy. I don't want to link the two in people's minds."

"Trella," Ramon growled.

"I'm handling this!"

"You're not. A baby doesn't go away, *hermana*."

"Oh, you think? You're just mad I'm not letting *you* handle it."

"Trella," Isidora interjected. Once these two started arguing they could go on for days. She had heard it with her own ears. "Do I say whether the prince knew it was you? Is he likely to comment one way or another?"

Trella dug her hands through her hair, and groaned, "Don't say. We'll see if he comments and deal with it if he does."

"That's hardly 'handling it,' is it?" Ramon said. "The more you play coy, the worse this will get. I will—"

"What?" Trella challenged. "Make out with Izzy on the bow of the boat? Let them catch her topless? *Stop trying to fix this*. You *can't*. It's *my* problem, Ramon." She ended the call without another word.

With a feral noise, Ramon gripped his phone tightly and gave it a small shake. *"Braguillas."* Brat. He made a noise of disgust and set down the phone with a clatter.

Isidora scratched her upper lip. "Just to be clear, we're not, um, going to do those things, are we? I get to keep my top on?"

His gaze flicked across like a whip, his expression fierce. "Do you honestly think I would expect that of you?"

That arrogant tone got under her skin.

"I don't know, do I?" In the back of her mind, she knew she was deliberately provoking him, looking for any sort of reaction beyond flat disinterest. "It's something you *would* do. You always deflect attention from her. That's how I wound up in this fake engagement, if you recall."

She reached for her phone as a small shield, tensing with apprehension that he would come back with something about her chest not being enough to interest anyone.

His thundering silence was worse.

CHAPTER SEVEN

THIS WOMAN. SHE was driving him insane, revealing exactly what kind of fire burned inside her before tearing him down and locking him out.

The things she had revealed the night of the party had been a shock, and he hadn't dealt with it well in the moment, had been too sexually frustrated to process all that she had revealed—and how much shame she had sent crawling up inside him. But he'd had plenty of time for self-castigation since.

He had underestimated her feelings for him over the years, thinking them superficial because from the time he had become sexually active, he'd been treated as a trophy. Even the racing fans who "preferred" him over his brother were more interested in the driver than the man. Besides, Isidora hadn't been mature enough for anything more than surface infatuation, he had always believed.

But he couldn't stop hearing her say "*if I thought you wanted* me." Like she believed herself interchangeable with the women he'd encountered over the years.

She wasn't. Deep down, he had always known an affair with Isidora would be the furthest thing from impersonal. That's why he had held her off so uncompromisingly. Emotional intimacy made him close up inside.

He had told himself he was protecting *her*, denting her

ego, not her heart, but he wasn't so devoid of conscience he would pimp her out with topless photos, and it wasn't just because the idea of any man seeing her naked was abhorrent to him.

Really abhorrent.

"No, I wouldn't ask you to strip down to divert attention from my sister," he stated, biting out each word. "Effective as that might be."

She took up her fork and dipped her head, brows pulling with consternation as though she wasn't sure whether he was complimenting her or what.

It struck him afresh that his discouragement over the years had affected her far more seriously than he had intended. Looking back, he could see that a young woman's confidence could be impacted by such things, but at the time— He sighed with self-disgust.

"I shouldn't have taken advantage of your loyalty as badly as I have. I know what a precious commodity it is. Anyone else would have sold us out, or pushed me into traffic by now."

"If the doors to the terrace had been open the other night..." She stuffed a cherry tomato into her mouth, sealing her lips over the threat she didn't finish. But even as she chewed, he saw the faint tremble in her lips. His few words of culpability affected her.

He wasn't someone who apologized, and barely had just now, but she was moved. In that moment, he understood, really understood, what kind of power he had over her.

Maybe he had always known, because he tensed even now, wanting to turn away. He had the intelligence to know that the flip side of a power coin was responsibility. He already carried a lot of obligations. He didn't want more.

But there she perched, teetering in the place between his conscience and his sense of duty, whether he wanted to accept her presence or not. Something unsteady see-sawed in his chest, making him look to the horizon, hoping it was only the yacht listing on the waves.

He heard her draw a breath as though preparing to say something, but when he looked back at her, he saw hesitation. A change of mind.

"What?" he prompted.

"Nothing." She pushed at the greens on her plate with the tines of her fork. "I know that my loyalty is both my strength and my weakness, that's all."

That hadn't been what she had been about to say, he was sure of it, but now he wondered if that was why she hadn't pushed her mother out of her life, despite how much anguish Francisca's actions had caused her. Her mother was still keeping a secret that could devastate her, he recalled, and wished like hell he didn't know about it. If she ever found out he knew and hadn't told her, she really would push him into traffic.

"For instance, my loyalty to Trella demands that I ask why you're still playing human shield for her, even though I know you'll say it's not my place to ask."

"I do take a zero-tolerance approach to discussing my family." He felt like an ass as he said it, especially when she nodded, as if he had behaved as expected, but still slid her attention sideways to hide that she was stung.

"Even though I'm directly affected in this case." Her voice quavered with emotion. "I mean, I know you and Henri have reason to be protective, and I know she was hiding her panic attacks from the press. That's why she stayed out of the public eye all those years, but she has that under control now, right? So after all those years of her struggling to get a handle on things, she's finally ready to steer her own life. Why don't you want to let her? Why go the route of keeping me here, doing this? Don't say it's because she'll make mistakes. We all kiss frogs on the way to growing up."

Like him?

She cleared her throat, not meeting his gaze, but her chin took on a haughty angle. "For what it's worth, I agree with you. I think the prince is the father and that she should tell him. But it's not my life and it's not yours, either." "So there" was heavily implied.

She dropped her gaze to the face of her phone, chin set with belligerence, but he had the distinct feeling she was sitting there braced for a blast.

His knee-jerk reaction was to not just nip that sort of intrusion in the bud, but yank it out by the roots.

Yet here he sat, using a woman who only wanted to defend his sister. On the brink of hurting Isidora again, because she dared ask why he was using *her*.

The fluttering snap of the flag at the stern filled the silence.

"Whatever," she muttered, shoving aside her plate. "I'll chalk it up to that childish contrariness you two have been locked in all your lives and get back to doing my 'job.'"

She started to rise.

"I've been called a lot of things. 'Childish' is not one of them."

"But you're willing to own 'contrary?'"

He curled his lip, not exactly warm to the idea, even though there was some truth to it. He and Trella *were* contrary. If he said black she had to say white. To this day, his little sister would always claim "*he* started it," even though she invariably picked their fights.

"I don't have brothers and sisters. I've never understood why you fight so much. I've always thought you two were lucky to have each other and should be nicer. Especially—"

She didn't finish, but he knew what she meant. He *was* lucky to have Trella, considering how close they had come to losing her.

"I don't fully understand it, either," he admitted, not sure if he was relieved or dismayed when Isidora let her hands and napkin fall back into her lap as she stayed to listen. "Henri has the patience to deal with Trella being headstrong and impulsive. Gili is so sensitive, she cries if they disagree. With me, Trella seems to challenge every single thing I say. There's six years between us. I don't antagonize her for the sake of it, but she has never accepted that I might know a few things."

Isidora's brows went up. She set her elbow on her armrest and propped her chin on her fist, wearing an expression of polite interest, but she rolled her lips inward to suppress a smile.

"Why is that funny?"

"I'm just wondering how much you know about being pregnant? By accident. By a prince."

He let out a heavy breath, *hating* this, but supposed he owed her an explanation.

"I left her to deal with her own problems once before. It didn't work out well." He moved his gaze to the endless horizon of blue on blue, holding that blankness inside him so he didn't have to deal with the roiling emotions beneath the surface.

"Ramon! No, you didn't." Her touch settled on his wrist, her fingertips cool against his skin, far more profound than her voice. He found himself holding very still, not wanting to startle her into lifting her hand and removing that tentative contact.

"Don't ever blame yourself for not catching up to that van before they got away."

"I'm not talking about the kidnapping." They'd all had therapy ad nauseam after Trella was recovered. He knew in his head he wasn't responsible for Trella's kidnapping. Gili's math tutor was. Ramon had been fifteen, a top athlete, and had chased the van until he collapsed with exhaustion. He still had sick moments when he went over and over that memory, thinking *maybe* and *if only.*

Therapy could only accomplish so much, but for the most part they had all put that trauma into the past. They had still been coming to terms with the rest, however, when Trella had been pulled into a fresh hell and they had all been sucked in with her.

"I mean later," he clarified, using the measured, disembodied voice he used when he had no choice but to go back to the dark times. "After our father died."

He had the unnatural urge to turn up his palm and invite her hand to slip into his grip, but tensed against needing support. He *needed* to be strong, because as much as Trella exasperated him, she was also deeply vulnerable. He had to be a pillar for her. For all his family. Impervious.

"Grief isn't something you can fix for anyone." He could hear the confusion in her voice. "All you can do is be there and I know you were. Weren't you? I know you were racing…"

"I took time off from racing after Papa died. Henri and I were dealing with…*everything.* Grief. The board. They refused to hand the keys to the castle to a pair of new adults still wet behind the ears. Henri was going through our father's records, doing the sort of tedious work I can't stand. I was doing what I could to support Mama and the girls. Trella and Gili were supposed to start back at school, but Trella kept making excuses. Things were happening online that she didn't tell us about. Emails. Photographs and sexual harassment. Things that make me sick as a grown man. You can imagine what they did to a teenage girl with Trella's history."

She absorbed that in a beat of thoughtful silence, then murmured, "I always wondered why she was so adamant against starting social-media accounts. Is that what started her panic attacks?" Her hand stayed on his arm, was soothing despite just resting the light weight of her fingertips against his skin.

"Gili was getting the same messages, but neither of them wanted to worry us. She knew something was up with Trella, though. That it was worse for her. I kept saying she was just being Trella. Moody and obstinate. She had made so much progress since the kidnapping, I didn't see—I didn't *want* to see—that she was falling apart. Going past rock-bottom and not coming back. Like if I ignored it, I could keep it from happening."

He wanted to go back and shake that ignorant young man he'd been. If he had listened to Gili, if he had pushed past Trella's insistence that she was *fine*…

"She was supposed to come watch one of my races and changed her mind at the last minute. We argued and she told me to leave her alone. I took her at her word. It was the worst possible thing I could do."

He thought he heard Isidora's breath catch in apprehension, but he was lost in that awful moment of fearing that history had repeated itself.

"Gili was hysterical even before we got home, convinced something was wrong. We walked in the house and Trella was gone. I called the police, then checked the security footage. That's how I figured out where to look.

She was curled up in the back of her closet, biting a towel to keep from screaming, soaked with sweat."

"Oh, Trella," Isidora whispered, and moved her hand from his arm to cover her heart. "There were so many times when I would ask if I could come see her and she would say it wasn't a good day. I had no idea it was ever *that* bad."

"No one but family does." He looked around, realized where he was, but no one was on deck except the two of them. Perspiration coated his back as he leaned forward, letting the breeze ripple his shirt and pull him back to the present.

"I would never tell anyone."

"I know." He was still impatient with himself. "I shouldn't have said anything regardless. It's her secret to tell, not mine. I wish I could say that was the worst of it, but those same panic attacks happened again and again, sometimes as night terrors, other times hours straight of racing heart and deep anxiety. She didn't get them under control until she pulled out of the public eye completely. Even then, it's been a long haul to get here. We're all holding our breath and is she keeping a low profile, taking things slow? Hell, no. Not Trella." He flung up an exasperated hand. "She's sleeping with strangers, getting pregnant by a damn prince who has his own publicity nightmare to manage. That is why, *cariño*, I have forced you into the spotlight with me. I never want her to go through that again."

Ramon's tormented profile twisted her stomach into a knot.

In so many ways, this man had stolen her heart by being strong. The very first time she had ever seen him, he had picked her up off the grass at an executive picnic for Sauveterre International. She'd been five or six and he had set her on her feet like it was nothing, then called out to the boys who had rushed past and knocked her down that they should be more careful.

After the kidnapping, when her father had made house calls to his, she hadn't understood why her friends were so different, so sad. Even some of the grown-ups cried sometimes, but if Ramon or Henri wept, they did it behind closed doors.

By the time she had begun to stir with a more primal, feminine understanding of male strength, Ramon had been a godlike figure who dominated her imagination. He'd been a dynamic alpha who tamed a thousand horses with the pedals of one car. There were no contests he didn't win, no weights his broad shoulders couldn't carry.

In truth, she had set him up for a role he was too human to live up to.

No wonder he had pushed her away. Who needed that much pressure? He had enough on his plate conquering his personal demons.

But until this moment, she hadn't seen them. Not this closely. Not this nakedly.

She had sat with her hand on his arm while he had revealed the dark space inside himself. Now he had retreated into it and she wanted to respect that need for privacy, but more than anything, she wanted to pull him out of that grim place. There was no way to fix his bleak past, though. No way to guarantee bad things wouldn't happen in the future.

All she could do was let him know he was not alone in this moment. He had drafted her into the role of his fiancée. She loved his sisters and owed his family, so she was willing to continue this engagement, but she knew in her heart, she was doing it for his sake, too. Because she was who she was and she did want to make the world a better place, one tiny ray of light at a time.

"I *would* let myself be photographed topless—"

"Like hell." His head snapped around so fast, and his voice was so dour, that her heart clenched. It skipped at the same time, buoyed by a giddy urge to laugh.

She was such an idiot to think he was being protective, to like it, but she still grasped at it as she continued.

"To take the heat off this latest news about Trella."

"I said *no*."

"But we'd probably have more success if we pretended I dropped my engagement ring overboard."

His thunderous expression eased into a faint smirk.

"You're starting to think like me. I'm not sure that's a good thing." He nodded once. "Let's eat, then go fishing."

They managed an uneasy truce as they finished their travel into Málaga. Since they were the guests of honor at their engagement party, they stayed at the hotel where it was being held, rather than at Sus Brazos with the rest of his family.

The hotel was a completely refurbished nineteenth-century structure. All the five-star amenities had been added, but the rooms described as "charming" and "authentic" were actually "small" and "snug." Ramon had taken their best suite, but with their own guest list competing for rooms with wealthy vacationers from across Europe, he hadn't been able to take any extra space.

They were back to either sharing a bed or arguing, until he volunteered to take that torture device the decorator no doubt called "a delightful period piece." It looked no bigger than the average love seat and sported fili-greed armrests.

Isidora gave the bed a circumspect glance and asked if he needed the bathroom before she started getting ready.

He nursed a Scotch on the balcony, watching the waves against the beach, trying not to think of that bed behind him. Yesterday he'd spent the afternoon lusting after her in a bikini as they'd spent a couple of hours diving for an engagement ring that was in the safe in his onboard office.

Damn it, if he wanted sex, Isidora was right. He didn't have to go very far. He turned down more offers than he accepted. Finding someone to discreetly take the edge off behind the back of his "fiancée" would not be difficult. But as he glanced over the topless, golden bodies wandering in from a day on the sand, he found himself turned off by the idea of a quick frolic with a stranger.

He wanted Isidora. Since that night in Monaco, he had been obsessively imagining bringing her to the same kind of shattering orgasm she'd had in his lap, but pumping into her while it happened, intimately feeling her contractions of ecstasy, finding his own pleasure at the same time.

Damn, but it was hot this summer!

With a soft curse, he drained his Scotch and chewed an ice cube, then moved into the air-conditioning, finding no relief as he changed into his tuxedo.

He had never been so preoccupied by a woman. It was uncomfortable. Especially when he wanted… He shook his head at himself. He wanted to be friends. When he had opened up about Trella, Isidora hadn't offered platitudes like "I understand," or "it will be all right." She had sat with her warm touch on his arm, waiting to lead him out of his own closet of fear.

That patient contact had been so profound it seemed to reach all the way to his heart. He had *felt* understood.

He couldn't ruin that tentative trust by asking her again for an empty affair.

Tying his bow tie, he heard a noise behind him and turned.

And swore.

Isidora was flawless in a black-velvet, one-shoulder gown that hugged her breasts and hips. It might have bordered on unremarkable if not for the faux diamonds that traced the shoulder strap and followed the cutout beneath her left breast, drawing the eye to where the creamy skin of her rib cage and waist was exposed.

He didn't want to just touch that bare skin, he wanted to feel the soft heat of it against his open mouth, taste it, feel her squirm under butterfly kisses and arch as he sucked.

"No?" Her hand went to her middle. "I have a red gown—"

"No. I mean yes. You have completely emptied my brain, woman." He ate up her slender arms, her upper chest, the flex in her throat as she swallowed. Her hair was gathered with a line of sparkling diamonds, exposing a blue stone dangling from her earlobe. "You look fantastic."

"Ramon—" Her shy face twisted into a drawn, anxious expression.

He hurried forward, like he could save something falling from a cart.

"That isn't flattery. I'm not being polite. You have never escaped my notice, Isidora. I wanted to ignore you. I *tried*. But even when you were just a chatty, flat-chested sprite of a thing, I couldn't overlook you."

He stopped her hands from wringing by taking them in his own.

"If I hurt you—" He swore. "I know I've hurt you."

He circled his thumb over the tip of her pointed knuckle, aware of the way her fingers fluttered against his loose grip, like a nervous bird's wings. "I'm sorry."

It surprised him how hard it was to say the words. A lot of remorse came with the admission, leaving a tightness in his chest that caused a scrape in his voice.

"Sometimes yours was the only laugh we heard in our house all week. It bothers me that I might have cut that off. I don't think I've heard you laugh since…"

Hell, probably since before her mother's lounge five years ago.

He closed his eyes in regret and brought her bent fingers to his lips, pressing his apology into them.

Her breath caught. The cool stone in her ring grazed near the corner of his mouth and the backs of his thumbs touched the prickle on his own chin. He grimaced, releasing her to rub at his stubbled jaw. "I should shave before I forget."

"You should." Her voice was thick with emotion. "Thank you, Ramon."

"For shaving?" He knew what she meant, but the moment was too charged for his liking. "I don't want you to be uncomfortable when we kiss at our party."

Completely leveled, Isidora tried to gather her composure.

I'm sorry. Such small words, spoken so quietly, but the impact was huge. Her throat felt swollen and her heart ran like a freight train in her chest.

When she heard him come back a few minutes later, she still couldn't look at him, too moved. Too overwhelmed. She checked that she hadn't chewed off her lipstick and swept out the door he held open for her. It wasn't until they were in the elevator with their guards that her gaze tracked to his in the mirror they faced.

"I thought you were going to shave?" He looked quite the ruffian in a tuxedo with that five o'clock shadow. Very devil-may-care. If he loosened his bow tie her knees would unhinge completely.

He made a face and scraped his palm against his cheek. "My razor broke."

"We could have one sent up. Do you want to go back?"

His guard, Oscar, extended a finger toward the panel.

"There's no point. I know what the problem is and something else will happen to stop me. Resistance is futile."

"What do you mean?" She turned from the reflection to the man. "I noticed you've been wearing stubble more often lately. I thought it was a fashion choice."

"A fashion choice," he repeated with a choked noise, clearly offended. "*No.* I'm not being lazy, either."

"What then?"

"I don't want to tell you. You'll laugh." His lip curled, but the way he eyed her sent rising bubbles of amusement into her chest.

She made a show of holding a bored expression and glancing at her nails. "I heard a rumor that was a goal of yours, but whatever…"

The doors opened to the lobby, putting an abrupt end to what had been the beginnings of very enjoyable, light-hearted flirting. The dull roar of conversation filled the space on the second floor, where a chandelier hung amid a gallery of masterpieces in gilded frames.

They stepped out and Ramon halted her with a touch on her arm.

"Come here, then." He veered her from the throng crowding the marble floor around the fountain and drew her into a small kiosk. It had probably held a telephone at one point, but now housed a terminal for airline check-ins and other online tasks.

It was close quarters. She brought her hands up to rest on his lapels, conscious of the hard wall of his chest.

"What, um—" She hadn't been this close to him since sitting astride him. The sting of a blush crept into her cheeks. She looked to the sliding door he had pulled closed behind them.

"It's new-father syndrome. I've seen it with our executives. They look like they're coming to work after a terrific bender, but it's just a fresh baby at home."

That surprised her into looking up with a confused frown. "Is there something you haven't told me?" She cocked her head. "Because I must say you're being very hard on your sister."

"Not me. My brother." He lightly cupped her elbows and his thumbs drew restless patterns against her skin, making a shiver run up her shoulders and into her chest, sensitizing her nipples. She tried to ignore it.

"You want me to believe that Henri is forgetting to shave so you are, too?" She shook her head. "The universe broke your razor?"

"Do you think we dress alike because we think it's cute?"

"You're businessmen. The uniform is a three-piece suit. Of course you'll grab the same white shirt now and again."

"And the same tie? And the same shoes?"

She shook her head. "I'm not as gullible as those people who think twins are psychic." Lowering her brow, she asked with suspicion, "*Are* you psychic?"

"No." Amusement played around his mouth.

He really had a beautiful mouth. The seam of his lips

was quite wide, but his upper lip was defined with two strong peaks, while his bottom lip was smooth and full, inviting a nibble.

"Isidora."

She'd never heard her name spoken in such a husky, sexy tone. When he cupped the side of her neck, she felt as though her body fell away. She became something ephemeral, pulse throbbing against the heat of his hand on her throat as his green, green eyes held her in thrall.

"You accused me of wanting you because you're convenient, but that is so far from the truth. My brain is telling me not to wreck the peace we've finally made, but I can't stop thinking about what we started. About how passionate you are. *You*. It's not convenient at all."

She grew hotter with every word. Beyond the door, one of the guards said something.

"I think someone wants in here," she said, desperate for escape before she did something stupid, like fall all over him again.

Ramon's hand dropped from her neck, leaving a chill that increased as he opened the door.

The indirect lighting against the yellowed facade of the hotel, along with the candles floating in the pool, cast a warm glow over the bricked area that had been roped off all the way to the beach. A string trio played for the reception portion, to be replaced by a livelier dance band after the champagne toast.

Paparazzi had already bribed their way into positions along the velvet rails and off some balconies, determined to snap photos of the celebrities Ramon had deliberately invited. He could have held the party in the privacy of Sus Brazos, but that ultrahigh security would have defeated the purpose. This party was the event of the year, intended to dominate the society pages so Trella wouldn't.

His sister arrived in a subtle maternity gown, choosing to let a picture speak a thousand words. Ramon sincerely hoped her plan to bury the news amid the spectacle of his engagement worked.

Letting go of his responsibility toward either of his sisters was easier said than done. At least Angelique was in good hands. Ramon had no doubt Kasim would die before allowing harm to come to her. He certainly had the resources to kill anyone who tried, but Ramon still did a quick scan to note where his sisters stood with their mother, a collective of guards on hand. Kasim, unruffled yet ever alert, stood at Angelique's side.

His shy little sister was a queen. Ramon still hadn't taken it in. Along with Henri and his babies, she now had too much responsibility to drop everything and rush to Trella's side when necessary. It was all on him.

The weight of that might have pushed him into grim introspection, but a sudden burst of laughter from Isidora yanked like a sweet hook in his heart. It wasn't just the tinkling sound that turned his head. He wanted to catch the way her eyes sparkled.

His breath stalled and he found himself smiling in reaction. Satisfaction and something more tender rolled through him. He hadn't destroyed that light in her after all.

"You knew!" she accused, squeezing his upper arm through his jacket and bumping into him at the same time, so he felt the press of her breast. "Did you call him?"

"Who?"

She waved at where Henri was coming toward them with Cinnia.

"Ah." It could be argued that all tuxedos looked alike,

that pleated shirts were de rigueur with one, but he and his brother both owned several penguin costumes. Despite that, he would bet their collective fortune that the same designer label was sewn into every article they both wore tonight. And Henri had *not* shaved.

They looked as they too often did—like mirror images. Their sisters regularly turned themselves out with individual looks unless they consciously chose to copy each other. Why the hell could he and Henri not manage it?

As was often the case, Henri knew without a word being spoken what Ramon was thinking. He shrugged. "I had to get Cinnia out of the house before they woke up and noticed she was gone. There wasn't time to shave."

Cinnia was a little more voluptuous than she had been before pregnancy, but it suited her. She rose on tiptoe to press her cheek to his and wrinkled her nose at his stubble. "He had a different shirt on. Then Rosalina spit up and he had to change."

"This is a setup, isn't it?" Isidora looked between the identical men, skeptical. "I mean, it was a safe bet that Henri might not have shaved, but…"

"I've seen it happen more times than I can count," Cinnia assured her, then picked up her husband's hand and said cheekily, "Be careful, Ramon. Henri wears a ring now."

Cinnia knew the engagement was a stunt. She didn't speak so loudly she risked exposing the ruse, but none of them laughed. Isidora blushed and dropped her gaze. Ramon felt a familiar clench of protectiveness, but it was directed toward someone different, which was such a new sensation it was disconcerting. Like the sensitive skin beneath a freshly removed cast.

"What—?" Cinnia began.

Henri tucked her under his arm and spoke over her. "I'll get the speeches done quickly. I want to dance with my wife while I have her to myself. Especially since we can't stay long." He squeezed her and drew her away.

Isidora's parents chose that moment to arrive, but the awkwardness only increased.

"My angel! We're so happy for you!" Francisca cried. "Have you set a date?"

"Hija preciosa," Isidora's father said as her mother moved along to fawn over Ramon.

"Papa." She leaned into her father's barrel chest to accept his enveloping hug.

"Estás bien?" He drew back to give her a searching look. Others had laughed at her puppy love for Ramon, but he never had. He didn't know about That Day, but he knew her reservations against taking this position at Sauveterre International had been motivated by a strong desire to avoid Ramon.

"I'm fine," she assured him. It felt like only a small lie. She was telling the truth in this moment, especially since she and Ramon had cleared the air in many ways, but she suspected that when this pretend engagement was over, she would not be "fine" by any stretch of the imagination.

Because he wouldn't marry her. That's why Cinnia's joke had landed so flatly, like a gob of mud on the bricks at their feet. She shook off the painful reminder and patted her father's lapel.

"How about you?" she asked with gentle concern. Every time her parents had reunited in the past, a painful breakup had soon followed, usually caused by her mother's tendency to wander.

Their experience was a cautionary tale, she reminded

herself, thinking of all the things Ramon had said that replaced her hurt and anger with wistful yearning and a blind desire to believe in miracles.

"Excelente," her father assured her with confidence.

Isidora wanted to believe him. As she watched them through the evening, staying close and sharing affectionate touches, she found herself hoping that this time they really would find happiness. But deep down, she knew she was just trying to believe in fairy-tale endings for her parents so she could buy in to one for herself.

Like her engagement dinner in the Paris restaurant, this evening was agonizing in its perfection. The moonlight turned the gentle foam on the sea to a veil of lace. The late summer breeze caressed like down. Henri and her father said warm things about how close their families had always been. Some of her dearest friends raised their glasses, genuine in their happiness for her, believing she was marrying the man of her long-held dreams.

When she looked up at Ramon, she almost believed it—which was so very dangerous, but how could she not be inexorably drawn to him? He was so confident, with features painted by a master into an archangel's, mouth curled in private amusement, body disciplined and still while his restless gaze moved across all he surveyed.

He was aloof and hard for a reason. Knowing those reasons only made caring for him more perilous. He wouldn't bend and nothing could break him. She knew better than to expect anything but heartache from him.

When they toasted with champagne, however, and the partygoers tapped their glasses, demanding a kiss from the happy couple, her heart raced with excitement. He took her in his arms and she knew that no matter what happened in the rest of her life, this man would always possess a piece of her heart.

She tensed slightly, as she had before all of his kisses, bracing herself to hide the way she reacted. She feared the blaze of need that flared when he touched her. It had only grown worse with proximity. This man had always had the ability to pull her outside herself and leave her standing without defenses, bare to the world. In the last few weeks, each and every time they had kissed, no matter how generic the peck, she had wanted to sob out at the pleasure-pain of it.

His embrace was too great a power to withstand, making her feel pried open.

But not being near him, not feeling his touch, *not* kissing him, was worse.

Until this moment, she had used fury and hurt to suppress all those feelings, but so much of her anger and agony was defused. She had little left to protect her. She was tingly and soft. Without conscious decision, she *yielded*.

He noticed. His gaze flashed as he slid his hand along the bare skin exposed by the cutout of her gown. He tucked his fingertips beneath the fabric as he drew her into him, the sheer propriety of his action making her heart stumble.

Other men had held her and kissed her, but no man except this one made the soft crash of their bodies feel like an implosion. All the energy was sucked from the surrounding area. It gathered tight inside her, releasing as a blast of excitement as his mouth claimed hers.

She really hadn't stopped thinking about their night. She tasted the memory on his lips, sipped again at the passion in the sweep of his tongue into her mouth. She hadn't stopped thinking about it, either, and abandoned chagrin in favor of welcoming the sensual storm he sent whirling through her blood.

In that moment, she knew he must possess *her*. It wasn't a clear-headed decision to make love with him tonight. It was a far more primal knowledge that whether it was tonight, or next week, or some point in the future, she would lie down with this man. Had to. Her mouth opened wider to accept his plundering kiss. Her body *yearned*. She wrapped her arms around his neck and stopped fearing he would destroy her.

She looked forward to it.

CHAPTER EIGHT

IF SHE HAD been a little bit drunk the last time she was in Ramon's arms, tonight she was high on natural chemistry. Pheromones. The imprint of a particular man's touch that never seemed to lift from her body even if it was only his eyes across a dance floor.

Not that he let other men monopolize her. No, he cut in shamelessly more than once, and reserved all the slow dances for himself. He said nothing, but he knew. He was too experienced not to.

She felt obvious and callow, but she was supposed to be a besotted fiancée, right? No one knew she was a virgin, though, least of all the man who would relieve her of that label.

They slipped away from their own party while it continued to rage, waiting until family was gone, then leaving the who's who to their follies.

With a signal, Ramon ensured the guards didn't let anyone else onto their elevator. The men stood at the front, giving her and Ramon the privacy of their turned backs.

Ramon didn't draw her into a hot embrace, though. He leaned his shoulder into the wall and gently drew her into the loose cage of his hands on her waist. His one hand moved against her skin within the cutout. His gaze went to where he traced that lazy pattern.

"I like this dress."

She choked out a laugh that sounded equally like a sob. The compliment was so bland. *Seduce me.*

His expression was solemn. He lifted one bent knuckle to stroke up her throat, then caressed beneath her chin, the action surprisingly tender.

The doors opened, startling her.

Ramon linked their fingers as they walked to their room and waited for it to be checked. Then he drew her inside and released her.

She stood for a moment in stasis, confused, aching, while he turned the lock behind her. Anxiety started to creep in at the edges of her consciousness. He was going to reject her. Again.

"Be sure, Isidora." The weight of his hands, solid and grounding, possessive, settled on her bare shoulders. For a moment, that's all it was, then he stepped closer, so she felt the graze of his tuxedo jacket, then the movement of his breath as he spoke against her hair. "I want to give you pleasure. I want that so badly you can't even imagine." His head rested briefly against hers. "But I don't want you to hate me after."

Because he wouldn't marry her.

She looked down at the clutch she held, then made herself move away from his touch to set the purse aside and face him. It wasn't easy. His focus on her was like a live wire, pulsing electricity through her in painful beats.

"I'm not a reckless person. I try not to do self-destructive things." She'd grown up watching it and knew better. She would proceed very carefully, she told herself. She wouldn't let herself get in too deep. "But I would always wonder."

She looked at where her hands tangled themselves together, not admitting the harder truth, that she feared she would never get over him until she had gone as far as she could with him.

"I know it would only be an affair." Her throat tightened, making the words rasp.

He flinched and the green of his eyes cooled to silver before he looked away. "You deserve better."

"I know I do."

That brought his attention back with a flash of reassessment that made her heart race into the base of her throat.

"I'm not a child, Ramon. Not anymore. You're right that you never could have met my expectations back then. But I do know what I'm worth and what I should expect from a man now, as a woman."

She turned the ring on her finger.

"I wouldn't normally go into something so intimate without at least the hope of long-term or permanent, but..." She sighed. "Maybe I am still a little naive, but I want to believe that even though this...arrangement is temporary, that we can be friends after."

A beat of silence before he made a jagged sound that wasn't quite a laugh.

"I left naive a long time ago, but I want to believe that, too."

"Then, yes. I'm sure." She held out her hands.

Ramon took her hands and pulled them behind his back, then his palm hooked the slenderness of her neck and he covered her mouth like he owned it.

And thrilled when she let him. She surrendered exactly as she had when he had kissed her downstairs. He had wanted to feast on her then and let himself do it now, kissing her hard, deep, taking and taking, allowing his hunger to consume him.

He wasn't a brute. He would have backed off if she had signaled he was moving too fast, but she worked her hands against his back, pulling herself tighter into him.

He caught fire under the friction, burning in a sudden conflagration that had only subsided since Monaco, waiting for the sough of her breath to burst into life again. He released her long enough to shed his jacket, dropping it to the floor, then growled like an animal as he caught her close and pressed her toward the bedroom.

The bed.

He was going too fast, he knew he was, but he'd never felt so greedy. So pressed for time. He wanted so *much*— the tendons in her neck, which made her gasp when he scraped his teeth there, the thrust of her mound against his aching erection, the fullness of her breasts weighing into his palms. Releasing her zip, he was able to draw down the one shoulder and find her braless, naked and firm, yet soft. So soft. And hot. Her skin scalded his hand as he cupped her breast, plumping it so her nipple sat high on the creamy swell. He bent to taste the hard bead, playing it against his tongue and loving her sob of pleasure.

Yes. Pleasure. He wanted to ask what she liked, how he could intensify this for her, but his voice was gone. He was barely able to form a thought beyond his desire to make her writhe and cry out and shudder the way she had in his lap.

Pressing her to sit on the bed, he climbed her gown up her thighs.

She gasped and her hand closed around his wrist.

"I only want to kiss you." He leaned to cover her mouth again, penetrated her lips with his tongue and groaned as she sucked on it. She shivered under the caress of his fingers over her breast. He let his touch linger there as he lowered to his knees between hers, kissing her and kissing her while he caressed and stroked and finally moved his hands to rub up the insides of her thighs.

When he found the silk between her legs and lightly stroked over it, she made a mewing sound, like music. He drew back to admire her swollen, parted lips, the dazed glow in her eyes, the way she bit her lip as he worked a finger behind the silk into heat. So much wet, slippery heat.

He pressed his finger into her honeyed channel, nearly out of his mind with how soft and ready she was.

She made a keening noise and her lashes fluttered. He stroked his thumb in a way that made her tighten all over, and she panted, "Oh, yes."

"Lie back," he commanded, feeling like a god when she sank onto the mattress and threw her arm over her eyes.

He worked black silk down her ivory thighs, taking his time unwrapping this gift. That's exactly what she was, with her thatch of red-gold and her nervous twitch as he slid his arms beneath the weight of her thighs. Pink and perfumed and heady. He wanted to make her scream.

Then he wanted to plunge into her and make her his. Indelibly.

Isidora was burning alive, driven crazy by the slide of Ramon's tongue, the way he pleasured her with his hand. Her fist knotted in his hair and she pinched her thighs against his ears, her abdomen twisting as an orgasm contracted in her. She lifted into his mouth, crying out, not caring how abandoned she was. It was too good, too fiercely good.

As her climax subsided, she lay there as a puddle of spent muscles and melted bones.

He rose over her, gaze avid as he studied her while roughly stripping his clothes.

She didn't move, only had a distant thought that her dress was the wrong color. It should be white. This was supposed to be a sanctified moment, not something raw and primal, where her thighs still burned with the scrape of his beard and he carried a condom in his pocket so he could roll it on without stepping away.

He pulled off her gown and pushed her higher on the bed as he covered her.

"My shoes."

"I like them." He guided her ankle to the small of his back, bit her earlobe and said something dirty about wanting to be inside her.

She had thought this moment would come on her wedding day, with declarations of love and a sweeter, more romantic deflowering.

But as imperfect as this was, lying atop a made bed, a man who would never promise forever pushing her legs apart, she couldn't deny she wanted this, too. She had never wanted anything so badly in her life.

He moved his tip against her slick folds, parting and teasing until she moaned, "Ramon," and lifted, offering herself.

He muttered something against her mouth and kissed her as he found her opening. He pressed in with a firm, deep thrust, pelvis coming up tight against hers as an inner burn seared and made her gasp.

He lifted his head, the haze from his eyes clearing. "Hurt?" He started to pull out.

"It's okay," she whispered hurriedly, trying to draw his head into the crook of her neck. Her heel instinctively pushed against his buttock, keeping him from retreating.

"Isidora," he breathed, eyes closing.

"Don't say anything stupid, Ramon. Don't—"

His eyes opened and realization was in them. Something golden and amazed that made the connection more than physical. Profound. It was like he saw inside her soul, glanced once, reached out and took possession of it. She had nothing left to shield herself. Everything she was had become his. It terrified her.

Something she couldn't decipher moved behind his eyes. He said something that was too soft and stark to catch. Dismay?

"Don't say you want to stop." Her voice was barely there.

"I am not that noble." He shifted, rocking their hips from side to side, settling deep again in a way that made her gasp. A little shudder went through her at the rush of sensations. Not pain, but acute sensitivity. Undeniable intimacy.

There was no pretending she was swept away. It was real. Indelible.

Yet strangely tender and sweet.

He propped on his arms, cupping the sides of her head in his hands. "This does change the tempo." He moved in a slow retreat and return, watching her. His eyes glittered, sharp and bright in the slanted light from the lamp. "I want to make it so good for you."

"You *like* that you're my first," she accused softly, biting her lip as a particularly sharp sensation glittered into delightful places.

"I do," he admitted, unabashed, dipping his head to suck her nipple, smiling with dark satisfaction when he provoked a wriggle and a gasp from her. He bent toward the other, and when she forced his head up, he added, "I like it more than I should. I can't wait to feel you come."

That sounded like he was impatient, but he took his

time, let her get used to the intrusion of a man while he caressed and kissed and complimented her.

It wasn't until she arched into him and said, "Ramon, I can't take this," that he laughed softly and moved with heavier, more wicked thrusts, giving her what she had unconsciously begged for. What she longed to keep each time he slid away, and welcomed with a noise of gratification each time he returned.

She didn't know what she thought sex would be, but she hadn't expected to flush all over, to want his teeth against her skin, his weight, his animalistic dominance over her.

It was base and elemental and made her moan and writhe and arch to offer herself until he pushed her into that glorious space where release burst over and around her, leaving her shivering and feeling like the most beautiful woman alive.

But she was alone again.

Still panting and dazed, she opened her eyes, betrayed yet again. "You didn't—"

"I will," he promised, shifting slightly so he could caress where they joined.

She sucked in a breath as fresh desire shot into her loins, making her clasp at his shaft. A latent pang of climax pulsed through her sex. She wouldn't have thought that could make her feel so turned on, but her limbs drew close around him of their own accord, trying to pull him more fully atop her, not even thinking, just knowing that she needed more of him.

"Tell me if I get too rough," he said as he loomed over her, voice gravelly and lips hot against hers. His kiss held nothing back and neither did his body as he pressed deep, quickly sucking her back into the whorl of mindless passion.

When he moved faster and harder this time, she wasn't sure she could take it. Not because it hurt, but because the intensity was so great, drawing her tight, threatening to cleave her in half. She needed this from him, though. Needed his unbridled desire, the possessive grasp of his hands on her shoulders. She wanted it. Gave herself up to it—to him.

And when the world exploded around her, she clung to his shuddering, damp form, listened to the echo of her cries in his hoarse shout and knew that once again, he had given her everything she had ever craved.

And still, it wasn't real.

CHAPTER NINE

FOREPLAY. AFTER-PLAY. SEX was play for him. At least it always had been.

Not with Isidora. Nothing in him felt light or humorous as he came back from the bathroom and found her naked, on her side, clutching a pillow to her chest. Her wary, sideways glance speared his throat, his gut.

He dragged down the blankets, shifted her feet, then the rest of her as he pulled her beneath the covers with him. He grabbed the pillow and sent it to the floor so nothing was between them but naked skin and silence.

After a second, she gave a shuddering sigh against his chest and relaxed in his arms. He relaxed at that point, too, oddly relieved.

"Did I hurt you?" There'd been a streak of red on the condom.

"A little. It's okay."

It wasn't. He didn't know how to react, but brushing off her virginity as trivial wasn't right. He knew that much.

"I wasn't, like, waiting for you or anything," she murmured. "Don't think I expect anything. There just hasn't been anyone I was that interested in doing it with."

"You let me believe you'd slept with Etienne."

She didn't say anything, only shifted her face against

his shoulder. He rolled onto his back so she could settle more comfortably against his side, and pulled her leg up so her thigh was across his waist, smooth and soft under his absent touch, twitching as he found a ticklish spot.

Should he tell her how closely he'd been watching Etienne, looking for an excuse to fire him?

"It was nice," she said so quietly he barely heard her. "Thank you."

"You're the Queen of Understatement, aren't you? It wasn't 'nice.'"

Her head came up and she looked appalled. "You didn't like it?"

She was a bright, confident woman, but still such an innocent.

"Of course I liked it," he grumbled, cuddling her into him again. "It was exquisite. *You* are exquisite." He wasn't a sensitive man. He knew how to charm, but rarely shared his true thoughts or feelings. Nevertheless, he admitted, "I will never forget it."

"Oh." He felt the word more than heard it. She swallowed and relaxed against him again. "That's sweet of you to say."

But she didn't believe him. Maybe that was for the best. He didn't want to lead her on, but it still bothered him. Their lovemaking had been incomparable. He'd been riding painted horses on a carousel all his life, then suddenly found himself atop a wild stallion. No, steering a purring race car. Flying a fighter jet. A rocket into space.

She wouldn't know how remarkable their connection was, though. Not until she moved on.

An uncharacteristic possessiveness struck him as he thought of her climbing into bed with other men, sharing her body, abandoning herself to passion, finding pleasure from *their* touch.

It was never going to be that good with anyone else. Did she realize that?

Was it fair for either of them to believe it?

He unconsciously tightened his arm around her, causing her to start, and she said, "Mmm?"

"Nothing. It's fine." He turned his lips against her hairline and inhaled her scent. He wanted her again. His body was hardening, longing to be inside her, but he reminded himself she was new to physical intimacy, so gently ordered, "Sleep."

Isidora had never slept with a man. They took up a lot of room. When she woke in the early hours, in a room so dark it was nearly black, she almost fell out of bed she was so close to the edge. She searched with a hand across the mattress for her pillow but found only warm, naked limbs. One snaked out to pull her tight against him. He was sinewy and hot, muscles flexing beneath satin skin. Hard.

"Where are you going?" he growled sleepily.

"Nowhere. I just…" She touched him. Couldn't help herself. She drew away enough to follow the line of silky hair down his tight stomach, then took his shape in her fist. He was smooth and ultrahot, his textures fascinating to her curious fingers.

He made a noise as she traced the arrowed ridge at his tip and pulsed under her touch.

"Did that hurt?"

"Hell, no. Don't stop."

She swallowed, surprised to feel a throb and rush of heat between her thighs. She was tender from their lovemaking, but in a way that made her feel secretive and luxurious and sensual. She stretched against him, wanting to feel him with every inch of her nude body. She thrust her nest of hair against his shaft and pressed him with her hand to firm the contact.

"I was trying to show some restraint, but if you're going to do that..." He kissed her and his hand stroked her thigh. He grew harder in her hand and shifted to suck her nipple, then asked, "Sore?" as he stroked into her wetness.

"No. It feels good." So good.

He rolled away and came back, then he was there, carefully pushing into her, thrusting lightly, then, when she moaned, with more power.

Somehow it kept getting better. The buildup was faster and more sure, the pinnacle higher, the release more complete. Maybe because he said, "Isidora!" like an incantation. The waves of pleasure expanded to her fingertips and toes, going on and on, both of them moving with it, playing out their mutual orgasm until they both settled to rest.

It happened again in full daylight, after they rose and showered. They fell onto the unmade bed for an energetic tussle that left them washed up like storm survivors, panting and damp, on their backs.

"This is insane. I can't keep my hands off you."

His words caused a pang under her heart. It was nice of him to say sexy things, but she expected he did the same for every woman he bedded. It was all part of his love-'em-and-leave-'em routine. Maybe he was even trying to make up for past hurts, wanting her to feel desirable.

She did, but she couldn't let the remarks mean anything beyond face value. Her father's eternal optimism where her mother was concerned was proof enough that some people were not a good risk.

Ignoring the slant of agony that pressed on her heart, she forced a wry tone and sat up, patting his thigh as she

said, "You've been going without since our engagement.
I wish I'd known sooner what I was missing. We're kind
of experiencing a perfect storm. But now I need another
shower. We really should get going or we'll be late for
your mother's."

She paused as a thought occurred.

"I think we should, um, keep this on the down low."
She waggled a finger between their naked bodies. "Do
you mind? I don't want things to be weird with your sisters."

"Why would it be weird?" He curled his arm beneath
his head, but she had the impression he wasn't nearly as
relaxed as he looked. His glorious chest was tense despite their recent release, his gaze hooded by his spiky
dark lashes.

Her hand lifted, wanting to pet him. He was so gorgeous, with his brown nipples on his toasted almond
chest, his defined abdomen and his sex relaxed but still
lengthened against his powerful thigh. She wanted to
rise over him, straddle—

"What?" *Focus.* "I don't know. I just don't want them
to think I'm still nursing a crush."

She would *die* if they teased her. It was bad enough
that Trella had said last night that their kiss had looked
"very convincing." Isidora had quipped something about
practice making perfect, adding a roll of her eyes, pretending it was all a huge act. Trella had moved on to
other things, but Angelique's gaze had lingered thought-
fully on her.

"Surely my privacy carries the same weight as yours?"
Isidora said to Ramon.

Something flashed in his gaze, then he used a slow
blink to hide his thoughts. "It does."

A stab of insecurity went into her belly anyway. She

didn't know why. Because this was new, she supposed. And it wouldn't last.

"Thank you," she said, lungs tight as she rose. She kept her back to him until she was putting on her face and able to keep her anxious thoughts hidden.

Ramon wasn't the sort of man who needed to keep his arm hooked around a woman, proclaiming to the world she was his. When he was in any sort of prolonged dalliance, however, like a week on his yacht, he enjoyed the affection that came between the bouts of sex. It was like petting a cat. The physical touches, the textures and warmth of her body, were as enjoyable for him as for her. He liked to keep them purring and content.

Isidora was right that they should keep things simple, but Sus Brazos was where he and his siblings came to unwind. It was the place they could be themselves without subterfuge or judgments.

And Isidora looked infinitely touchable with her hair loose—something she almost never seemed to do during the day. It tumbled in a mass of rich burgundy around shoulders bared by a sleeveless top in burnt orange. The color made her skin glow, especially where the collar was open down her breastbone.

He wanted to play with her hair and trace that narrow vee and draw circles with his palm on that firm ass of hers. She wore a pair of pants that looked like chamois, soft and buttery. They snugly cupped her figure and ended in narrow cuffs over sassy little boots that laced up like a spinster's, teasing him to find his lover behind the conservative facade.

Dios, he genuinely had to fight the urge to keep his hands to himself.

She forgot about him completely, enraptured by his

infant nieces. As she gathered Rosalina against her chest and buried her nose in the baby's neck, eyes closed blissfully, he caught a glimpse of what her future husband would see. His heart took a sharp corner, veering toward a cliff's edge. He had to look away.

And found Angelique watching him.

She was the intuitive one among them. A pulse of guilt went through him, like he'd been caught doing something he shouldn't.

He turned away from her and looked for Henri. He was speaking to Melodie, the family's official photographer, who was beginning to arrange everyone in front of the painting of their father.

Since the whole family happened to be here today, and Angelique was now married, their mother wanted a family portrait. It was a perfectly reasonable request, since Melodie had already been commissioned to snap Henri's new family.

Isidora came up to them and handed off Rosalina to Henri. "I want to check in with my mother," she said to Ramon. "She and Papa should be back in Madrid by now."

She slipped outside, but her weak excuse and even weaker smile stuck like a burr in Ramon's chest.

"Where did your fiancée go?" Melodie asked, stalling in surprise as she positioned Ramon.

"She's making some calls. Don't wait." He sounded peeved to his own ears, but this felt...inconsiderate. Isidora didn't belong in the portrait. She was never going to be part of this family in such an official way.

But he didn't have to rub her face in it.

Melodie blinked, astonished. "I see. Um, Trella, you stand here, then." She positioned Trella in front of him.

"He's engaged in image management, not marriage,"

Trella explained. "He's *helping* me." Glancing over her shoulder, she added, "Don't glare. You'll break the camera."

"If you're happy to tell the world that much, why not the rest?" He nodded at her prominent bump.

"Oh, please. Melodie isn't going to say anything to anyone."

"It doesn't change the fact you're being a hypocrite. Quit telling her my business and tell the father of your child he has one. Or let him off the hook if he's not. He's leaving messages with all of us, you know. *Return his calls.*"

"Did you just air *my* business in front of company? Now who's the hypocrite?"

"Faire taire," Henri growled. He was the last to move into position, along with Cinnia, and they each held an infant. "Do you know how hard it is to get two babies clean, fed and happy? Smile."

"Why do I even have to stand by him?" Trella growled, throwing an elbow into Ramon's diaphragm.

This was why he had always paired up with Gili. He glanced over at her, serene beside Kasim, glowing with joy. No doubt she would produce a new Sauveterre herself very soon.

He hadn't figured out how to handle this domesticity his siblings were embracing. It was far beyond what he imagined for himself. It wasn't a traumatic change, but it was still an enormous shift in his most comfortable dynamic. The foundation he depended on was rearranging itself.

Gili caught his eye and canted her head, expression concerned. Questioning.

He dropped his gaze. Trella's loosely curled hair cascaded down her back, too tempting to ignore. He re-

verted to when their lives had been simplest and gave
one tendril a tug.

"He just pulled my hair!"

"Tattletale."

Everyone laughed. Melodie blinded them with a flash
and said, "Perfect!"

A few more snaps—and snipes from his sister—and
Ramon stepped away to nod at Henri. "*Así*. We need to
talk."

Henri grimaced. "Rio. *Oui*."

It was their typical shorthand. They both knew that
politically and financially, one of them should go to Rio
for the commissioning of a port project Ramon had been
overseeing for the last two years. The enterprise was Sauveterre's foundation in South America, establishing their
expertise and credibility there.

"What are you talking about? Rio? You have to go."
Sometimes they joked that if Trella had been old enough
when their father had died, she would have pushed the
two of them aside and taken over Sauveterre International herself. Maison des Jumeaux was the world's leading design house because she has a business degree in
artist's clothing.

Certain things had held her back from reaching her
potential, however, and Henri was as aware of them as
Ramon. The trip had been planned before Cinnia delivered early and Gili had married and left Paris.

"You're not canceling. Not for me." Trella's jaw set.

Ramon ignored her, just held his brother's gaze. Their
mother could step in if necessary, but she was better at
helping Trella stay grounded. She wasn't as good with
actual attacks, found them distressing and often fell apart
herself.

"It's not that far if I have to fly back to Paris," Gili

said, setting her hand on her husband's arm. "Kasim understands."

"I'm right here," Trella interjected. "Telling you all that I don't want to be that person who needs hand-holding. How do I learn to cope on my own if you all keep rushing in? I *want* Ramon to *go*."

Ramon shook his head. He'd been down this road. "Bella—"

She spun to confront him. "If I want a man to be the boss of me, I will call the father of my child. You need to butt out."

"Ça va," Henri said, holding up a hand. "Do not start World War Three. If something comes up, Gili and I will handle it. Go. Or you'll wake Colette and this will fall apart before Mama gets the rest of the pictures she wants."

Whatever Isidora had conjured in her innocent dreams as the perfect romantic honeymoon didn't come close to the reality of a week with Ramon in Rio de Janeiro. It was so much better and she knew that all future vacations with a man had been spoiled for her, along with all the rest of the things he'd ruined. Nothing would ever live up to this perfection.

The temperatures in South America were balmy, not hot, but the weather was glorious all the same. Not that the weather mattered. It could have been cyclone season and Isidora still would have been floating on a cloud of joy.

It didn't even bother her that they were working. They went into the company offices most days, at least for a few hours, then she ran to the site with him, smiled for photo ops, or stood by while he courted local officials at cocktail parties.

Ramon was as popular as ever with the paparazzi, having raced in São Paulo, but the animosity toward her was dying down so the attention felt quite friendly. She supposed people were beginning to believe it really was true love that had motivated him to quit racing. He certainly gave that impression, acting attentive, playing the part of enamored fiancé very convincingly when they were in public.

Heck, she was falling for it. She told herself it was nothing more than a revival of her old crush, this time more of a sexual infatuation, but she couldn't help feeling connected to him and he made it seem like it was reciprocated.

Because he wasn't putting on a show. At least, she didn't think he was. He was every bit as thoughtful and charming in private as he was for an audience. They retreated to his penthouse as often as they could, where he lavished her with attention. Whether they drank coffee in robes as they overlooked the ocean, or drank wine under the stars in his jet tub, his bare foot might seek hers, or he might pull her to sit with her back against his front. It was seduction, but at a slow pace. They made love constantly, but he was just as prone to maintaining physical contact afterward as before and during. He said sweet and sexy things, but they talked about other things, too. They debated world events and types of music and theater versus film. They bantered and rolled their eyes at each other and sent each other cheeky texts.

And then, when they had been scheduled to leave two days ago, he had said, "Why don't we stay and do the final coffee reception with the team. The view is something everyone should see if they've come all the way to Rio."

It had meant another night of lovemaking, another

day of feeling like a spoiled bride on her honeymoon because he wanted her to experience something he knew she would like.

Now she stood at the rail of Páo de Açúcar, Sugarloaf Mountain, and the view *was* amazing. She looked back on the cable car that had brought their team up. Wispy clouds decorated an intense blue sky, and far into the distance Rio de Janeiro sprawled in a river of concrete gray through the valleys between high, green-coated peaks. A lazy line of sandy beach drew a border between the land and the green-blue water that stretched endlessly into the horizon.

She felt as though she stood on the top of the world.

She loved him for extending their stay and bringing her up here. For wanting to spend more time with her. For making her feel like she was loved back.

She loved him.

Oh, no.

As she took in the dizzying view from what felt like the top of the world, fingers clinging to the rail, everything fell away below her. It was nothing but down, down, down.

Which was how far she had fallen for Ramon. Not a crush this time. The real thing. The most devastating kind of love. The all-in, heart-surrendered kind of love.

Oh, no.

Ramon's warm hand settled beneath her clipped hair, finding the crook of her shoulder at the back of her neck. "Good thinking—"

She knew immediately it was him, but was so deep in thought, instantly so fearful of him finding out, she reacted with a flinch and a startled gasp.

He gave her a little frown. "I only wanted to say it was good thinking to arrange this as a thank-you. They're all taking selfies and posting to social media, exactly the sort of excitement we want to convey. Are you all right? You're pale."

"Vertigo." She turned away from the view of paradise, stomach still plummeting into the abyss. "That was the idea when I suggested it," she murmured, feeling like that day he had proposed to her in front of the cameras was a million years ago. So much had changed, yet nothing had. "I didn't expect to be here enjoying it with them, though."

"I'm glad you are. Here, I brought you one."

Was he glad to be with her? Or had she been conjuring happiness all week, wanting to believe in a mirage?

She accepted the mug he held and watched him pick up one he'd set on the rail. She sipped, needing the rush of sugar and caffeine to help her get a grip on her composure.

"I don't know if I'll be able to go back to my French press after this."

"I only drink *cafezinho* when I'm here. It doesn't taste right anywhere else."

"Ah. Well, since this is our last day, and I probably won't be back, I'll have to appreciate this last taste, won't I?"

A beat of silence followed. She went over her words in her head, wondering if he heard the parallel. How much longer would she enjoy *him* and then never taste him again?

"I was thinking about extending our stay again. Would you like that?" He squinted into the view. A muscle pulsed in his jaw. "You haven't seen the statue."

Christ the Redeemer, he meant.

Her pulse skipped and she was windmilling her arms over the gorge again, anxious to latch on to what sounded like feelings of being equally enamored on his side.

"That's up to you, isn't it?" She stung as she said it. She had completely handed him the keys to their relationship. He steered it. He decided how far they went. Now she really did feel sick and heavy, the ground rushing up at her.

She opened her mouth, not sure what to say, how to recover, when an unusually loud jangle brought his hand to his chest pocket and a fierce, terrifying look to his face.

"What—?"

"That's the emergency ringtone." His hand slid to her upper arm and he drew her toward a quiet space away from the edge, where they had a semblance of privacy while he flicked through his phone.

His teeth bared. "Every. Damn. Time."

"What's wrong?"

"The prince of Elazar has Trella."

CHAPTER TEN

RAMON COULDN'T BELIEVE he'd let himself become so distracted. Lingering an extra two days was bad enough, but he'd been on the brink of adding to that shirking of responsibility. He was furious with himself.

In silence, he got them back to the penthouse, where they gathered their things for the flight he'd just moved up. They would take off the minute they could get themselves to the tarmac.

He packed light at the best of times and had been coming and going from this penthouse for twenty-four months. He was ready in minutes, but Isidora had managed to imprint herself all over the place. A pair of shoes here, a lipstick there.

As he moved around, picking up various items, he tried not to think of his participation in littering them about. He had pulled that hair clip from her tidy daytime chignon as she had shyly taken him in her mouth. That scarf on the end table had made a loose figure eight around his wrists as she straddled him and playfully took control for an erotic hour. He had even left a pair of her silk cheekies in the pocket of his suit, when she had let him bend her over his desk the other day at the office. They had fought groaning aloud so they wouldn't be heard and he had to bite back a mixture of frustration and renewed desire now.

This *had* to stop.

He found the scrap of lace in the jacket in the closet and threw everything he'd collected into the open suitcase.

"Thanks." Her mouth quirked and she blushed self-consciously, turning away to gather tubes and small color palettes off the dresser to put into a cosmetic bag. "Were you able to reach Trella?"

"No." Trella had given Henri her security code herself and seemed to be staying with the prince voluntarily, but she was having an attack, according to Gili.

Isidora glanced at him. "Is Angelique going to her?"

"No. And she shouldn't have to. She's the queen of Zhamair. *I'm* the one who should be on hand for that."

Isidora paused in pulling the drawstring on a shoe bag. Her lashes swept low across cheekbones that darkened with color.

"Am I being blamed for that?" She threw the bag into the suitcase and closed it.

"Not directly."

"Ah." She smiled flatly as she reached to zip the case. "I'm the enabler."

"I shouldn't have let my libido do my thinking. I know better."

She breathed out sharply, as if she'd taken a hit to the solar plexus. "Look, I know you're upset, but—"

"You *don't* know. This is why I will never have a woman in my life. This—" He motioned to the space between and around them, the crackling physical connection that had been so enthralling he had ignored the world outside it. "This ends now."

Her head went back, taking it on the chin with a flare of shock in her gray eyes.

He braced himself for an argument. Wheedling. Some kind of resistance.

She only offered a slow blink of acceptance, and somehow that was worse.

"Bueno," she said softly and turned to lift her case off the bed.

He was so shocked, he didn't move. He listened as she took it to the door herself, the rolling wheels loud across the ceramic tiles. When he finally moved to join her at the door, his joints felt stiff, words jammed sideways in his throat.

The silence wasn't an angry one, but it blistered as they traveled with their security detail to the airport and boarded his private plane.

He told himself not to dwell on whether he had stepped on her feelings. She understood. She had gone into this with her eyes open. His fixation on her was the root of his problem right now. He shouldn't have started their affair.

The flight was twelve hours. They both dozed in their seats rather than moving into the state room, as they'd done on the way over. No lovemaking this time.

As they touched down in Paris, Ramon arranged for Isidora to be taken to his apartment while he continued to Elazar alone. He didn't ask her if she minded. Her reaction was a quiet "Please call me if there's anything I can do."

There wasn't. He saw her off the plane, then carried on to see his sister, aware of the empty seat beside him. Isidora's presence had been strangely calming, he realized. She hadn't intruded overtly. She didn't pretend to understand the monsters in his emotional closet. No one except those as deeply affected by his past really understood that part of him, but Isidora had still been sincere in her concern. She had been a quiet light, keeping him from losing himself to the dark scenarios exploding in his mind.

Those grim thoughts threatened to overtake him as he arrived at the palace in Lirona, the capital of Elazar, where he had to wait thirty minutes for security clearance. It was another twenty before someone escorted him to a private suite, where his sister was curled on the end of a sofa, looking like hell.

Failure coalesced in a metallic taste on his tongue.

"Why are you here?"

That took him aback. He studied the ravages of a bad attack. Her cheeks were hollow beneath swollen eyelids. Her lips were chapped where she tended to lick and chew them as she waited out her symptoms. She wore a thick, man's cardigan over a pair of loose silk pants and ballet slippers. She always retained a cloak of insecurity and low body temperature after coming down from the worst of it. She hugged her arms tight across herself, seeming pale and slight despite the bump at her middle.

"What do you mean, 'why am I here'? I'm here to *get* you."

"I told you not to come."

"You told Henri and Gili not to come."

"Well, I didn't expect you to drop everything, did I? You were in South America, screwing your brains out with Izzy."

He balked at having his affair with Isidora described in such base terms, and was shocked enough by Trella knowing they had been sleeping together to ask "You talked to her? When?"

"I didn't. Gili said she thought something was going on between you two and you just fell for the oldest trick in the book. Seriously? How *could* you?"

He pinched the bridge of his nose. "I just traveled

twenty hours to come *save* you." That's why his wits were so dull. It had nothing to do with a strange, gnawing ache that kept marking the absence of that sliver of light he needed like fire needed air. "You don't get to make me into the bad guy here."

"No." She jabbed the air with a finger. "You keep saying you're doing me a favor with this engagement of yours, but if you want to sleep with Izzy, that's on you. Don't claim it's something you're doing to benefit *me*."

"Look, what happens between me and Isidora is our business. Why don't you tell me what's going on here?" He waved his hand at the elegant parlor. It was a very well-appointed prison tower.

"How many times do I have to say this? What's going on is my business, not yours. At least I'm not taking advantage of Xavier's feelings. I'm doing the opposite of nursing false expectations. What are you letting Isidora believe?"

"Stow it," he growled. "I don't answer to you."

"Oh, you do. For some crazy reason Isidora has decided she would die for us, which none of us deserve, and you think that gives you license to sleep with her and break her heart?"

"I'm not breaking her heart." His memory flashed with the look in her eye as they left Rio, the slam of emotion that she had hidden by turning her back on him. Again.

The pit of his stomach grew heavy. He had pushed her away because he felt guilty. He couldn't have her *and* be what his family needed. The push-pull had made him snap.

But she had known they weren't going to last forever. She hadn't invested her heart in him. Not again.

Had she?

"No, you broke it a long time ago," Trella accused.

"She never said how. She has never once said a word against you to me, because that's who she is, but I know you did something."

"That was a misunderstanding." He sliced the air with his hand, ashamed when he thought back on how he had treated her. "We sorted it out."

"Isidora is a *good person*. She's *kind*. You don't get to hurt my friend and say it's my fault. Quit leading her on. Quit—"

"Shut *up*, Bella."

"You shut up."

"No, *you* shut up—"

The door flew open. A man of about his own age strode in. His commanding air would have made him the crown prince of Elazar even if Ramon hadn't recognized his blond hair and red sash beneath a tailored business suit. Three guards entered behind him.

"Leave quietly or I'll have you removed."

Ramon snorted, hands on his hips, heart pumping hard enough with agitation to want to accept the rougher side of that ultimatum.

"Don't." Trella's weight landed against him and she looped her arms tightly around his middle, protective for once, not clinging with fear. "I was saying things he didn't want to hear. We almost never manage to speak in a civil tone, do we? It's not our way." She dug her chin into the place above his heart as she batted a sugar-sweet look up at him. "But we love each other dearly, under all the cussing and yelling. Don't we?"

Her wrinkle-nosed grin infuriated him, but the vestiges of an emotional storm still haunted her eyes. He wanted to hug her and yell at her to quit making his life difficult, same as always.

He looped his arm around her and squeezed gently,

mindful of his unborn niece or nephew. "Who would I fight with if I didn't have you? Gili? She cries."

"Henri? He lectures. I guess we agree on one thing." She gave him another hug, then drew back, expression solemn. "Sometimes I need you, Ramon. All those times you showed up when I called makes it possible for me to work through this on my own now. I know that you *will* come if I ask. That means everything." Her brow lowered to a dark, stern line. "But until I ask, you *have* to *butt out*."

He dropped his arm and held up his hands. *"Bueno."*

"And be nicer to Iz—"

"No." He held up a finger. "Butting out goes both ways. And you *will* introduce me to your host." Her keeper?

Ramon shared a perfectly civilized meal with his sister and Prince Xavier. He touched base with his family, texted Isidora, then slept off some of his jet lag in a room with an exalted past-occupant list that went back four hundred years. By the time he was leaving, Isidora still hadn't replied.

He probably deserved that, but it bothered him, especially when Trella said, "The palace is handling my PR from now on. Whatever stunts you pull with Izzy could do more damage than good. Tone it down."

He left in a state of discontent, ears ringing with the knowledge his primary reason for cornering Isidora into their fake engagement was gone.

He tried calling her twice more while he was in transit, but she declined to pick up.

Quit leading her on.

Had he been? He hadn't let himself examine too closely what they were doing, which wasn't unlike him.

He didn't deconstruct the good things in his life. He enjoyed them until they reached their natural end.

Enjoyed didn't come close to his state of mind while he'd been with Isidora, though. Yes, the sex was out-of-this-world, but there had been something enormously relaxing about being in a relationship recognized by outsiders as inviolate. The pretty birds of prey who'd circled all his life had kept their distance. The weight of boring small talk at parties was cut in half. She made him look better than he was and when they were alone, she was equally witty, stimulating his intellect, keeping him on his toes.

She had known it was temporary, he reminded himself. But his chest felt tight. Had he let things become too intimate? Had his drawing it out made it seem likely to become permanent?

Maybe it was better he had scorned her again.

Another searing pain went through him, resisting that truth. If he needed convincing, however, the sick feeling that had accosted him when Trella's alarm had gone off was it. He hated being so vulnerable. He didn't want to feel so worried for yet another human being.

It was stressful enough that she was refusing to answer his calls.

He checked her security report, but everything was listed as normal. Even the social-media reports had calmed down as his fans began fixating on when their wedding date would be announced and whether they would produce twins, as Henri had.

Ramon clicked off his phone and tucked it in the pocket over the ache of regret that hung in his chest.

Definitely better to end things before she began to wonder about wedding dates herself, he thought bleakly.

Since it was office hours when he arrived in Paris, he went to work, but only found Etienne at Isidora's desk.

"Where is she?" he asked, scanning the empty room, accosted by a weird premonition that grew worse as Etienne blinked in bewilderment.

"She didn't call you? Bernardo had a heart attack. She's gone to Madrid. I've been waiting to hear if he'll pull through—"

Ramon walked out, already speed-dialing his pilot.

"Why didn't you call me?" Ramon's voice came in with his footsteps, behind her, dragging her from a sea of worry to a boatload of pain. When his hand settled on her shoulder, she stiffened in defense, not able to cope with both sources of anguish at once.

His hand left her and in her periphery she saw it curl into a loose fist. He moved to stand closer to the bed, his expression tightening as he took in how her vibrant father was gray and still beneath his light sheet. His face was obscured by breathing equipment, his arm tied to an IV bag. The room was eerily quiet. Just that low sough of manufactured breath, the muted blip of equipment a lonely signal, proclaiming his heart still functioned. Barely.

"Was your mother with him? Where is she?" He glanced around.

She gave her father's limp fingers a reassuring squeeze, only able to reply with a faint shake of her head, not willing to go there. According to her father's housekeeper, who had been the one to call Isidora, Francisca had packed a few days ago. She wasn't at her own home. Isidora had tried to reach her without success, which suggested she was away. Far away. With someone else. On a yacht, beyond coverage, perhaps.

So much for this latest reconciliation.

Isidora wasn't ready to face any of it. She would have to wonder if her mother's fickle soul had caused her father's cardiac arrest and that created such a division of loyalty in her, she thought it might break her clean in half.

Focus on the positive.

"He made it through the surgery. They say that's a good sign." Her voice was desert-dry, thin and arid.

He transferred his attention to her, frown deepening as he studied her. "You look exhausted. Have you slept? Eaten? How long have you been here?"

She vaguely recalled a nurse giving her a canned protein drink while she waited for her father to come out of surgery. She had meant to finish it, but couldn't remember if she had taken more than a few sips.

"Can you please stop asking me questions? I was talking to Papa in my head. I want him to know that I love him. You can go, if you want. I'm just going to sit here."

Ouch.

He wasn't going anywhere, not that he wanted to be in a hospital again. It hadn't been very long since he'd sat vigil with his brother, waiting for news on Cinnia. It was the most helpless feeling in the world.

But he couldn't let her face it alone.

He did what little he could, checking with a nurse for a prognosis, which was at the grim wait-and-see stage. He shared the update with his siblings, who were all troubled by the news, then found a coffee station. He made a cup for Isidora, heavily sweetened and creamed.

"Gracias." She sipped and set it aside, all her focus on her father.

Time crawled for several hours, then suddenly her mother fluttered in.

"Ah, mi ángel! Lo siento mucho. I should have been here sooner. I didn't have my phone. How is he?" Her tearstained face contorted with fresh anguish as she looked at Bernardo. She burst into fresh tears, one hand on the bed rail, the other going around Isidora's waist as her daughter rose to stand beside her. She turned her face into Isidora's shoulder and cried without reserve for several minutes.

Silent tears slid out of Isidora's closed eyes, but even he could sense her mixed feelings, her distancing as her mother came up for air.

Francisca's expression grew even more stricken. "You're upset with me. Why?" Her gaze swung to Ramon with alarm. "Did you—?"

He jerked his head in swift denial. Now was *not* the time to reveal Isidora's parentage.

He braced himself for Isidora to catch on and demand to know what they were hiding, but she didn't even look at him.

"I'm upset that you left him, Mama." Isidora's voice was that heavy, anguished thing that wrung out his heart.

"No para un hombre. To a spa. I swear." She grasped at Isidora's arms. "We argued and I needed time—"

"No, Mama." Isidora tried to shrug off her mother's touch. "I don't want to be in the middle of it."

"There's nothing to be in the middle of! You have to believe me, *querida.*" Her mother gave her a little shake as she searched her daughter's expression, her own growing frantic. Fearful. "He asked me to marry him again. I said I would move in, but he insisted on marriage. Now he may die—"

"He won't," Isidora quickly said, shoulders caving as she reached for her mother. "He'll pull through. He has to."

Francisca looked like a lost child as Isidora comforted her, completely the wrong way around.

Ramon looked away, dismayed by all of it. Suspicious that Francisca had been with a man, but he wasn't about to throw accusations around a room like this.

Not long after, the doctor told them Bernardo's vitals had improved.

Ramon convinced Isidora to let him take her home to rest. She was so exhausted, she didn't have any fight left in her and fell asleep in the car. She woke when they arrived and said plaintively, "I thought we were going to *my* home."

"Your mother's?"

"My apartment. The one I bought when I requested a transfer. I sent all the things you removed from my place in Paris. I was going to start unpacking."

"That will have to wait." She was a wreck. "We're here now." In Salamanca, at the villa built by his mother's ancestors in the nineteenth century, not that that made an impression on her.

She moved like a zombie as she accompanied him up the front steps of the family mansion, barely looking around.

This home was one of the places few people except immediate family ever entered. He had lived here as a child, until Trella's kidnapping had prompted their father to create the heavily guarded compound, Sus Brazos, in southern Spain. Like all their homes, this one had been retrofitted and secured to the nth degree, but retained its exemplary architecture and original grandeur. Their father used to say it was more stairs than house, but it had tremendous charm, with its stained glass windows, ornate scrollwork and marble columns. The staff took care of him very well and seemed genuinely pleased to see him. He felt good to be home.

"I know you're tired," he said to Isidora. "But I called ahead. The soup is ready. You need to eat."

She sighed with resignation and let him guide her into the stately dining room, where she lowered onto the velvet-covered chair he held for her. She smiled weakly as their *cocido madrileño* arrived, fragrant enough to make his own stomach pang.

As they were left alone, and the only sound was the quiet clink of spoons against bowls, she said softly, "It's okay. I already know."

"Perdóname?" He paused with his spoon in midair.

"Mama told you when you were sharing secrets that night, I suppose?" The low light cast shadows over her hollow cheeks, making her look that much more haunted with her bruised eyes and cloak of anguish.

His mind went first to how blindly he had walked into Trella's trap. He liked to think he learned from his mistakes.

"You'll have to be more specific. I'm not sure what you're talking about."

The corners of her mouth trembled as though she tried for a cynical smile, but didn't have the strength. He suspected there was disappointment there, too. In him, for making her spell it out.

"My mother has never had it in her to be exclusive to anyone. She cheated on my father a lot, right from the beginning. He married her because she was pregnant. He thought it would get better, but it didn't. He blamed himself. He traveled so much, working for your father." She waved her spoon toward him. "I don't say that to imply your father is responsible for her infidelity. Papa has no regrets about working so closely with him. When Trella was taken… He had a daughter. He wanted desperately to help, not be one of the vipers who tried to capitalize."

"We know." The words seemed to vibrate in the still, empty cavern that his chest became. "Bernardo was one of the few to take our side after our father passed, supporting us against the board. He has always been highly valued by our family. We're all upset he's in hospital."

"I know." She dropped her gaze to her bowl as she stirred her soup. "And he was an ambitious man when he was younger. He wanted to work that hard. When he did come home, he wanted that home to include his daughter, so he didn't confront Mama about her infidelity. He didn't want to divorce her. He knew she had been molded into what she was by her childhood. He didn't want a replay of custody battles and risk turning me into the same thing. But by the time I was starting school, he couldn't ignore any longer that I looked nothing like him."

Ramon set down his spoon and sat back.

"He knew she must at least suspect I wasn't his. He had a DNA test done and knew for sure."

"But he didn't confront her."

She shook her head. "He was angry enough to divorce her outright, but…he loved me." She smiled through a sheen of tears. "He knew he would lose me in a custody battle. I wasn't his. He didn't know what to do. He asked your father for advice and your father asked him, 'Who will be her father if not you?' So he stayed a little longer."

Her smile wobbled and turned down.

"I owe your father for that," she said huskily. "It wasn't easy for Papa."

He watched her swirl her soup, eating nothing, thinking of Trella saying "For some crazy reason she has decided she would die for us."

"This is why you agreed to our engagement." He

wanted to be alone then, to deal with the roaring, howling shame in him. Somewhere, in his past, his father had done something so noble and kind for this girl, it filled him with a swell of pride. His father had ensured Isidora had something she desperately needed, that she deserved, and he, Ramon, had come along years later, grabbed it roughly and used it without remorse.

"I love him so much." Her voice cracked. "I knew Mama was…not like other mothers. I used to lie to him about the men in the house, about where she had been. I lied to people all over the city, trying to cover up for her. I was so afraid he would find out and leave us. Leave me." She bit her lips together to still their tremble.

He drew a measured breath into lungs that burned.

"When your father died…" Her lashes came up and sent empathy to him that compressed his chest even further. "It hit Papa hard. He reassessed his own life, the sacrifices he was making in staying married. I think he thought if he divorced my mother, he would stop loving her, but that never happened. He told me everything once they started their proceedings, in case it came up. He didn't want me to be blindsided by it."

"But if you all knew at that point, why didn't you take it up with Francisca?"

She shook her head in a hopeless little gesture.

"Mama doesn't process relationships the way other people do. She didn't have parents who loved her so she doesn't know how to be a parent, doesn't understand how love works. That's why I needed Papa so badly. If I could have, I would have gone to live with him after they divorced. It was so disruptive to live with her. But if she had known that I knew he wasn't my father yet preferred him over her…? It would have killed her. I mean that almost literally. She's a broken person. She's desperate to feel loved and counts on me to love her no matter what. It's something that keeps her from completely self-destructing. To take that away from her, and reveal that I know she did this awful thing to my father... And what is the next step? Ask her about my biological father? Make her admit she doesn't *know*? She would expect that I would never forgive her. Maybe I wouldn't. I would lose her, that's for sure. One way or another she would disappear from my life. I can't risk that."

The slant of her shoulders, so heavily weighted, made his own ache. He carried a lot of pain himself, but in that moment, he took in the scope of hers and he was humbled.

"I'm really tired. Can I go to bed now?" She set aside her spoon.

He gave her barely dented soup a dismayed glance. "I'll take you up."

He put her in his own bed, watching her move like a robot on autopilot as she stripped her pants, then pulled her bra straps down her arms before digging under her shirt and throwing her bra to the floor. She was asleep before her head hit the pillow.

He watched her for a long time, wondering what would happen to her if *she* lost the one person she counted on to love her.

It had all been a bad dream. They were still in Rio and she had dreamed that he had ended things so ruthlessly. He hadn't dumped her in Paris like soiled laundry. She hadn't received a call that had shaken her to her very foundation.

Part of her knew that she was kidding herself, that she was in his bed in Madrid, but as her hands skimmed over the warm satin that was Ramon's hard body next to hers, she let herself travel back in time a mere few days, to when she had believed their future was bright and endless.

He responded by gathering her into his heat, murmuring something about her needing sleep.

"I am sleeping," she whispered against his neck, nuzzling the stubble under his chin with her nose. Her hand found his length, slowly worked up and down as he grew under her touch. "I'm dreaming. Don't wake me."

He said something she didn't catch, an imprecation, and dug his hand into her hair, pulling her closer as he searched for her mouth with his own. His heavy body rolled, tucking her beneath him.

Time slowed. He drew out each kiss, each caress, peeling open one button at a time down her shirt, then parting it to spread kisses across her chest. When he finally found her nipple, she was practically weeping, all of her skin sensitized, all of her being expanding with love for him.

"Touch me," she begged, pushing his hand between her thighs, where she was wet and aching.

He growled with appreciation, then stroked his hand on her inner thigh, spreading her legs wider to accommodate him as he settled between them. When he climbed his fingertips back to where she yearned, she gasped into his mouth.

He slid away, down and down, mouth following a leisurely path through the valley of her breasts while his hands cruised in tender caresses across her skin. His lips grazed the ridges of her ribs, played into the trembling plane of her belly, and finally his hot breath fogged the humid grove between her thighs.

He pleasured her, driving her up and up the rise of tension.

She stroked her fingers through his hair, blatant in

how she offered herself to him, joyous in her abandonment. No man would ever give her this again. She had to take it now. *Now.*

She cried out as a climax rocked through her, anguished that it was over so quickly, but he rose over her, moving away briefly for a condom, then settled on her again. As he slid into her, she sighed with repletion. All of her folded around him, drawing him in deeper.

He made love to her like that for a long time, slow and easy, as if he, too, wanted to prolong this connection. As if he knew, as she did, that this was their last time.

But it couldn't last forever and their bodies were too responsive to each other's. The friction of his movement was building to a screaming pitch inside her. She was so mindless in her arousal, her hands moved in uneven patterns across his shoulders and back. They slid of their own accord to his flexing buttocks and urged him to thrust harder. Deeper.

He pushed his hands beneath her buttocks and took her with him, driving ruthlessly. She closed her legs across his back and lifted herself into him, glorying in the animalistic act, thrilling to the roughness of it. The implacable imprinting of his body into hers.

On and on she clung to him, everything obliterated from her mind except him. This. Them. Timeless. Forever.

Then, suddenly, the world exploded. They both released jagged noises as a powerful climax overcame them both in a rush of culmination and abject loss.

CHAPTER ELEVEN

ISIDORA FELT LIKE an exposed nerve as they arrived at the hospital. She and Ramon hadn't spoken much, just exchanged the mundane things. Breakfast was ready. What time should he order the car, that kind of thing. She had showered alone, which had made her feel bereft.

Neither acknowledged their lovemaking, which had made her feel like it was something shameful that needed to be hidden, at least from herself.

She felt like her father, going back to her mother again and again, hoping for a better result. She had judged Bernardo at times, thinking him foolishly optimistic and a glutton for punishment. Now she judged herself the same way.

At least they would have a clean break.

Her father was awake when they arrived, still very weak, but the doctor was there and pleased with how things were progressing. He was recommending a move out of intensive care and discussed the plan for his recovery at home when he was discharged in a week or two.

"I'll stay with him," Isidora said, smiling through her relieved tears at her father, not looking at Ramon as she said it. He couldn't argue. It was a perfectly legitimate reason to end their pretend engagement.

"Oh, no, *querida*," her mother protested. "You have

a wedding to plan. So do I." She smiled, glowing as she gazed at Bernardo. "Of course I'll be your father's nurse. In sickness and health, *correcto, mi amor*?"

"But you said—?" From the way her mother had spoken yesterday, she had thought Francisca didn't want to marry again.

"I told you, that's why I went away. I needed to think. To be sure, but yes. Almost losing my one true love has convinced me." She leaned to kiss Bernardo's waxen forehead. "Of course I will marry you, *mi amor*."

Her father's breathing tube was gone and his white lips managed a small, cherishing smile.

"Papa—" She stopped herself, unable to protest their trying again. Her mother would take it as a lack of support.

She didn't know where to look as she fought letting all her bitter, angry, confused, angst-ridden thoughts fly out of her tight throat.

Ramon moved in close behind her and rubbed his hands on her upper arms.

"Congratulations," he murmured over her shoulder to Bernardo. "We're both very happy for you. Francisca, did you spend the night here? You must be exhausted. Let me order a car, so you can go home for some rest. We're in no hurry to get back to Paris. Isidora will want to sit here awhile and assure herself Bernardo is on his way back to fighting form." He walked her mother out.

Once they were alone, Isidora met her father's eyes. Her brimming eyes overflowed in a pair of tracks down her cheeks.

"Papa… She *left*." Her hands locked around the bed rail, blurred eyes taking in the equipment that had kept him alive when his heart had given out. Did he not see that this time her mother had, in actual fact, *broken* his heart?

Still, the way her breath caught in a hiss made him feel cruel. He wanted to apologize, but she nodded distantly and turned away.

She didn't see his hand lift, clench into a fist and get forcibly pushed into his pocket.

She disappeared into thin air.

She went from his apartment to the secure flat above Maison des Jumeaux. He knew that much, but a week later, he realized she had slipped out of Paris and he had no way to trace her. She took over paying her security team and that was that.

It threatened to drive him mad.

Ramon knew this feeling. He hated it above all others. It was precisely the reason he was so careful about allowing people into his heart. Worry gave him a vulnerability, a pressure point. It was a type of gnawing pain that never ceased.

He barely slept, either spending the night conjuring a kind of hell he didn't want to contemplate, or recalling the heaven he'd had. He woke in an empty bed and checked his phone, saw no messages from her and was forced to wonder where the hell she was. With whom.

Her father said she had taken a PR position with a very exclusive client. He didn't know who it was, but she had assured him she was happy and well looked after.

After another two weeks, Ramon broke down and called Killian, their security specialist. "I want you to locate Isidora for me."

After a beat of surprise, Killian admitted with a hint of reluctance, "I can't fulfill that request."

"Why the hell not?" Then, with suspicion, he asked "Is she working for you?"

"No."

"A client?"

"You know I don't discuss clients."

"I love this conversation we're not having, Killian. Can you give me proof of life? Is she well?"

"Yes."

It was a relief, but a very small one. Killian wouldn't say where she was or how he knew. He had clients all over the world so Ramon had to continue to speculate.

When Angelique called a few days later, claiming to be homesick, and begged him to visit, he complied. She was always comforting to be around when he was unsettled, but the minute he landed, he was uneasy, wanting to be in Paris in case Isidora turned up there, looking for him.

Why the hell would she look for him? He had savaged her heart yet again.

"I was surprised you agreed to come," Gili said as he was shown into her obscenely lavish private apartment inside the palace of Zhamair. "When we were here for Sadiq and Hasna's wedding, you were quite put out at the cultural restrictions, if I recall."

Her gentle teasing came with a hug that contained volumes of an embroidered dress with a cape. Her head was loosely covered in a beaded scarf, her forehead graced with chains of gold. Her eyes were made up with dramatic dark liner and thick lashes, but this was no stranger. His compassionate sister lurked in her searching gaze as they drew apart.

"Chatting up women doesn't interest me the way it used to," he admitted grimly, making a restless turn past an ottoman to a tinted window that overlooked the well-watered grounds. "Have you spoken to her?"

"Who?"

He sent her an impatient look. "Isidora. Trella said

you suspected more was going on with our pretend engagement. Has she been in touch? Said anything about where she is? What she's doing?"

Gili adjusted the fold of her scarf alongside her face. "When she called to ask to use the Paris flat, she said things didn't work out between you, but she has always drawn a line between our friendship and her feelings for you." She moved to sit and carefully arranged her skirt. "She has never once tried to prevail on us the way other women have, to try to get near you and Henri. That's why we love her."

Love. He shoved his hands in his pockets, fearful that that was the root cause of his discontent. He used to like using Gili as a sounding board, but suddenly he was loath to open up. The things he had shared with Isidora, the way she made him feel, were far too personal to reveal to even his most trusted sibling.

"It's why I wanted to help her when you broke her heart yet again," she murmured.

He whirled around. "You— What do you mean? You sent her somewhere?" His brain clicked to the answer very quickly. It made perfect sense, but he still couldn't believe it. "She's *here*? Working for *you*?" The sense of betrayal was startlingly sharp. "Why would you keep that from me? Does Henri know? Does Trella?" His tone was a lot harsher than he would normally take with her.

Rather than tear up, however, his sister folded her hands in her lap and set her chin, regal in the way she regarded him. Angelique was always toughest when defending those she loved and right now, he knew exactly whose side she was on. Not *his*.

"She deserves a chance to heal in private, after you made such a spectacle of her."

He grimaced and looked away.

"But when Killian said you were concerned about her, I thought I should let you know that she's perfectly safe. She has a room here in the palace and forms part of my entourage when I have royal duties. We're all under royal guard. She's safer here than she would be anywhere," she mused. Then she grinned like her old self as she confided, "I almost miss the tourists and the selfies. The press is so respectful here, it's kind of funny."

He was glad for her and wanted to hear more about that, but not right this second. "I want to see her."

She sobered. "Why? Just because she hasn't given me details doesn't mean I can't see how miserable she is. If I thought you loved her—"

"I *do*." It came out through clenched teeth—he'd resisted to the very last second. It came with a wrench that reframed his heart, cracking the vault, spinning the dials, opening to allow her in, then sitting agape. That aching sense of exposure was nearly more than he could stand. "Take me to her, Gili. *Now*."

Isidora was living a fairy tale, the kind that took place over a thousand and one nights.

Her job was much the same work she'd been doing for all the Sauveterres, but she focused on Angelique now. Kasim had a team that handled his palace concerns, but she had been hired to comb the English-language sites, addressing rumors that specifically affected his wife, especially anything that had the potential to reflect poorly on her, his country, or his ability to rule.

From a career standpoint, the job outshone even the Sauveterre name on her CV. On a more personal level, while her boss was a man, she rarely needed to speak directly to him. She had two female coworkers and, since fraternization between the sexes was discouraged, rarely spoke to any men at all.

She was making new friends and helped keep Gili from feeling homesick. They lunched together a few times a week, practiced their Arabic on each other, visited the spa together and traded opinions on the designs Angelique's team sent from Paris. Sometimes, if Kasim was tied up for an evening, they ordered a Western movie and watched it in Angelique's private chamber.

Isidora thought her own lodging plenty fit for royalty. It was ridiculously beautiful for a midmanagement PR clerk, not that she would dare to say so and risk being kicked out of it. More of a bachelor suite, the sleeping area was part of the main room, but the space was enormous. It had marble floors, a lounge and dining area, and a pretty screen to hide the dressing area that also led to an attached bathroom.

It was like living in a hotel. She ordered food by speaking to her personal attendant and her meal was delivered hot and fresh at the requested hour. Tonight she said, "I'll call you when I've finished my swim."

Her private bathing pool was too tiny for laps. She could walk end to end in its waist-deep, kidney shape in less than ten steps. It sat under a trellis in a walled garden, where a handful of birds sang and fluttered amid a riot of colorful blooms from climbing roses to dangling fuchsias. The fragrances off the lavender and lemongrass, cloves and saffron, were exotic and dream-inducing—it was the perfect place to relax.

She poured herself a glass of cordial, stripped naked next to the pool and waded down the steps. As the water lapped at her knees, then her thighs, she sat—as she did every evening—and let the agony she ignored all day overtake her.

Because this beautiful life did not make her happy. She missed Ramon. So badly. The tears coming out of her eyes were drawn directly from her heart, squeezed out with each clenched beat.

With her elbows sitting in the water, braced on her submerged thighs, she let her tears run through her fingertips, certain she was what filled this pool every day, not the underground spring her attendant claimed.

And when she heard a footstep, and flung up her head, mortified to have her attendant catch her like this, she was even more appalled to see a man. *The* man who had reduced her to this.

She cupped some water, splashed her face to clear her eyes and, yes, Ramon still stood there in a pair of his scrupulously tailored pants. His crisp button shirt was open at the throat and strained across his chest as he set his hands on his hips.

She couldn't meet his eyes. She ducked her head, crossed her arms across her front and drew her feet up a step. "What are you doing here?"

"Visiting my sister," he said flatly.

"Wrong room."

"I've been worried about you."

"I don't want to talk to you, Ramon. Not like this. Let me get dressed."

In her line of vision, she saw him toe off his shoes, then his pants skimmed down and landed in a ball of charcoal, quickly topped by navy colored shorts and a pair of black socks.

She clenched her eyes shut, not watching the rest. "What are you *doing*?"

"You sounded uncomfortable that you were naked and I was clothed." The water rippled and he sighed. "This is nice."

"You are *such* an impossible man." She hid her face behind her hands, huddling to protect her nudity, still feeling teary, but for an entirely different reason. Some horribly sick part of her wanted to hope, but it was so futile. "They have pools elsewhere, you know. With your connections, I'm sure you could get your own right here in the palace."

"I spoke to your father. He sounds well."

Her parents were muddling along, waiting until her father was fully recovered to plan their wedding. They weren't yet falling apart, but it was early days. She wouldn't get her hopes up any more than she would with Ramon. Why was he here?

"Isidora. Look at me."

"No."

"Why not?"

"Because you'll talk me in to whatever stupid thing you want me to do and I refuse, okay? You have come to the well once too often."

The water swished and she mentally pictured his strapping form gliding toward her. Her pulse tripped. Water swayed against her, licking sensually, teasing her into wanting to open her eyes.

"Ask me why I spoke to your father." His voice was at the far end of the pool.

"No."

"No matter what I ask of you, you're going to say no? Is that what I'm hearing?"

"That sounds like a trick question. I refuse to answer."

"The trouble with an intelligent woman," he muttered.

"Better than being a stupid one."

"Do you feel stupid for loving me?"

Present tense, like he knew how deeply she had fallen for him. Fresh tears pressed the backs of her aching eyes.

"No." She finally lifted her head and opened her eyes.

He had his arms outstretched against the pool's edge, shoulders gleaming, hair wet, cheeks stubbled and rugged. The desert sky was fading to mauve and the pin-prick strings of white lights that wound through the trees were coming on.

It was magic, pure magic.

Not real.

A line of fire stretched from the back of her throat to spread burning fingers around the walls of her heart. "But I would be stupid to let you take advantage of my love again. I won't, Ramon."

"I want you to marry me, Isidora."

"That's—" Cruel. "Why? What happened? Never mind. I don't want to know. *No*, Ramon." She started to rise.

He pushed off from the end, striking through the water like a crocodile, barely giving her time to react beyond pressing backward into the hard edge of the step behind her before he was right there, eye-to-eye, arms caging her, water sluicing a pattern down his chest hair between them.

"Why not?"

"Because I won't go through that again." She put up a hand to ward him off, but he eased onto one elbow, then another, so he bracketed her very tightly, practically nose-to-nose.

"We're good together."

"Sexually? You can get that anywhere."

He sizzled with temper as he pierced her with a hot, green stare. "No. I can't. It's different when you love someone."

Her heart flipped and tumbled, creating such a jumble of emotions in her that she pressed his shoulder, silently begging for space to assess and understand. To keep her head so she wouldn't follow her foolish heart into believing the impossible.

"Don't—don't say that. You don't even know me. You don't—"

"I *know* you." So askance.

"You know what I like in bed." She couldn't say it without her stupid voice creaking and, yes, she was starkly aware they were naked. Why the heck was he doing this to her like this, keeping her off-kilter and completely defenseless? She was half seduced by his nearness alone and refused to look down, even though she was quite sure she knew what that firm shape was that was nudging her thigh.

"You—" She cleared her throat and kept her hand firmly on his shoulder, holding him off. "You know that you can talk me in to anything. You don't want a wife. You want a PA who puts out."

His expression edged toward thunderous. "Is this you demonstrating how well you know me? Because I'm beginning to doubt *your* love."

She narrowed her eyes. *Her* love had been born so long ago, it was celebrating double-digit birthdays.

The corners of his mouth curled, which almost scored another hit, but then he said gently, "That won't do, will it? The absolute worst thing I could do to you is underestimate how much you care for me, isn't it? You see? I do know you."

He moved backward, but somehow he gathered her off the step and pulled her with him. She instinctively clung, expecting to sink, but his hard, warm body kept her afloat.

"I know that when you eat, you start with the vegetables. You eat as much of what's good for you as you think you have to, then switch to what you really want before you get too full and abandon what's left. You're always trying to find the balance between what you think you *should* do against not cheating yourself. Which is why you became my lover. It's also why you walked away when the cost became too high."

She wriggled, trying to find her feet, but he was in control, tapping a side wall so they gently rotated back to the steps. A moment later, he settled on a stair low enough to submerge them to their shoulders, and gathered her into his lap.

She kept herself sitting up straight, perched on his thighs, trying to ignore the light play of his fingertips against her hip.

"It's why you're holding me off right now, even though I would bet my fortune that you are as physically ready to make love as I am." A slight shift let her drift in to feel his hard flesh against her buttock.

She gasped and tried to angle herself away.

Even though he was hideously correct. A secretive throb was pulsing between her thighs and she had to fight the urge to let her arms twine around him, to let their lips meet and their bodies rub, and deal with the reality of such foolishness in the morning.

His expression sobered. "I also know you have a capacity for forgiveness that scares me, because I know you're going to be hurt—by me, by your parents, by some other person who I'll want to kill for treating you carelessly… I can't prevent it, though, because you lead with your heart. You'll always put yourself out there, trying to save the world one bolstering hug at a time. Emotional pain doesn't scare you. Hurting people, letting them down, scares you. Why is that?"

She looked down, shocked by that. Profoundly shaken.

"Was it because your mother was so easily hurt? Because you saw how traumatized Trella was? How broken we all were, and you had to do what you could? That sounds like you, doesn't it?" His thumb kept up that lazy pattern against her upper thigh. "Generous. So easy to love."

"Ramon," she protested weakly, closing her eyes to hold the burn inside her lids.

"Why else would I have gone to such lengths to push you away? Hmm? I was half in love with you, scared to death. I didn't *want* to love you. No, don't let that hurt. Listen."

He pulled her close even as her face contorted and she tried to press away, trying to turn from the anguish.

"Listen to me," he said, mouth against her temple, arms strong around her cringing body, holding her together as the seismic shifts he was sending through her threatened to crumble her apart. "I didn't want to add to my list of people to worry about and fear for. I didn't want to put a woman at risk by giving her my name. How could I ask anyone to make children with me so we could fear for them? All of that scares the hell out of me, Isidora. *But my love for you is bigger than that.*"

She drew back, mouth pulling at the corners so she had to bite her lips to still their tremble.

"It's true," he said gently, beautiful face open and grave. "I can even tell you the day when my feelings began to overtake my fear. When you refused to dance with me at your father's birthday, I realized that I might have lost you. You weren't dead, but I was. To you. I told myself it was for the best, that I didn't care." He traced a wet thumb along her jawline. "But I cared. I felt dead."

She tucked her chin, sheepish. "I was pretty mad. I really did want to get over you."

"I know you did." He was very, very solemn. "And when Henri hired you, I was so grimly pleased you were being forced back into my life without my having to chase you."

"You never chase women."

"No, I don't. But I've been hunting for *you*. I thought I knew how badly I would miss you, but it's been a living hell, Isidora."

She made a scoffing noise and let her body melt into his, seduced by his words, one arm going up to his neck. "You miss the hero worship."

"Is that what that abuse was during our engagement?" His mouth quirked as he nuzzled his nose against her chin. "I happen to love that you aren't afraid to take me down a peg. I'm not an easy man. Living with our kind of attention and security can be a nightmare. You have to be tough to withstand it and the fact you can find a smile in all of that, and make me smile…I'm the one in awe of you, Isidora."

She balanced on a razor's edge, but this time she knew she would fall. One side was hope, the other belief.

"Is this real, Ramon? Because if—"

"It's real, Isidora. Ask me why I spoke to your father."

"To ask him where I was?"

"To ask his permission to marry you."

"Did you really?" She teared up, incredibly moved. "He must have been so touched. Thank you for that."

She gave in to desire and slid from her balance on his thigh, using the buoyancy of the water to inveigle between his legs, so they were chest-to-chest, her knees bumping between his flatly planted feet.

She would have kissed him, but he drew back a little. "Is that a yes?"

"To marriage? Kiss me and I'll think about it."

"Not good enough, *mi amor*. I want—"

"I know what you want." She used her arms around his neck to draw herself up and down his length, pleased when his breath hissed in and his hands tightened on her.

In a sudden move, he gathered her as he stood. "*Bueno.* When in Rome…"

"What?" she prompted as he carried her into the apartment. "You'll carry me to bed like a concubine?" She could work with that.

"I declare us married."

"You're not the king. Do you really think it will stick?"

"I do." He came down on the bed with her, then lifted his head. "I love you."

His expression reflected the vast feelings contained behind the visage, all darks and lights, fears and ferocities and love. Endless, true-as-gold *love*.

Her heart had always been his, but in that moment she released it to him, freely and without reservation, confident he would protect it with everything in him.

"I love you, too."

Even though he had known she loved him for what must have felt like centuries, his face spasmed with emotion. He closed his eyes as though savoring the words.

"And?" he prompted quietly.

Bossy, bossy man.

Resisting the urge to roll her eyes, because this was very serious and very real, she said very sincerely, "I do."

EPILOGUE

Isidora was wearing only a black bra, underpants and garters when Ramon walked into their bedroom.

He came up short, green eyes searing her to the spot as he took her in.

Heart skipping with instant reaction, she playfully ticktocked her hips as she walked across and stepped into the shoes she'd chosen to go with her dress. They were erotically tall with a hint of bondage in the thick black ankle straps. She slanted him a sultry look over her shoulder.

"You approve?"

"Hell, yes. Now I really don't want to go out tonight."

"Oh." She pivoted to face him. One of Paris's hottest new nightclubs was having a grand reopening and they were one of the "it" couples always begged to show up at such events. "Why not?"

He swore under his breath. "I didn't mean that to sound— Of course I want to take you dancing. It's your birthday. I've even gone shopping. That's why I'm late." He brought across a small box of indigo velvet embossed in silver.

She opened the box and caught her breath, dazzled by the earrings. "Spoiler!" She went on tiptoe to kiss him.

His arm went around her, possessive and edging toward dominant as he clasped her close. His kiss was thorough and hot, deeply passionate, leaving her breathless when they finally came up for air.

"Trying to convince me to stay in? I'm listening." She leaned into him, enamored as ever, and let her fingers begin to work on his tie.

But something in the way his mouth flexed into a tight line made her sober.

"What's wrong?" She tried to draw back so she could see him better.

"Nothing." He held on to her. His familiar expression, usually so readable, was disconcertingly cautious. "Absolutely nothing is wrong. I'm being...impatient."

"About what? Did I do something?" Her heart lurched. Their marriage was everything she had ever wished it to be and more. They always seemed to be on the same wavelength, even managing to continue working together despite both having demanding schedules. To hear something was off threw her back into old insecurity.

"Everything you do is perfect. I'm the one." He released her and shrugged out of his suit jacket. "I told myself I would wait until you turned twenty-five and this morning, it was all I could do to let you sleep in without saying something."

"About what?" He had made love to her before he left for the office, telling her to enjoy her day off, and promised to take her out to celebrate tonight. She had drifted off blissfully, thinking she really was living happily ever after. "Ramon, you're scaring me!"

"*I'm* scared. But I still want to do it. I want to have a baby, Isidora."

It took a moment for the words to penetrate, for the meaning to sink in. For her to believe he had actually said them.

"What do you think?" he prompted, watching her closely.

She thought he had just given her the best birthday gift ever. Pushing her knuckles against her lips, she tried to keep them from trembling while a bubble of joy pressed for release in her throat. Her whole chest was expanding, putting an excited sting of moisture into her eyes.

"I don't know how to read this silence." His brows lowered with concern as he came closer. "I know it will be hard. Parenting is hard already without that." He pushed his splayed hand toward the window, where the outside world was always a pressure on his family. Then he took her hand from her mouth and pressed it to his own. "Having you is enough, Isidora. I love you with everything in me. If you think raising a baby in our circus is too much risk, that's okay. But I've been thinking about it for months and had to ask."

"Why on earth did you think you had to wait until I was twenty-five?" Her voice came out as strained and unsteady as she felt. Her legs were so weak, she wobbled in her heels.

"Because you're that much younger than me. And we're not a normal family. You needed time to get used to being a Sauveterre. It's a big ask, Isidora. I know that."

"But I love you. Of course I want your baby. I have since…" She shrugged, not the least self-conscious anymore about the way she had idolized him as a child. That love was mature and real now. Strong and eternal on both sides. "Forever."

He frowned. "Why didn't *you* say something?"

"Because it's a big ask." She slid her arms around his neck, warming her near nude body against his clothed one, loving how he wrapped his arms around her in response, always welcoming her into closeness against him.

"It's been nice having you to myself, being auntie and uncle, running around to see everyone else's children on a whim. Having *you* is enough for me. But if you want a baby? *Yes, please.*"

"You're sure? There's a decent chance it'll be twins," he said dryly.

"Even better."

"You say that now…" He picked her up and she clasped her legs around his waist as he took her toward the bed.

Ten months later, they had a gorgeous little boy with dark hair and green eyes, the spitting of his father and uncle. Two years after that, however, girls arrived with identical auburn locks and gray eyes. Their father shook his head in wry delight.

* * * * *

If you enjoyed
BOUND BY THE MILLIONAIRE'S RING,
why not explore the first two parts of
Dani Collins's
THE SAUVETERRE SIBLINGS *trilogy?*

PURSUED BY THE DESERT PRINCE
HIS MISTRESS WITH TWO SECRETS
Available now!

'Dario, are you even listening to me?'

He forced his gaze back to Megan's face. Her pale skin had acquired a healthy sun-burnished glow in the last week, her cheeks now a bright scarlet hue even more tempting than that damn bikini. He wanted to lick that fluttering pulse in her collarbone so much that he could almost taste her sweet, spicy aroma on his tongue.

The way he had every night in his dreams.

Her eyes had widened. Was that trepidation or shock he could see in them, their misty green bright with stunned knowledge? Then she rolled her lip under small white teeth and everything inside him shattered. All the smart, practical, moral reasons why he couldn't taste her seemed to explode in a cloud of nuclear fallout.

'Stop biting your lip,' he said, his voice a low, husky croak he barely recognised as his own.

'Dario! Don't speak to me like that.'

He wrapped his hands around her upper arms and hauled her to him.

Then all coherent thought fled as his lips landed on succulent skin and his hands captured the lush curves that had finally pushed him over the edge into madness.

One Night With Consequences

When one night…leads to pregnancy!

When succumbing to a night of unbridled desire
it's impossible to think past the morning after!

But, with the sheets barely settled,
that little blue line appears on the pregnancy test and it
doesn't take long to realise that one night of white-hot
passion has turned into a lifetime of consequences!

Only one question remains:

How do you tell a man you've just met
that you're about to share more than just his bed?

Find out in:

Look for more **One Night With Consequences** stories
coming soon!

THE VIRGIN'S
SHOCK BABY

BY
HEIDI RICE

First Published in Great Britain 2017
By Mills & Boon, an imprint of HarperCollins*Publishers*
1 London Bridge Street, London, SE1 9GF

© 2017 Heidi Rice

ISBN: 978-0-263-92542-5

Our policy is to use papers that are natural, renewable and recyclable
products and made from wood grown in sustainable forests. The logging
and manufacturing processes conform to the legal environmental
regulations of the country of origin.

Printed and bound in Spain
by CPI, Barcelona

Books by Heidi Rice

Mills & Boon Modern Romance

Vows They Can't Escape
One Night, So Pregnant!
Too Close for Comfort

Mills & Boon Modern Tempted

Beach Bar Baby
Maid of Dishonour
Cupcakes and Killer Heels
The Good, the Bad and the Wild
On the First Night of Christmas...

Visit the Author Profile page
at millsandboon.co.uk for more titles.

To Bryony, who made sure I gave this story
the depth it deserved.

And Daisy, who talked me off the ledge a few times
while I was doing that!

Dario, Megan and I thank you both sincerely.

PROLOGUE

'DARIO DE ROSSI IS escorting you to the Westchester Ball tomorrow night and you need to seduce him while you're there.'

'What? Why?' Megan Whittaker was fairly sure she'd just been transported into an alternate universe. An alternate universe that was two hundred years past its sell-by date. Either that or her father had lost his mind. Whichever way you looked at it, the demand he had just levelled at her from across his walnut desk in the Manhattan offices of Whittaker Enterprises, without even the hint of a smile on his face, was not good news, because he did not appear to be joking.

'To save Whittaker's from possible annihilation,' her father snapped. 'Don't give me your whipped puppy look, Megan,' he added. 'Do you think I would ask this of you if there were another option?'

'Well, I…' She wanted to believe him, even though she knew his love for Whittaker's had always taken precedence over his love for his daughters.

But unlike her sister, Katie, Megan understood that. Having spent the last four years working her way up to head her own tiny department at Whittaker's, she didn't begrudge him his dedication to the company that had been in their family for five generations.

She also didn't really begrudge him a request so outside the norm for a father to a daughter, or indeed a boss to his employee. She knew that to be successful in business your personal life had to suffer, and personal loyalties could be tested. But this was… Well… It wasn't even rational. What possible reason could there be for her to seduce any man? Let alone a man like De Rossi, a corporate wolf who had risen through the ranks of New York business society in the last ten years to become one of its prime movers and shakers.

Quite apart from anything else, if her father was looking for a femme fatale, surely he must know Megan was not the best candidate for the job.

She simply did not have the necessary temperament, equipment or experience. She had always been more comfortable in business suits and flats than cocktail dresses and heels. She found going to the beauty salon tedious, the concentration on her appearance a waste of time and money. Her intellect and her work ethic were so much more important. And after the few fumbled encounters she'd had at college, she'd been beyond grateful to discover she comprehensively lacked her mother's voracious and indiscriminate libido. At twenty-four, she was still technically speaking a virgin, for goodness' sake! These days she would much rather spend her small amount of free time watching TV boxsets with a nice glass of Pouilly Fuissé, than finding a man—especially as the judicious use of a vibrator could take care of her needs without all the awkwardness and disappointment.

'Someone's buying up all our stock,' her father said, the vein pulsing at his temple starting to disturb Megan. 'I'm almost certain it's him. And if it is him, we're in serious trouble. We're exposed. We have to stay his hand. That means making sacrifices for the good of the company.'

'But I don't understand how…'

'You don't have to understand. What you have to do is get an invitation back to his penthouse so we can discover if it is him. If you can find out which of our shareholders he's targeting that would be even better. Then we might have some hope of keeping the bastard off our back until I can secure new capital investment.'

'You expect me to seduce him for the purposes of industrial espionage?' Megan tried to clarify where her father was going with this, as something became devastatingly obvious to her. He had to be exceptionally stressed to believe she could pull such a plan off with her limited skills, which meant the company must be in serious financial difficulties.

'You have your mother's face and figure, Megan. And you're not a lesbian… Are you?'

Her face coloured, the heat racing up her neck, the impatient enquiry mortifying her. 'What? Of course not, but…'

'Then what's the damn problem? Surely there must be enough of that oversexed bitch in you somewhere to know how to seduce this bastard. It's built into your DNA, all you have to do is locate it.' Her father was becoming increasingly frantic. The bitterness in his voice at the mention of her mother made Megan's stomach knot.

Her father never mentioned her mother. Not ever. Alexis Whittaker had abandoned all three of them—her father, herself and her little sister, Katie—not long after Katie's birth, and had died ten years ago when her Italian boyfriend's Ferrari had plummeted from a clifftop road on the island of Capri. Megan could still remember her father coming to tell her the news at her boarding school in Cornwall, his face white with an agonising combination of grief, pain and humiliation. And she could remember the same hollow sensation in her stomach.

Her mother had been a social butterfly, stunningly beautiful, flamboyant and reckless—with everyone's life including her own. Megan could barely remember her; she'd never come to visit her daughters, which was why their father had shipped them off to board at St Grey's as soon as they were old enough.

The hollow confusion had turned to panic though, when paparazzi photos of her and Katie at the funeral had appeared on the Internet. They had been forced to leave the only real home they had ever known, chased out by the photographers wanting to get a glimpse of the 'grief-stricken' Whittaker sisters, and the salacious whispers about their mother's infidelities, spread by some of the other girls at St Grey's. Her father had moved them to an apartment ten blocks from his own on Fifth Avenue in New York, employed a housekeeper and a security guard, enrolled them in an exclusive private school and made the effort to visit them at least once a month. And eventually the media storm surrounding Alexis Whittaker's wicked ways and her untimely death had died down.

But ever since Megan had been ripped away from St Grey's, she had promised herself two things: she would protect the sister she loved from the fallout of her mother's disgrace, and she would work herself to the bone to prove to her father that she was nothing like the woman who had given birth to them.

And up until this moment, she had thought she'd succeeded. With her second objective at least. Katie, unfortunately, appeared to be almost as wild as their mother, despite Megan's best efforts to tame her rebellious temperament.

Megan, though, had concentrated on making her father proud. She'd got a first at Cambridge two years ahead of her peers in computer science. And then an MBA at

Harvard Business School specialising in e-commerce. To prove herself worthy, not just to her father but to her colleagues at Whittaker's, she'd refused his offer of a vanity position and had instead started on the ground floor of the building in Midtown. After six months in the mailroom, she'd applied for an internship in the tech department. It had taken her three years to work her way up the ladder from there, rung by torturous rung. Her recent promotion had put her in charge of the company's small three-person e-commerce department, finally proving once and for all that her mother's shameful behaviour had no bearing on who she was. Until this moment.

How could her father even consider asking her to seduce De Rossi? Did he expect her to have sex with the man, too?

'I can't do it,' she said.

'Why the hell not?'

Because I'm about as far from being De Rossi's ideal woman as Daffy Duck is from Jessica Rabbit.

'Because it wouldn't be ethical,' she managed, recoiling from the hot flash of memory from the only time she'd ever met De Rossi in the flesh.

He'd certainly made an impression.

She'd heard of him, but the gossip hadn't prepared her for the staggeringly handsome man who had arrived at the Met Ball with supermodel Giselle Monroe hanging off his arm like the latest fashion accessory. The brute force of his powerful body had barely been contained by the expertly tailored designer suit, and his bold heated gaze had raked over her when they'd been introduced by her father. The knowledge in his ice-blue eyes had disturbed her on a purely visceral level. And set off a thousand tiny explosions of sensation over every inch of exposed skin.

She'd been careful to avoid De Rossi for the rest of the evening, because she'd known instinctively the man was not just tall, dark and handsome, but also extremely dangerous—to her peace of mind.

'Don't be naïve.' Her father flicked a chilling glare at her. 'There are no ethics in business. Not when it comes to the bottom line. De Rossi certainly doesn't have any, so we can't afford to have any either.'

'But how did you even persuade him to take me to the ball?' Megan said, becoming desperate herself.

'It's a charity ball. He's paying for a table. You're going to be Whittaker's representative there. I asked him to escort you as a courtesy to me; he's a member of my club.'

So she had officially become a pity date—which would have been mortifying, if her father's ulterior motive wasn't a thousand times worse.

'De Rossi's only weakness that I could find is for beautiful women,' her father continued in the same deceptively pragmatic tone. As if he were talking sense, instead of insanity. 'Not that it's exactly a weakness. He's never been foolish enough to marry one of them, unlike me. And he never keeps them longer than a few months. But he's between women at the moment, according to Annalise, who keeps up with this nonsense,' he said, mentioning his mistress. 'And he never has one out of his bed for long. Which gives you all the opportunity you need. He'll be on the hunt and I'm putting you in his path. All you need to do is get his attention.' The dispassionate statement had shame burning the back of Megan's neck. 'Get an invite to his penthouse on Central Park West,' her father continued. 'Once he takes you there, you can get access to his computer and his files. Computers are your forte, are they not?'

That he'd thought this scenario through in such detail wasn't helping the chill spreading through Megan's abdomen—or the flush of awareness flaming across her scalp.

'But anything he has on there will be password protected,' she said, trying to be practical.

'I have his passwords.'

'How?'

'It's not important. The important thing is to get access to his computer before he changes them. Which means acting quickly and concisely.'

And setting her up as some kind of Mata Hari? The idea would almost be funny if it weren't so appalling.

'You can't ask me to do this,' said Megan. She'd always strived so hard to please her father, to prove herself worthy of his trust. There weren't many things she wouldn't do for him, but this request scared her on so many levels. 'You wouldn't ask me to, if I were your son,' she added, trying to appeal to her father's sense of justice. He wasn't a bad man, he was fair and, in his own gruff, distant way, he loved her and Katie. Obviously he was so stressed he had completely lost his grip on reality. But he had to be under a huge amount of pressure, if De Rossi was sniffing about the company.

She knew enough about De Rossi's business practices from the financial press to know that once his conglomerate got their hooks into your stock you were as good as dead in the water. He was famous for asset stripping. If he really was planning a hostile takeover, he could reduce Whittaker's to rubble in weeks, a legacy company destroyed in a heartbeat simply to feed his insatiable appetite for wealth at any cost. But her father's solution was beyond desperate, not to mention illegal, and doomed to failure. She had to make him see that, and find another way.

'If I had a son and De Rossi was gay, that would be an option.' Instead of looking persuaded, the tic in her father's cheek went ballistic. 'As neither is the case, it's a moot point.'

The blush seared her skin, the knot in her stomach tightening into a hollow ball of anxiety. It was no good, she was going to be forced to state the obvious.

'De Rossi might as well be gay for all the interest he's likely to take in me. He dates supermodels.'

And I'm hardly supermodel material.

At five-foot-five, and with the lush curves she had inherited from her mother, Megan had felt like an over-endowed pixie next to the slim, stunning woman who had fawned over De Rossi at the Met Ball.

But Megan's lack of appeal to men had always felt like a boon. She didn't want to become any man's decorative accessory. Especially not a man like De Rossi, who even on their brief acquaintance she suspected was as ruthless with women as he was in his business dealings.

She could control those mini explosions. They were nothing more than a biological reaction.

'Don't sell yourself short.' Her father huffed, looking exasperated now as well as desperate. 'You have enough of your mother's charms to attract him if you put your mind to it.'

'But I—'

'If you don't do it, there's only one other person I can ask.'

Megan's panic downgraded. Thank goodness, he had someone else he could ask. She would not have to even attempt something that was bound to humiliate and degrade her, and was extremely unlikely to be successful. 'Who?'

'Your sister, Katie.'

The panic went from ten to ninety in a nanosecond.

'But Katie's only nineteen,' she cried, shocked. 'And she's in art school.'

After an endless string of school expulsions and acting out against their father's authority, Katie had finally found her passion as a talented and brilliant artist. And she didn't give a fig about Whittaker's.

'An art school I pay for,' her father remarked, the dispassionate expression chilling Megan to the bone. Katie and her father had been at loggerheads for years—ever since the sisters had moved to New York after their mother's death. It had taken Megan months to persuade their father to pay for the exclusive academy that had only offered Katie a partial scholarship—something she had never told her sister. She didn't know how Katie would react if she discovered their father was paying some of her tuition fees and was prepared to pull the plug on the dreams she'd worked so hard for to save Whittaker's. But Megan doubted it would be good.

'Your sister is also as reckless and wild as your mother,' her father added. 'Given the right incentive, I think we both know she'd pass this assignment with flying colours.'

No, she wouldn't, she'd be crushed, Megan thought.

Katie was as lively and spirited as Megan was cautious and grounded. But for all her recklessness, she also had an open and easily bruised heart—and absolutely no regard for business ethics or expediency. Katie would be appalled that their father could ask such a thing of either one of them. And Katie's own worst enemy was usually Katie. She was volatile and unpredictable, especially if she was hurt. So much so that Megan had no idea what she'd do if forced into this situation by their father. She could have a mad passionate affair with De Rossi or annoy him so much he'd destroy Whittaker's just for the hell of it. But one thing was for sure, putting a hothead like Katie into the path of someone as ruthless as De Rossi would be a car crash of epic proportions, and Katie would be the one who got destroyed.

'The only reason I haven't already asked her is because

she knows nothing about computers,' her father said. 'And De Rossi likes his lovers more mature, according to Annalise,' he added. 'You've got a better chance. But if you leave me with no choice I will have to explain to your sister that if she wants to stay at her fancy art school she will have to—'

'Okay, I'll do it,' Megan jumped in, before her father could state the unthinkable. 'I'll give it my best shot.'

Even if her best shot had very little chance of being a success, her pride and her ethics felt like a small price to pay to save her sister from heartbreak—and Whittaker's from guaranteed annihilation.

'Good girl, Megan,' her father said. 'Take the day off tomorrow. Annalise will accompany you to select an outfit suitable for the occasion and take you to her beautician to get you properly prepared.'

'Okay,' she said, feeling dazed at the enormity of what she had just agreed to—and how ill-prepared she was for the challenge. Annalise's alluring sense of style and supreme sexual confidence had always intimidated Megan.

'Don't disappoint me. Whittaker's is counting on you,' her father finished, dismissing her as he turned back to the papers on his desk.

'I know and I won't,' she murmured, trying to sound confident.

But as she returned to her small office on the building's tenth floor, the pressure of what she had to achieve sat in her belly like a brick. An annoyingly hot brick seeping an uncontrollable and completely unregulated warmth throughout her body.

She didn't feel confident; she felt like a sacrifice, about to be staked out in the wolf's lair, with nothing to protect her but a designer gown and heels and an overpriced beautician's appointment.

CHAPTER ONE

'NO WAY, KATIE. You need to stay in your room when he gets here.' Megan's hand trembled as she picked up one of the diamond drop earrings Annalise had loaned her to match the sleek, blue, satin, floor-length gown it had taken her father's mistress an eternity to select during their endless shopping expedition that afternoon. The sting as the thin silver spike penetrated the rarely used hole in her lobe did nothing to calm the rapid flutter of Megan's heartbeat. She breathed deeply and picked up the other earring. She needed to stop hyperventilating or she was liable to pass out before De Rossi even arrived.

'But I want to meet him, to make sure he doesn't take advantage of you,' Katie said, the fire in her eyes accompanied by a petulant pout. 'He's rich, arrogant and scarily gorgeous. You've got zero experience of guys like him. Did you see the cover shot of him on that boring business magazine you get? He even looks hot in one of those stuffy suits.'

Yes, she had seen the magazine, she'd even re-read the interview with De Rossi to give herself some useful topics of conversation. But all the article had really done—illustrated with all those photos of him looking broad and muscular and indomitable—was make her panic increase. And Katie's misguided attempts to protect her were not helping.

'What if he tries to ravish you?' Katie added, the battle she'd been waging for the last two hours—to stand between Megan and De Rossi's super-human seduction skills—starting to wear on Megan's already frazzled nerves.

De Rossi was due to arrive in less than five minutes and Katie's misguided reading of the situation was the last thing Megan needed. But she would never tell Katie the truth. That the only thing standing between them and financial ruin was Megan's mission to seduce De Rossi—not the other way around—because that would only make Katie worry more about Megan's date in the lion's den. And Megan was already panicking enough for both of them.

She'd spent most of her life shielding her sister, ever since the day she'd stood beside a nine-year-old Katie at their mother's graveside and held her as her little sister shed real tears for a woman who had abandoned them.

She was not about to stop now.

But sometimes shielding Katie from the realities of life could be very trying. Megan poked the second earring into her earlobe with an unsteady hand and absorbed the sting, attempting to tune out Katie's next offensive.

'I can't believe you won't even let me meet him. All I want to do is make sure he knows not to mess with you.' Katie stood defiantly behind her, every sinew in her slim, coltish body fraught with challenge and righteous determination. 'At least promise me you won't let him lure you back to his love nest on Central Park West.'

'His *what* nest?' Megan would have laughed at the term, if her heart hadn't just jumped into her throat.

'Don't look like that.' Katie rolled her eyes, frustrated. 'That's what they called it in Giselle Monroe's piece in the *Post*. Didn't you read it?'

'No, I did not, and you shouldn't have either. It's sala-cious gossip.' The last thing she needed to read was the model's kiss-and-tell account of De Rossi's sexual prow-ess when she was nervous enough already.

'According to Giselle,' Katie continued undeterred, 'the guy's insatiable in the sack. He can make a woman—'

'Katie, for goodness' sake, shut up!' She swung round on the stool. 'I didn't read it, because I didn't need to. This isn't a proper date.' Even if the memory of one look from the man was still giving her goosebumps a month after the fact. 'Dad asked him to escort me. He may not even turn up.' The hope that he might have forgotten the arrangement had guilt coalescing in her stomach to go with the panic.

She was Whittaker's only hope. She'd promised to do this thing, even if the computer codes buried in her purse were burning a hole in her conscience.

The sound of the front door buzzer made them both jump.

'So he's not gonna show, huh?' Katie said, looking tri-umphant.

Megan cursed under her breath, and stood to check out her reflection. The gown was sleek and simple in its elegance, the bias-cut satin snug enough to enhance her curves without offering them up on a platter. Or at least, that was what Annalise had insisted.

Diamonds sparkled in the thin straps that held up the bodice, which plunged low enough to entice but not low enough to give Megan an anxiety attack. Yet. A faux-fur wrap to hold off the night-time chill in late April, and four-inch heels—which were as high as she could go without risking a twisted ankle—an elaborate up-do that held her unruly hair in some kind of order, a five-hundred-dollar make-up session and the delicate diamond drop earrings completed the outfit. Annalise had told her the ensemble screamed sophistication and purpose, rather than panic and desperation.

Megan wasn't so sure.

She heard the front door of the apartment being opened by their housekeeper, Lydia Brady, and the low murmur of a deep masculine voice.

Awareness rippled up her spine and she grasped her sister's wrists. 'Stay here, Katie, I'm warning you. This is going to be humiliating enough without you there making me feel even more self-conscious.'

Katie pulled her hands free, the spark of defiance disappearing for the first time in hours. 'Why would it be humiliating?'

'Because I'm not his type and he's only taking me as a favour to Dad.'

And Dad expects me to seduce him. Somehow. And then commit a crime to save Whittaker's.

'What do you mean, you're not his type?' Katie's gaze travelled over Megan's outfit, the appreciation in her wide green eyes making Megan's heart pound even harder. 'You look absolutely stunning. Just like Mum. I wish I had at least a few of your curves.' She flung her arms around Megan's shoulders, holding her tight for a few precious seconds. 'You're going to knock his designer socks off, you silly moo,' Katie whispered in her ear, before she drew back. Warmth suffused Megan.

Even when she was being a pain in the backside, Katie was Megan's greatest cheerleader and her best friend.

'Which is precisely why you need me there to make sure he doesn't get any ideas,' Katie added, in case Megan hadn't figured that out already after the four-hour campaign. 'Are you absolutely sure you don't want me to threaten him with my kick-boxing skills?'

'You gave up kick-boxing after two sessions,' Megan pointed out.

'What if I threaten to macramé him to death instead, then?' Katie offered—probably only half joking. 'I did a killer macramé piece for my course.'

The chuckle that popped out of Megan's mouth was part gratitude and part hysteria. Whatever happened with De Rossi, her life was likely to be irrevocably changed once tonight was over. Because she'd either be in his bed, or in a prison cell. Her sister's silly joke helped to ground her, though, and confirm what she already knew: that protecting Katie and her dreams, and protecting Whittaker's, were worth sacrificing her self-respect and throwing herself at De Rossi tonight.

All Megan had to do was figure out how to do that without having a nervous breakdown.

Lydia Brady stepped into the room. 'Mr De Rossi has arrived, Megan.' The older woman smiled. 'You look beautiful, dear.'

'Thank you, Lydia.' Nerves screamed across her bare shoulders, and the hot brick in her stomach sank lower.

Letting go of her sister's hands, she walked towards the dressing-room door, affecting the expression she had practised in the mirror for hours last night. Polite, confident and, she hoped, at least a little alluring.

Her heels echoed on the marble flooring as she made her way down the corridor, but as she turned into the apartment's plush lobby area all the air seized in her lungs and her steps faltered.

Dario De Rossi looked up from adjusting his cuffs, his crystal-blue eyes locking on her face like a tractor beam, and sending a sizzle of electric energy through her body.

The man looked devastating in a tux. Tall and broad, his powerful body only made more intimidating by the classic black tailoring, which emphasised the magnificent width of his shoulders, the leanness of his waist and the length of his legs.

How tall was he? At least three inches above her father's six feet.

She took a careful breath and forced herself to carry on walking, grateful her wrap covered her cleavage when the assessing gaze roamed down, setting off a series of mini explosions and making her insides grow hot.

'*Buonasera*, Megan.'

His English was so perfect, with only the slightest hint of his Italian heritage, it felt strangely intimate to have him greet her in his native language. The way the deep husky rumble of his voice skated across already oversensitive flesh, though, was not as disturbing as the dark flash of hunger in his eyes as she drew level.

'*Buonasera,*' she said, answering him in Italian automatically.

He lifted her fingers to his mouth, startling her, and pressed his lips to the knuckles.

The gesture should have been polite, gallant even, but for the way his thumb slid across her palm as he lowered her hand, sending arrows of sensation darting up her arm, and into her torso.

She tugged her hand out of his grasp, shocked by her response, as his gaze roamed up to her hair.

'The colour is natural?' he asked.

'Yes,' she replied, disconcerted by the approval shining in his eyes.

His firm lips lifted in a smile that managed to be both amused and predatory, as if he were a panther, toying with his prey.

'I hope I did not offend you,' he said, the intimacy of his gaze contradicting his apology. The bright blue gaze then dipped to her toes and back, sending seismic ripples over her skin and igniting every pulse point like a firework.

'Relax, *cara mia*.' The rough chuckle scraped across her nerve-endings.

A fiery blush crept up her neck. Was he mocking her?

She looked down at her hands, and forced her fingers to release their death grip on the diamond-encrusted purse. Annalise had told her that looking like a lamb being led to slaughter would not entice any man.

Breathe. Remember to breathe. Breathing is good.

But when she raised her head, he was doing that laser-beam thing again, as if he could see right through her—to the soon-to-be felon beneath.

'I'm sorry, I'm tired,' she mumbled. 'I've had a very busy day.'

Could she actually sound any *more* inane? Where was all the scintillating conversation about his business acquisitions that she had been working on for hours?

'Doing what?' he asked.

'Shopping for this dress, mostly. And getting my hair and nails and stuff done,' she replied honestly. Until today she'd had no idea that trawling the designer boutiques of the Upper East Side and spending four hours getting waxed and plucked and pampered to within an inch of her life was more exhausting than hiking up Kilimanjaro.

'Have you, now?' he said, the wry tone making her realise the statement made her sound like a spoilt debutante fishing for a compliment.

Humiliation washed over her.

She knew from the articles she'd devoured about him in the last twenty-four hours that he had been born into one of Rome's most notorious slums. He had to know what true exhaustion was. Everything else about his origins was sketchy, something he refused to talk to the press about, but that simple nugget of information had only intimidated her more. She could well imagine how hard De Rossi must have fought to escape his origins—and how hard he would fight now to keep hold of what he had. And what he wanted to acquire.

Her skin burned, her nipples tightening as his gaze met hers. The cool blue was not as icy as she remembered it from their first brief meeting. His lips quirked.

'It was time and money well spent,' he said, the casual compliment making the flush flare across her collarbone.

Then, to her astonishment, he lifted a hand and tucked his forefinger under her chin. The soft brush of the knuckle was like a zap of electricity, firing down to her core as he lifted her face.

She stiffened, stunned by the enormity of her response to a simple touch. She struggled not to jerk her head away, to submit to the proprietorial caress, despite being brutally aware of the heat now blazing on her cheeks.

What was going on here? Because the amused quirk on his lips had disappeared. Why was he looking at her so intently?

He drew his thumb across her bottom lip.

'You are very beautiful in your own unique way,' he said, his gaze lifting to her chignon. 'Especially that hair.'

He sounded sincere. Why did that make tonight seem all the more terrifying?

She forced a smile, trying desperately to pretend she wasn't burning up inside. But she couldn't resist the involuntary flick of her tongue to moisten lips dried to parchment. He focused on her mouth, and a soft indrawn breath escaped her at the hunger in his eyes.

'The colour reminds me of a naked flame,' he said. 'I wonder if you're as fiery in bed?'

The heat swelling in her abdomen settled uncomfortably between her legs at the boldly sexual comment. She ought to say something provocative back.

But she didn't feel provocative, she felt stunned. And hopelessly aroused. And completely out of her depth. Already.

Dario De Rossi wanted her. And while that should have been very good news, because she was supposed to be seducing him, the power dynamic did not feel as if it was in her favour. Surely her thighs wouldn't be trembling under that hard, heated gaze if it were? She searched her mind for something to say that wouldn't clue him in to how inexperienced she was.

Annalise had told her in no uncertain terms that De Rossi would not find her gaucheness appealing.

Think, Megan, think. What would Mata Hari do?

'That's for me to know,' she finally managed, allowing the desire her body couldn't seem to control to show in her voice. 'And for you to find out, if you dare.'

'There's not much I wouldn't dare, *cara*,' he said, the cynical edge in his tone disturbingly compelling.

His hand dropped, and she couldn't prevent the tiny sob as her body softened in relief.

She was playing a very dangerous game. But she had no choice. She had to brazen this out, pretend she was much more knowing and experienced than she actually was.

Sweeping his hand out in front of him, he smiled, and she became a little fixated on those firm sensual lips.

'Let's get you to the ball, Cinderella.'

She pushed out a strained laugh and walked past him, only to tense as his hand settled on the base of her spine. Sensation flashed down to her bottom, but she carried on walking, acting as if the feel of his hand wasn't burning through her clothing.

The ride down in the lift was excruciating, the deceptively light touch driving her insane. He kept his palm there the whole time, guiding her where he wanted her to go, and not letting her stray more than an inch from his side with the subtlest of gestures. But even so, the heat grew.

As they walked out of the apartment building, past the doorman, her nerves were screaming, the controlling pressure so light it was torture not to stretch against his hold. Her body waged a battle between wanting to kick off her heels and race away from him down the street, while another, much more elemental urge had her longing to ease closer to him and let the heat of his body overwhelm her.

The night chill caught her hair, making the tendrils the stylist had spent an hour carefully teasing out of the chignon dance against her neck. She shivered, the skin there already oversensitised by the feel of his gaze boring into her from behind.

The sleek black limousine was parked at the kerb, a man in a dark suit and a cap waiting for them. The chauffeur opened the door and tipped his hat, giving her a polite smile.

She eased into the shadowed interior, the split in the long skirt of her dress pushing open to reveal her thigh almost up to the hip.

She heard a gruff intake of breath. And had to tamp down on the desire to escape out of the other side of the vehicle. The cool leather pushed against the backs of her knees through the dress.

'The guy's insatiable in the sack...'

'What if he tries to ravish you?'

Katie's foolish observations came back to haunt her as De Rossi folded his big body into the seat beside her. His wide shoulders filled up the opposite side of the car and made the spacious, luxury black leather interior feel unbearably cramped and claustrophobic.

He leant across her to grasp the seat belt. She pulled back, his face inches from hers, his scent surrounding her. Sandalwood and musk and man. But as his eyes met hers he only smiled again and pulled the seat belt down to click it into place, his knuckles brushing her hip.

'Why are you so skittish, Megan?' he asked.

'I'm just a little nervous, Mr De Rossi,' she blurted out, then glanced around the car searching for a plausible excuse. She was supposed to be flirting with him, making him think she was available for a quick fling, not quaking like someone standing on a fault line. 'About the ball. I don't want to let my father or the company down. It's my first time representing them at such a prestigious event.' Which was actually true; ordinarily that responsibility alone would be reason enough for her nerves.

The warm proprietorial palm settled over her leg, and gave her knee a quick squeeze, touching her again in a way that made her feel owned.

'My name is Dario.' His jaw clenched and she noticed the bunched muscle, twitching. Was it possible she was affecting him as much as he was affecting her?

The thought thrilled her on some visceral level, but disturbed her more.

The possibility of playing him at his own game was almost as terrifying as the endorphins careering through her for the first time in her life.

'We are on a date, remember,' he murmured.

'Thank you for agreeing to escort me,' she said, finally remembering her manners. 'It was nice of you.'

'Nice?' He seemed amused and surprised by the suggestion. 'Not many women have accused me of that.'

She could well imagine. 'My father really appreciated you doing us this favour.' More than De Rossi would ever know. Hopefully.

'There is nothing to appreciate,' he said, cryptically. 'I only do favours when I expect something in return.'

'What do you expect from me?' she said, then realised how suggestive it sounded a moment too late. 'I don't mean…' she stumbled. 'I just…'

'I expect nothing from you, Megan.' He cut into her rambling denials with the skill and precision of a surgeon wielding a scalpel. 'I did this favour for your father.'

Those staggeringly blue eyes studied her, the knowledge in them unnerving her even more. Sensation skittered down her spine, making her breath seize in her lungs, the car's interior now devoid of oxygen. Did he know the real reason her father had asked him to escort her tonight? Was this charade already doomed to failure?

'Don't look so terrified, *cara*,' he said, and she tried to school her features not to give away her fear.

'I promise not to bite. Unless you want me to,' he said, before touching the intercom button to inform the driver to proceed.

Pinpricks rioted over her skin as the car whisked away from the kerb and she imagined those straight white teeth nipping at all her most sensitive places.

She forced a smile, attempting to shake off the sensual fog he seemed to weave around her so effortlessly.

This was going to be the longest night of her life. Her physical reaction to him was too intense, too overwhelming. How was she supposed to survive an evening in his company without telling him every one of her secrets?

CHAPTER TWO

DARIO DE ROSSI WATCHED AS his date finally appeared from the bathroom on the far side of the ballroom. That was the third time in the last hour that she'd deserted him to go to the powder room. And freshen up, as she'd put it.

She didn't need freshening up. Her dewy skin was lightly flushed, the colour riding high on those apple cheeks, on the rare occasions when she'd been close enough for him actually to see her face. And when she wasn't in the powder room, she was engaged in the most vacuous of conversations with everyone but him, her light breathy laughter making every pulse in his body stand on high alert.

She was not what he had expected.

He had known, of course, the second that Lloyd Whittaker had approached him in the club yesterday morning and asked him to escort his daughter to the ball, that the request was part of the man's last-ditch attempt to save his company. The fool had finally realised who was buying up his stock and had probably thought throwing his daughter at Dario would soften the blow. It wouldn't be the first time a business rival had believed that he could manipulate Dario through his enjoyment of the opposite sex—or believed the garbage written about his love life in the tabloids. Giselle's recent hissy fit in *The Post* hadn't helped in that regard.

It also certainly wouldn't be the first time a powerful man had used and degraded a woman he was supposed to love and protect.

The brutal flash of memory had his gut twisting sharply. He took a sip from the bottle of Italian lager the hosts had imported especially for him and waited for the sensation to pass, while he watched Megan Whittaker make her way towards him.

She took the most circuitous route through the crowd, he noted, stopping to talk to a series of her father's acquaintances, every one of whom, Dario observed as his fist plunged into the pocket of his trousers, seemed to think it was okay to look down her cleavage.

The dress—plunging low enough at the neckline to leave not nearly enough to the imagination—had made his heart slam into his throat and dried up every molecule of saliva in his mouth when she'd walked down the hallway of her apartment. And quite literally taken his breath away when she'd eased onto the seat of the limousine and revealed a mile of toned, tanned thigh. Which had to be an optical illusion, because the woman, despite all those impressive curves, didn't even reach to his collarbone in her ice-pick heels.

He downed the last of the beer, and dumped the empty bottle on a passing waiter's tray, deciding that he'd let Megan off the leash long enough.

He'd only agreed to this date out of curiosity. Because he was bored. He'd wanted to see what foolishness Whittaker had planned—especially as he had remembered the daughter from a tedious event a month ago that he'd attended with Giselle. Strangely he had remembered her eyes, that deep intense green had captivated him, but only for a moment, before she'd ducked her head. She'd avoided him for the rest of the evening. So he'd found it amusing that Whittaker had decided to push her into his path to-night. To do what exactly? Seduce him into releasing his stranglehold on a company her old man had been running into the ground for years?

The idea was so preposterous he had been convinced it couldn't actually be true. That such an apparently inexperienced girl should be used for such a purpose seemed beyond even Whittaker's ability to mismanage the situation. But he'd decided to play the scenario out, mostly for his own entertainment. He'd had no date for the ball, Megan Whittaker had already intrigued him, and he would enjoy proving that he was not the barbarian her father obviously assumed him to be. He was perfectly capable of resisting the charms of any woman—even if he hadn't had one in his bed for over a month.

But then his date had surprised him. Stunned him even. And he didn't like to be surprised, much less stunned. She was nervous, yes, and had an artlessness about her, which might have been why he had considered her so inexperienced a month ago, but beneath that was an awareness, a physical response to him that was so intense and unguarded it had done a great deal more than simply captivate or intrigue him.

He didn't like it. He hadn't expected to want her. Or certainly not this much.

But now he had to decide what to do about it.

If Whittaker had sent her on some cock-eyed mission to seduce him, he wasn't about to take advantage of that. But on the other hand, if her response to him was genuine, why shouldn't they enjoy each other for an evening? She couldn't possibly be *that* inexperienced. She was twenty-four, well-travelled, and she'd dated at university in the UK, according to the background check he'd had done by his friend Jared Caine, the owner of Caine Securities.

And he'd felt the way she'd stretched against the palm he'd rested on the slope of her back as they'd left her apartment—like a cat desperate to be stroked.

She wasn't an accomplished flirt, but her instinctive response to a simple touch suggested a rare chemistry. What if she was as wild and vibrant as that russet-coloured hair if he got her into bed?

He hadn't had such a basic reaction to a woman in years, maybe never. He liked sex, he was good at it, but something about Megan had sunk claws into his gut, tearing at his self-control, which he was finding it increasingly difficult to ignore.

He'd sensed her nervousness in the car, so he'd backed off when they'd arrived at the ball, deciding to observe her, and give himself time to figure out what exactly he was supposed to do about the driving need inside him.

But that had obviously been a mistake, because all it was doing was frustrating him more. Truth was, he hadn't expected the avoidance tactics, but as he watched her pause to strike up a conversation with Garson Charters, the senile old judge who seemed to be as fixated on his date's cleavage as every other man in the place, Dario knew that was exactly what her frequent trips to the powder room were about. She was wary of him, not all that surprising if her father had told her to come on to him.

The conniving old bastard probably expected her to wheedle information out of him about their business dealings.

So now he had two choices: he could escort her home, or play with the fire between them regardless of her father's ulterior motives. Whatever happened, though, backing off wasn't an option, because it went against every one of his natural—and a few unnatural—instincts.

He heard the string orchestra in the adjoining ballroom

start up a waltz as he marched through the throng of guests sipping champagne and whispering loudly, and made a beeline for his date.

Her head popped up as he approached, almost as if she had a radar ready to alert her to his presence at a ten-metre radius. Her gaze locked on his for a millisecond and then flicked away, but not before he saw the jolt of awareness cross her features.

Her hunger was as real as his.

She said something to the elderly judge, who still had his beady eyes focused on her cleavage, then began to edge past the guy, heading back towards the bathroom.

No way, not this time.

He caught up with her in a few strides and hooked her wrist, drawing her to a halt. 'Not so fast, *cara*. Where are you going?'

The colour in her cheeks deepened, her eyes widening like those of a startled deer. The smoky perfection of her make-up and the hint of glitter on her eyelids did nothing to mask the unguarded sparkle of awareness in the emerald-green gaze.

'Hi, Dario,' she said breathlessly. 'I think I left something in the restroom.'

'What did you leave in the restroom?'

She scraped her teeth over her full bottom lip, for less than a second, but it sent a shot of heat straight to his crotch.

'Um…my…' She paused, obviously casting around for something.

Unlike her father, she wasn't an accomplished liar.

He stowed the thought. She might be Whittaker's daughter, but he'd seen little evidence this evening of any deviousness on Megan's part. She couldn't even seem to flirt with any degree of sophistication—her desire for him as blatant as her nerves whenever he got within a few feet of her. He could feel the slight tremors in her arm and the pounding beat of her pulse beneath the fingers he had on her wrist.

'Whatever it is, it will be fine in the restroom until after this dance,' he said, linking his fingers with hers as he made his way towards the dance floor in the adjacent ballroom.

She followed behind him as they weaved their way through the crowd, her reluctance palpable. Almost as palpable as the quiver of reaction in her fingers. He clasped her hand harder, not sure why he was seeking to reassure her.

'What dance?' she gasped. The confusion in her voice was almost as much of a turn-on as the tremor in her fingers.

He drew her into the ballroom and swung her into the crowd, deftly joining the other dancers as he lifted her arm high and then placed his other hand at the dip of her waist. 'This dance.'

She matched her steps to his instinctively. He gave her waist a light squeeze, leading her effortlessly into the turn, and dragged her closer. 'Put your hand on my shoulder, Megan,' he ordered, pulling her easily into his body, until the length of her pressed against him from shoulder to hip. Those impressive breasts plumped up against his chest.

She did as she was told.

He swallowed around the renewed jolt of lust, willing his crotch to behave itself. At least until they were off the dance floor and he could get her somewhere private. His decision had been made.

Playing with fire it is, then.

CHAPTER THREE

MEGAN WAS IN TROUBLE. In big, broad, six-foot-three trouble. And she didn't have any viable strategies left to get her out of trouble.

Because her first and only strategy, of hiding in the bathroom until she came up with a better strategy, had just gone down in flames, even though De Rossi had been surprisingly co-operative at first.

But now that strategy had crashed and burned. And she was far too aware of him to come up with another. The deliberate beats of the waltz reverberated in her ears, the sprinkle of light from the chandeliers dazzling her as he swung her around with practised ease.

With his body plastered against hers, she felt overwhelmed by the heat coming off him, the bunch and flex of his shoulder muscles as she clung to the fabric of his tuxedo; and the flare of arousal in his darkened pupils— all proof she wasn't the only one caught in this maelstrom.

His big body surrounded her, his heady scent frying the few functioning brain cells she had left and sending her hormones into meltdown. She could hardly breathe, let alone think.

The hard planes of his chest pressed against her breast as he whisked her round again. And she stumbled. His muscular forearm braced across her back, lifting her off the floor for a beat.

'Steady,' he murmured against her hair as her heels clicked down on the polished parquet. 'Follow my lead.'

She surrendered as he propelled her round the dance floor, past the envious stares of the women around her. He looked magnificent, lean and graceful in the tuxedo but with that air of raw, rugged masculinity that made the other men stand back.

She felt light-headed, her caution and control obliterated under the tractor-beam gaze she'd felt on her all evening, even when she was busy scurrying off to the bathroom for the umpteenth time.

The music swirled around them, the twinkle of light above them as they weaved in and out of the other dancers disorientating her. It was as if she were in the heart of a kaleidoscope, the colour and light dazzling her and leaving her dazed. Every inch of her skin stretched tight over her bones, so that she could feel each millimetre that touched his: the controlling press of his large palm on her hip, the rise and fall of his breathing, slow and steady against her own ragged pants; the thud of her heart, audible above the glide of cello strings marking the beat.

At last the music ended and he came to a halt. She stepped back as he let her go. Grateful for the space, even if his scent still enveloped her.

'You dance very well.' She forced the words out. Wondering if inane chatter might be a viable strategy.

'Do you wish to leave?' he replied.

Obviously not.

'Yes.' The word popped out on a breathless sigh.

He took her hand to lead her off the dance floor. A few people tried to waylay them, but he marched past as if he hadn't noticed. Maybe he hadn't, but she had. She felt as if she had a sign on her forehead—'woman being claimed'.

Her father's suggestion came back to haunt her. He'd wanted her to seduce this man, and she'd agreed to try, but why did what was happening now feel as if it had nothing to do with her father, or Whittaker's, or even rescuing Katie's dreams?

She wanted De Rossi for herself. No one else.

Her pulse battered her collarbone, her fingers clasped tightly in his rough palm, the prickle of awareness shooting all over her body. He paused briefly to pick up their coats from the cloakroom attendant at the entrance to the elaborate Westchester town house where the ball was held.

The chauffeur-driven car was waiting at the kerb as they descended the steps. Megan's heels clicked on the paving stones like gunshots, shooting down the last of her caution and control.

Dario didn't wait for the driver but pulled the door open himself. The dark interior beckoned, but she held back, scared to take the next step.

If she entered the car, this man would be her first real lover. And while that hadn't felt like an event of any significance up to this second, it felt significant now. Obviously this was just lust, some pheromonal trick her body was playing on her. She wasn't a hothead like Katie, and she wasn't a romantic either. She didn't need the conceit of hearts and flowers to justify a purely physical urge. But she'd never had this urge with any other man. And because of that, she couldn't do this thing while there was still so much deception between them.

'Get in the car, Megan,' he murmured, his voice deep with purpose. 'Or I'm liable to do something that is going to get us both arrested.'

She turned to find herself surrounded by him again, his arm braced against the roof of the car, her back flush against the door frame; she could feel the thick ridge touching her belly through their clothing.

'I can't… I have to tell you something first.'

'If it's about your father, and the reason he set up this date, don't bother. I already know.'

'You do?' She pressed a palm to his chest, shock overlaid with bone-deep relief.

The clatter of his heartbeat through the starched linen felt like a validation, silencing the cacophony of objections in her mind. He was as blown away by their chemistry as she was. That was all that mattered, surely? If he knew about her father's plan, this wasn't seedy, or underhand, or unethical. It was nothing more than two healthy adults fulfilling a need.

He nodded, his dark hair shining black in the streetlamp. 'Tell me, are you here for him, for his company, or for me?'

'I…'

For me. I'm here for me.

But even as the truth rang in her head, she couldn't voice it. Paralysed by words whispering across her consciousness from another April night, spiced with the juniper scent of gin and selfishness, the words her mother had whispered to her before she left. The last words her mother had ever spoken to her.

'I have to leave with him, baby. He makes Mummy so happy. Daddy will understand eventually.'

'I… I can't,' she finally blurted out.

She didn't want to be like her mother, she couldn't be. Maybe she had the same biological urges, urges she'd tried to deny for so long, but she couldn't sleep with her father's enemy and do nothing to try to save him.

'Why can't you?' De Rossi asked.

'Because it would kill my father if you destroyed Whittaker's.'

The dark scowl on Dario's face would have been frightening, if she still had some control of her faculties. Instead it only seemed to spike the fire in her blood. Would a man as ruthless in business as Dario consider changing his mind? Would he stop his pursuit of her father's company for her? Did he want her that much?

'I promise you, I have no intention of destroying your father's company.' He ground the words out.

She tried to control the foolish spurt of emotion at the concession. But she couldn't help it. As smart and sensible and grounded as she had always been about life and business, and as aware as she was of De Rossi's ruthlessness, and his cynicism, she was still moved that he would give her this, because she'd asked it of him.

'*Grazie,*' she said.

His brow quirked, then his lips tipped up in a feral smile that should have been terrifying but was instead terrifyingly exciting.

'Don't thank me yet.' He gave her a firm pat on the backside. 'Now get in the car.'

She laughed, she actually laughed, as she scrambled inside. All the stresses and strains of the last twenty-four hours floated off into the Manhattan night as the car sped through the evening traffic towards his home—his love nest—on Central Park West.

Whittaker's would be saved. Her father could stop freaking out about losing the company that had been in their family for generations and she could have this night of erotic exploration with a man who made her blood bubble and fizz beneath her skin, without a single regret.

It took ten minutes to drive through the moonlit park, a few hardy and fearless joggers still peppering the well-lit streets as they passed Belvedere Castle's fairy-tale tur-rets. Megan felt almost as fearless as those intrepid joggers when the car drew to a stop and Dario got out. He hadn't spoken during the journey, and neither had she. But the fever of anticipation stirring her blood made her fingers shake as he helped her out of the car.

'So this is your love nest?' she said.

'My what?' he asked as she tilted her head to take in the two towers of the art deco building, the ornate and op-ulent architecture a luxury statement from a bygone era.

But the laugh at his puzzled expression got trapped in her throat as he escorted her into the building, past the doorman and a receptionist, until he reached the antique lift. The intricate iron filigree gates opened as the uni-formed operator beckoned them inside.

'Good evening, Mr De Rossi.' The man in his late-fifties tipped his hat at Megan. 'Miss.'

'*Buonasera*, Rick.' Dario's tone was clipped, his hand gripping hers so tightly she could feel her pulse punching. 'This is Megan Whittaker.'

'Nice to meet you, Rick,' she said, her voice distress-ingly husky. Heat scorched her neck. How many other late-night lovers had Rick been introduced to on their way up to Dario's love nest?

The term felt quaint instead of romantic—which was for the best, she decided. She wasn't here to make love, but to have sex for the first time.

Suddenly the enormity of what they were about to do occurred to her. They hadn't even kissed yet. What would that firm sensual mouth feel like on hers? How would his body look naked? She assessed the width of his shoulders in the perfectly tailored designer coat. He was a well-built guy; what if all of him was as generously proportioned? Would it hurt?

Should she tell him she'd never actually gone all the way before?

Her pulse rabbited against her collarbone as she watched the gold arrow above their heads swing in an arc signalling the floors.

Despite the antique design, the lift whisked them up to the twenty-sixth floor without a single creak. Too soon, and yet not soon enough. Dario bid the operator goodnight and led her into a palatial lobby area. Fresh flowers stood on a side table, the only touch of softness against the sleek modern lines.

Shrugging off his coat, he dumped it on an armchair, then lifted her wrap off her shoulders. Despite the warmth pumping out of a central air system, she shivered.

Callused hands settled on her bare shoulders and he turned her to face him.

His handsome face, rigid with desire, should have frightened her, at least a little bit. But somehow it felt compelling, for him to want her so much. His thumbs glided over her collarbone. His fingers curled around her nape with exquisite tenderness. And trapped her in place. Then his lips. Firm, sensual, and unapologetic, slanted across hers, triggering a tsunami of sensation.

Her breath got trapped somewhere around her solar plexus. The hard, unyielding line of his body imprinted itself on her curves, making her want to yield. Instead of demanding or devouring, his lips were coaxing, gentle, until her mouth opened on a huff and his tongue plundered.

He explored, exploited, taking control of the kiss. Shivers of awareness reverberated in her core, then his fingers fisted in her hair to angle her face so he could go deeper, take more. Her heart beat violently against her ribcage, like the wings of a trapped bird trying to escape. She plastered herself against him, absorbing the heat of his body, and kissed him back, her tongue darting out to duel with his. The sudden feeling of weightlessness was as terrifying as the desperate flare of longing, the shocking well of desire surging up her torso to obliterate everything but the sight, the sound, the taste of him. Earthy and raw and so staggeringly real.

The kiss could only have lasted for a few moments, but still she staggered, unsteady on her feet, when he lifted his head abruptly. His brows lifted, his eyes flaring hot, and she wondered for a second if he were as stunned as she was by the intensity of feeling that had passed between them.

Taking her hand, he led her down the corridor and into a huge, double-height room. A majestic sweep of stairs led to a mezzanine level, the deep leather sofas along the back wall the only furnishings. Huge floor-to-ceiling leaded windows looked out over the dark expanse of Central Park, the lake and the twinkle of lights from the East Side skyline beyond.

She could see her own reflection in the mullioned glass, her breath heaving in and out, her satin curves shimmering in the light from the hallway as he stood behind her. He glided his thumbs under the gown's diamanté straps.

'Yes?' The low question shattered the silence.

'Yes,' she managed around the thickening in her throat.

He eased the straps over her shoulder blades. The rasp of the gown's zip seemed deafening. Satin caught at her waist, and then slid down to pool around her feet, revealing the lacy royal-blue lingerie Annalise had insisted on buying to go with the gown.

Her breath hitched painfully as she heard the click of her bra releasing. He dragged the lace straps off her shoulders to slide down her arms. Her heavy breasts were released from their confinement. His lips caressed her neck, suckling on the pulse point as his hands covered the swollen mounds, his fingers circling her nipples.

Sensation tugged at her sex as he rolled the rigid peaks between thumb and forefinger, plucking then squeezing. Her knees went liquid, and a strong arm banded around her waist to hold her up. Her pale flesh shone white against his darkness.

His lips caressed the side of her neck as he growled. 'I can't wait any longer to have you.'

She pulled away and turned to face him. Her pulse was going berserk. She dragged a precious lungful of air into her lungs and tasted him, the subtle aroma of sandalwood and clean laundry detergent.

His thumb skimmed her cheek. The gentle touch had all her nerve-endings springing to high alert.

No man had ever looked at her with such hunger in his eyes. She absorbed the heat and intensity and it felt like a benediction, a celebration of everything she was that she had always been terrified to admit to.

The heat between her legs melted into a puddle of need, making her skin sensitive and her senses alert to the scent and taste of him, the rough sound of his breathing.

She squeezed her thighs together. 'Neither can I,' she said.

Dario stared at the girl in front of him—an artless seductress whose acute awareness of his touch had been torturing him all evening.

He had become spellbound by his own lust. He'd never wanted a woman this much, so much he wasn't sure he could be gentle—and that frightened him. He could actually read every one of her emotions as they flitted across her face, her attempts to wrestle them under control almost as bewitching as the hard peaks of her breasts, which begged for his mouth.

Need coiled hard in his gut, the pounding in his crotch unbearable.

He cupped her breast. She jolted but didn't draw away.

'Are you sure, *cara*?' He wanted no lies or obligations between them. He'd promised not to destroy her father's company. But it had never been his intention to destroy it, only to take it from the man...tonight, when the final deal with the last of Whittaker's shareholders went through at midnight.

'Yes,' she murmured.

He threaded his fingers in her hair, loosening the up-do. As the soft, silky strands teased his fingertips, her scent curled around him, fresh and vivid, and heat powered through his body. Her eyes widened, her breathing coming in harsh pants now. And he knew she felt it too, that tug of yearning, the driving need to finish what they'd started.

Her teeth sank into her bottom lip, mesmerising him, and calling to every one of his baser instincts, instincts he'd spent a lifetime trying to control.

Need overwhelmed him as he lifted her into his arms. Placing her on the couch, he lowered his head, unable to resist the pull of that lush mouth a moment longer.

He heard the soft gasp, tasted her excitement and her trepidation. It could only be a trick of the night, this veneer of innocence. No woman could be innocent and drive him this insane, but even so he enjoyed the challenge as he coaxed and cajoled, tempting her with his tongue.

Her lips opened at last on a shuddering sigh. His tongue swept into her mouth, exploring. Then she began to explore back. Tentative at first, then bold. Matching his hunger with her own. Driving them both mad. She tasted glorious, sweet and eager and new.

Her fingers glided beneath his jacket to cling to his waist. Heat slammed into him. He lifted himself up, yanking off his jacket and flinging it on the floor, pressing her back into the cool leather. Lifting her hands above her head, he bracketed her wrists in one hand to palm the pouting tip of her breast.

The nipple poked against his palm, standing proud as she arched her back, her breathing coming in desperate gasps as she pressed into the caress. He circled the tight bud, all thoughts of caution obliterated by her seductive response.

He trapped the peak between his teeth, tonguing it and then sucking it into his mouth. She sobbed something incoherent in the darkness, the desire in her voice rasping across his skin and sending the need spiralling out of control.

He wanted her, more than he'd wanted any woman, her artless response tapping into some primal desire to claim her, brand her, devour her.

'Please, I can't…' She jolted against him.

'Shh…' he crooned, desperate to relieve the throbbing ache in his crotch. She wanted him just as much. He could feel it in her body, which was tight as a bowstring, and in the staggered rise and fall of her breathing; he could see it in the flush of arousal spreading across the delicate skin of her collarbone.

'That feels so good—' Her voice choked off as he sucked the nipple against the roof of his mouth, tugging hard. She jerked against his hold, and pulled her hands free to plunge them into his hair.

The thin thread on his control snapped, primal desire charging through his system. Damn thought and sense and reason and anything that would stop him from making her come apart in his arms.

The madness to have her consumed him. He inhaled the delicate floral fragrance, like a narcotic drug. Pressing the heel of his palm between her thighs, to test her readiness, he felt her warm and wet through the lace. She quaked with need, daring him to take her, claim her, control her. Here. Now. And satisfy the need driving them both insane.

He plunged beneath the damp fabric of her panties, circling the tight bud. She cried out, bucking against the intimate touch. But the slick folds told a different story. She needed this. Needed him.

Ripping her panties, he grasped her thighs, spreading them wide to press the aching ridge against her centre.

'Let me have you,' he growled, the ferocity of the demand foreign to his own ears.

She looked dazed, her eyes unfocused, but she dropped her head in the tiniest hint of a nod.

The madness took over. He grappled with his zip and released his erection, then, positioning himself against the swollen folds, he thrust hard.

But as he surged deep, he heard the cry of pain against his neck, felt the tiny barrier, before she tightened on him like a fist.

He stopped dead.

He was buried to the hilt, the orgasm already licking at the base of his spine. But the hot clasp of her body was so tight. Too tight.

'What the…?' He swore viciously, shocked and sickened by the evidence of her innocence. 'You are a virgin?' he said, the shock only countered by the fierce unstoppable desire to move, to finish.

Megan buried her face in his neck, her whole body reeling from the shocking invasion. It had been so good, so bright, so beautiful, but now she felt impaled. He was too big, filling up every space inside her, all those empty places that had ached for so long.

She stiffened as he shifted, the thick heat branding her insides, stroking a place so deep inside, it spun her mind away from coherent thought again and back towards that glorious heat that had consumed her just moments ago.

'*Cara…*' He cradled her cheek. 'Answer me. Why you did not tell me I am…your first?' His perfect English seemed to have deserted him, the words clumsy, those deep blue eyes alive with stunned disbelief and raw aching need.

'I'm sorry,' she said, not sure why she was apologising, but he looked so horrified, she didn't know what else to say.

He held her hips, easing back, withdrawing that glorious heat. She gripped his buttocks, felt the muscles jump.

'Don't stop. It doesn't matter, really it doesn't. And it feels good.' It didn't exactly; it felt sore, and overwhelming.

'I don't want to hurt you.' He bit out the words, torn between temper and what sounded like torment.

Why did this matter to him so much? She wanted to ask.

But what she wanted more was for the bright, beautiful feeling to return. So that she felt empowered and special, not crushed and broken.

'I'm not fragile. I won't break,' she said, determined to make him believe it.

He swore softly in Italian, his fingers holding her thighs, poised at her entrance. 'Are you sure?' he asked.

She nodded, unbearably moved by the torment in his voice. 'Yes, I'm sure.'

He sank back into her to the hilt.

Her breath clogged in her throat. She could feel him everywhere, the stretching feeling unbearable again, but with it came the swift surge of pleasure as he nudged a place deep inside. He rocked his hips, and nudged it again.

'*Si sente bene?*' he asked, his English apparently having deserted him entirely.

'Yes, it feels good,' she said as the pleasure began to build in fierce undulating waves, sweeping away the pain, the confusion, until all that was left was the glorious swell of ecstasy, pure and perfect. The sensitive tips of her breasts rubbed against the hard contours of his chest through his linen shirt, sending arrows of sensation surging into her sex.

The slick sounds of their bodies slapping together, the scent of pheromones and sweat heavy on the air, the soft bump of her spine against the leather, faded into the background until all she could hear were the pants of her breathing and the grunts of his. He established a punishing rhythm, forceful, relentless, unstoppable. Then reached between them to press his thumb to the heart of her.

The huge wave crested, her whole being now focused on the burning core of her body, clambering for release.

She held on to him, terrified, frantic and overjoyed, all at the same time. He grew to impossible proportions inside her, his thrusts jerky and uncoordinated in their desperation.

She rode on that high wide plane between intense pleasure and unbearable pain for what seemed like an eternity, but could only have lasted a heartbeat. And her body soared.

Her thin cry cut the still air as the wave crashed over her, overwhelming in its intensity, and his shout of release echoed in her ear, the hot seed searing her insides.

What the hell just happened?

Sensation came back in small increments as Dario waited for his heart to stop battering his ribs like a wild stallion trying to kick its way to freedom.

The sultry scent of orange blossoms and sweat, the weight of her hands on his waist, the clinging cotton of the shirt he hadn't bothered to take off. The tight clasp of her surrounding him as the iron-hard erection finally began to soften and the ache in his groin subsided.

He buried his face against her neck, the soft skin damp and fragrant, and felt the hummingbird flutter of her pulse, as wild and erratic as his own.

He couldn't move, didn't want to move, grateful for the shadowy light as they lay cocooned together on the couch.

He'd had good sex before. Hell, he'd had spectacular sex before. He'd never had sex like that before, or an orgasm so intense it had felt as if it were ripping out a part of his soul.

Who is this woman? And what has she done to me?

He eased up on his elbows and felt her flinch beneath him. The sob of discomfort whispered against his face, making shame twist in his gut.

She had been innocent, and he'd ravished her like a man possessed. Not only that, but he had taken her without protection. Spilled his seed inside her. He should have stopped, withdrawn, but she had transfixed him somehow. And he had been unable to focus on anything but her. And the need to possess her.

Why hadn't she told him? She should have told him she was a virgin. He would never have—

Stop lying to yourself.

No force on earth would have stopped him, once she had given him her consent and unleashed the wild hunger inside him.

He climbed off her, careful not to jostle her. He couldn't make out her expression in the shadowy light, but he could see the tremors raking her body.

Lush and lovely, her pale skin looked somehow ethereal

in the soft glow of light from the lobby. He felt the renewed stirring of desire, and shame mixed with anger in his gut.

You are not an animal.

The admonition seemed like another lie though as he zipped his trousers and walked to pick up the jacket he had discarded. He returned to the couch to find her seated, her arms wrapped around her waist. He laid the jacket over her shoulders, and drew her close under his arm.

'Why are you shivering? Are you cold?' he asked, his voice hoarse.

She had to be sore, but was she also scared of him?

He tucked a riotous curl behind her ear, relief assailing him when she turned to him and smiled. The urge to kiss her gripped him again at the guileless tilt of her lips.

He resisted it. Not a good idea, given that kissing her would lead to other, more dangerous pursuits.

'No, I'm not cold. I just... I think it's a reaction...' She hesitated, biting down on that full bottom lip that had driven him wild, was still driving him wild. He forced himself to look away from her mouth.

'A reaction to what?' he prompted, determined to distract them both with conversation. He didn't usually like to talk much after sex, but this was different. He'd never been a woman's first before. It wasn't a responsibility he wanted or would have chosen, but he felt it nonetheless.

'A reaction to...' She hesitated again, but she didn't look embarrassed or unsure, just as if she were searching for the right words. 'Well, the orgasm, I guess. It was pretty intense. You're much better than my vibrator.'

The chuckle rumbled up from his chest, part amusement, part desire, but mostly relief. Her blunt honesty was ridiculously charming, especially when she blushed.

'*Grazie*, that is quite a compliment,' he murmured.

She gave a shy smile, looking embarrassed now but also amused. 'Sorry, I'm not very good at this.'

He looped the wayward curl behind her ear again, let his thumb linger on the smooth skin of her jaw, the laughter dying on his lips. 'On the contrary, you are very good at it, especially for someone with so little practice.'

The blush climbed up to her hairline, but she seemed pleased with the compliment. He felt a strange sensation in his chest and dropped his hand. What was he doing? Behaving like a besotted fool, when he needed to make sure that there would be no fallout from his irresponsible behaviour.

'Megan, we must talk about practicalities.'

'What practicalities?' she said, the guileless expression making him feel uneasy. Could anyone really be this innocent? Was this whole scenario some kind of set-up? Had Whittaker been devious enough to offer up his virgin daughter as a means of trapping him?

'I did not use a condom,' he said bluntly. 'Are you on the pill?'

The flush fired across her cheeks and her eyes widened. Either she was an actress worthy of an award, or the shocked reaction was not faked.

'No, I'm not, I'm sorry, I didn't—'

'There is no need for apologies.' He cut off her stumbling words, feeling oddly ashamed at the cynical direction of his thoughts.

Megan Whittaker was that rare thing, a person as genuine as they appeared to be—just as he had originally suspected.

'We are both responsible for the error,' he added. 'I am clean, I have a regular check-up and testing for my company insurance—and I never usually have sex without protection,' he continued, suspecting the threat of disease was probably the reason for her horrified reaction. His conquests after all had been well documented in the press, and made to seem much more indiscriminate than they actually were. Because, until Megan, he had always chosen his sexual partners with exquisite care. Which was precisely why he had never found himself in this position before. 'If you need proof,' he said, when she didn't respond, 'I can get my doctor to contact you.'

'No, that's not necessary. I trust you,' she said, marking out her innocence even more. He wanted to tell her not to trust him, not to trust any man, but before he could find the words she added, 'I don't either, by the way... Have sex without protection, I mean. Just in case you were wondering, and were worried too.'

The gauche statement was so earnest, his lips tipped up in a wry smile. 'With your vibrator, you mean?'

'Um, well...' The blush intensified on her cheeks, before she buried her hands in her face and groaned. 'Oh, God, I feel like such a clueless muppet.'

'Not at all, *piccola*.' He laughed, he couldn't help it; her found her reaction charming. 'We do still have one problem though,' he said, sobering. 'When did you have your last period?'

'Oh, I...' She raised her face, the blush still burning brightly. 'About a week ago. I think.'

'Then we are not quite in the middle of your cycle,' he said. 'But you should take emergency contraception. Yes? As a precaution.' He watched her intently for her reaction to the request, his anger at himself increasing. What would he do if she refused?

'Yes, yes, of course. I'll go to a pharmacy.' She jumped up from the couch, her panicked reaction easing the tension in his gut. 'I better go now. I'll need to find an all-night pharmacy. I don't even know if you can buy it across the counter.'

'Megan, there is no need to panic.' He rose from the couch too and tucked a knuckle under her chin. Raising her face to his, he touched his thumb to her mouth, the heat powering through him surprising him. 'And stop biting your lip. Or I will not be responsible for the consequences.'

She released her lip instinctively. 'But I should go, Dario. I need to get the contraception. I don't want...'

'You have up to a week to take it.'

'I do?'

'I believe so. Don't look at me like that, *piccola*.' He smiled again, captivated once more by how easily she was to read. 'I promise you, I don't make a habit of making love without contraception.' The truth was he had never made this mistake before, even as an untried boy, but she didn't need to know that. 'But I am a cautious man.' Or he had been until now. 'As I have no desire to father a child.'

'Yes, of course.' She nodded, her cheeks still as bright as beacons. 'I'm sorry, I'm making a hash of this, aren't I?'

'Not at all. This is new to you, I understand.'

She shuddered slightly, his tux jacket dwarfing her as she tucked her arms into the sleeves and held it close. 'I should probably leave now anyway though. I'll make sure I go to a pharmacy first thing in the morning.'

She was correct, of course, this had just been a chance for them to slake the lust that had sparked between them as soon as they had met.

But as she stood before him, beautiful and beguiling in the half light, he knew the spark hadn't yet been extinguished. And tonight would be their only opportunity, because he would not be contacting her again.

In a few hours, his agents would complete the hostile

takeover of her father's company, giving their encounter a one-night embargo.

It was of course dishonest of him not to clarify his earlier statement about Whittaker's, so there could be no confusion about what he'd meant. But he didn't mix business with pleasure. And for that reason, he did not feel guilty for giving her the cryptic answer he had. What happened in the boardroom had no bearing on relations in the bedroom—or rather the couch. What had passed between them, however wild and uncontrolled, could never be more than a physical attachment after all.

Once she discovered the truth, she would be upset. She might even feel he had got her here under false pretences. After all, his reply to her request had been deliberately ambiguous. But as his gaze drifted down her bare legs and he remembered the sweet shudder of her release, the feel of her thighs clasping his hips as she came, he knew he didn't want their one night to end so soon.

In fact, he almost felt regretful that she would no doubt hate him in the morning.

She picked her gown up from the floor and clasped it to her chest. 'Is there somewhere I could wash up,' she said, looking shy again and unsure.

He walked over to her, his mind made up. They would have this night.

He would show her the finesse, the reverence he had failed to show her so far. She deserved better than a frantic romp on a couch. He wasn't a romantic or a sentimental man, but he was a good lover.

The last of the shame drained away. He could keep the wildness in check; he would not ravish her again.

'There is no need to leave,' he said, tugging the cool satin out of her hands.

'But I...'

He placed a finger on her lips. 'No buts. We have all night. Why not let me show you all the other things your vibrator cannot do for you?'

The blush intensified, and he found the lightness, the laughter threatening to roll up his torso again. Not a response he was used to when in the process of seducing a beautiful woman.

No wonder this woman was so damn captivating. She was simply the opposite of his usual type. Her uniqueness would wear thin quickly enough, but he was enjoying himself for now. And he planned to enjoy himself a lot more tonight. While making sure Megan enjoyed herself too, of course. She might hate him in the morning, but eventually she would thank him for showing her that sex was much more enjoyable when not compromised by emotional entanglements.

'I'm not sure that's a good idea,' she said.

'Why not?' He cradled her cheek, enjoying the way she leant into his palm instinctively. And her pupils darkened dramatically. Did she know he could see exactly how much she wanted him?

'Because, to be perfectly honest, I'm a little sore.'

The delightfully gauche statement, delivered with complete sincerity, had him throwing back his head and laughing out loud for the first time in longer than he could remember.

'What's so funny?' she asked, grumpily.

He scooped her up into his arms.

She grabbed hold of his neck, her frown of protest only making him laugh harder as he headed to the stairs and the deluxe king-size bed and lake-size bath with power shower he planned to make good use of in the next few hours.

He placed a kiss on her forehead, enjoying the feel of

her bottom against his forearm. Why not keep her naked and wanting the rest of the night?

Why had he never considered before how arousing it would be to help a woman discover the frontiers of her own pleasure?

'Do not look so worried, *cara mia*,' he said as he took the stairs two at a time. 'There are many ways to make love, not all of them require penetration. Clearly your vibrator does not help with this either.'

'I wish I'd never told you about my vibrator,' she said. 'Now you're never going to stop making fun of me.'

'I am not making fun,' he said, although of course he was. 'But I do intend to remedy the situation. With your permission?'

She huffed out a breath, but the excitement and arousal dancing in her eyes told a different story, especially when she tightened her grip on his neck and said, with mock severity, 'Oh, all right, then—if you insist.'

CHAPTER FOUR

Didn't the man ever eat?

Megan stared at the dazzlingly clean and startlingly empty shelves in the huge double wide fridge. Apart from a couple of bottles of pricey mineral water, a bottle of expensive champagne, some imported Italian lager, some milk and an untouched box of expensive chocolates, there was nothing to eat. She searched the cupboards a second time. Nope, still nothing there except some strong Italian coffee.

She turned in a circle. The oversized Italian football shirt she'd fished out of a drawer in Dario's walk-in closet skimmed her bare thighs as she took in the acres of granite and polished steel. The tingle of sensation as the material brushed her nipples had a memory flushing through her. Of Dario ravishing her breasts in the shower.

Moving swiftly on.

She concentrated on the sun, which had begun to climb over Central Park, shining off the lake and adding to that magnificent view. She'd woken up with Dario's big body wrapped around hers in sleep. He'd tucked her against his chest after he'd brought her to a stunning orgasm for the fourth time in one night... She lifted the glass of mineral water she'd poured herself from the meagre supplies in the fridge and took several gulps to ease the dryness in her throat.

Dario De Rossi a snuggler. Who'd have thought it?

She smiled to herself, feeling a little giddy. It was a Saturday, so she didn't need to go to work today. She knew her father would want her to call him to confirm if she had discovered anything, but there would be no need for that now. Dario had told her he wasn't going to go after Whittaker's. Maybe he had never intended to.

But unlike last night, she didn't feel the need to run off and hide. He'd been so solicitous after they'd made love that first time. And so devoted for the rest of the night. He'd soaked with her in the bathtub, then done things to her body that had proved that, yes, vibrators could not replace a flesh-and-blood man.

The sex had been hot, intense and unbelievably intimate. But she had adored every minute of it. Was this what her mother had been so addicted to? Now she understood. Something fluttered in her chest. Something sweet and seductive and more than a little bit silly.

She set about figuring out the state-of-the-art coffee maker and ignored the feeling. Their liaison was unlikely to last past this morning—so there was no point in getting carried away. She needed to be pragmatic. Really, she ought to be heading home. She had to find a pharmacy en route and take care of the practicalities—as Dario had put it. Her cheeks heated as she recalled their excruciating conversation from the night before. Her hand strayed to her belly. And she wondered, just for a split second, what it would be like to have the child of a man like Dario De Rossi.

Not going there.

She shook off the foolish, fanciful thoughts and let her hand drop.

She didn't want Dario's baby. She didn't want anyone's baby. She was fairly sure she wasn't cut out for motherhood, any more than her own mother had been. And if by chance Dario's seed had found fertile ground last night, she would remedy the problem as soon as she got back home. But first she needed coffee.

She concentrated on filling the machine's in-built grinder with coffee beans. It didn't take long to have the strong, chicory scent filling up the kitchen. If only she had more clothing, she could pop out and get something for breakfast. She liked to cook. And she felt she owed Dario. He'd made last night magnificent. And she hadn't exactly held up her end, so to speak. She frowned as she poured a steaming cup of coffee into one of the demi-cups in the cupboard. He'd been so controlled, so focused, it had been flattering and exhausting and beyond amazing. But somehow the times after that first time hadn't felt quite as, well, quite as equal. She'd felt oddly like a pupil, being played by a master. Her attempts to touch him, to caress him, to drive him crazy back, rebuffed.

'I'm impressed.'

She jerked round, sloshing hot coffee over the counter, to find Dario standing behind her, his broad, muscular chest making her pulse race. He wore a pair of sweat pants low on his hips—revealing the most mouthwatering V she had ever seen in her life—and nothing else. His olive skin was deeply tanned, even down to the line of his low-riding pants. His dark hair stood up in clumps on one side of his head, but unlike her hair—which probably resembled Frizz City this morning—the rumpled, just-out-of-bed look only made him sexier. Add that to the jaw sporting a five o'clock shadow that had given her whisker burn in some interesting places last night, and the man wouldn't have looked out of place in a million-dollar cologne ad.

'Still skittish, Megan?' His sensual lips tipped up on one side in a boyish smile as he leant past her to pour himself a mug of coffee and the giddy feeling in her chest fluttered again.

She breathed in his scent, the sandalwood aroma a brutal reminder of everything they'd got up to together in the shower.

'You have a habit of creeping up on me,' she said in her defence, but she smiled. Had she actually spent all night in this man's arms? This god among men? No fair.

He laughed, that deep rusty chuckle that had enthralled her last night, when she'd had the oddest sensation that he didn't laugh nearly often enough. It had made her feel special. When she knew she wasn't. But still.

'Why do I impress you?' she asked, shamelessly fishing for a compliment.

The tanned skin around his eyes crinkled, as if he knew exactly what she was up to. 'You figured out the espresso machine without an hour-long tutorial.'

She laughed and glanced back at the complex contraption. 'It's not that hard for a computer geek.'

He sipped his coffee, hummed low in his throat, the sound sending the familiar pinpricks darting down to her sex. Heavens, she was a hopeless case.

'Sexy and smart *and* a great coffee maker.' He leant down to kiss her, the teasing licks sending her senses reeling, his rich coffee taste making the hunger in her gut intensify. But as she opened her mouth to take him in, he pulled back.

'Damn, what do you do to me, *piccola*?'
Little one.
He'd used the same endearment last night. It was probably something he called all the women who slept with him. It didn't make her special or different—she needed to remember that. But even so, the deep blue of his irises seemed to sparkle just for her when he said it. This play-

ful, provocative side of him made her feel as if she was getting a glimpse of something he never showed to anyone else.

'Nothing you don't do to me,' she replied, because it was true.

'Hmm, I doubt that,' he said enigmatically, before he walked round and perched on one of the bar stools by the kitchen counter.

'I thought I could cook us breakfast, before I go,' she said, trying not to sound too eager. 'But you don't have any food.'

'I use a caterer when I entertain. Otherwise I eat out.'

'I see.' Although she didn't really. Surely for any house to be a home, you had to eat in occasionally? 'Well, I guess I should be going, then.'

'There is no need to leave yet. I can get groceries sent up. I like the idea of you cooking me breakfast.' He glanced at her shirt. 'Especially in my Roma shirt. Maybe I will ravish you afterwards on the countertop.'

The arrogantly male statement and the wicked intention in his eyes should have unsettled her, but instead it only excited her. But then every damn thing about the man turned her on.

'If you're going to be a caveman about it, I may have to rescind my offer,' she teased back.

'We will have to see if I can persuade you,' he said and she knew she was sunk. They both knew her resistance when it came to him was zero. 'How much time do you have?' he asked.

She glanced at the clock on the glass wall next to the eight-ring cooker...that he never used. And blinked, shocked to realise it was inching towards ten o'clock. She had to get back to her apartment before Katie woke up. Katie was not an early riser on a Saturday when she didn't have to go to college, thank goodness. But she didn't want her sister asking probing questions about where she'd been all night. And she definitely didn't want her finding out about the morning-after pill debacle—which meant making sure she bought it and took it before Katie got out of bed.

'I didn't realise it was so late,' she said, unable to keep the regret from her voice. 'I really need to go home and change and handle the other…um…practicalities we talked about last night.'

'This is a shame,' he said, and seemed to mean it—which didn't help with the giddy flutter in her chest.

But then her phone buzzed on the counter. She picked it up. A message from her father.

What the hell happened with De Rossi last night?

Guilt washed over her as she glanced up at Dario. Her father sounded as if he was freaking out again. This couldn't be right. Dario had told her he wasn't pursuing Whittaker's, that there would be no takeover.

'I should probably take this,' she said.

A strange chill settled in her stomach as she walked to the other side of the room and texted her father back.

Don't panic Dad, everything's okay. Dario assured me he's not attempting a takeover. I spoke to him.

She stared at the text, then quickly scrolled back to delete Dario and replace it with Mr De Rossi. Then she pressed send. She'd done a lot more than speak to Dario, but her father did not need to know that. Their liaison had nothing to do with the company. Not now.

The reply came back within seconds. And the sinking

feeling in her stomach became a black hole. The vicious words felt like a punch in the gut she couldn't defend herself against.

Stupid little slut! You slept with him, didn't you? After he stole my company. You're no better than your bitch of a mother.

'He shouldn't say such things to you.'

She swung round to find Dario watching her, his expression grim. She whipped the phone behind her back, humiliated and sick at the same time. Had he read that?

'He's upset. I think… He's under a lot of stress at the moment,' she said, instantly jumping to her father's defence. He didn't mean to be cruel. He wasn't a bad man, just an extremely stressed one. 'But I should go, and explain things to him. He's obviously got the wrong end of the stick. He thinks De Rossi Corp is involved in a hostile takeover. And obviously that's not the case, because you promised me yesterday you have no interest in Whittaker's.'

Dario took the phone from her and grasped her hand to lead her to one of the kitchen stools. 'Sit down, Megan. I need to explain something.'

She sat down. Confused now and wary. Why did Dario look so serious? Where had the sexy man of a moment ago gone to? The man who had worshipped her with his mouth, his hands, his body, last night? And why had her father texted her so viciously? None of it made any sense. The company wasn't under threat; it had all been a misunderstanding of some sort.

'Megan, you must understand, I never mix business with pleasure.'

'I know. I'm sorry, I shouldn't have brought it up, it's just he texted me and I—'

'You misunderstand me.'

'Sorry?'

'Last night was about us enjoying each other, not about your father, or his company.'

'I know that, but you promised me that—'

'What I promised you was that I would not destroy Whittaker's. That is what you asked me and I answered truthfully.'

'I know, and that's good.'

'I have no plans to destroy it. Because, as of last night, I now own it.'

She blinked rapidly, the black hole in her stomach opening into a huge pit. A huge gaping pit full of vipers. As he continued to speak in that calm, pragmatic voice, his words became barely audible above the hissing in her head.

'Whittaker's is still a viable company with the right management. It is a heritage brand with excellent prospects. The right management, though, is not your father. E-commerce is the way forward. He has refused to develop that side of the business to any great degree. I only asset-strip companies that have no future.'

He had taken the company away from her father.

He hadn't lied, but he had been economical with the truth. And she'd fallen for it. Because she'd wanted to. She'd heard what she'd wanted to hear in his qualified denial, because she'd wanted him. Her father had every right to call her a slut. Because that was exactly what she was. She'd put her own pleasure above the good of the company. The good of the family. Just like her mother.

Tears stung her eyes, making her sinuses throb. She wouldn't cry. She didn't deserve that indulgence. She had to get back to her apartment, get changed and then go to

see her father and try to make this right. She and Katie
had the money from their mother's trust fund, but her father administered it. He was bound to withdraw Katie's tuition now, to punish Megan for this folly. For this betrayal.

She sniffed, struggling to pull herself together, to ignore the hollow ache in her gut. The same sick feeling that
had paralysed her the night her mother had left, when she
was convinced her mother's departure was somehow her
fault, because she hadn't been a good enough daughter.

She clambered off the stool, but as she tried to walk past
Dario he held her arm, and pulled her round to face him.
'If you are angry with me, you should say so.'

'I'm not angry with you. I'm angry with myself. I've
betrayed a man I love and now I have to tell him what I've
done and hope he doesn't hate me.'

'Why would you love a man who speaks to you like
that?' He sounded annoyed. She didn't understand.

'Please, I have to go.' She tugged out of his grip, and
rushed over to pick up her gown. She would have to wear
it home. The walk of shame really did not get any worse
than this.

'He doesn't deserve your loyalty,' he said, the cynical
edge in his voice cutting through the last of her defences.
'No man does who would use you in such a way.'

But you used me, too.

She pushed the self-pitying thought to one side. Dario
hadn't used her, he had taken what she had offered freely.
But even so, she couldn't bear to look at him as she took
off his football shirt and slipped into the satin sheath. She
should have been embarrassed that he was watching her.
That having those eyes on her, cool and blue and full of
heat, still aroused her. But she was way past embarrassment—everything she had ever known or believed about
herself and her own integrity ripped to shreds.

She deserved her father's scorn.

'We slept together,' she said, pushing her feet into the torturous heels. 'I made a choice to sleep with you. It was the wrong choice. I see that now. I let what I wanted get in the way of what was right.'

Not only that, but she'd allowed herself to believe that a man as ruthless as Dario would put his desire for her above a business deal.

She wasn't just a clueless muppet. She was a hopelessly naïve and narcissistic clueless muppet.

'Don't be foolish,' he demanded. 'This isn't about right or wrong. Or you and me and what we did together last night. This is about your father and his inability to run a company competently. The two circumstances are not related.'

'They are to me.' She picked the wrap up from the floor of the living room and took one last glance at the wide green canopy of Central Park. There would be families down there, on this bright spring day. Families who loved and respected each other. But her father would never respect her again. She'd failed him. Failed herself. Thanks to her hunger for a man who was so far out of her league it was ridiculous.

He snagged her arm again. 'This is madness, Megan. We satisfied a perfectly natural urge last night. Nothing more. There is no need to punish yourself.'

She shook her arm free, blinking furiously to stop the tears from falling—because she would feel even more wretched if he ever found out the truth.

That somehow during their wild night together, she had come to believe she and Dario were doing more than just satisfying a perfectly natural urge.

'I have to go.'

She rushed down the long corridor towards the door,

pathetically grateful he didn't try to stop her. The sound of her heels clicking on the inlaid wood flooring mocked her. Along with the scattershot beats of her heart. And the nausea rolling in her belly.

As she took the lift down, she felt sick at her own stupidity.

But as the cab drove away from the art deco apartment building, she also felt a strange sense of pity. For Dario.

Because for all his wealth and power, for all his good looks and potent sex appeal, his indomitable confidence and charisma, it was clear he did not understand the importance of family.

CHAPTER FIVE

'MEG, WHERE HAVE YOU BEEN?' Katie pounced on her forty minutes later as she let herself into their apartment.

'Oh. My. God. You spent the night with him, didn't you?' Katie hissed as she took in the creased satin gown, the haphazard wrap, and the hastily knotted bundle of frizz on Megan's head. 'Sheesh, is that whisker burn on your cheek?'

Megan placed a hand over the raw skin, ashamed all over again. 'I can't talk about it now.' *Or ever.*

Her head hurt, the deep ache matched by the smarting pain in her tear ducts from the disastrous end to her wild night with Dario De Rossi—and all the tears she refused to shed.

That was nothing though compared to what the company would face now. She would lose her job, and she'd deserve it. A part of her—the small, sane part of her that could still think straight—had reasoned that it wasn't her fault De Rossi had targeted Whittaker's, or that her father's wild scheme to discover Dario's intentions through some sort of computer hack wouldn't have made a difference. But even so, she felt unbearably guilty. For sleeping with a man who had destroyed what her family had spent years building.

'Actually, you don't have to talk about it, I already

know...' Katie grabbed her hand, and tugged her into the alcove off the hallway. 'Dad's here, and he's behaving like a lunatic. He called you all sorts of horrid names and dismissed Lydia. Just sacked her on the spot.'

'Oh, no.' Was Lydia going to be made to pay for her mistakes too?

'Did he say anything about your tuition?' Megan asked, praying that she might be able to limit at least some of the damage.

'Yeah, he's pulling the plug on that. You could have told me he was paying for it,' her sister said, but she didn't look nearly as devastated as Megan had expected.

'Don't worry, Katie, I'll find a way to fund it.' Somehow.

'Forget it, I'll figure out a way to fund it myself,' Katie said dismissively. 'Believe me, that's the least of our worries. We have to deal with Dad first. I think he's lost his marbles. I'm not kidding. He's been ranting and raving about Mum, and you and De Rossi. He's behaving like King Lear on a bender. I think he's on something. He's dangerous.'

'What?' The vice around Megan's temples tightened.

'I tried to call you, to warn you.' Katie's head swivelled round to peek past the column that edged the hallway and gave her a direct view of the living-room door. 'But I kept getting the answer-machine.'

Because Megan had switched off the phone when she'd left Dario's—too much of a coward to bear her father's wrath before she had to. She'd delayed the inevitable still further by stopping at a pharmacy en route. But the chemist's judgmental look as she'd bought the emergency contraception in a crumpled satin ball gown had been more than enough of a guilt trip to remind her of all her transgressions.

'Don't worry,' Megan murmured wearily. She really didn't need Katie's ongoing battle with their father resurfacing and turning this crisis into a catastrophe. 'Dad's mad with me, that's all. I did something he may never forgive me for…' Just the thought of that had the guilt clawing at her insides like a rabid dog. 'He's lost Whittaker's.' Of course her father was distraught. He must have just found out about the takeover when he'd texted her this morning. 'But he's not going to hurt either one of us.'

'Don't be so sure,' Katie whispered, her eye darts and head swivels becoming increasingly frantic. 'Please, you have to go. Don't let him catch you here. He smashed up the living room already. You have to run away and hide until he calms down. I can stall him. He hardly knows I exist. He won't hurt me. But you…'

'Megan, get in here now!'

Katie shuddered as their father's voice boomed down the hallway.

Weariness and regret added to the guilt tying Megan's stomach into tight greasy knots. But as she went to step into the hallway to face her fate, and the dressing-down she no doubt deserved, Katie grabbed her arm. 'Don't go, Meg. For God's sake, what's wrong with you? He's nuts.'

'He's not nuts,' she said, although he did sound a bit deranged. But losing a company that had been your father's, and his father's before him, could probably do that to any man. 'And he's not going to hurt me.' Their father had always been distant, preoccupied with the company and his commitment to making Whittaker's a success, but he had never raised a hand to either one of them.

She dislodged Katie's fingers from her arm and walked down the hallway to the living room. The first shock came when she walked into the room. For once, Katie hadn't exaggerated. The room Lydia Brady always kept so spotless looked as if a hurricane had hit it. The photos of her and Katie growing up that she'd framed and hung on the walls had been smashed. A table had been up-ended, leaving fresh flowers crushed and water splattered over the broken glass, but it was the wanton destruction of one of Katie's artworks—the beautiful painting was lying in tattered pieces across the floor—that shocked Megan to the core.

Her father stood by the window, with his back to her. She had expected him to look bowed, to look devastated, had been willing to apologise profusely and then try her best to soothe and persuade and maybe even come up with some kind of solution, if he would let her. But when he turned, his fists clenched at his sides, his usually perfect appearance horribly dishevelled, he didn't look sad, or angry, he looked wild; the whites of his eyes were blood-shot.

'About time the little slut got home.' He strode across the room, the broken picture frames cracking beneath his shoes.

Megan stepped back, the pain in her temples scream-ing now. He leant past her and slammed the living-room door shut on Katie, who was hovering outside the room. Then propped a chair against the door knob.

'Daddy?' Megan said, the first darts of fear combining with the guilt sitting like a lump of lead in her stomach.

The blow came from nowhere, cracking in the air like a missile shot. She reeled backwards, the pain excruciat-ing as it exploded in her cheekbone.

'You stupid bitch! I'm not your daddy. I kept you two around because I had to—'

She scrambled onto her hands and knees, ignoring the pain in her jaw, the prickle of glass in her palms. He stood over her and hit her again, his fist knocking her shoulder and forcing her down. His foot glanced off her hip then caught the hem of her gown, the blue satin now spattered with blood. Was that her blood?

The metallic taste permeated her mouth.

She couldn't move, the gown twisted around her legs. She could hear her sister's cries, the pounding of her fists against the blocked door.

'Megan? Megan? Answer me, are you okay?'

She tried to shout back, but no sound would come out, the scream locked in her throat as she rolled and saw her father, standing over her, yanking the belt out of the loops on his trousers. He flexed it, snapped it against his palm, as if testing it.

'It was a condition of the damn trust fund your slut of a mother left you.' He was talking, his voice tight with bitterness, but so calm, almost conversational, unlike the wild light in his eyes.

Katie was right. He had gone mad.

'I'm calling the police.' Katie's muffled shouts came through the door. 'Hang on, Megan. I'll get help.'

She heard Katie's running footsteps retreat into silence.

Run, Katie, run. Don't come back.

Her mind screamed as her father ripped away the wrap she had clutched in one hand, then wheeled his arm back. She rolled onto her front, so as not to take the blow on her face.

Pain sliced across her back, the leather biting into her shoulder. She raised her hands, trying to protect her head and the belt cut into the skin of her arm.

'Please, stop.' The plea burst free of the blockage in her throat.

'You deserve this, Lexy,' he screamed her mother's name. 'You did this to me.'

Megan curled into a ball, trying to escape the barrage

of blows. His grunts of exertion, the brutal slap of leather against skin, the scent of lemon polish and blood swirled around her, retreating into darkness, nothingness.

Dario's face appeared, the memory sultry and vivid.

What do you do to me?

The jagged pain in her heart was the last thing to fade as she fell down, down—away from the agony, and the shouts of her mother's name over and over again—into a safe place where no one could find her. Unless she wanted them to.

CHAPTER SIX

'COULD YOU INFORM Miss Megan Whittaker I'm here to see her?' Dario announced to the officious-looking building receptionist.

He didn't like the way Megan had run out on him. He needed to speak with her again. She hadn't done any of the things he had expected of her. He'd been prepared for temper, recriminations, even a guilt trip for deliberately misleading her. He had been ready for all those things and had had all the arguments on hand to explain to her, sensibly and dispassionately, why she was wrong to have read too much into their liaison.

But she hadn't done any of those things. And he couldn't get the picture of her, looking devastated and furious, not with him, but with herself, out of his head. It was foolish of him to feel guilty. He really had nothing to feel bad about. But still he couldn't shake the feeling that he owed her at least a visit.

The memory of her sobs of fulfilment, her sighs of pleasure, her body so sweet and trusting nestled in his arms all through the night, couldn't quite allow him to leave it the way it had ended.

He didn't have to explain himself. They were adults, consenting adults, and everything they'd done together during the night had been mutually pleasurable. But still he felt responsible.

'I'm sorry, sir, there's no answer from the apartment.' The receptionist frowned, the officiousness dropping away to reveal concern. 'Which is odd, because I saw Miss Whittaker go up there ten minutes ago and I know Mr Whittaker and Katie are there, too.'

'Try it again,' he said, the back of his neck prickling.

Something wasn't right. The lift pinged and out of it flew a girl dressed in skinny jeans and a scanty top that left her belly bare. 'De Rossi!' she yelled, racing down the steps leading to the lift and coming to a shuddering halt in front of him. 'You have to rescue her! He's going to kill her, and it's all your fault!'

She grabbed a fistful of his sweater, the fear in her eyes, deep green eyes so like Megan's, searing him to his soul.

'Who are you?' he demanded as he marched towards the lift. But he had already guessed. The prickles became a swarm.

'What's wrong, Katie?' the receptionist shouted out, jettisoning the formality as she confirmed that the frantic girl was Megan's younger sister.

Dario broke into a run, stabbing the lift button ahead of the girl, who shouted to the receptionist, 'Call the police, Marcie. And an ambulance.'

'Which floor?' Dario demanded as they entered the lift together. Cold hard dread gripped his insides—as the memory of another time, another place, assaulted his senses.

Megan's sister punched the button herself. And kept stabbing it as the doors closed, tears streaking down her face now.

'Hurry up, hurry up,' she said in a broken mantra.

'Stop it.' He gripped her shoulders as the lift travelled

up to the tenth floor, her fear forcing him to push the flood of memory and his own terror back.

She collapsed against him, her whole body shaking, and wrapped her arms around his waist. Burying her head against his chest. 'Thank God, you're here. I couldn't get the phone to work in the apartment.'

He rested his palms on her thin shoulders, drew her away, her blind faith in him almost as disturbing as his own irrational fear. 'When we get there, you need to show me where they are.'

'He's locked the door. I couldn't get in.'

The lift finally arrived at the floor. She charged out ahead of him, leading the way to an open apartment door. He heard the sounds first, the rhythmic thuds. He raced down the hallway, kicking open the door the girl indicated at the end with all his might.

The wood shattered and the door flew inward. The explosion of sound startled the man inside, his fist raised, a belt wrapped around it.

Whittaker.

But then Dario saw the woman curled in a foetal position at Lloyd Whittaker's feet. And his mind stalled, the horror gripping his torso so huge and all-consuming he couldn't breathe, couldn't hear anything but the terrified screams in his own head.

'Wake up, Mummy. Please wake up, Mummy.'

'Megan!' The scream from behind him shocked him out of his inertia. The fear was replaced by a feral rage that obliterated everything it its path. Until he couldn't see Lloyd Whittaker any more, or the young woman he'd held in his arms all through the night. All he could see was the man he had fought so many times in his nightmares.

His fist connected with Whittaker's jaw and pain ricocheted up his arm. Whittaker flew backwards and crumpled into a heap, the one punch sending him sprawling into an already broken table, which shattered beneath his weight.

Dario wanted to follow him down, to keep on pounding until the man's face was nothing more than a bloody pulp, but the small mewling cry, like a wild animal caught in a trap, stopped the rage in its tracks.

He watched Katie crouch beside her sister. Megan's beautiful gown, the one he'd eased off her body last night, was torn, the red welts of Whittaker's belt scoring the delicate skin of her shoulders and back.

'She's hurt.' Katie's cries pierced the fog in his brain, dulling the choking fear, the incandescent rage. 'He hurt her. I hate him.'

The fury finally dissolved into a mist—the surge of adrenaline retreating to leave Dario feeling hollow and shaky. He knelt on Megan's other side and gathered her into his arms, determined to concentrate on the task at hand.

They had to get Megan downstairs, to an ambulance. She needed medical care.

Her fragile body curled into his chest as trusting as a child, the bodice of her dress drooping to reveal the dark blue lace that had captivated him the night before.

Ave, o Maria...

He prayed to the virgin mother, the prayer that had been drilled into him as a child by his own mother as he carried Megan's unresisting body through the wreckage of the apartment.

This is not your fault. You are not responsible for the behaviour of a madman.

He kept repeating the words in his mind, his throat dry, his knuckles raw, his arms trembling as he used every ounce of his strength to keep the dark thoughts under control.

As he held her in the lift—Katie stroking her hair and begging her to be okay—Megan shifted in his arms.

He thanked God and all the saints.

'*Cara*, can you hear me?' he asked, gently.

Her eyelids fluttered open, the vicious mark reddening on her cheek making the rage and pain gallop back into his throat.

'*Stai bene, piccola?*' he said, and willed her to be all right.

Please let her be okay.

'*Grazie.*' Her bruised lips tipped into a shy smile— guileless and innocent. She winced, as her eyes closed again.

And the crippling guilt he had been holding so carefully at bay stabbed him right through the heart.

CHAPTER SEVEN

'WE'VE PUT HER into an induced coma, Mr De Rossi. The CT scan was inconclusive and we want to be certain there is no swelling on the brain from the head injury she sustained during the assault.'

Head injury?

The doctor's words whipped at Dario's conscience.

He hated hospitals—the chemical aroma of cleaning fluids and air freshener almost as disturbing as the feeling of powerlessness. He'd been waiting for nearly twenty minutes to see the doctor, his self-control on a knife-edge for a great deal longer—ever since the paramedics had whisked Megan away from him in the foyer three days ago.

After watching Whittaker being treated by paramedics and then taken away in handcuffs, he'd spent hours dealing with his team of lawyers and the police to ensure any assault charges against him would be dropped. He'd then spent further hours being questioned as a witness to Whittaker's assault on his daughter. And after that he had been forced to give a press conference, the media swarming around the hint of a juicy story like flies on a rotting carcass. There had already been a barrage of reports on the Internet, and photographs of him and Megan dancing at the Westchester and their subsequent departure. All of which had fuelled speculation about how Megan had ended up being rushed to hospital the next morning, and how her father had ended up in handcuffs.

As soon as the press conference was over, Dario's first instinct had been to rush to Megan's bedside at the exclusive private hospital in Murray Hill where he'd insisted she be transferred to avoid the press hordes. But he'd forced himself not to give in to that knee-jerk reaction.

Going to see Megan in the hospital would only increase the press speculation about them, he'd reasoned. He and Megan were not a couple, they were never meant to be anything more than a one-night stand—and, despite the horror of her father's attack and his own cursory involvement in it, he was not responsible for her.

But after he had been waiting three torturous days for news of Megan's recovery, Dario's ability to be patient and circumspect about the situation was at an end.

He wanted to know what the hell was going on, because the reports he'd been getting had been inconclusive, contradictory and wholly unsatisfactory. She should be awake and lucid by now, surely?

Unfortunately, the decision to go to the hospital and see for himself how she was had not helped calm his temper in the slightest—because he'd been thwarted by a brick wall of white coats and medical jargon as soon as he'd arrived and now the good Dr Hernandez, all five feet nothing of her, was the last straw.

'I wish to see her,' he reiterated.

The truth was, he *had* to see her, to be sure she was okay. The faraway look in her eyes, that bruised cheek and bloodied lip, the welts left by her father's belt on her shoulder blades had been tormenting him for days. He needed to touch her, feel her skin warm beneath his fingers, before he would be able to breathe again.

'Her sister is her only authorised visitor, Mr De Rossi.'

'Is Katie with her now?' he asked.

'No, I insisted she went home to rest.'

'Then Megan's alone?' He didn't want her to be alone. What if she woke and no one was there? Wouldn't she be scared after everything she'd been through?

'Miss Whittaker is still unconscious and will remain so, until we're ready to bring her out of the induced coma later today.' The doctor continued dispassionately, 'But when that happens I am only going to authorise close family to visit her.'

And of course she had no other family than Katie, and her bastard of a father. Every protective instinct Dario possessed, instincts he'd never even realised he had, rose up inside him. They had been as close as any two people could get four nights ago, but he could see that wasn't going to wash with Dr Hernandez.

'I am paying for her treatment. I insist on seeing her.'

Maybe it was irrational, the fear that had gripped him ever since he'd stormed into her apartment building to find her being brutalised by her father, but he couldn't wait to see her any longer.

Dr Hernandez drew herself up to her full height, which did not reach his chin, and levelled a sanguine look at him. She didn't look intimidated in the slightest.

'This isn't about what *you* want, Mr De Rossi. It's about what's best for my patient.'

'And leaving her alone is best for her?' he demanded, his frustration increasing. This woman hadn't seen her curled on the floor like a terrified child.

'That doesn't alter the fact that you're not related to her, Mr De Rossi, and I can't authorise a—'

'We're engaged,' he said, grasping at the only connection he could think of to give him the access he needed. 'And I'm not leaving until I see her. Does that alter things?'

The doctor's features softened and she gave a weary sigh. 'Okay, Mr De Rossi, you can see her when she wakes up. But that could be a while.'

'I'll wait.'

She tucked her hands into the pockets of her white coat, the sympathetic look annoying him more. 'Why don't you go home first and get some rest? You look exhausted.'

Of course he was exhausted; he hadn't slept for three damn days. 'I'm not leaving.'

'It could be several hours before your fiancée wakes up.'

The quaint, romantic term gave him a jolt, but he ignored it. Seeing Megan was the only way to make the anxiety that had been lodged in the pit of his stomach ever since the attack go away. 'And I intend to be here when that happens.' On that point, he refused to budge.

If he returned to his penthouse, the memories of that night would be waiting for him. Memories he couldn't seem to shake. The sweet sighs of her release, the hours spent touching and tempting her. And worse still, if he closed his eyes, the nightmares would chase him. He would see her bruised and battered body, feel her dead weight in his arms as he carried her into the lift, trying not to hurt her more.

'Then sit down before you fall down,' the doctor said, not unkindly, indicating one of the waiting area's leather armchairs. The pity in the woman's warm brown eyes added discomfort to his frustration—and the dazed feeling that had started to descend without warning.

'I'm not going to fall down,' he said, locking his knees, just to be sure.

'Good, because I have no intention of catching you,' the doctor returned. Gripping his elbow, she led him to the armchair she had indicated. 'What Miss Whittaker needs now most of all is rest,' she added, her voice floating somewhere over his head and not quite coming into complete focus any more. 'She's suffered a terrible trauma.'

'I understand that,' he said, his knees giving way as the adrenaline that had been charging through his veins for days finally deserted him. 'Which is why I intend to stay.'

'I suppose it can't do any harm to have her loved ones close by.'

Her loved ones?

The doctor's softly spoken words made no sense.

But as she left the room Dario sank his head into his hands. He raked his fingers through his hair and gripped his head to stop it dropping off his shoulders. He didn't have time to worry about the doctor's misconceptions. He'd said what he had to say to give him the access he needed.

He had to make sure Megan was okay. And that Whittaker paid for his crimes. Then he would be able to forget about the attack—and get a decent night's sleep again.

His smartphone buzzed and he fished it out of his pocket. He scrolled through the list of missed calls and texts. His gaze snagged on Jared Caine's text.

Saw the news. Nice work knocking that creep unconscious, buddy. Here if you need me.

The simple, succinct message made his chest tighten—which had to be the exhaustion.

He and Jared were friends. They went way back. Ten years back to be exact, to a dark rainy night in the West Village—when Dario had been a twenty-year-old Italian upstart with a fledgling investment corporation making a name for itself on Wall Street and Jared had been a fifteen-year-old street punk who'd made the mistake of trying to pick another former street punk's pocket.

Dario had taken Jared under his wing after that night because the boy's cynicism and street smarts, his thirst for something better in life and his too-old eyes, had reminded Dario of himself.

But somewhere in the last decade, as Jared had forged his own path, shearing off all but a few of his rough edges, to become a smart, erudite and ambitious security advisor with a growing portfolio, Dario had come to rely on the younger man's friendship and loyalty.

And right now he could use Jared's professional help, because his buddy owned and operated one of the best, and certainly the hungriest, private security and investigative firms in the city.

Dario keyed in a quick text, requesting a meeting soon to discuss Whittaker's case. Not that Dario didn't trust New York's Finest, but the NYPD didn't have the resources of De Rossi Corp. Dario wanted Megan's father prosecuted to the full extent of the law.

He had seen the look in Whittaker's eyes when he'd punched him. He knew exactly what that wild glassy sheen indicated. And if the fifty-something CEO had a substance-abuse problem he had managed to keep secret, there would no doubt be other stuff they could use to crucify him.

Jared's reply came back.

I'll get working on it. Then we can arrange a meet at my place. More private.

The tightness in Dario's chest eased.

He laid his head back against the armchair, his galloping pulse slowing to a canter, but blinked to keep the foggy feeling at bay.

No sleep yet, not until he'd seen Megan. And assured himself once and for all she was okay.

Because only then would he be able to get the picture of her cowering at Whittaker's feet, beaten and brutalised, out of his head.

CHAPTER EIGHT

SHE COULD HEAR VOICES.

The first was her sister's.

'Meggy, please come back, you have to wake up now.'
She could hear the panic and fear in Katie's voice. But she
didn't want to come back just yet. Couldn't she stay here?

But then she heard another voice, much lower and more
assured, which didn't plead, it insisted.

'Open your eyes for me, *cara*.'

She frowned. She wanted to be a little bit annoyed. Why
did she have to come back? Staying where she was felt so
much easier. But that voice, it was so compelling. It made
her feel important. Significant. Special. It sounded so sure.
And so safe. And so deliciously seductive.

The tingling sensation in her fingers became something
more. A ripple of sensation. Warmth spread over her hand
and her eyelids fluttered open.

Dario?

Heat flushed through her at the memory of that seductive mouth on hers. But why did he look so different from
the last time she'd seen him, in his penthouse apartment,
after they'd made love?

His hair had been dishevelled then too, but it looked a
mess now. His jaw was covered in dark stubble and his

eyes… He hadn't had those bruised smudges under his eyes, had he?

'*Ciao*, Megan. *Come va?*' The lyrical Italian washed over her. But then his sensual lips tipped up at the edges as he translated. 'How are you feeling?'

That smile, she remembered that smile. So sexy. Heat settled in her abdomen and she tried to speak. But all that came out was a husky croak.

He held her hand and pressed it to his lips. The prickle of stubble against her knuckles made her aware of a few other aches and pains. A lot of other aches and pains. Where had they come from? She remembered being sore after their lovemaking, but not this sore.

'Water?' he asked.

She nodded.

Cradling her head, he held a cup to her lips, directing the straw into her mouth. She took a sip, the cool water easing the rawness in her throat. Why was she so thirsty?

'Okay?' he said.

'Yes,' she said, despite all those unexplained aches and pains. 'Where are we? Is this your bedroom?' Had he taken her upstairs? She was sure he had. She could remember the slow glide of his fingers over sensitive flesh, the prickling spray of the water in his power shower, the scent of sandalwood soap that had clung to his skin and hers later, much later, as they lay together on Egyptian cotton sheets. But everything else felt so disjointed. And this didn't feel like his bedroom, the cloying scent of roses and the persistent sound of something beeping confusing her.

'You're in hospital,' he said, placing the cup back on a bedside table.

'I am? Why?' That didn't sound right. What was she doing in a hospital? 'Did I have an accident?'

'You don't remember?' he asked.

'No, I... I remember being with you and...' The heat suffused her skin. Should she tell him? But he looked concerned. She didn't want him to worry. She didn't want him to think for even a second that she hadn't enjoyed herself. It had been a little sore at first. Just as she had suspected, he wasn't a small man...anywhere. But it had been glorious after that. She wanted him to know that. She thought she'd told him this already, but maybe she'd only thought it.

'I remember it was wonderful. You were wonderful. But that's all I can remember.' Had she made a complete muppet of herself? Fallen over in his power shower? Tripped down the stairs leading up to the mezzanine? That would be just like her, to knock herself unconscious after the best sex of her life. The only proper sex of her life.

'What accident did I have?' she asked, when he simply stared at her, his gaze searching her face as if he was looking for something. Something important.

'Meg, you're awake.' Katie's excited voice pierced her aching head before her sister bounced into view beside Dario.

He started to move aside to make room for Katie, who looked overjoyed to see her. But as he went to let go of her hand, Megan's grip tightened.

'No, don't. Don't go.'

She didn't want to let go of him, not yet. She liked having him there. Something dark and scary seemed to be lurking just out of reach, and she didn't want to let it come any closer. With Dario there, holding her hand, she knew it wouldn't be able to. He was such a force of nature. He would never let it hurt her, whatever it was. And he cared about her. She knew he did. Because she could hear his voice in her memory telling her everything would be okay.

He squeezed her hand back. 'What is it, *cara*?'

'Could you stay with me?'

He hesitated for a moment, but then he sat back down, still holding her hand. 'If you want.'

She could see Katie swivelling her head between the two of them, her eyes widening. But she didn't have the energy to care. She had known she would have to tell Katie about Dario, and everything that had happened last night at the Westchester Ball, because it was impossible to keep anything secret from her sister. But she was more than happy to let Katie draw her own conclusions now, because she wasn't exactly sure herself what had happened any more. Except that it had been glorious. And just having Dario look at her like that, as if he would keep her safe no matter what, was enough to make the aches and pains from her mysterious accident fade away.

Along with the dark, scary thing lurking in the shadows.

A short, rotund, middle-aged Hispanic woman with a friendly face and gentle hands appeared and introduced herself as Dr Hernandez.

She checked Megan's pulse, shone a light into her eyes and then spoke to her in a soft, even voice.

She asked Megan all sorts of silly questions, like her age and her name, and Katie's name and their relationship. And where they lived. And what year it was. The doctor asked her about Dario and if she remembered him. Of course she did, she said, as the blush spread up her chest.

Thank goodness the lighting was muted in here. Or this interrogation could become really awkward, especially with Katie sitting there listening to every word.

But then the questions became more confusing.

'Do you remember your relationship to Mr De Rossi?'

She felt Dario's hand clench hers, his jaw stiffening.

'I...' She wasn't sure how to answer that. She didn't want to seem even more gauche, or clueless, than she did already, but at the same time he was here, holding her hand, so maybe he wouldn't mind her mentioning it. 'We're lovers,' she said, deciding that sounded a little less embarrassing than *We shared a night of the hottest sex I've ever had.*

'Do you remember that you're engaged to Mr De Rossi?'

Huh?

'What? Seriously?' Katie said, echoing Megan's confused thoughts. 'You're kidding?'

Her little sister crowded in on her and Dario and the doctor again.

Really? They were engaged? That was, well, surprising. Astonishing even. She couldn't remember the exact details, but hadn't they only met last night?

Dario's grip stayed firm, though, and he didn't jump in to deny it. The look on his face was guarded somehow but intense.

Even though she couldn't remember falling in love with Dario—which was probably a bad thing—being engaged to him, having him fall in love with her, felt like a good thing. Or at least not a bad thing. It made her feel protected, coveted, the way she hadn't felt since she was a little girl and her mother— She cut off that thought.

No, she wasn't going to think about her mother. Because it would take away the happy, floaty buzz, the giddy excitement in her chest that thinking about Dario gave her.

And being with him. Now. For ever. That felt pretty good too. Because as well as him being there to protect her, he could give her lots more of the hot, sexy times that she *could* remember from their night together—their apparently very eventful night together.

Really, it was all good. Except the not remembering part. But that would come back in time. Surely no woman would forget falling in love with Dario De Rossi for long?

'I...' She paused. She didn't want to lie to Dario, but she

didn't want to hurt his feelings either. And if they were en-gaged, she must have agreed to it. 'I think I remember it.'

'Do you remember anything about your father? About what happened?' the doctor said.

Thoughts butted into her head. Not happy, or floaty thoughts, this time, but sharp, discordant, jarring ones. Panic tore at her raw throat, and she began to shake.

The beeping in her ears got louder, more persistent.

'I don't...' She couldn't speak past the blockage in her throat, that dark, scary figure lurking nearby, encroaching on her peripheral vision. 'I don't want to think about that.'

She didn't know why, but she knew thinking about her father would be bad.

'Shh, Megan.' Dario leant over her, still holding her hand; he stroked her hair back from her forehead, the in-tense look pulling her away from the fear. 'It's okay. Look at me, *cara.*' He caught her chin in firm fingers, making her concentrate on him, that turbulent blue gaze forcing the fear back. 'You're okay. Do you understand?'

The words echoed in her heart, folding around her like a soft blanket, keeping her safe.

'Yes, but don't go.' She wanted to go back to sleep, but she couldn't stop shaking, the terror still too close.

'I won't,' he said, his voice so determined she knew he meant it. *'Te lo prometto.'*

I promise you.

'Relax, Megan,' the doctor said. 'I'm going to give you something to help with that.' A warm tingling feeling seeped into her vein, spreading up her arm and enveloping her in a beautiful fog. She floated on it, sinking into the cloud, soothed by the pressure of Dario's hand and his deep com-pelling voice telling her again that everything would be okay.

She held on to his hand, knowing it was true, as long as she didn't let him go.

* * *

'What just happened in there?' Dario could feel his frustration levels rising as he stalked after Dr Hernandez. He and Katie had been double teaming for ten hours, waiting for Megan to come out of her coma. And now this. 'How can she remember nothing of the attack?' he demanded as the doctor stopped at the nurses' station.

He shoved his fists into the pockets of his trousers, the fear on Megan's face still haunting him. How had this happened? He didn't feel less responsible now, he felt more so.

'Your fiancée has suffered a serious emotional and physical trauma, Mr De Rossi,' the doctor said with complete equanimity as she jotted something down on Megan's chart. 'It's quite possible she has blanked some of the events from that day.' The woman's clear brown gaze focused on his face. 'The good news is, she remembers you and your engagement. Your presence calmed her down considerably, which will be useful in the weeks and months ahead as she recovers.'

Months. He couldn't be responsible for her for months. He wasn't even her real fiancé. He knew he should point this out to Hernandez, but the memory of Megan clutching his hand and looking at him with such faith in her eyes made the words clog in his throat. He could not deny the connection now.

Until Megan was well again, and she had her memory back—*all* her memories back—she would be defenceless.

'I can't believe you proposed after one night!' Katie appeared at his elbow. 'That must have been some night.' The girl's scepticism was, of course, entirely justified, but the astonished look spiked his annoyance.

'Your sister is a remarkable woman,' he heard himself say.

'I know she is,' the girl said. 'But I'm surprised you do.'

He could hear the bite of cynicism in her tone. And it occurred to him that, although Katie was the younger sister, she had none of Megan's faith in the inherent goodness of people.

'He certainly never did,' she added.

'I am not your father,' he said, the comparison annoying him more. 'I appreciate your sister.'

'I get that, or I guess you wouldn't have asked her to marry you,' she said, not sounding convinced. 'But you still don't strike me as the sort of guy to fall hopelessly in love in the space of one night.'

She was certainly correct about that.

'Who said anything about love?' he asked, his temper kicking up another notch. He didn't need the fifth degree from a teenager. 'Megan and I are well matched. And she understands this engagement is one of convenience.' Or she would, as soon as she regained her memory and he could break it off.

But until then he would have to maintain this fiction. He could not leave Megan so vulnerable.

There was the police investigation to consider, the subsequent trial and, on top of all that, the press, who had been camped outside the hospital for days. How could he leave the young woman who had gripped his hand with such fear in her eyes to fend off all that alone?

Maybe he had not wanted the job, but who else was there? A nineteen-year-old art student was the only other candidate.

'I don't believe you.' Katie interrupted his thoughts. 'Underneath all her pragmatism and business savvy, Megan's a romantic. If she agreed to marry you, she must think she's in love with you.'

'She needs someone to protect her. I have the money and resources to do that until she is well. She understands that.'

Megan had struck him from the first as a pragmatic young woman, astute and intelligent. Maybe she had a blind spot where her father was concerned, but however fragile her mental state she must have made a choice to agree with Dario's deception in there. A subconscious choice maybe, but a choice nonetheless. However faulty her memory, she could hardly have remembered a proposal that did not occur.

He flexed his fingers, recalling the feel of her hand, so small, clasping his, as she begged him not to leave her. And another memory swirled in his consciousness, making his lungs squeeze in his chest.

Please save me, Dario.

He took a steadying breath, forcing himself to shake off the debilitating images from his past.

He had to concentrate on the present. The way forward was simple. He could not abandon Megan until she was well. But their situation had nothing to do with love. He and Megan understood that, even if Megan's sister did not.

'I'm sorry. I don't know why I'm having a go at you,' Katie said, as the fluorescent lighting caught the bluish smudges under her eyes. The girl was exhausted. She'd been keeping this vigil a great deal longer than he had, he realised. She dragged her hand through her hair. 'I'm the one who let her walk into that room.'

'It is pointless to blame yourself.' He gave the girl an awkward pat on the shoulder. Then shoved his hand back into his pocket.

Consoling distraught teenagers was as far out of his comfort zone as pretending to be someone's fiancé.

'You should go home, get some sleep,' he said. 'I will stay and ascertain what is to be done next and contact you in the morning.'

Katie looked at him, then back at the door to Megan's

room, clearly torn. He was struck by the closeness of the bond between the two sisters, despite their personality differences. He would do well to remember that.

'There is little more either one of us can do now,' he added. He might not want this responsibility, but he was not about to shirk it—until he had come up with a coherent plan for Megan's recovery.

'Okay, I guess she trusts you,' she said. 'And you did save her life.'

The words should have made him feel more burdened, but, oddly, instead he felt strangely relieved as he watched Megan's sister leave. As long as he had complete control of the situation, he would be in a position to resolve it, to everyone's satisfaction.

'Dr Hernandez...' He turned to the doctor, who had been scribbling on Megan's chart while he and Katie talked. 'Can you tell me when Megan's memory will return?' The first order of business was to discover the depths of the problem.

'I'm afraid not. Medicine is not an exact science, Mr De Rossi. We'll run some more tests, have her speak to a psychiatrist to ascertain as much as we can about the amnesia. If there is no neurological cause, though, I would expect Megan to remember the events in more detail once she is emotionally strong enough to deal with them.'

'Get her whatever she needs. Money is no object,' he said, prepared to pay whatever it took.

'Either way, she should be ready to leave the hospital in a week or so,' the doctor continued. 'Her physical injuries are healing well. And she'll be able to get the rest and recuperation she needs much better in a home environment.'

He swore under his breath. The doctor was right, of course, but what home environment did she have? She could not return to her old apartment, which had been repossessed as soon as Whittaker had been arrested and the state of his finances revealed. And anyway, it was the site of the attack. Katie was now staying with the girls' old housekeeper in Brooklyn, having refused his offer of financial aid. But Megan couldn't stay there—it was too small and would not protect her from press attention. He and Katie had been running the gauntlet of photographers and reporters while taking it in turns to visit the hospital. Megan would need somewhere far away from the media spotlight.

'By the way, Mr De Rossi,' the doctor cut into his thoughts as she finished writing on Megan's chart and handed it back to the nurse. 'You mentioned the possibility of Megan being pregnant. We ran the test as requested and it came back negative.'

Thank goodness.

Dario's lungs released, the relief making him light-headed. He'd requested the test a few hours before, his mind finally functioning well enough to realise that Megan might not have had time to take the necessary precautions before her father attacked her. Maybe she hadn't even needed the emergency contraception. Either way, this at least was good news.

But before he could suck in another calming breath the doctor added, 'Of course, there's always a slight chance of a false negative this soon after possible conception, but it's unlikely.'

A false negative? What on earth did that even mean?

CHAPTER NINE

'Hey, man, wasn't expecting you tonight.' Jared yawned, then squinted at Dario out of sleep-deprived eyes.

Dario glanced at his watch. And winced. Two a.m. 'Sorry, I did not realise the time.'

'No problem. Come on in.' His friend wearing only a pair of sweat pants pushed open the heavy metal door to his loft apartment. 'Want a beer? You look like you could use one,' Jared added, padding into the apartment ahead of Dario.

He probably shouldn't have come over at this hour. But for the first time in his life, he needed help and complete confidentiality, and Jared was the only person he trusted that much.

The guy was the closest thing Dario had to family. Or what Dario figured a brother would be like. Someone who would help you out in a jam, no questions asked, but didn't pry into your private life. And that was what he needed right now. Because he'd been roaming Murray Hill like a zombie for a couple of hours, ever since he'd left Megan at the hospital, trying to figure out a workable solution.

'You look terrible,' Jared said as he cracked open a beer and handed it to Dario.

'It's been a long four days.' Dario took the beer and

chugged a mouthful of the yeasty lager. Had it really been only four days since he'd had Megan in his arms? Soft and sweet and sobbing for release?

Stop right there, amico.

He took another long pull of lager, struggling to ignore the inevitable swell of heat.

He needed to stop torturing himself with thoughts of that night, because he wasn't going to have Megan in his arms again. The only way to square the subterfuge with his conscience was if he didn't sleep with her. She was fragile, emotionally as well as physically, so until she was fully recovered he couldn't even consider making love to her. He swallowed. Sleeping with her *again*, he corrected.

And not even then.

She was trusting and innocent and this situation had become far too complex already. He preferred women who knew the score, so that he could keep his sex life simple and his affairs shallow and short-lived. Megan had got under his skin to an extent that no other woman ever had, and circumstances had done the rest. All of which made him supremely uncomfortable.

'Yeah, I gathered that from the press reports on late-night TV.' Jared took a swig of his own beer and leaned against the counter top, the searching look only winding the knot in Dario's gut tighter. 'How's the new fiancée doing?'

The beer hit Dario's tonsils and he jerked forward in mid-sip.

Jared gave him a hearty thump on the back.

'The press got hold of that already?' Dario managed at last, his voice a hoarse whisper. Someone at the hospital must have leaked the information—which was all the more reason to get Megan out of there, out of the city, as soon as she was well enough to travel.

'So it's true?' Jared said dispassionately, but the relaxed pose was history. 'You guys are engaged?'

'Yes,' Dario said, his tired brain starting to knot along with his gut. He needed to get some sleep. He'd been running on adrenaline for hours; it was dulling his thought processes.

'You want to tell me how that happened?' Jared said.

'It's complicated,' Dario said.

'I gathered that.' Jared picked his beer back up off the counter, and used it to point at the long leather couches that made up the apartment's seating area. 'Let's take a load off.' He led the way across the large open-plan living space. Dario followed.

Jared settled on one of the luxury couches. The leather creaked as he propped his bare feet on the coffee table. And waited for Dario to speak. The younger man's pragmatic presence helped to settle the nerves dancing in Dario's stomach as he stared out at the night time NoHo cityscape visible through the wall of glass that had replaced the old loft's loading bay doors. But the compulsion to explain the situation to Jared still surprised him.

He never talked about his personal life to anyone. He'd been a self-contained unit since he was eight years old. Had forced himself to be. Leaning on other people, relying on them, just made you weak. But his personal life hadn't been this complicated ever. And he hadn't been blindsided like this, by events beyond his control, since he was that eight-year-old boy. And he didn't like it, because that was a feeling he'd promised himself he'd never have again.

'Megan doesn't remember what happened with her father,' he said, fixing his gaze on the blinking light of a plane above the dark shapes of the city's skyline. 'They ran some tests, got the opinion of the top psychologist in NYC and a head trauma specialist from Baltimore who's supposed to be the best in her field.' He'd had the woman flown in especially, to give a second opinion. 'They don't think the memory loss is to do with her head injury, which was minor.' The relief he felt at that piece of information was still palpable. 'More likely it's to do with the emotional trauma. A form of PTSD. A man Megan loved and trusted turned on her like an animal, so she's blacked it out.'

He drew his thumbnail through the label on the beer bottle, watched it tear into jagged pieces.

There was only one thing to do. It didn't matter if it would complicate his life for a while. Seeing Megan's anguish when Hernandez had mentioned her father, her vibrant hair rioting around that alabaster face and her deep emerald eyes wild with terror, had pulled at something deep inside him that he could not deny. She'd gripped his fingers as if he were the only solid object in the midst of a hurricane. She needed him and he couldn't simply desert her.

'I see what you mean by complicated,' Jared said.

Dario looked up from his contemplation of the beer bottle, remembering his friend was there.

'She needs rest and as little stress as possible, according to the doctors,' he said. 'The press furore is only going to get more insane when Whittaker is charged. I think it is best if I take her out of the country. If she is my fiancée I am in a position to make those arrangements, to keep her safe and protected until she recovers.'

Jared sent him a level stare. 'If? So this isn't a real engagement. Does she know that?'

'Maybe, maybe not. But she has accepted it without question, so it hardly matters,' Dario said. Maybe it was complicated and confused, but it all made perfect sense if you looked at it rationally.

Megan was in no position to make these decisions for

herself. And even if she hadn't been assaulted, Dario didn't trust her to make sensible decisions about her own safety. She was far too trusting at the best of times, and these were not the best of times.

'Okay.' Jared leant forward, resting his elbows on his knees—accepting Dario's reasoning.

But then, he hadn't expected Jared to question him.

His friend was even more cynical about relationships than he was. To the best of Dario's knowledge, Jared had never kept a lover for more than one night. Manhattan high society was strewn with the bruised hearts of women Jared had cast off before they could mean anything to him. He suspected that emotional isolation had something to do with Jared's childhood, or rather the lack of it, but he'd never asked; any more than he had asked about the cigarette burns on his friend's forearms, which were barely visible now, or the other scars that had faded in the years since he'd offered Jared a bed for the night in his apartment, before referring the homeless boy to the proper authorities. Because Jared's past was none of his business.

'I was going to work up a report for you on the case,' Jared said. 'You want the high points, before we discuss the particulars of how you're going to get your new fiancée out of the country?' Jared asked, the efficient, down-to-earth approach reassuring.

Dario nodded. 'Yeah.'

'Just as you suspected, Megan's father was high as a kite when he attacked her,' Jared began. 'According to my contact in the NYPD he's had a major cocaine habit for years. His girlfriend Annalise Maybury—now his ex-girlfriend—told the detectives as much under questioning. And there's something else, something I found out on my own after doing some digging,' Jared continued, the cynicism in his voice even sharper than usual. 'They're not his daughters.'

'What?'

'Megan and her sister, they're not his biological kids. He's known for years—got them paternity tested without their knowledge when they were children after the mom ran off with one of her lovers. Whittaker only kept them around, pretended he was still their old man, because he was busy mooching off the trust fund their mom left them. Which is all gone now, just in case you were wondering.'

'Bastardo!' Dario's anger curled around his heart, turning from red-hot rage to ice-cold fury.

He'd known Whittaker was a poor excuse for a CEO, and an even worse excuse for a father. But he'd never suspected the cocaine use, or the violence, so adding embezzlement and exploitation to that didn't seem like much of a stretch. But how much more vulnerable did this make Megan?

Megan and her sister had no money. And the press were bound to find out the truth about her parentage and splash it all over the papers and the Internet to feed the public's insatiable hunger for scandal. He'd seen the paparazzi shots of her as a teenager at her mother's funeral. She'd been scared and alone but also fiercely protective of her little sister.

When the press got hold of this story, it would be worse.

The memory of the welts on Megan's shoulder blades leapt out from the recesses of his tired mind, only to blur into a bloodier, more terrifying image. The sickening thuds of fists hitting flesh, the high-pitched sound of his mother's screams and the scent of stale cigarette smoke and cheap chianti assaulted him.

'Hey, man, are you okay?'

Jared's question drew him back to the present.

He blocked the image out, the way he had learned to over the years. But the return of the old nightmare left him shaken. His hand trembled as he took a last swig of his beer. Something he did not need Jared, or anyone else, to see.

'Yes.' He placed the bottle on the table between them. 'Can you give this information to the police?'

'Sure. I'll send them a copy of my report. Anything else you need on this?'

'I need your help to get Megan and her sister, Katie, out of the country without alerting the press as soon as Megan is well enough to travel. And me as well.' His mind was made up. There was no other solution. And with Katie there as a chaperone, he ought to find it easier to keep his mind out of the gutter.

Megan's memory would return soon, he had to believe that, because he intended to do everything in his power to ensure she felt safe and secure and well rested enough for that to happen—which included him being by her side. And when her memory did return, he wanted to be there. Just in case there were other complications.

The possibility of a pregnancy was small, according to Hernandez, after she had dropped her bombshell about a false negative on the test, and he wasn't going to worry about it overmuch. But he also wasn't taking any chances.

'I'd advise against taking the kid sister with you,' Jared said, interrupting Dario's thoughts.

'What? Why?'

'She might need to be available for Whittaker's arraignment,' he said.

'But surely our sworn statements are enough until the case comes to trial?' Dario asked. Witnesses weren't usually called for an arraignment.

'True enough, but I wouldn't risk it. Whittaker might

be low on funds, but he's no fool. He's managed to beg, borrow and steal enough for a top-flight legal team. He's saying you inflicted the wounds on your lover in a jealous rage. Neither the police nor the prosecutor's office are buying that. But if Megan's lost her memory, Katie is the only reliable witness to the actual assault. You can make a good case for taking Megan out of the country to recuperate until the trial, and if you're her fiancé it makes sense for you to go with her. But you spirit Katie out of the country too, just before the guy's arraigned, and I guarantee you Whittaker's defence team will try and use it. The kid sister stays, or you're taking a risk of this case not even getting to trial.'

Dario swore, his head starting to pound. 'Okay, Katie stays. I'll tell her tomorrow. She won't like it.' And neither did he. Being alone with her big sister wasn't going to make resisting Megan any easier. 'We cannot risk having Whittaker weasel out of paying for what he has done. Katie will understand that.' Because he suspected, unlike Megan, Katie had never had any delusions about their father. Or rather, the man who had pretended to be their father. 'Can I ask you another favour in that case?'

'Fire away,' Jared said.

'Can you protect Katie from the press once we're gone?' The girl was brave and bold, but she was also reckless and unpredictable and young.

Jared nodded. 'Consider it done.'

'I should warn you though,' Dario said, recalling his run-in with Katie earlier that day. 'She may not be co-operative. She is not as trusting or as amenable as Megan.'

'I think I can handle a hot-headed kid,' Jared said. 'I happen to be a professional.'

Dario's lips lifted in what felt like his first smile in days at the wry tone. 'Thanks.'

Downing the rest of the beer, Dario got up from the couch and shook Jared's hand. 'I'll speak to Katie tomorrow.' Not a conversation he was looking forward to. 'In the meantime, can you liaise with the police and the prosecutor's office to let them know what's going on? Then work up a plan to get us out of the country undetected.'

'Got it,' Jared said as he walked Dario to the door of the apartment. 'Where are you guys headed?'

'Isadora.'

He'd bought the island off the coast of Sicily five years ago, when the company had made its first billion in turnover. And had finished renovating the five-bedroom villa on it over a year ago. He'd already had a visit scheduled to the island once the Whittaker takeover was finalised, to check up on the many investments he was making in the island's infrastructure. And get some much-needed R and R.

'Nice,' Jared said, before bidding him goodbye.

Dario wasn't so sure. When he was not so tired, he might appreciate the irony that his visit to the island was now likely to be the opposite of relaxing.

CHAPTER TEN

THE HELICOPTER TOUCHED down on a helipad hewn out of volcanic rock. Megan breathed in the scent of sea salt and citrus, her eyes expanding with wonder at the heart-stopping view as the blades whirled to a stop.

A path meandered through terraces of lemon groves to a white sand beach. Dario's villa stood on the clifftop, its elegant stone walls adorned by grapevines and wisteria, the dark wood shutters open to let in the sunny spring morning, which was a good ten degrees hotter than Manhattan.

Dario leaned over her to undo her seat belt. 'You're awake? Are you feeling well?' he asked, solicitous and concerned.

'Yes, I woke up a while ago,' she said. She'd noticed him sitting beside her when she opened her eyes, busy keying in data on his smartphone, apparently uninterested in the staggering view as the helicopter swooped over the Mediterranean and then hugged the coastline of the stunningly picturesque island.

She hadn't wanted to disturb him, so she'd gazed out of the window and absorbed the breathtaking vistas while trying to get her careering pulse and erratic heartbeat under control.

It all seemed like a strange and wonderful dream. So strange and wonderful, she didn't know what to make of it.

Everything had happened so fast. Ever since Dario had told her they were engaged in the hospital three days ago. And yet at the same time, in a sort of delayed motion, each new and astonishing experience leaving her struggling to make sense of them. Frankly, it was all a bit too wonderful. As if she couldn't quite believe it was real.

She had led a privileged life, having attended private schools and lived in well-appointed homes in London and New York. She considered herself to be fairly cosmopolitan, with a smattering of Italian and French, having spent her childhood and adolescence living on two continents.

But nothing could have prepared her for the opulence and luxury of the world Dario lived in.

They'd been whisked from the hospital to JFK in a fleet of limousines in the middle of the night, then transported across the Atlantic on a private jet. The cordon bleu meal served on bone china crockery with sterling silver cutlery, followed by a night—alone—on a king-size bed in the sleek aircraft. The helicopter ride had been yet another new experience—as exhilarating as it was unsettling. But by far the most daunting thing had been having Dario by her side during every waking hour.

He'd been so careful with her, as if she were made of spun glass and might break at any minute. But while his care had made her feel cherished and safe in the hospital, now it was starting to feel stifling. He was such a commanding man, both physically and professionally. And she knew she wasn't yet one hundred per cent, because she still couldn't remember a thing about their engagement, or her accident. She didn't want to seem ungrateful, but she couldn't help wondering how Dario had managed to fall in love with her, when he obviously thought she was a bit pathetic.

She also couldn't quite fathom how she'd agreed to

marry him, when he made the air seize in her chest and her stomach do backflips every time he looked at her with those piercing blue eyes.

How were they going to have any kind of married life together, when his presence by her side made it hard for her to breathe?

Then again, at least she wasn't the only one who found him a bit intimidating.

He never raised his voice, but everyone they came into contact with on their journey—his PA, the drivers, the pilots, even the passport authorities—did his bidding without question. Everyone except his friend Jared, who'd talked to Dario like an equal when he had come to tell Megan he would be keeping an eye on Katie while they were away, on Dario's instructions.

She had wondered why Katie would need anyone keeping an eye on her, and debated warning him that Katie wasn't the easiest person to handle. But, in the end, she'd decided not to say anything. After all, Katie was more than capable of speaking for herself, and it had been so thoughtful of Dario to worry about her sister's welfare.

A car and driver arrived at the heliport as Dario helped her down from the cockpit. His firm fingers on her arm made her pulse jump and jive. She concentrated on the spurt of adrenaline as he left her side to go to talk to the pilot.

Gift horse—mouth? Hello? Stop looking! Why can't you just enjoy the thrill? You're tired and a little overwhelmed, that's all. A staggeringly gorgeous man is in love with you. This is not something to have a panic attack about.

A team of staff members arrived in a fleet of SUVs to unload a series of bags, boxes and trunks from the helicopter's hold. Luggage Megan had never seen before.

'*Cara*, are you ready?' Dario said, returning to lead her to the car.

'Yes, but… I just realised I didn't pack anything for the trip.' She didn't recognise the luggage, so it must be Dario's. 'Do you think I could order some clothes?' There had been some expensive clothes waiting for her on his private jet to change into when she'd arrived from the hospital, which had been wonderful and had made her feel a little teary—her fiancé appeared to think of everything. There had even been a ton of expensive creams, make-up and haircare products for all her toiletry needs, and a designer negligee in the plane's bedroom—although the seductive confection of silk and lace had seemed a little pointless when Dario had worked through the flight on his laptop instead of joining her.

But she couldn't expect the luggage fairy to keep providing her with everything she needed.

Dario had told her they would be staying for at least a fortnight as he had a series of meetings planned with his business contacts on the island. He was a busy man, and she knew she had a demanding job too. Although every time she tried to think about her job, the dark shadow lurking at the edge of her consciousness threatened, so she had decided not to worry about that. But if Dario had brought all this stuff with him, she would need more clothing, too. She didn't want to embarrass him with her paltry wardrobe.

'I've only got the hospital gown, and my negligee and this,' she said, sweeping her hands over the ensemble of slim-fit jeans, a camisole and linen shirt he'd already provided.

She sank her teeth into her bottom lip. Dario's lifestyle was extremely glamorous, way too glamorous for a woman with no luggage. No wonder she felt overwhelmed.

'Stop worrying, *cara*,' Dario said, his thumb glancing over her bottom lip.

She stopped biting it, the goosebumps going haywire at his tiny touch.

'There is nothing you need that isn't already purchased.'

'But I didn't bring...'

'The cases are mostly yours.' He swept his hand to encompass the luggage still being transported by several burly men to the fleet of cars. 'Della, my PA, assured me it was all you would need.'

Megan gaped, feeling like Alice, having just plopped down the rabbit hole.

All she would need? There was enough luggage here to dress the entire catwalk at Paris Fashion Week.

'But I... I'm not sure I can afford it,' she said, desperately trying to scramble out of the rabbit hole, and plant her feet on solid ground. Or solid*ish*.

'Shh... Do not concern yourself with money.' He captured her chin, forcing her gaze away from the never-ending parade of designer suitcases. The slow sexy smile that spread across his handsome face wasn't any less disturbing. 'I can provide what you need while we are here.'

She knew he was just being thoughtful again, but the insistence in his voice brought back the flutter of frustration. 'That's very generous of you, but I prefer to pay my own way.'

In the hospital, he'd told her she was his responsibility, and, while she'd found it comforting then, it was way past time she let him off the hook now. She still had some interesting bruises—her back was covered in them, which made her sure she must have fallen down his stairs. Obviously, he'd taken the whole responsibility thing too far because she'd had her accident in his home—which was touching, but it was getting a bit over the top.

'I certainly don't think you should pay for my clothes. I can do that.' Of course, she wasn't sure she could pay for those clothes, because from the logos on the bags they looked way out of her price range. 'You must let me pay you back.' *Once I've secured a loan.*

Dario's brows furrowed, the offer clearly confusing him. Obviously Giselle hadn't been much of a pay-your-own-way kind of gal. Maybe she didn't have Giselle's supermodel face and figure, but she did have financial integrity. And an unimpeachable work ethic.

Or at least she thought she did.

One of the luggage handlers arrived to tell them everything was ready.

Dario replied in Italian, instructing them to take the luggage to the house and have the housekeeper unpack it in the bedroom.

She got momentarily fixated on the word *bedroom*, his rich, resonant voice making it sound ludicrously seductive.

The thought of what they would be doing together in the bedroom in the coming days, and possibly for two whole weeks, cheered her up considerably.

She couldn't wait to get started. Her body's constant hunger for Dario, the desire to feel his touch again—the one thing about their engagement that was straightforward and uncomplicated. Maybe she wouldn't need to wear all the clothes. Then she could return a few and get a refund.

'Come, we will talk about this on the drive,' he said.

'Okay,' she said, although she couldn't see what else there was to discuss.

But then he put a palm on the small of her back, caressing the base of her spine, to direct her to the car—and she had to bite her lip to hold back the purr.

As the car sped down the track towards his magnificent home on the clifftop, an infinity pool came into view nestled amid trellises of flowering vines as the road climbed towards the house.

'The clothes are a gift, Megan,' he said, in the velvet-over-steel voice she recognised as the one he used when instructing his employees. 'I am a very rich man. I enjoy purchasing things for you. Payment is out of the question. Do you understand?'

'Um…okay?' she said, because she was distracted by that delicious voice, and the thought of all the things they were going to be doing in his *camera* tonight.

The villa was beautiful. But she didn't get much chance to examine the sweep of living and dining rooms on the ground floor, before Dario had directed her to the second floor and a suite of rooms with a terrace that offered an awe-inspiring view of the pool and the terraces of lemon groves that led down to the sea.

The men carrying her luggage trooped in behind them.

But all Megan's attention was on the enormous bed. The four-poster, draped with gauzy muslin curtains, was the room's focal point, both romantic and exciting and a tiny bit intimidating. Her heartbeat throbbed in her throat—and a few other key parts of her anatomy.

'Megan, this is Sofia,' Dario announced and she turned to find a tiny bird of a woman in her fifties with lush chestnut hair standing beside him. 'She is the villa housekeeper and in charge of all the staff; she will take care of your needs. I have instructed her to serve you your meal in your rooms tonight, so that you can rest.'

'*My* rooms?' she asked, confused now. Wasn't this suite of rooms for both of them? Where was Dario planning to sleep? 'But…?' Her cheeks coloured. How could she ask him such an intimate question in front of all these people? 'Won't you be joining me?' she managed at last.

'Not tonight, *piccola*,' he said.

He cupped her face and gave her a proprietorial kiss on the forehead, making her feel like an over-eager puppy. 'You must rest. And I must work.'

He dropped his hands and stepped back so quickly she might almost have imagined the perfunctory peck, but for the prickle of sensation on her cheeks left by the calluses on his palms. '*Buonanotte*, Megan. I will see you tomorrow, at suppertime.'

At suppertime?

He marched out of the room, his back ramrod straight.

What about the rest of the day?

She stood in the centre of the beautiful room, feeling dazed and desperately disappointed.

Sofia chatted away in a halting mix of English and Italian about how overjoyed they all were to have their boss's *fidanzata* in residence, while directing a couple of maids to fold away the dazzling array of designer clothing and making menu suggestions for Megan's evening meal. But as Megan watched Dario, tall and indomitable, disappear down the steps of the terrace, she'd never felt less like a *fidanzata* in her life.

CHAPTER ELEVEN

'*BUONGIORNO,* SOFIA. *DOVE* DARIO?' Megan asked the house-keeper, hoping she'd got her tenses right—and trying not to be embarrassed by the all too familiar enquiry. Because she'd been asking the housekeeper every morning for almost a week where Dario was that day.

'*Buongiorno, signorina.*' Sofia smiled, busy stretching and pulling the fresh pasta dough, as she did every morning. '*Il capo?* He is with the fishermen, today,' she said. 'Tonight we will have *Pesce spada.* How you say that in *Inglese?* Swordfish? Yes?'

Megan nodded as her heart sank to her toes.

The swordfish season had started that morning. She had spotted the traditional long boat with its twenty-five-foot mast from the veranda in her suite of rooms as the sun turned the deep blue sea a ruddy pink.

So Dario had got up at dawn and would no doubt be gone all day. Again. She had hoped today, with no business scheduled that she knew of, he might be able to stay at the villa.

'*Delizioso.*' She did a smacking action with her lips and Sofia laughed.

'Only if the fish smile on us,' the housekeeper said. 'If they do not we have sardine ravioli.'

Megan smiled back, but it felt forced and tight.

She adored Sofia. The woman was friendly and efficient and had been happy to spend the afternoon yesterday teaching Megan how to make fresh tagliatelle, which
had gone a long way in keeping her anxiety at bay. But
she didn't think pasta making was going to cut it today.

She'd been at the villa for nearly a whole week now. And
each day had begun to blend into the next. At first she'd
forced herself to appreciate the chance to rest and heal,
and had tried not to let Dario's absences from the villa—
and indeed her bed each night—upset her.

The villa was in a stunningly beautiful location with
every possible luxury at her fingertips and Sofia, along
with her two young maids, Donella and Isa, were more
than happy to accommodate Megan's every whim. She'd
made herself relax and enjoy the late mornings spent lazing
in bed or sitting on the veranda with strong coffee and a
tray of Sofia's fresh pastries; the light lunches spent loung-
ing by the pool reading the books she'd downloaded from
the Internet; the afternoons spent swimming and exploring the secluded coves, picking wildflowers, and trying
to identify the local fauna. It had all helped to fill up the
empty hours and stop her from obsessing about getting
the chance to talk to Dario. About their engagement. And
about all the things she could not remember about him.

To be fair, the complete lack of any stress had been
welcome at first, as her body healed from her accident.

She also called Katie using Skype each afternoon, but
that had become an exercise in avoiding all Katie's probing questions about how everything was going with Dario.

In the last few days, she had tried to be content seeing
Dario each evening, when they would sit down to the lavish
four-course meal Sofia and her helpers prepared each day.

Last night, as the citronella candles burned, illuminat-
ing his harsh, handsome face, Megan had watched her fi-

ancé devour Sofia's delicious food and finally drummed up the courage to ask him about himself.

But he had directed the conversation away from anything personal, and in the end she was just so pleased to see him, she had decided not to push.

The hunger inside her, though, had been like a dragon, breathing fire into every single erogenous zone, as she'd watched Dario's firm sensual lips consume a mouthful of Sofia's light, tart lemon zabaglione. She thought she'd caught his dark hooded gaze on her cleavage, but it had flicked away again so quickly she wasn't sure if she had imagined it.

Her confusion and desperation had increased as he had escorted her once again to her suite of rooms and bid her goodnight at the door. So much so that she had been unable to hold back the suggestion that he spend the night with her.

She'd waited patiently for him to make the first move. But her patience was at an end now. Instead of taking her up on her offer, though, he'd said nothing at all, his jaw rigid.

So she'd ended up babbling on about how much better she felt now and if she relaxed any more she'd turn into a narcoleptic… A very fat narcoleptic, because Sofia's cooking was to die for.

For a split second she thought she'd seen the flare of desire, burning even hotter than her own, but then he'd politely refused her offer and walked away—leaving her breathless, anxious, and hopelessly frustrated.

And now this.

After waking up feeing tense, confused and even more frustrated this morning, she discovered he'd gone again.

It was too much.

Ordinarily, she did not have a confrontational bone in

her body—that had always been Katie's forte. But after over a week of rest and recuperation at Dario's command she didn't think she could survive another night alone without exploding.

Bidding Sofia good day, she returned to her rooms and rifled through the swimwear she had found among all the other clothing. She picked out a stunning scarlet bikini, which she had shied away from wearing because of the purpling bruises on her hip and back. But the bruises were as good as gone now.

She squeezed herself into the two swatches of red Lycra, dismayed to discover that whomever had bought the clothing had underestimated Megan's bust size a fraction. Either that, or Sofia's pasta blow-outs had added a cup size.

Didn't matter. Dario needed to see the evidence for himself—that she was fully recovered from her accident. It was way past time she demanded more of his time and attention.

She packed her e-reader, some sun lotion and a towel into her beach bag, and headed to the two-tiered pool situated on the terrace below the villa, prepared for a long wait. Dario would have to walk up through the lemon groves from the harbour and past the pool when he got back from his fishing expedition—by which time she would be more than ready to confront him. She hoped.

Dario trudged up the last few stairs through the lemon grove, calculating the hour as close to four o'clock. He would wash the fish smell off, then take the Jeep over to Matteo Caldone's farm, to check on the new irrigation system he'd financed for Matteo's groves of blood oranges. His shoulders ached from reeling in fish for ten straight hours. And he was ready to collapse. But after last night, he was not about to risk seeing Megan any sooner than was absolutely necessary.

After today's back-breaking work, surely tonight he'd be able to sleep without being visited by the erotic visions that had woken him hard and aching every night since they'd arrived.

Walking away from her last night had nearly killed him. Once he'd returned to his own room, he'd had to resort to the sort of self-servicing that he hadn't indulged in for some time.

Unfortunately, it hadn't done much good. He'd woken sweating and swearing, with images of Megan on their one torrid night together turning his hunger into a ravening beast.

The salt air, perfumed by the tart, citrus scent of the lemon grove, filled his lungs. He let it go, the heavy sigh almost as weary as his aching body. Tonight he would sleep and he would not dream of Megan. Those high, full breasts with their pale, pink peaks as she begged for...

He blinked and wiped the layer of sweat off his forehead.

Dio! Basta!

Then he rounded the drystone wall that led to the pool terrace and all the air left his lungs in a rush. Sitting on a sun lounger, her wet hair tied on top of her head in a loose knot, her full breasts barely covered by the world's tiniest bikini, was the star player in every one of those erotic fantasies.

A small voice in the very recesses of his brain was whispering that he should step away, disappear behind the wall and then trek across the fields to approach the villa from the other side, before Megan spotted him standing there like a besotted teenager getting his first glimpse at a nude centrefold.

But he couldn't move, the blood powering down to his groin silencing that small voice while making the rest of his body scream in agony.

Then her head rose and she saw him.

Too late.

'Dario, I've been waiting for you,' she said. Or that was what he thought she said, because it was hard to tell over the sound of the blood plummeting out of his brain to destinations south.

Standing up, she walked across the sun-warmed terracotta tiles towards him, her gorgeous curves threatening to spill right out of the minuscule patches of scarlet fabric with each seductive sway of her hips.

After getting up at dawn to spend an entire day hauling fish so he could get a stranglehold on his libido, everything south of his belt buckle had lost the plot in less than a second. The throbbing ache in his groin was now even more pronounced than the aching pain in his over-tired muscles.

Next time I see Della I am going to murder her. What was she thinking, ordering Megan that pitiful excuse for a bikini?

'I need to speak to you about…' She paused. 'About what happened last night… I don't want to spend another night alone, Dario. I understand that you are busy, that you have work commitments. But there are so many things I need to talk to you about and I've hardly seen you since we arrived.' Her voice drifted through his mind but he could make no sense of what she was saying.

Was that excuse for swimwear actually *wet*? He could see the clear outline of her nipples through the fabric.

Madonna! Please kill me now.

Her conversation drifted into one ear and then right out of the other as he became fixated on taking each of those ripe, responsive peaks between his lips and torturing them until she begged for release.

'Dario, are you even listening to me?'

'Scusami?' he mumbled, forcing his gaze back to her face. Her pale skin had acquired a healthy sun-burnished glow in the last week, her cheeks now a bright scarlet hue even more tempting than that damn bikini. He wanted to lick that fluttering pulse in her collarbone so much he could almost taste her sweet, spicy aroma on his tongue.

The way he had every night in his dreams.

Her eyes widened. Was that trepidation or shock he could see in them, the misty green bright with stunned knowledge? Then she rolled her lip under small white teeth and everything inside him shattered. All the smart, practical, moral reasons why he couldn't taste her seemed to explode in a cloud of nuclear fallout.

'Stop biting your lip,' he said, his voice a low husky croak he barely recognised as his own.

'Dario! Don't speak to me like that.'

He wrapped his hands around her upper arms and hauled her to him.

Her eyes popped even wider as his heat and hardness rubbed against her naked belly through confining denim.

Then all coherent thought fled as his lips landed on succulent skin and his hands captured the lush curves that had finally pushed him over the edge into madness.

Megan sucked in a shocked gasp, the pulse point in her neck battering her collarbone as Dario bent his head to press his mouth to her neck.

Everything burst inside her, all the hopes and needs and wants that had been escalating for days.

Pulling free of his controlling hands, she plunged her fingers into his thick hair, and dragged his face up.

He wanted her too. She hadn't imagined it. She hadn't.

The truth felt like a sunbeam, bursting inside her, as hunger darkened his hot blue eyes to black.

'Kiss me,' she demanded.

His tongue thrust into her mouth as he massaged her bottom, notching the apex of her thighs against the mammoth ridge in his jeans.

She almost wept for joy, kissing him back for all she was worth, her heart ready to explode right out of her chest.

He held her easily, forcing that thick ridge against the one place where she needed it the most. A guttural moan seemed to reverberate in her chest. Was that her or him? Did she even care?

The pleasure mounted, her whole body on fire now, her melting core seizing into greedy knots of desperation, coiling tighter and tighter.

She wanted him inside her, but before she could think or talk or even respond the wave crashed over her in one titanic surge of pure unadulterated bliss.

She tore her mouth from his, her broken cry shattering the harsh grunts of his breathing.

He swore suddenly and let her go, his eyes still turbulent with need. But instead of taking her back into his arms the way she wanted, the way she was desperate for him to do, he looked stunned.

'Don't stop,' she begged. 'Please don't stop.'

Her chin and cheek stung from the rough abrasion of his stubble. Her whole body shuddered from the force and fury of the spontaneous orgasm.

'I should not have touched you,' he said, his voice brittle.

'Why not?' What was he talking about? 'I wanted you to,' she added, in case he hadn't realised it. But surely he must have realised it. She'd had a climax from little more than a kiss, for goodness' sake.

She felt herself flush at the gaucheness of that. But she refused to care. Why should she be embarrassed by her wildfire response to this man? They were a couple, engaged to be married.

He raked his hands through his hair and took another step back. Why did he look so tortured? 'This cannot happen.'

'Why not?'

'I…' He hesitated, and for the first time ever he seemed unsure of what to say. 'I could have hurt you. I should not have put my hands on you.'

Oh, for— Not that again.

Temper, rich and fluid, and surprising in its intensity, rose up. 'I'm not made of glass, Dario. And I'm going to be your wife. I want your hands on me.'

He stared at her, as if he were lost for words. She could see the huge erection outlined by battered denim. Then he said, 'You have bruises still.'

'No, I don't. You can see, they're as good as gone.'

His gaze went all glassy again, before he suddenly jerked his head up.

'I smell,' he said, his voice a harsh croak now. 'I must wash off the scent of the fish.'

'You smell of the sea. And of you. Both scents that I love.' As much as she must love him in order to have agreed to marry him. Did he doubt her commitment to him? Was that it? Because she couldn't remember why and how she had fallen for him? But how could she know if he would share nothing of himself with her? Not even his body.

'Please don't do this,' she said, determined to find out why he was so reluctant to repair what seemed to be broken between them. 'Don't shut yourself off from me.'

She reached out a hand, wanting to stroke that rigid cheek, to reassure him. But he jerked back, out of reach.

'I must go and shower. I will be out this evening.'

'Why? Where are you going?' she asked, trying to stifle the bitter stab of rejection. And hurt.

'I have important business to discuss with Matteo Caldone, a local farmer... A new irrigation system. I will eat when I return, but don't wait for me.'

Before she could get in a word of objection, or shout at him that she did not want to wait any longer, he had marched past her and headed up to the house.

She stood by the pool, stunned by the encounter. But as she dug her teeth into her lip she remembered that flash of pure unadulterated need that had darkened his eyes to black before he'd swooped down on her, and she realised one incontrovertible truth.

The only way to bridge the huge chasm that had opened up between them was to get Dario back into her bed. Everything else would surely follow. Because wasn't that how they'd fallen in love in the first place? Through their shared passion for each other?

And if their mad kiss a minute ago had proved one thing above all others, it was that Dario De Rossi still wanted her as much as she wanted him.

All she had to do now was make him admit it.

There would be no more polite requests. No more sitting meekly every evening while he directed the conversation, staying obediently in the villa all day or standing silently while he gave her that one peck on the forehead and left her alone for another night.

The only way Dario would ever see her as an equal, the only way he would ever open up to her, was if she started behaving like an equal. And started demanding that he satisfy the hunger that was eating them both up inside.

No way was she going to let him run off to yet another crucially important meeting. A crucially important meeting she was fairly sure he had made up on the spot.

Rushing over to her bag, she stuffed everything inside. She dashed across the pool terrace and headed towards the villa.

Time's up, Dario. You're not running away from me again.

It took her ten minutes to find his suite of rooms in the opposite wing of the villa from hers. Rooms she had never been invited to. That was going to stop too. What was the point of her being here, if they spent no time together? She wanted to know everything about him—all the things she must have discovered that first night in order to have agreed to this engagement, but which she had forgotten about because of her accident.

She passed through a simply furnished but beautifully appointed office, equipped with all the things necessary to run a multinational business. That he'd had all this equipment installed in a holiday home gave her pause for a moment. Dario was a workaholic. But she had no idea why he was so driven.

Shouldn't she know about these parts of his life? She wanted to know why he couldn't settle, and what had turned him into a man so determined to succeed that he could never take a break.

She found the door to his bedroom closed. She knocked but there was no answer.

Gathering her courage, she pushed the door open.

A bed even bigger than her own stood in the centre of the room, but it had none of the romantic flourishes of hers. It suited him, she decided. The open shutters on high windows afforded him a glorious view of the cliff tops and the path leading towards the harbour. The room was enormous, but Dario was nowhere in sight.

Had he left already? Had she missed him?

But then she jumped at the sound of splashing water coming from a door in the far wall. She noticed a pile of clothes that had been discarded in a heap on the floor.

Her throat thickened, the eddying heat making the skimpy bikini feel tight and restrictive on her swollen breasts.

He was in the shower. Should she go and join him?

Vague memories of him naked and fully aroused, the muscle and sinew slicked with water from a different shower, blasted into her brain.

Don't overthink this. Just do it.

She knotted the summer wrap around her waist, and inched open the bathroom door.

Her breathing hitched, her heartbeat thudding against her ribs. The hot melting sensation detonated between her thighs and spread throughout her body like hot lava. Her knees shook, the sight before her bringing the dragon in her belly to scorching life.

Dario stood ten feet away in the walled shower, naked, with his back to her, the pounding of multiple jets of water meaning he hadn't heard her come in.

He had one hand braced against the mosaic tiles, his head bent, obviously concentrating on what his other hand was doing. Steaming water slicked down bunching muscles, making her throat close the rest of the way.

His masculine beauty was so breathtaking, each hard plane and muscular bulge so perfectly sculpted, it staggered her.

He was pleasuring himself. Heat flushed through her. Had their kiss done that to him?

What a waste.

'Dario?'

His head whipped round and the hot blue gaze locked on her face. His motions stopped. He turned as his hand fell away and her gaze dropped to the huge erection standing proud against his belly.

'You should leave,' he said, but the command in his voice was tempered by the rasp of longing.

She shook her head, unable to speak. Or move. Everything inside her gathered into that harsh, aching desperation to feel the thick length buried deep inside her again. Because the one thing she could remember with complete clarity was how glorious he could make her feel.

He turned fully now, allowing her to look her fill. He was magnificent. Moisture pooled in her sex, dampening her bikini bottoms.

'If you do not leave, I will have you,' he said, his voice so husky she could barely hear it against the beat of the water. 'Is that what you want?'

'Yes.' She found the strength from somewhere, even though her whole body was trembling now with desire and longing.

He nodded, his jaw hardening. His eyes took on a harsh glint that was both terrifying and exhilarating in its intensity. 'Then prove it to me.'

Wrapping long fingers around the hard shaft, he stroked himself—not fast this time, but with agonising slowness. The erotic display was almost more than she could bear.

'Take off your clothes for me,' he said, the tone harsh with demand.

Undoing the knot on the belt with clumsy fingers, she obeyed him without question. The wrap slid off her shoulders, the silk feeling like sandpaper as it whispered over her sensitive skin.

'All of it.' The commanding tone tightened the desire in her gut. 'I want you naked.'

She reached behind to undo the hook—unable to deny him now even if she had wanted to. The scarlet triangles dropped from her breasts, and the swollen, tender flesh burst free from its confinement. The breeze from the open window tightened her nipples into hard, aching peaks.

He dipped his head, still stroking that huge erection, to indicate she must lose the bikini bottoms too.

She plucked the tie on one side, and the fabric dropped away.

She couldn't breathe—anticipation warring with panic—as he finally released his erection and turned off the water. Wrapping a towel around his hips, he walked towards her.

Gripping her face, he forced her gaze to meet his and stroked his thumb across her cheek. 'Are you scared of me, *piccola*?' he said.

The nickname stirred a new memory of their first time. She had been a little scared then, of his size and what was to come, but she wasn't scared now.

'No,' she said.

'Then why are you shaking?'

'Because I want you so much,' she said, knowing if there was one thing she was sure about, this was it.

He swore, but then said, 'I want you too. Very much.'

Bending, he scooped her up and carried her quaking body out of the bathroom and into his bedroom. Another memory assailed her, of being in his arms before. Of being carried up the stairs in his penthouse... Bright, exciting, arousing. But something darker tickled at the edges of her mind. Not in his penthouse, but her apartment, the crunch of broken glass under his feet...

The shadow she had been avoiding lurched into view and she slammed the door shut on that memory.

Don't go there. Concentrate on the wonder of now.

Placing her on the bed, he dragged off the towel, releasing that magnificent erection. Reaching past her, he found a condom in the bedside cabinet and rolled it on.

She folded her arms over her breasts as he climbed onto the bed.

'Don't hide from me, Megan.' He moved her arms above her head, bracketing her wrists in one hand.

She cried out as he circled one swollen peak with his tongue, then nipped at the tip. The exquisite spike of sensation darted down to her already molten sex.

He played with her breasts, circling and sucking, releasing her wrists to stroke her slick folds.

Her moans turned to sobs of need, deep and guttural, almost animalistic as he circled and caressed, right at the heart of her.

He raised his head, releasing her tortured nipples, his erection prominent against her thigh. 'I must taste you. It has been too long,' he said.

'Yes,' she heard herself beg, not sure if he was asking her permission but desperate for him to know he had it.

Parting her thighs, he held her bottom, then knelt between her legs and lifted her. She arched, offering herself to him as his stubble brushed against her inner thigh. His hot tongue licked at the heart of her, delving and exploring.

Her sobs turned to ragged pants, the pleasure coiling tighter and tighter. His mouth found the pulsating nub at last and suckled hard.

She cried out his name as she shattered, the orgasm crashing over her in undulating waves.

He licked her through the last drops of her climax, as if gathering her taste. Then he let her go, to settle on top of her. Capturing her hips, he thrust deep in one shudder-ing glide. She stretched for him, the pleasure returning in a titanic rush as he rocked her back to orgasm with stag-gering speed.

His hands anchored her, forcing her to take the full measure of him. His penis butting that perfect spot he had found once before. The second orgasm swept through her, obliterating everything in its path—the trail of fire sear-ing through her from her head to the tips of her toes. She clung to his shoulders, her broken sobs matched by his shout of release as he followed her over at last.

It felt like a month but could only have been a few sec-onds before she returned to her senses, every part of her aching with the exhaustion of a body well used.

He shifted, still so huge inside her. And then lifted his head.

Why did he look so guarded? Surely he must know he'd just given her a multiple orgasm.

'You are okay?' he asked. As if he really didn't know.

'Are you kidding?' she said, even though she could see he was deadly serious. 'I'm spectacular.'

The deep chuckle—although slightly strained—was like music to her ears.

'Are you sure I did not hurt you?' he murmured.

'I told you, I'm not fragile,' she said. 'I love having sex with you. I really, really love it.'

His eyes narrowed, but the shadows retreated as he cra-dled her cheek and then kissed her nose.

'Ditto,' he said. Then he rolled off her.

She felt the loss of his warmth, his heat, immediately. Was this the moment when he told her he had to leave, to go to his irrigation ditch meeting? She was all ready to protest, to finally demand that he stay with her for the rest of the day. But instead of getting out of the bed, he hauled her close, wrapping his arms round her, and tucking her against his body, her back to his front.

She could feel the hard length of him nestled against her backside.

'You're not leaving to go to the lemon farm?' she asked tentatively, afraid to remind him of the engagement.

'It is an orange farm. But no, not tonight,' he said.

He leaned over her to grab his smartphone off the bedside table. Then keyed in a text.

Snuggling against her back, he nibbled kisses along her shoulder. Incredibly, after that shattering orgasm—make that two shattering orgasms—she felt the sleeping dragon wake again in her belly.

'Are you hungry?' he asked.

Talk about a loaded question.

'Yes,' she said.

'What are you hungry for?' he asked, and she could hear the smile in his voice.

'For food and for you, not necessarily in that order.'

The deep chuckle reverberated against her, sending a ripple down her spine as he cupped her breast and played with the nipple. The arrows of sensation shot straight back to her still tender sex.

'Sofia will leave us food in the kitchen for later. But first you must rest.'

The tenderness in his voice, and the feel of his thumb teasing her nipple, made her feel warm and languid, but far too turned on.

'Why must I?' she asked.

She didn't want to sleep. She'd had over ten days to sleep and now she finally had him where she wanted him, why would she waste time sleeping?

'Because you will need your strength for what I plan to do to you next.'

She shifted around, so she could look over her shoulder to gauge his expression. 'Really? You're going to make love to me again?' She could hear the eagerness in her voice and hoped she didn't sound like a nymphomaniac. But already the renewed stirrings of hunger in her belly were becoming unbearable.

Clearly satisfaction was a relative term, and, when it came to Dario De Rossi, she might never be satisfied.

He sighed against her hair. 'I have no choice. My will is not my own any more.'

It seemed a strange thing to say. Why would he choose not to make love to her, when he now had conclusive proof she was fully recovered from her accident?

Before she had the chance to debate the puzzling thought, or ask any of the many other questions that had tormented her about him, his hand slid off her hip, and sure seeking fingers found her sex, blasting into oblivion everything but the renewed surge of longing.

CHAPTER TWELVE

'CAN I ASK you a question?' Megan's eyes brightened, her voice eager, as she laid Sofia's antipasti onto an earthenware platter.

It was late, and Dario was ravenous. Unfortunately, it wasn't just for the array of cold food his housekeeper had left out for them.

How could he still want her? When he'd spent the last six hours with her in his arms—none of it catching up on the sleep he had lost in the last week.

He tore off chunks of the sesame seed bread Sofia made fresh each morning and added it to their midnight feast.

'You may ask,' he said, reserving the right to refuse her, the anticipation in her eyes making him instantly wary. He should never have touched her. He had promised himself he wouldn't. But ultimately he had been unable to stop himself from taking what she offered so eagerly. And now he would have to pay the consequences—by finding a way to deflect her curiosity again, without feeling like a bastard.

'There are so many things I want to ask you about that night.'

Dario carried the platter and their glasses to the moonlit terrace, the fresh scent of sea air and citrus fruit doing nothing to appease the clutching sensation in his gut.

Was her memory about to return at last? Perhaps the sex had finally jogged something loose?

'What do you wish to know?' he asked, cautiously.

Lloyd Whittaker had been charged and arraigned, thanks to Katie's testimony. He had been refused bail and would be standing trial in a few months. Megan hadn't mentioned him though, not since she had woken up in the hospital—convincing Dario her memory loss was centred exclusively on her father. If she asked about him now, it would surely mean her mind was finally healing as well as her body. But as she sat down opposite him at the table and began to serve them both from the platter, her vibrant hair the colour of rich red flames in the light from the citronella candles, he didn't feel as pleased at the prospect of her memory returning as he should.

Here was a chance to finally end this charade. To free them both from the obligations brought about by Whittaker's attack and Megan's subsequent amnesia.

But as he watched her tuck into Sofia's *verdure misti*— clearly considering what she wanted to ask very carefully—his mind spun back through the events of the past week. Against all the odds, and despite the knife-edge of sexual frustration that had been driving him insane for days, he had looked forward to seeing her each evening.

At last she looked up from her plate. The sheen of olive oil on her lips made them look even more kissable than usual. Dario licked his own lips.

This was just sexual desire, nothing more. His hunger for her was clouding his usually crystal-clear judgment. Anything she wanted to know he would be happy to tell her—because it would bring her memory back sooner and that was what he wanted.

'Would you tell me about yourself?' she said.

Anything except that.

His shoulders tightened. 'What do you wish to know?' he said, stalling.

She smiled shyly, the subtle shift of her lips as sexy as it was beguiling. 'Everything. All the things you told me that night about your hopes and dreams and where they came from.'

'But I told you nothing.' He never talked about his past, his childhood, because it had no part in who he was now. He'd made absolutely sure of that, erasing all but the most basic facts about his life from the media narrative of his success.

'Don't be silly.' She seemed amused at his attempt to correct her. 'You must have told me something for me to have fallen in love with you.'

The happy expression on her face made his heart kick against his chest in hard, heavy thuds.

They weren't in love. He had never loved anyone—not since... He shut down the thought.

'I expect I told you loads of stuff too,' she added in that effortlessly optimistic tone. As if love were something you would want, instead of something that would only hurt you. 'But I can't seem to remember that either. So you're going to have to help me remember.'

But there is nothing to remember.

'I don't know what you would want to know,' he said, still stalling.

'Then how about I ask you all the things I'm curious about now, because that's probably what I asked before?'

He didn't know how to reply to that, but she didn't really give him much of an opportunity before she had launched into her first question. 'The article in *Forbes* said you grew up in Rome.'

'I grew up outside Rome, in one of the government-funded housing projects constructed for the Roma community,' he said, reluctantly. The snap of bitterness in his voice that he couldn't control, though, surprised him.

He'd realised a long time ago that the experience of waking up to the scrabble of rats outside the trailer window and the sound of his own teeth chattering during winters in the slum, or the fetid smell of rotting trash and effluent from the urinals that marked the summer months, were the very experiences that had driven his need to succeed. He'd long ago come to terms with the terrible privations of his childhood. He wasn't embarrassed or ashamed of his origins, but still he had no desire to revisit that time in his life.

'You're of Roma descent? That's amazing,' she said, as if this were something to be proud of.

He frowned. Didn't she know that the Roma people had been treated like the scum of Europe—ghettoised and vilified, their way of life stigmatised for generations?

'My mother was.' The information slipped out, as he recalled the woman who had been so proud of her heritage, despite the hovel they'd lived in.

'She *was*?' Sympathy and compassion clouded Megan's eyes, making the antipasti in his stomach threaten to revolt. 'I'm so sorry, Dario. Is your mother dead?'

For a moment, the memories threatened to flood in on him. Memories he had spent a lifetime forgetting. 'Yes, but it was a long time ago.'

'Oh, no, were you a child?'

'No,' he said, because he had never been a child, not in the sense she meant. Grasping his fork in stiff fingers, he scooped up a mouthful of Sofia's grilled aubergine. It tasted like chalk as he swallowed.

'What about your father?' she asked.

'I never knew him,' he said, the lie coming much more easily this time.

He heard a groan, and looked up to see Megan digging a knuckle into her temple as if trying to erase something from her mind.

'Are you okay?'

'Yes, but… It's like there's a darkness lurking at the edge of my consciousness and I don't want to let it in.' Had the question about his father made her think of her own? And all the things she was trying so hard to forget?

He got out of his chair. 'Then don't.' Smoothing the unruly hair back from her brow, he took her other hand, and tugged her out of the chair. 'It has been a long day. You must get some rest now.'

'Really, it's nothing. I'm fine.' She dropped her hand. 'It's gone now.'

'I insist. You must rest.' Despite her protests, he scooped her into his arms, the desire to protect her from the demons that might be chasing her foolish in the circumstances, but there nonetheless. He needed her to remember, but if remembering still caused her pain…

She gripped his neck, looking a little perturbed. 'Put me down, Dario,' she said. 'You're overreacting. I can walk.'

He tightened his grip, taking her into the house. 'Let me carry you. It is my fault you are over-tired.'

She held on to his neck and stopped struggling, but the look she sent him was one of frustration. He didn't care. He was right. They had overdone things because where she was concerned he was incapable of keeping his libido in check.

'I don't see how it's your fault when I seduced you,' she said, indignant now.

'That is debatable,' he said, but he couldn't help smiling at the stubborn lift of her chin, or the combative light in her eyes. He was beginning to discover how brave and spirited she could be, for a woman who had been brutalised. Unfortunately, it only turned him on more.

He felt the familiar response in his groin and took a turn once he'd mounted the stairs towards her suite of rooms.

'Stop right there. I'm not going to my own rooms,' she shouted, and all but threw herself out of his arms—a bit too brave and spirited for his liking.

He swore as he scrambled to gather her back up. 'Come back here.'

'No.' She batted his hands away.

'You need to sleep. You must do as I tell you.'

'I'll do no such thing. You have to stop treating me like a child, Dario. I'm a grown woman. I can make decisions for myself.'

He could feel his own frustration kicking in. 'Not when you make the wrong ones.'

Like believing even for a second you could have fallen in love with a man like me.

'Will you listen to yourself?' Megan propped her hands on her hips.

How could she want to kiss him and strangle him at the same time? Seriously though, they were getting this straight once and for all. No more excuses and no more distractions.

'This is not the nineteenth century and you are not in charge of me.'

'You need rest. It is past midnight and you have reached orgasm six times today,' he shot back.

So he'd been counting. Why did that make her feel so much better?

He crossed his arms over his chest, looking like the poster boy for stubborn manhood, strong and indomitable. He who should be obeyed at all costs.

Well, not by me, buster.

His biceps bulged deliciously beneath the short sleeves of his T-shirt.

Her sex clenched.

Fine, maybe some distractions were going to be impossible to ignore. But that didn't mean she was going to let him get away with his high-handed attitude a moment longer. They'd come so far this evening.

The sex had been awesome, but the tantalising glimpse of intimacy had been even more so. Because the few things she had discovered about him tonight had intrigued and moved her in ways she couldn't explain.

Who would have believed that beneath the charming, charismatic sex god lurked a man who could look stricken when he was asked about his mother? He'd masked it quickly, but she'd seen enough to be touched—and compelled to wonder about so many things. Things she hoped to be able to discover about him in the days ahead. But she couldn't do that if she allowed him to push her away again—to compartmentalise their time together and keep her at arm's length.

'And I enjoyed every single one of those orgasms,' she said, something rich and empowering surging through her when his face flushed with aggravation. Sex was the key.

She knew sex, even great sex, didn't necessarily translate into emotional intimacy—especially with a man who was so adept at hiding his feelings. But it was a very good start. Not to mention rewarding in its own right.

'But we wouldn't have been at it for six hours straight if you hadn't denied us both the pleasure of sleeping together for a whole week,' she added.

'You were recovering from your accident,' he said.

'And now I'm not recovering any more. I'm recovered. I think we proved that comprehensively this evening.'

Something flickered across his face again, before he looked away. She touched his forearm, felt it tense beneath her fingers.

'How about a compromise?' she murmured. She didn't want to argue with him.

'What compromise?' he said grudgingly.

She smiled, amused by the muscle bunching in his jaw. For a moment he reminded her of a petulant child, so used to getting his own way he had forgotten how to bend. Only he wasn't a child, not in any sense of the word. Because...biceps.

'This is funny somehow?' The muscle in his jaw started to throb.

She bit down on her lip, trying not to let loose the smile that wanted to burst over her face.

Because instead of finding his taciturn show of temper intimidating, she found it exhilarating...and unbearably arousing.

His gaze glided down to her mouth, and she felt the spark of awareness leap between them.

'Here's what I suggest,' she said, deciding to ignore his rhetorical question. 'I'll consider taking your advice about my welfare, if I think it's warranted, but only if you agree to let us start behaving like a couple.'

No way was she letting him confine her to her own bedroom again.

'What does that mean? We are already together here.'

'I want to share a bed with you.'

His eyes narrowed and she could see he was about to refuse, so she jumped in before he could.

'I want us to sleep together...' She hesitated. Would this make her sound too needy? She frowned. How could it when they were engaged? Since when did engaged couples sleep in separate rooms? 'I like being in your arms. I want to go to sleep with you and to wake up with you. It's important to me.'

Dario knew he should refuse. She did not know what she was asking. They weren't a couple.

But before he could force the words out, she said, 'You make me feel safe, Dario. I don't want there to be so much distance between us. Or why are we even considering getting married?'

The plea in her voice made him feel like a bastard. He should tell her now that the engagement had been a ruse. A ruse that had got out of control. But somehow, he couldn't bring himself to do it. Something about the way she was looking at him, as if he could harness the moon and the stars for her if she asked him to, made him want to say yes.

She trusted him. When she learned the truth, it would crush that trust. But until then, he wanted her to feel safe and secure.

He cupped her cheek, his heart thundering in his chest when she leant into the caress and smiled.

'I can accept that compromise...' he said, touching his thumb to her bottom lip. 'But only if you promise to let me seduce you when we get to my bed?'

Maybe it had been a mistake to deny them both the physical pleasure that flared so easily between them? Perhaps this physical closeness was what she needed to find the strength to battle the darkness lurking at the edges of her consciousness. And really, what better way was there to distract her from her foolish desire to get to know him better? Which was all part and parcel of her foolish delusions that she loved him—or had ever loved him.

She smiled, the quick grin captivating and full of mischief. 'Absolutely—assuming of course I don't seduce you first,' she said, batting her eyelashes outrageously.

'Dio!' He reached for her hand and marched towards his own bedroom. Her seductive chuckles spurred the aching hunger in his groin.

Somehow or other he'd completely lost the upper hand in this negotiation, but the feel of her hand in his—and the thought of having her in his bed tonight, all night—was like a heady drug, making it hard for him to remember why exactly he had ever insisted on keeping her out of it.

CHAPTER THIRTEEN

MEGAN SQUINTED AT the sun shining through the shutters and stretched, disappointed to find Dario's side of the bed empty. Again. After over a week of waking up in Dario's bed she still hadn't managed to wake up before him. Her body protested, the desire to slip back into sleep almost overwhelming. She yawned, forcing the tiredness back. And grinned. Too much spectacular sex could be exhausting.

As she rolled over onto her belly, her grin widened at the sight of Dario's smartphone on the bedside table. He couldn't be far, probably in his study next door catching up on emails while she slept the day away.

Thank goodness he hadn't left without her. He'd mentioned a speedboat trip to the lagoon on the other side of the island today—one of the many trips and excursions they'd been on ever since she'd moved into his suite of rooms.

She'd used her newfound boldness to insist he start taking her with him each day on his different trips. And although he'd been reluctant at first, she was so glad she had insisted—because she'd discovered so many amazing things, not just about the island but about Dario, too.

Isadora had only a small fishing village on the other side of the peninsula on which the villa sat, many of whose inhabitants had to commute to the mainland to find work.

Dario had invested a lot in rejuvenating the island's once thriving community—building a new dock, constructing the villa itself and resurrecting the old olive, lemon and blood orange groves that had once thrived in the volcanic soil and had been a mainstay of the island's economy.

Each day, Megan would discover a new aspect to everything he was doing on the island, as he oversaw those projects with her in tow.

For a billionaire with a portfolio of international companies and investments, Dario had no qualms about getting his hands dirty. And the islanders hero-worshipped him, while also being comfortable treating him like one of their own.

Maybe she hadn't made much headway getting him to talk more about himself, or his past, but everything else she'd discovered had only made her fascination with him increase.

He was still bossy, but she had begun to realise that was all part of how focused and intense he was. He would never ask something of someone he wasn't prepared to do himself. And maybe he was still guarded about personal information. But his focus and intensity each night in bed—and on the occasions when they snatched a chance to make love in the daylight—showed a care and concern for her pleasure that made her sure what they were forging together was much more than just a physical connection.

She could make him laugh, lighten that dark, brooding quality that had once intimidated her, but now made her love him all the more.

And today she had a plan. To make a much bigger dent in that wall he seemed determined to keep erected around his emotions. And her plan was simple. Today was the first day they would be alone for one of their excursions. She would seduce him into a puddle and then pounce on him while he was floating on a cloud of afterglow—unable to resist her brilliantly subtle interrogation.

Of course, her plan was a risky one, because up until now she'd been the one who could barely remember her own name after they made love. But today she planned to get sneaky.

She'd asked Sofia to provide a picnic for their trip—to lull Dario into a false sense of security and satisfy his boundless appetite for food—and she was going to wear her scarlet bikini—to torture him with his boundless appetite for her.

She picked up the phone on the table to check the time.

Nearly noon? She frowned. How could she have slept so late when she had something so important to do today?

Throwing back the cover, she sat up.

Mission: Puddle of Lust, here I come.

The nausea came in a rush, the wave heaving up from her stomach so suddenly she was already gagging as she raced into the bathroom. She made it just in time before she lost last night's dinner in the toilet bowl.

Finally empty, her stomach settled into an uneasy truce as she sat on the cool tiles. Her whole body ached as she reached to push the flush button.

'*Cara*, what happened? Were you sick?'

Dario knelt down beside her and wrapped her robe around her shoulders to cover her nakedness.

'Yes, I think I must have picked up some kind of bug.' She placed a hand on her stomach. 'Although it feels a bit better now I've been sick.'

'Has this happened before?' The fierce expression made her heart bobble in her chest. Why did he look so disturbed? She hoped he wasn't going to use a little bit of nausea as an excuse to start treating her like an invalid again.

'No, not really.'

'No or not really?' he said.

Her stomach had been a bit queasy yesterday, and the day before when she'd woken up. But she hadn't been sick. And it had soon gone away. His brows drew down as he waited for an answer and she decided a white lie might be in order.

'No, it hasn't happened before.' Using the toilet bowl, she pushed herself to her feet, steadfastly ignoring the pitch and roll of her not-completely-calm belly.

She tied the robe around herself and brushed her teeth, before walking past Dario, who still looked concerned.

She escaped into the walk-in closet.

'I'll be fine,' she said, her voice deliberately light and cheery. 'All I need is a swim in the lagoon to make me feel better. I'm sorry I slept in so long.'

But when she came out of the closet, he'd disappeared into his office. She heard him talking in rapid Italian on his smartphone. She tuned it out. Thank goodness, he'd found some business thing to keep him occupied. She slipped on a summer dress and sat at the dressing table to slick on sun cream and a touch of lip gloss.

But when Dario returned to the bedroom, his face was still set in the same unforgiving lines. 'How is your stomach?'

'It's wonderful. Really, I'm great now. How long will it take to get to the cove?' she asked, still trying to inject as much brightness into her voice as she could, while subtly changing the subject.

'We're not going to the cove. The helicopter will be ready in ten minutes, to take us to the hospital in Palermo.'

The forbidding expression had her already dodgy tummy jitterbugging. 'Don't be ridiculous. I'm not going to hospital over a bit of nausea.' Why was he overreacting?

'Tell me, Megan,' he said, his jaw so tense she wondered he didn't break a tooth. 'Have you had a period since we arrived?'

'No,' she replied.

'Then we must go to the hospital for a pregnancy test.'

Shock came first, her stomach jumping right into her throat. 'But I can't be pregnant, we've used condoms the whole time. It's not possible.' It couldn't be possible. Except... The evidence started to reel off in her mind: her increased bust size, the tiredness and now her upset tummy. But more than that, something else niggled her memory.

Sofia tapped on the bedroom door. 'The helicopter is waiting, *signor*. Do you still want the picnic?'

The nausea charged back up Megan's throat at the mention of food.

'*No, grazie*, Sofia,' she heard Dario murmur as she shot back into the bathroom.

CHAPTER FOURTEEN

'You are indeed pregnant, *signora*.' Dr Mascati smiled benignly at Megan. Dario tensed beside her, his expression as guarded as it had been throughout the never-ending helicopter ride from Isadora to the heliport on the roof of the exclusive private maternity centre.

'Are you sure?' Dario said, his voice curt. Not angry but not happy either.

Megan understood. This was shocking news. No wonder he'd hardly said a word to her since they'd boarded the helicopter. She hadn't known what to say either. However whirlwind their engagement, they hadn't even talked about their wedding yet, so introducing a pregnancy into that was bound to put huge pressure on them both.

But after the last week, the last two weeks, ever since waking up in the hospital, she'd come to terms with why she had agreed to marry him in only one night. Maybe it was mad. But the more she discovered about him, the more she got to know him, the more sure she was that she could love this man.

'The test is unequivocal,' the doctor said in his perfect English. 'There can be no doubt. We can do a scan in a couple of weeks so you can see your baby for yourself.'

'Okay,' she murmured, acknowledging the leap of joy despite her shock.

She placed a hand on her stomach, imagining the tiny life growing inside her. However unprepared for this they both were, this pregnancy felt so positive on some elemental level.

Perhaps it was her hormones talking. Or the endorphin high she'd been riding on for the last seven days. But whatever it was, she knew instinctively that despite the challenges and problems ahead they would be able to deal with them.

Maybe it had only been a few weeks, but Dario—so protective, so caring, so solid and sure of himself—would make an amazing father, and she… She would do everything within her power to be the mother this tiny life deserved.

Dario spoke to the doctor in rapid Italian, but the conversation floated somewhere over Megan's head as she caressed her invisible baby bump. And tried to contain the secret smile in her heart.

Dario was obviously unsure about this development; she could tell that already from his reaction to her sickness, which she realised now had been panic. Pure and simple. She just hadn't recognised it as such, because he always seemed so confident and commanding. But once they were alone together, they could talk about his misgivings. This pregnancy didn't have to be a bad thing.

'Megan, we must go now.' Dario's words jolted Megan out of her reverie.

'Oh, yes, thank you, Dr Mascati,' she said, trying not to sound too spacey. Even if she felt as if she were flying somewhere above the cosmos at the moment.

Dario rested an arm around her waist to guide her out of the doctor's office. They made their way back up to the roof, Dario gripping her hand as they crossed the heliport to the waiting chopper. He said nothing, his face now an implacable mask.

She stared out of the window on the flight back. The noise of the chopper's blades made it impossible to speak and she was grateful for that, because she wanted to get her thoughts together. He would need reassurance. Understanding.

But she was confident he would come around to the idea given time and encouragement. If he was sure enough of his feelings to ask her to marry him after only one night, no way would he be too scared to take on this responsibility once he knew how positive she was about it.

The sun dipped towards the horizon as they swooped over the villa and came into land on the cliff-top heliport.

Dario led her back to their suite of rooms in silence. Sofia arrived to lay out a meal for them on the terrace. The housekeeper sent her a gentle smile and Megan smiled back at her. Did she know already?

She stared out at the sea, the sky lit in a redolent array of red and gold and deep darkening blues. Isadora was such a beautiful place. What a wonderful place this would be to bring up a child.

No, that was silly, Dario had a life in New York, and so did she. But surely they could spend summers here— with their baby. She had to tell Katie. Her sister would be an auntie.

'Eat, Megan. You must be hungry.' She glanced back to find Dario watching her. She dialled down her excitement.

She was getting way ahead of herself. There was still so much to talk about. So much to discuss. She mustn't try and second-guess Dario's feelings. The doctor had said the pregnancy was still in the very early stages.

'Yes, of course,' she said, although the truth was she was far too nervous to eat. 'This looks delicious.' She picked up her fork and forced down a few bites of the aubergine and cherry tomato pasta she was sure Sofia had produced for her delicate stomach on Dario's orders.

'Do you want to talk about the baby?' she asked, as nonchalantly as she could, while she watched him closely, to gauge his reaction.

The impassive mask cracked, revealing something she didn't understand until he said, 'It is not a baby yet. It is a collection of cells.'

The flat words tore into the excitement that had buoyed her up through the helicopter ride.

Her fork clattered onto the plate. 'I know I'm only a few weeks pregnant, but…' She stalled, suddenly scared to say what she thought.

'But what?' he asked, not unkindly.

'It feels like a baby to me,' she managed around the feeling of dread suddenly pushing against her throat.

What would she do if he wanted her to have a termination? She hadn't even considered that option. Wasn't sure she could go through with it even if that was what he wanted. Had she been foolish, expecting him to be as happy about this unexpected event as she was? Probably, yes.

'Don't you want this baby?' she managed to say. Prepared for the worst, but desperately hoping for the best.

He looked away, across the terrace towards the sea, the breeze lifting the thick waves of his hair, lost in thought for a moment. But when he turned towards her, his gaze was shadowed and unreadable. 'That is not my decision. It is yours.'

The bright bubble of hope burst at the pragmatic tone.

Her hand strayed back to her tummy, and she looked down at the still invisible bump. Tears stung her eyes. She blinked furiously, desperate not to let them fall. It was just all so overwhelming. Not only the news about the baby, but how she felt about Dario. If she chose to have it, would it tear them apart? And if she chose not to, would it tear her apart?

Courage, Megan.

Dario was right: this was her choice to make and she'd already made it. She had to stand up for this child, and hope that, however early it was, this pregnancy wouldn't destroy what she was just starting to build with Dario.

Wiping away the errant tear that had slipped over her lid, she forced her gaze to his and smiled at him. 'I want to have your baby, Dario. Very much.'

He stiffened, and for once she could see his feelings written plainly on his face. He didn't look upset by her response—or particularly pleased either. He simply looked stunned.

He dipped his head, the nod almost imperceptible. 'I see,' he said.

She clasped her hands in her lap, but she couldn't stop her fingers from trembling, the emotion pressing on her chest too huge to deny as the bridge they had spent one glorious week building felt as if it were collapsing into a yawning chasm.

He didn't want this baby. She could see it in the rigid line of his jaw, the shadowed distance in his eyes.

'Dario, please tell me how you feel about it,' she begged, using every ounce of the courage she had left as another tear slid down her cheek.

He shook his head, then reached over to brush the tear away. The tender gesture made her heart ache even more.

Pushing back his chair, he stood up. 'You are tired, *piccola*. We can discuss this tomorrow.'

She should say something, anything—they needed to discuss this now, before he had a chance to retreat even further into that protective shell—but the last of her courage deserted her when he lifted her into his arms.

She clung to him as he carried her into their bedroom.

They would make love, she told herself desperately. That would make everything better. They were always so close when they made love.

He undressed her, but when she thought he would reach for her, he didn't. Instead he brought her one of his T-shirts, and helped her into it.

'Why do I need this?' she asked.

'Because your other nightwear tempts me too much,' he said. 'You need sleep, *cara*.' He tucked the thin sheet around her and stood up.

'Aren't you coming to bed, too?' she asked.

'Not yet, I have some work to do. I will be in later.' He kissed her forehead. 'Go to sleep. It has been an exhausting day.'

She wanted to argue with him, but her limbs were already melting into the bed. She curled up, taking in the comforting scent of sandalwood that clung to the sheets.

It was okay. She was still in his bed. And he would be back soon. Then they would make love. And all their differences would melt away.

'Don't be long,' she murmured as her eyes drifted closed.

But he had already left the room.

CHAPTER FIFTEEN

'SHE'S PREGNANT? FROM the look on your face, I'm guessing that's not good news,' Jared said, his voice as dispassionate as usual over the scratchy Internet connection.

Dario rubbed his forehead, trying to erase the picture lodged there of Megan crouched on the bathroom floor retching this morning. And the single tear drifting down her cheek this evening in the dusk as she told him she wanted to have his child.

He was shattered, the strain of trying to keep his emotions in check the whole day too much even for him. He had called his friend to get some advice. Even though he knew already, there was no advice that would fix this.

'No, it's not,' he said. 'It happened on our first night. We had agreed she would take the morning-after pill, but now she doesn't remember that conversation.' He raked his hand through his hair, and stared out into the starry night sky, the full moon reflecting off the bay.

The shock of this morning's discovery had left him reeling. He couldn't become a father. And Megan did not want to be a mother—something she would know when her memory returned. But as that hadn't happened, the way forward now was fraught with complications—and heartache.

And the last week had only complicated the situation more. It was all his fault.

He should never have given into his hunger for her and taken her back into his bed. And he should never have agreed to her requests to accompany him during the day. Because the time they'd spent together, instead of reinforcing all the reasons why they could never be a couple, had done exactly the opposite.

He'd become completely enchanted with her. Not just her enthusiasm and responsiveness in bed, but the way she behaved out of it.

He'd come to adore the bright, eager and surprisingly well-informed chatter about all the improvements he was making to the island. He'd been charmed by the way she had captivated the local fishermen with her faltering Italian or bonded with Matteo Caldone's wife over how to make gnocchi. And had come to rely on having her with him, having her by his side. She had made even the most tedious details of his working life an adventure. When he'd woken up this morning, he'd been stupidly excited about the prospect of taking her for a swim in a lagoon, knowing how much he would enjoy seeing her wide-eyed wonder at the cove's natural beauty. In the space of one short week, she'd managed to turn him into someone he didn't even recognise. Someone fun and playful and optimistic in a way he hadn't been in years. In short, a besotted fool.

But worse than that, in the past week, their fake relationship had started to feel real. Real enough that even the thought of her giving herself to another man had begun to torture him. And he had forgotten to be cautious and careful with her feelings as well as his own.

But this morning's bombshell had brought that illusion crashing down around his ears.

This relationship wasn't real.

He could never love Megan—however much he had enjoyed her companionship in the past week or the intense physical connection they shared. And Megan didn't really love him, because any feelings she had for him were based on a lie. But even knowing all this, when she had stared at him out of misty green eyes and told him she wanted to have his child, for one terrifying moment he had actually wanted it to be true.

It was all such a catastrophic mess, and he didn't know how the hell to get them both out of it.

'So she still doesn't remember that you were never engaged for real?' Jared said.

Dario shook his head.

'Maybe it's time to tell her the truth and see what happens, pal.'

Jared was right, of course. He should have said something tonight when he'd had the opportunity. Should have said something a week ago, before he'd taken her back into his bed. But still he kept second-guessing himself.

'What if I do that and it only confuses her more?' A tiny, foolish part of him almost wished she never regained her memory. It just went to show how far he had lost his grip on reality.

'Doesn't seem like you have much of a choice,' Jared said. 'It's either that or she has the kid and you pretend to love her for the rest of your life.'

'No, that is not an option, either.' His head felt as if it were about to explode, the fear that had haunted him since childhood making his heart kick his ribs in harsh erratic thuds.

'Sorry I can't be of more help, man,' Jared said, sounding as dejected as he felt. 'Good luck.'

Signing off, Dario turned off his laptop and walked back into the bedroom.

She lay curled on the bed, having kicked off the sheet. Her body looked small and defenceless as she moved restlessly in her sleep. He should sleep elsewhere, but as a small moan escaped he found himself taking off his clothing and slipping into the bed. He cradled her quaking body in his arms, and inhaled the flowery fragrance of her hair. Her breathing deepened as he stroked the soft strands to quieten her and the arousal that was always there became a dull ache in his groin.

'Shh, *piccola*,' he murmured as he struggled to find his own peace. And a way out of this mess—without hurting the smart, sweet, beautiful woman he had come to know.

'You stupid slut! You're worse than your mother.'

The darkness came to her in dreams, seeping into her consciousness where she couldn't defend herself against it. She saw her father's face contorted with rage, sweat dripping down his mottled skin as he screamed at her.

Pain rained down on her, striking her shoulders, her back, lancing through her heart, shattering everything she had ever known about herself and her place in the world.

'You're not mine! You and your sister were whelps from her lovers.'

Her broken sobs echoed in her head, as she begged her daddy not to hurt her any more. But her daddy wasn't her daddy now, and he hated her.

Just as the pain became unbearable, Dario's voice beckoned her out of the nightmare. 'Shh, Megan, it's okay, I'm here, you're safe.'

She awoke with a start in the darkened bedroom with Dario's arms around her.

Shapes formed in the moonlight. Familiar, comforting shapes. Dario's face harsh with concern. The giant bed where they had slept together in each other's arms. Luxury furnishings gilded by the light of the waning Mediterranean moon. The citrus and sea scented breeze brushed her naked skin through the open shutters. And for a moment she did feel safe. Secure. Loved… So happy.

But then the darkness unfolded as the dream returned. Not a dream this time though, but terrible reality: the kaleidoscopic colours of the ballroom as Dario spun her around in a circle on their pretend date; her sobs of fulfilment as he stroked her to orgasm; the wry tilt of his lips as they discussed emergency contraception; the shuddering humiliation as she received her father's text.

Nausea pitched and rolled in her belly. Clammy sweat covered her body. And horror hit her hard in the chest.

'*Cara*, are you okay?' he said, his voice gentle, coaxing.

But she knew the truth now. And his concern, his care, wasn't love. It was pity.

She could feel the phantom pain from her father's belt and see the dispassionate concern so clearly on Dario's face as he knelt next to her shattered body.

'Let me go.' Pushing against his hold, she wrestled with the cloying sheet, climbed off the bed.

'What's wrong?' he said, pulling back the sheet to follow her.

She scrambled away from him, her back hitting the wall of the bedroom, the cool plaster chilling her fevered flesh. 'You lied. Why did you lie to me? We were never engaged!'

For a moment he looked shocked, but then she saw the guilty flash of knowledge. Her thundering heart felt as if it were being crushed in her chest.

'Your memory has returned?' he said, his voice patient. And tightly controlled.

She gagged. Rushing into the bathroom, she heaved what little she'd eaten the night before into the toilet bowl. As she carried on heaving she heard him enter the bathroom behind her.

A dim light came on and warm hands settled on her shoulders.

She spun out of his grasp. 'Don't touch me.'

He stood in sweat pants, his magnificent body mocking her. How ridiculous she had been, to think for even a moment that a man like him would ever love her.

He had been nothing more than a glorious one-night stand—was never meant to be more than that—and because she had lost her memory, he had spun out a lie.

But why? Why would he do that?

He lifted a hand. Like a man trying to calm a frightened beast. 'You are over-emotional. Come back to bed so we can talk.'

She shook her head, trying to hold on to the tears making her sinuses ache. 'How could you pretend we were engaged? That we were in love? For all this time? Why would you?'

It had all been a lie. How could he justify it to himself? And how could *she*? She'd fallen in love with an illusion. None of this had been real. Her hand strayed to her stomach and the baby growing there. None of it except her child.

The child he didn't want, and now she knew why.

'You are overwrought. You need to calm down,' he said.

Anger flared. She clung onto it desperately, through the heartache and the weariness. 'Don't patronise me. Tell me the truth. Why did you tell me we were engaged? Why did you make me believe you loved me?'

He stiffened at the use of the word. And her already battered heart cracked silently in two.

'I never pretended to love you,' he said, and the last remnants of hope that she hadn't even realised she still clung to withered and died. 'I wanted you to get well,' he said. 'Which is why I brought you here. Away from the press, the trial, so you could recover. It was for your own good.'

'You slept with me, knowing I didn't know the true nature of our relationship. How could that be for my own good?'

His eyes darkened, his jaw tensed, and she felt the spark of electricity arc between them. She folded her arms across her chest, her swollen breasts tender and far too sensitive under that searing gaze. The T-shirt he had helped her into before bedtime suddenly felt see-through, every inch of skin prickling with the need to feel his touch as memories of that first night, of the past seven nights in his arms assaulted her.

'You offered yourself to me,' he said. 'And I should have resisted. But everything we did together we both enjoyed.'

It sounded reasonable, persuasive even. And of course, he was right. She had begged for him to make love to her. Except it had never been love. At least not for him. 'Did you ever care for me at all?'

'Of course I did,' he said, the frustration in his voice helping her to bury the agonising hurt deep.

'And what about the baby? Perhaps you should tell me how you really feel about that now.' But she already knew, the bitter truth turning her insides to jelly.

He heaved a deep sigh. Seeing the agony in his eyes made her want to weep. 'Megan, it is complicated. You must see that? Now you remember everything?'

He stepped forward, but she threw up a hand. 'Please don't, don't come any closer.' She couldn't stay strong, stay invulnerable, make any sense of this if he touched her. The chemistry between them had messed with her head all the way down the line. And made her fall in love with a phantom.

'My father attacked me because he hated me.' She pushed the words out past the thickness in her throat. The cruel, ugly words her father had said striking her all over again with more viciousness than the belt he'd used on her. 'He pretended to care about us for years because of the money in our trust funds. But this…' she swung her hand between them '…what you did, feels so much worse.'

Dario dragged a hand through his hair, cursed under his breath. 'I understand you are angry and upset,' he said. 'But let us talk about this in the morning. It's the middle of the night. You're tired. Come back to bed. I can make you feel better.'

'You think sex will make this better?' she said, stunned.

'I think it cannot hurt,' he said.

The wry twist of his lips made her heart shatter at her feet. That he had manipulated her with sex wasn't really the point, because she had revelled in her own destruction. That he thought it would make things better now, though, almost made her feel sorry for him.

How could anyone have such a jaundiced view of love and relationships that they thought sex was the only connection worth having?

He approached her.

But she held up her hand. 'No. I don't want to sleep with you, Dario.'

Of course, they both knew that wasn't strictly true. She only had to be in a room with him for her body to prepare itself for him. To yearn for him. It would be humiliating if it weren't so sad.

But she refused to give in to the yearning. She had to guard what little was left of her heart. In the hope that, one day, she would be able to heal. And move on from this.

'I need to think,' she said as her mind raced. She had to get away from him. Get away from Isadora. If for no other reason than to protect her child. 'I want to return to my own room.'

For a moment she thought he looked stricken at the suggestion, but it could only be an illusion like everything else. She had never been able to read him, or his feelings; her emotions had played tricks on her in the last few weeks, but that was the biggest trick of all.

She moved past him into the bedroom, pathetically grateful when he made no move to stop her. Her whole body began to shake, heat flushing through her, when she glanced at the bed, the rumpled sheets a testament to her foolishness and naiveté.

She had spent her whole life trying to please her father, a man who had never loved her. And if her memory hadn't returned, she might have done the same thing again with Dario.

'We will speak of this again in the morning,' Dario said from behind her. 'And find a solution.'

She turned around as she reached the bedroom door. The red fingers of dawn had begun to lighten the sky outside, shadowing his handsome face, and her heart squeezed tight in her chest. For just a moment, he looked like the loneliest man on earth.

'I never meant for you to be hurt,' he said.

The last tiny flicker of hope guttered out as she acknowledged something incontrovertible. Maybe he hadn't meant to hurt her, the way her father had. But the truth was he had.

She left the room as one of the tears she had promised herself she wouldn't shed slipped over her lid. She scrubbed it away with her fist.

After returning to her bedroom, she kept the exhaustion and the heartache at bay to dress.

She called Katie on her cell, and tiptoed out of the house, then rushed through the lemon groves down to the harbour, where the fishermen would be setting out for their morning catch.

As she stood on the deck of a small fishing boat, the aroma of fish and sea salt made her delicate stomach revolt. She retched over the side of the boat, but there was nothing left to throw up. As she raised her head she caught sight of the villa spotlighted on the hilltop in the early summer dawn.

She imagined Dario inside. And all the hopes and dreams that had never been real. Letting them go would be the hardest thing of all. But she had no choice.

While she had been falling hopelessly in love with a fantasy, he had managed to seal himself off from any emotion that would make him vulnerable.

So now she had to do the same.

Dario awoke, the pounding on his bedroom door disorientating him for a moment. He sat up, confused to find the other side of the bed cold. Then the details of the argument just before dawn came back to him.

He swore viciously, trying desperately to ignore the treacherous memory of Megan's face, white with shock and grief. And worse still, the deep sinking hole in his stomach when he had been forced to let her leave, and had lain in his empty bed alone.

But then he registered what his housekeeper was shouting through the door.

'Signor! Signor! La signorina e andato, ha lasciato con I pescatori.'

Megan has left with the fishermen? What the...?

He leapt out of bed, dragging a robe on as he raced to the door to find Sofia on the other side looking distraught as she explained in frantic Italian what she had heard from the young man delivering that morning's fish.

Dread spread through him. Megan had left? She had hitched a lift in a fishing boat in the middle of the night?

When she was still dealing with the emotional trauma of her memory returning? When she was pregnant? Was she mad?

He charged down the corridors until he reached her suite of rooms—to find the bed empty and unslept in, and a note addressed to him perched on the bedside table.

He picked it up, and flicked it open.

Goodbye, Dario.
I will take care of a termination.
Please don't contact me again.

No, no, *no*.

The note dropped from his numbed fingers and fluttered down onto the carpet.

He should have been relieved, he should have been grateful, that she had come to her senses, was going to do the sensible thing. But he felt none of those things as he clutched his head in his hands, and slumped onto the bed.

The cold, hard lump of devastation and grief in the pit of his stomach dragged him back to another time. He forced his mind to shut down as he lifted his head to stare out of the window at the new summer day, the dawn light spreading over the ocean.

And wondered if he would ever feel warm again.

CHAPTER SIXTEEN

Two months later

MEGAN SAT IN the chauffeur-driven car and watched the phalanx of photographers and reporters charging down the steps of the Manhattan courthouse towards them. Her sister, Katie, gripped her hand.

'Are you sure you're okay to do this, sis?' Katie's voice vibrated with the strength and maturity that she had gained ever since Megan had returned from Isadora.

Megan squeezed her sister's hand. 'We both need to do this to make sure Lloyd Whittaker stays behind bars as long as possible.'

The clamour outside the car became deafening as two burly security guards muscled their way through the crowd and one of them opened the driver's door.

He leaned into the interior. 'We have a detail to see you safely into the courthouse, Miss Whittaker. You both okay to go?'

The harsh flash of halogen lights blinded Megan as they stepped out of the car and were muscled into the courthouse, the noise becoming deafening as the reporters shouted questions.

'Are you here to testify against your father, Miss Whittaker?'

'Megan, tell us about your affair with Dario De Rossi? Are you two still an item?'

She clung to her resolve, tried to tune out the mention of Dario's name, to keep her nerves steady. But as they entered the main foyer she saw the tall, lean figure of Dario's friend Jared Caine standing beside the security checkpoint. And her heart careered into her throat.

'Well, if it isn't Mr Tall, Dark and Patronising,' Katie said, in a sing-song voice shot through with sarcasm as he walked towards them. Katie hadn't mentioned Jared before now, but she had never played nice with guys who told her what to do, so her animosity towards Dario's friend didn't really surprise Megan.

'Hello, Miss Whittaker, Katherine,' Jared said, in the confident, impersonal tone she remembered from the only other time she'd met him. If he'd heard her sister's jibe, he didn't let on.

'Why are you here?' Megan asked, anxiety gripping her insides.

'Dario's giving evidence at the moment,' he replied.

The news she had been dreading sliced through the defences she had been putting in place ever since running away from Isadora. But she maintained eye contact with Dario's friend, determined not to give away the turbulent emotions churning in her stomach.

She'd known this was likely. She'd just have to deal with it.

It didn't matter if she wasn't ready to see him again. He'd done what she'd asked, and hadn't contacted her since she'd left Isadora at dawn.

It didn't matter that she hadn't been able to stop thinking about him. Or stop going over every minute, every second she had spent with him since that first night. It was a weakness she would have to get over. Eventually. And it

seemed today was the day when she was going to be forced
to confront it. And him. For the first time.

She needed to move on from the time they had spent
together on Isadora. To accept that it had all been fake.
The way he obviously had. Coming to terms with the
truth about their relationship as well as the truth about her
father—or rather her ex-father—would eventually make
her a stronger, more resilient person.

If only she weren't going to be forced to take that next
step today, of all days.

One of the security guards who had helped them into
the building appeared to Jared's right. 'What's next, boss?'

'Stick around. Miss Whittaker and her sister will need
an escort when they leave the building,' Jared replied.

'Did Dario arrange the bodyguards?' Megan asked and
Jared nodded.

The protective gesture was like a new knife through
the heart—and her hard-fought-for composure. She didn't
want any evidence that he still cared, when he had never
cared enough.

'Please, tell Dario we don't need his help,' she said.

The tension in Jared's jaw drew tight. 'You should tell
him yourself. He's not exactly rational where you're concerned.'

What did that mean?

But before she could ask, the prosecutor's intern appeared looking harassed. 'Miss Whittaker, you're up next.
We need to get you into the courtroom.'

Her stomach continued to rebel as the intern ushered
them through the security line, leaving Jared behind.

As she walked into the courtroom her gaze immediately
connected with Dario on the witness stand. Her steps faltered, the blast of heat not nearly as disturbing as the pressure on her chest as his gaze swept over her.

From a distance, he looked as indomitable and intimidating as ever, the tailored designer suit, clean-shaven jaw and close-cropped hair a far cry from the intense and yet tender, even playful, man she had glimpsed on Isadora.

Her hand strayed to her stomach, but she forced herself to let it fall away as the intern directed her to the front of the courtroom and the seats behind the prosecutor's table.

But she couldn't take her eyes from the man on the witness stand. And as she drew closer, for a moment she thought she saw a flash of pain and longing in those pure blue eyes.

She broke eye contact, the pressure on her chest becoming unbearable.

You're wrong. Stop deluding yourself.

She needed to cut out that fragile, foolishly optimistic corner of her heart that still believed she loved him, or that he might have grown to love her.

She pressed her hand to her abdomen. She had her child to protect now. The child still growing in her womb.

The child she could never tell Dario about, because he had made it clear he had never wanted it, or her.

How can it still hurt so much to look at her?

Unable to detach his gaze from Megan's, Dario blanked out the defence attorney's questions.

But then Megan's gaze dropped away from his. And he felt the loss all over again, as he had so often since that fateful night on Isadora when her memory had returned and he'd seen the pain he'd caused in those expressive emerald eyes.

She looked pale and drawn in the tailored skirt and jacket. Had she lost weight? Her wild red hair was ruthlessly tied back. The style should have made her look severe and unapproachable—but only made her look more fragile and vulnerable to him.

His fingers clenched on the varnished wood of the witness box as he forced his attention back to the defence attorney. He had to concentrate on his evidence—as the man continued his campaign to convince the jury that Dario had been the one to attack Megan and not her father—and ignore the agonising parade of regrets that had plagued him since that night.

Stop trying to remake the past. She ran from you. And rejected your child. This was the outcome you wanted. Why can't you learn to live with it?

But then the defence attorney's mouth twisted in a grim approximation of a smile as he delivered a stream of questions that smashed into Dario's already faltering composure like physical blows.

'You maintain that you have never hit a woman, Mr De Rossi? That it is simply not in your make-up to do so? But is it not correct that you come from a family with a history of violence against women? That in fact your father was an extremely violent man, who hit you and your mother on numerous occasions? And that you indeed witnessed him beat your mother to death at a very impressionable age?'

Megan's head jerked up as the court broke into uproar—the barrage of questions, and Dario's shocked reaction to them, tearing away the stranglehold she had around her own heart.

Oh, please don't let it be true. Please don't let him have suffered like that.

Her chest imploded, the information delivered by the lawyer too traumatic to contemplate. But then her heartbeat rammed her throat in hard, heavy thuds as she registered the devastation on Dario's face—the mask of indifference ripped away to reveal the true horror of what he had once endured, clear for all to see.

And suddenly all the unanswered questions that had plagued her since that night, the questions that had made it so hard for her to move on, slammed into her all over again.

Why had he been so determined to protect her? How could he have made love to her with such passion, such purpose, and felt nothing?

Dario remained speechless, and utterly defenceless as the prosecutor's attempts to halt the line of questioning were dismissed by the judge.

'Mr De Rossi must answer the question. The prosecution can determine the relevance of this information in due course.'

The court fell silent, Megan's heart shattering.

'I did not consider him my father,' Dario said in a voice hoarse with raw emotion. 'The man was a monster.'

'Indeed,' the defence attorney said, the word laden with theatrical doubt. 'And yet it appears you resemble him in no small degree. Is it not the case that you seduced Lloyd Whittaker's daughter to secure a business deal? That you attacked her when she tried to return to her father? That you spirited her away while she had no memory to your private island in the Mediterranean? And then discarded her when she had outlived her usefulness to you.'

Dario's eyes met hers, the guilt and regret now so clear and unequivocal, the shudder of yearning and love that flowed through her was beyond her control.

'I did not leave Megan,' he said, the resignation in his voice destroying her. 'She left me.'

The poignant words pierced her heart. And the tug of war she'd been playing with her feelings for Dario was comprehensively lost.

Why had she run from him? Why hadn't she given him a chance? Given herself a chance?

What she had found with Dario on Isadora might have been built on a lie—but why hadn't she even considered staying and trying to make it real? Had what she thought was strength been nothing more than cowardice all along?

'Perhaps we should ask ourselves then why she would run from you, Mr De Rossi?' the defence attorney continued. 'And why she would choose not to inform you that she carries your child? Is it because she is terrified of what you might do to her?'

Megan leapt to her feet, her hand cupping her stomach, the puzzled shock on Dario's face at the news she still carried his child making the guilt lance through her.

What had she done to him? This man who had strived to protect her? The way he had no doubt once strived to protect his mother? All the lies he had told had been to protect her fragile mind from its own fears until she was ready to face them. But the lie she had told him had been to protect herself. Because she had been too weak, too scared, to admit she loved him. And now he was being crucified because of it.

'Stop, please stop,' Megan shouted. 'It's not true. Dario would never hurt me.'

Noise exploded around her, the judge's gavel echoing in her head.

'Meg, are you okay?' Katie's fingers gripped her arm as the surge of emotion threatened to choke her.

She swayed.

Her gaze remained locked on Dario's as he jerked to his feet in the witness box.

She heard the judge's call to order, the prosecutor's shouted demands for a recess next to her ear, but the blood buzzing in her head became a cacophony. Her knees dissolved as she dropped into the dark.

'I have you, *cara*, you are safe now.' Dario's voice beckoned her out of the darkness and into the light, as it had once before.

The clean, spicy aroma of soap and man enveloped her. The noise still surrounded her, but she was in his arms again as he shouldered his way through the crowd, protecting her from the shouted questions, the press of bodies, the bright flash of lights.

The sound of a door slamming cut out the noise until all she could hear was her heart hammering against her ribs.

They were alone in a cramped office, the large desk pushed into a corner surrounded by shelves loaded with leather-bound books.

The July sunlight shone through the window, lighting the dust motes in the air.

'Can you stand?' he asked.

'Yes, I think so.'

He put her down, holding on to her waist until he was satisfied she was strong enough to stand unaided.

'It is true?' he asked, his gaze focused on her belly, his fingers gliding over the barely visible bulge. 'About the baby? It still lives?'

She nodded. 'Yes, they... They think it's a girl.'

'Una bambina?' he said, the sound so full of stunned pleasure her guilt began to strangle her. *'Bellissima.'*

'I'm so sorry I lied to you in my note. It was cowardly and unforgivable and I—'

'Shh, *cara*.' He brushed the tears away with his thumbs. 'You are not the coward. I am.'

'Maybe we were both cowards,' she ventured.

His lips curved in a sad smile that melted her heart. 'I think, yes.'

She blinked, feeling the salty sting on her cheeks. 'Is it true, Dario? What he said happened to your mother?'

Dario stared at the woman in front of him, so brave, so bold, so beautiful. But the earnest question ate into the joy at the news their baby still lived.

He wished she hadn't heard about his mother, wished she would never have to know the truth of his past. But how could he tell her any more lies?

Guilt consumed him, not just for his part in his mother's death, but for his part in Megan's assault. A part he had never truly acknowledged to himself until now.

Maybe he hadn't been the one to wield the belt, but his actions had left her vulnerable. Left her at the mercy of a violent man—the way he had once left his own mother at the mercy of another violent man.

He stepped back, letting his hands fall from her waist. 'Yes, it is true. She died and it was my fault.'

'How could it be your fault?' Megan said, the sympathy and compassion in her eyes making him hate himself even more.

'I provoked him. My father.'

'I don't believe you,' she said, her dogged defence of him making him more determined than ever that she should know the truth. The whole bitter truth about who he was.

'And even if you did,' she added, 'it still wouldn't make what he did your fault.'

'You do not understand,' he said. 'He was a powerful man. A rich man with another family. He called me his gypsy bastard, and my mother his whore.' That the memory of his father's taunts still haunted and humiliated him only made him feel more ashamed. 'He enjoyed hurting her. When I woke that night, I saw him on top of her. And I could see how terrified she was.'

'Oh, Dario.' She touched his arm. 'No child should have to endure that.'

He shook his head, planted his fists into the pockets of his trousers, his insides churning with the long-forgotten memories—the hollow aching guilt that would never go away.

'I shouted at him to leave, to never touch my mother again. I was eight years old, nothing more than a proud, angry boy, and I thought I was man enough to protect her. He was furious. He lost all control, began to beat me with the belt he had used on me before. But this time, I don't think he would have stopped. My mother saved me. She fought him with the last breath in her body. She died protecting *me*.'

'Stop it.' Megan gripped his arms and shook him, her fierce expression forcing him back to the present, and away from the gut-wrenching guilt of memories. 'Don't you dare blame yourself. You were a child when your mother died. Do you understand me? And she died protecting you, because she loved you.'

He tried to absorb what she was saying. But he could not, because he knew his mother's death wasn't the only guilt he bore. History had repeated itself with Megan. Just as the defence attorney had implied.

He grasped her cheeks, looked into that brave face and forced himself to admit the final truth that he had been trying to deny for so long.

'Don't you see, Megan? I did the same thing to you. I lied to you to get you into my bed that night. I lied about my intentions towards your father's company. All I thought of was my own pleasure. And you paid the price. My actions provoked Whittaker, in the same way my actions once provoked my father.'

She reached around his waist and pressed her cheek into his sternum. 'Please stop it, Dario. It's not true. You mustn't blame yourself for what my father did to me.'

He placed his hands on her shoulders, wanting to believe her, yearning to hug her back, but terrified of all the emotions rushing to the surface. All the emotions he had spent two months struggling to comprehend.

She smiled up at him, the tender expression making his ribs ache, and his whole body feel as if it were perched on the edge of a precipice.

'I love you, Dario. So much.'

Gripping her cheeks in trembling palms, he pressed his forehead to hers, wanting to plunge over the edge, as the last of the walls shattered around him.

But how could he ever deserve her, or their child, after all that he had done?

'You cannot love me,' he said on a broken breath. 'I do not deserve it.'

Folding her arms around Dario's neck, Megan kissed him, tears streaking down her cheeks now. She had to make him believe her, had to make him see that he was worthy of her love.

At last, he opened for her and took her mouth in a deep, seeking kiss. She felt the emotion shuddering through him. And into her.

She loved him. And she suspected he loved her too. But he'd been too scared to acknowledge it to himself, let alone her, because of what had happened to his mother. She understood that now. She had to show him that he didn't have to be scared of love any more.

She drew back, taking in deep breaths as she saw the

torment still shadowing his eyes. 'Do you love me, too, Dario?' she asked. 'Do you want this baby?'

He sighed. 'Yes. And yes.' He rested a hand on her stomach as her heart filled with happiness. 'But I could not bear it if I hurt you again.'

She pressed her palm over his, hearing the raw emotion in his voice.

This was a struggle for him. A struggle that would take time and work to heal all the way, but knowing he loved her, and knowing where his anguish came from—knowing why it had been so hard for him to acknowledge his feelings—was surely the start of something magnificent. Something they could build a future on, with their baby.

'Dario, I know you're scared,' she said. 'And now I know why you're scared.' Because he had been traumatised by his mother's death as a child.

Her heart would always break for that little boy—who had learned to cope with the trauma by persuading himself he did not deserve to be loved.

She took a breath, her whole heart now lodged in her throat.

'I'm scared too,' she said, determined to get through to that little boy. 'Everyone is scared when they fall in love. Because love is a scary thing. But it's also a joyous, wonderful thing. And to have the joy, you have to overcome your fear. Can you do that, for me?'

'But what if I make a mistake?' he said, still unsure. Still scared. 'What if I cannot be a good father? A good husband? What if my love for you and our child is not enough?'

'There aren't any guarantees. Life isn't like that.' She gripped his hands, the love flowing through her so strong now she thought her heart might burst. 'And believe me— considering how new and untried this adventure is for both of us…' she smiled '…we're both going to make mistakes. The truth is we're probably going to make a ton of them. But it will be okay. As long as we make them together.'

He looked down at her belly. 'But I don't even know how to be a father. My own father was a monster.'

'And my mother was a woman who cared more about her next orgasm than she ever did about her daughters,' she replied, her smile widening. 'Look at it this way— however rubbish we are at this, we'll already be so much better than them.'

He nodded and let out a hoarse laugh, which had a wealth of bitter knowledge in it. 'This is true.'

'So what do you say, Dario De Rossi? Are you willing to go on this adventure with me?'

Her heart stopped beating, it simply stopped, as she waited for him to answer.

'You are sure you want to go on this adventure with me?' he said, the seriousness in his face making her heart jump and pound in her throat.

'Absolutely.'

He nodded again—the fierce passion that flashed into his eyes as he drew her into his arms choking off her air supply.

'Then I don't believe I have a choice,' he murmured against her hair. 'Even I cannot continue to be a coward in the face of your bravery.'

She wanted to laugh, the joy bursting in her heart almost more than she could bear.

He clasped her cheeks and lifted her head. 'I think now we must make this engagement real,' he said. 'Will you marry me, *piccola*?'

Her heart soared. 'Absolutely.'

His mouth swooped down to devour hers, the giddy

contentment making her head spin as warm hands cupped her bottom, and heat spread through her.

A loud thumping pulled them apart as Jared's voice came through the door. 'Sorry, folks, adjournment's over. And the judge is getting antsy.'

'Stall them a minute more,' Dario shouted back. Then he turned to her, his expression sober. 'Are you strong enough to take the witness stand after me?' he asked, searching her face for any signs of fatigue or fragility. 'If you are not, I will make them wait until tomorrow.'

'No. I can do it. I *want* to do it,' she said, knowing she was strong enough to do whatever it took to put the man who had pretended to be her father behind bars—because with Dario by her side, she was strong enough to do anything. 'For us.'

Cradling her head in his hands, he kissed her forehead, then her nose, then her mouth—the play of his lips full of sincerity and hunger.

'For us,' he vowed.

EPILOGUE

One year later

'SHH, *BAMBINA, PAPA* is here now.'

Megan stretched on the bed and plumped the pillows behind her as she watched her husband walk back into their bedroom, having retrieved their crying daughter from her crib in the room next door, which had once been his office.

She smiled as the baby quietened, happily settling into her favourite place in all the world, nestled on her father's shoulder as he rubbed her back with one large hand.

The little diva.

At six months old, Isabella Katherine De Rossi had her father—billionaire master of industry and feared corporate raider—wrapped firmly around her tiny little finger.

'She is not wet.' Dario frowned. 'Could she be hungry again?' he asked, rocking his daughter gently as he returned to their bed.

Megan yawned, and looked out of the bedroom window to gauge the time by the Mediterranean sun, which was barely creeping over the horizon. 'No,' she said. 'She had her morning feed less than half an hour ago.' Megan couldn't contain her grin at the confusion on Dario's face.

He was still sometimes unsure about his role as a husband and father, and so fiercely protective of them both it often led to him being a bit overzealous when caring for Issy. He was always the first to pick her up if she cried.

'Do you think she is unwell?' he said.

'I think she just likes having you hold her,' she said. 'And she knows that if she cries, you'll rush in there to pick her up.'

The frown eased from Dario's face and he chuckled as he lay down on the bed beside Megan. Lifting his daughter, he bounced her in his arms. The baby's delighted chuckle joined his deep laugh.

'You are a bad *bambina*,' he said, rubbing her nose against his own, the tone the opposite of chiding. 'You mustn't scare *papa* like that.'

He settled back, with the baby curled on his broad chest.

With her head tucked under her father's chin and her small fist stuck in her mouth, Issy dropped into sleep, secure in the knowledge that her father would hold her safe in his arms.

'Dario,' Megan said, smiling as Dario turned towards her. 'I need to talk to you about something.'

She'd held it off long enough. Had waited until they were on Isadora again, where the pace of life was slower, less pressured.

The last six months, heck the last year, had been idyllic. She'd never imagined when they'd made that commitment to each other, in the dusty clerk's office during her father's trial, that her love for Dario and their child would eventually become so overwhelming, so all-consuming. And because she'd been so content—and maybe also a little scared that this adventure was still so new and fragile, especially for Dario—she hadn't wanted to make any demands.

He'd changed so much though, from the cautious, guarded man she'd known. He'd been to therapy to help him deal with the lingering trauma of his mother's death. And they'd made a life for themselves in New York—in the huge brownstone he'd bought a block from Central Park. Their wedding had been a quiet affair on Isadora, with only the islanders and a few of his business associates as guests, plus Katie and Jared as witnesses.

Since their marriage, and even more so since Issy's birth, Dario had cut back on his business commitments, happy to spend long evenings and lazy weekends with her and Issy rather than building his business empire. Not that he wasn't still driven and focused, but he was now equally driven and focused about making his personal life as much of a success as his professional one.

And the bond he had established with his daughter was something that filled Megan with joy and wonder and gratitude every single day.

So the time was right to tell him about the interview she'd had last week in Brooklyn while their housekeeper Lydia Brady had looked after Issy. She'd held off and held off telling him about it, because she'd been concerned about his reaction.

Oh, just say it, Meg. For goodness' sake.

'Hmm…?' he murmured as he continued to stroke his daughter's back.

'I've been offered a job.'

His hand stopped moving as his head jerked round.

Well, that had certainly got his attention.

'A job where?'

'It's a charity in Brooklyn that administers a series of refuges for battered women and their children. They need someone to set up and then operate a new computer system to reduce the amount of time and money they spend on paperwork so they can spend more of it on setting up new refuges.'

He didn't say anything, but she could see the tension in his jaw. Instead of replying, he suddenly sat up and got off the bed.

'Dario? Where are you going?' she asked.

But he didn't turn to look at her, he simply walked out of the room mumbling, 'I should put Issy back into her crib.'

Okay, well, that didn't go according to plan.

Megan's heart sank as she flopped back onto the pillows, her excitement turning into a tangle of anxieties in the pit of her stomach. She didn't want to have a battle with him about this. But it looked as if she might have to.

Dario placed his daughter in her crib, and stroked the soft fluff of red hair on her head.

He wanted so much to say no.

He wanted to tell Megan she couldn't take the job. He didn't want her travelling to Brooklyn every day. Working for a charity that he could probably buy and sell several times over. He could fund the place himself. Throw money at them so they wouldn't need her computer expertise. If she needed a job, he could find her one at Whittaker's, preferably one that didn't require her to leave their house.

He wanted to insist that her daughter, their daughter, needed her mother at home. Where she would always be safe. And as their daughter grew, he would want to do the same thing to Issy. And all the other children he hoped they would have one day.

He wanted to wrap his perfect family in cotton wool and keep them locked away for ever from the outside world, so no one and nothing would ever have the power to hurt them. He wanted to protect them with his money, his resources and the last breath in his body. He wanted to cocoon them for ever in the love that still took his breath away every time he laid eyes on either one of them.

But that was the coward's way out.

Because he'd seen the look of excitement in Megan's eyes, seen how enthusiastic she was about this new opportunity. And he knew if he loved her, he could not kill that joy—however great his need to protect her from harm.

Damn it. But loving someone more than life itself— the way he loved Megan and Issy—was fraught with so many complications. Complications and difficult choices that he often found it extremely hard to even comprehend, let alone solve.

But then the words Megan had said to him a year ago, in the courthouse in Manhattan, echoed in his head. The words he had had to repeat to himself so many times since: when Megan had been curled over the toilet bowl and throwing up each morning through most of the months of her pregnancy; when he had endured the terror of watching her bring their child into the world through twelve gut-wrenching hours of labour; when he'd held the tiny, vulnerable and unbearably precious life they'd made together in his hands for the first time. The words he knew he would be repeating to himself for the rest of his life: when Issy took her first step; when he had to leave her on her first day of school; when he taught her how to ride a bike, drive a car, sail a boat, fly a helicopter; when she went off to Harvard or Yale—because, obviously, his daughter was going to be the smartest, bravest, most brilliant child the world had ever seen.

To have the joy you have to overcome your fear.

He kissed his fingertips and pressed them to the soft skin of his daughter's forehead; her tiny chest rose and fell in the regular rhythm of deep sleep. Relief eased some of the tightness in his chest. Thank goodness, he wouldn't have to face most of those fears with his daughter for a little while at least.

Walking back into the bedroom, he spotted Megan sitting up in their big bed, her arms wrapped around her drawn-up knees.

'Dario? I need to know what you think,' she said, her anxiety tempered with determination. 'About me taking the job?'

He climbed onto the bed, then gathered her into his arms. He held her tight, let the swell of arousal—that was always there when she was near him—help him to push out the words.

'You want to take this job?' he asked as he kissed her hair, even though he already knew the answer.

'Yes, I do.' She swung round in his arms, the eagerness on her face crucifying him a little more. 'I thought it all through about Issy's care while I'm at work. Lydia is fabulous with her, and she's happy to step in. And we've got more than enough other staff to take up the slack.'

He'd employed Lydia Brady as soon as he and Megan had moved into the new town house he'd bought on the Upper East Side—concerned that the penthouse apartment might not be suitable for a child. He'd also insisted on hiring three additional staff. Something he knew Megan still struggled with. He was forever coming home and finding the staff helping Megan with some charity project or other that had nothing to do with their domestic duties.

'And anyway, I'm only going to be working three hours a day to start,' his wife continued. 'I told them I want to take the time to wean Issy properly.'

'Shh, Megan.' He tucked her hair behind her ears, allowed his thumbs to skim down her cheeks. 'You don't have to say any more.'

Dio, *but I love this woman so much.*

'If you want to do this thing,' he added, 'I would never stand in your way.'

'Really?' She smiled. 'Because I thought… When you walked out with Issy like that, I thought you were upset about the idea. That you were going to object to it.'

He shook his head. He wasn't the only one with insecurities. Why did he find that so comforting all of a sudden?

'I could never refuse something so important to you,' he said, but then he smiled, enjoying the role of devil's advocate. 'But if I did, what would you do?'

The quick, seductive smile captivated him as she reached up to cradle his cheeks. 'Then I guess I would have to convince you,' she whispered against his lips.

She set her mouth on his. The heat surged at the seductive licks of her tongue.

He chuckled, the sound deep and so full of contentment. A contentment he'd never believed could be his. Her delighted answering smile made his heart thunder in his chest.

They would be okay. This job would be okay. He had to let her have her freedom despite his fears. And Megan need never know that he would hire one of Jared's security team to watch over her while she was in Brooklyn.

And if she did find out, they could always negotiate. Because if there was one thing his wife was an expert at, it was negotiation.

Scooping her up, he sat her in his lap, held her firmly when she wriggled, inflaming his desires still more.

'So you think you can convince me?' He cupped her breast, licking at the rigid tip through the sheer fabric of her nightgown. Arousal surged into his groin when she arched into his mouth, responding with enthusiasm to the erotic torture as always. 'Perhaps I will convince you first?' he teased.

She grasped his head and pulled his mouth up to hers. The kiss was long and deep before she drew back.

'You're on, big boy,' she said, clearly relishing the erotic challenge—even though she had to know she'd already won.

His loyalty, his trust and every single piece of his heart.

* * * * *

If you enjoyed
THE VIRGIN'S SHOCK BABY
why not explore these other
ONE NIGHT WITH CONSEQUENCES *stories?*

THE BOSS'S NINE-MONTH NEGOTIATION
by Maya Blake
THE PREGNANT KAVAKOS BRIDE
by Sharon Kendrick
A RING FOR THE GREEK'S BABY
by Melanie Milburne
ENGAGED FOR HER ENEMY'S HEIR
by Kate Hewitt

Available now!

MILLS & BOON®

MODERN™

POWER, PASSION AND IRRESISTIBLE TEMPTATION

MILLS & BOON®

EXCLUSIVE EXTRACT

When chauffeur Keira Ryan drives into a snowdrift, she and her devastatingly attractive passenger must find a hotel…but there's only one bed! Luckily Matteo Valenti knows how to make the best of a bad situation—with the most sizzling experience of her life. It's nearly Christmas again before Matteo uncovers Keira's secret. He's avoided commitment his whole life, but now it's time to claim his heir…

Read on for a sneak preview of Sharon Kendrick's book
THE ITALIAN'S CHRISTMAS SECRET
One Night With Consequences

'Santino?' Matteo repeated, wondering if he'd misheard her. He stared at her, his brow creased in a frown. 'You gave him an Italian name?'

'Yes.'

'Why?'

'Because when I looked at him…' Keira's voice faltered as she scraped her fingers back through her hair and turned those big sapphire eyes on him '…I knew I could call him nothing else but an Italian name.'

'Even though you sought to deny him his heritage and kept his birth hidden from me?'

She swallowed. 'You made it very clear that you never wanted to see me again, Matteo.'

His voice grew hard. 'I haven't come here to argue the rights and wrongs of your secrecy. I've come to see my son.'

It was a demand Keira couldn't ignore. She'd seen the brief tightening of his face when she'd mentioned his child and another wave of guilt had washed over her.

'Come with me,' she said huskily.

He followed her up the narrow staircase and Keira was

acutely aware of his presence behind her. She could detect the heat from his body and the subtle sandalwood which was all his and, stupidly, she remembered the way that scent had clung to her skin the morning after he'd made love to her. Her heart was thundering by the time they reached the box-room she shared with Santino and she held her breath as Matteo stood frozen for a moment before moving soundlessly towards the crib.

'Matteo?' she said.

Matteo didn't answer. Not then. He wasn't sure he trusted himself to speak because his thoughts were in such disarray. He stared down at the dark fringe of eyelashes which curved on the infant's olive-hued cheeks and the shock of black hair. Tiny hands were curled into two tiny fists and he found himself leaning forward to count all the fingers, nodding his head with satisfaction as he registered each one.

He swallowed.

His *son*.

He opened his mouth to speak but Santino chose that moment to start to whimper and Keira bent over the crib to scoop him up. 'Would you…would you like to hold him?'

'Not now,' he said abruptly. 'There isn't time. You need to pack your things while I call ahead and prepare for your arrival in Italy.'

'What?'

'You heard me. You can't put out a call for help and then ignore help when it comes. You telephoned me and now you must accept the consequences,' he added grimly.

Don't miss
THE ITALIAN'S CHRISTMAS SECRET
By Sharon Kendrick

Available November 2017

www.millsandboon.co.uk